The Fine Society - Information

By A. H. Kent

The Fine Society is available in e-reader format. For additional information visit the website;
thefinesociety.com

For additional background and on-going updates visit The Fine Society blog. A link to the blog is available at:
thefinesociety.com.

Supplemental videos are available at;
thefinesociety.com

Your comments are welcomed on FaceBook at
facebook.com/TheFineSociety
or
thefinesociety@gmail.com

Copyright 2016

ISBN   978-0-9849956-2-2

Print Edition
Abridged Edition

Foreword

You are likely to find that The Fine Society is not what you normally associate with the classification, Science Fiction. The characters are fictional but as real as you, I and people around us. Their surroundings, primarily Chicago, public events and landmarks are real. You will easily be able to place yourself in amongst the characters as an unseen observer and share their mysterious adventure.

The science is real as well, well most of it. If you have a reasonable background in science, a fun challenge for you will be able to determine what is true.

If you do not have a science background, no problem, the story its self is an enticing mystery. Some of the characters are in the same position in that they do not have a physics or math background. They simply deal with it on a high level and leave the details to those with the necessary background.

What happens in The Fine Society that is compelling? Well I cannot answer directly because that would ruin the story for you. I will say that one of the things you will experience could go something like this: Wow, this is so simple. Why didn't I think of it?

Now what could these folks be up to? Read on and find out.

Acknowledgements

The Fine Society started out as a daydream that I would play in my head as I lay in bed unwinding for sleep. Each night I would refine the story and carry the development a little further. It was fun, like watching my own private movie. And it had the desired effect, sleep.

On several occasions, I recalled the essence of the story to my wife and a few friends. They liked what they heard and urged me to write it down. Primary encouragement came from my wife, Megan, and a professional acquaintance of hers, Lora Sanberg. I thank them for their encouragement.

Not being a professional writer, my first scribblings were, from a writing perspective, painful to read. However, once again my wife, her friend Lora, Alice Biggers and my son Philip stepped up to review the first draft. They confirmed that my writing was severely lacking but that the story was compelling. I thank them for their endurance.

To better understand the process ahead, I turned to Jack Palmer and Georgia Kohart of the Defiance Crescent News for advice and direction. The tips, contacts and references they supplied were what I needed. Thanks for being on target.

A partial re-draft was done and submitted to my wife and an old physics teacher friend of mine, Myron Bok. Their responses were again encouraging that I had made some of the necessary changes to breathe life into it. I thank them for her honestly and effort.

Emboldened with the idea that the story was well worth more effort, but fully aware of the shortcomings of my own writing skills, I sought an editor. I found a perfect fit, Sarah Logue. She not only fixed the myriad of mechanical problems, she became engrossed in the story and the characters. As a result, she provided volumes of suggestions for inclusions (and a few deletions). She made me work hard. I thank her for being more than just an editor.

I submitted a summary of The Fine Society to Sue Grafton.   I was amazed at the points she picked up on from just those few paragraphs. I thank her for the good questions she raised.

For the videos I needed some equipment not readily available. For that I turned to my alma mater, The Ohio State University and the physics department. Harold Whitt, lab supervisor, knew what I needed but did not have that demo piece. However, he put me in contact with Pete Gosser, machine shop supervisor, to see if they could help. Indeed they could, and did. In a few days, Pete and his instrument makers Josh Gueth and Jon Shover had fabricated the spring-coupled pendulums that I needed. I thank them for their fast and fine workmanship.

For finding and fixing those last elusive mistakes that are like gremlins, you think you have eliminated them all and another appears; Betty and Ed Burns, Nick Hainen, Alice Biggers my wife, Megan were troupers. I cannot thank you enough for indulging my fantasy.

Finally, Brad Griffith and his staff at Buckeye Interactive have my profound thanks. Their support in bridging a semi-geek, me, to the totally geeky world of e-books, website creation, widgets and a lot of other details necessary to get The Fine Society into the e-reader world was truly invaluable.

5

The Fine Society

By A.H. Kent

1. AUTUMN 1938

Zelig, his wife Sarah and his father, Jacob had been gathered around a small table for quite some time. It was evening and the room was illuminated only by a solitary oil lamp on the table. They were speaking in hushed tones so that their six year old son, Isaac who was playing nearby on the floor could not determine what was being said. Even at his age he could recognize the tone as troublesome but gave no outward indication that he sensed their stress. As he sat on the floor building arches and bridges over imaginary streams with an assortment of plain wooden blocks, suddenly the adults were silent. Almost simultaneously the adults reached across the table to one another and clenched hands. The dim light of the oil lamp revealing the tears that had welled up in their eyes. Unknown to young Isaac a painful decision had been made.

In his short years Isaac could remember many trips from his home in Munich to his grandfather's farm near the Austrian border. The mood was always happy and playful until the last few visits and now they were not having fun anymore. He saw his mother crying many times and his father and grandfather would be yelling.

Zelig was a well-regarded professor at the Institute of Science in Munich. The Institute had a long standing reputation for its excellence in teaching and research. Not only had Zelig been a success there but his grandfather, Isaac for whom his son was named, years earlier had enjoyed a rewarding career at the Institute as well. With just a few weeks before the end of the fall term Zelig was informed that he would no longer be employed after the term ends. He was given a vague and lame excuse for his impending termination. Completely dumbfounded by the action Zelig had immediately consulted with his colleagues to see if they could help explain the sudden and unfounded action. His answer was clear and swift. Four of his colleagues were being terminated as well, all Jewish.

It was 1938 and the winds of discontent were blowing across Europe. Zelig and his family had heard stories of persecution and intimidation fomented by emerging radical groups but not this close to home. Now he was sure these were not just rumors, now they were the victims. The visits to Grandpa Jacob's when it was no longer fun began when Zelig was given the news.

At the Institute Zelig was appalled at the lack of outcry by other faculty, staff and students. Most turned away when asked if they knew specifics about the firings. Stammering and incoherent statements were typical responses Zelig received if at all. Many could be seen turning away down side hallways so as not to come face to face with Zelig. Salacious rumors began to surface, no doubt the works of the rampant spread of the Nazi movement. Even more hurtful and diabolical were the damning assertions about his grandfather who had an illustrious career at the Institute. He died many years ago. What was the point of defaming him?

The only person who was willing to listen and provided a sympathetic ear was a former colleague who had recently retired from teaching at the Institute, Rene LaFrance. Rene always seemed to be the person around at the right time to provide assistance or an answer when a difficult situation arose. A quite shy person who never sought the limelight, his second role in life seemed to be the perfect facilitator, making it possible for others to succeed. Somehow Rene had found out about the terminations and had returned to the Institute from his retirement activity, a Swiss farmer.

As Rene had approached his own retirement some years earlier, he decided to take up farming in Switzerland. In many respects it would mirror his boyhood farm upbringing in western Switzerland bordering on France.

Rene knew all of the people being let go, especially Zelig and his family. He would often stop at Jacob's farm as he traveled between his Swiss home and Munich. He and Jacob would share farm stories and enjoy them as only a fellow farmer could. Rene was a man of small stature and not what you would typically associate with farming. However, having grown up on a farm, he knew how to compensate for what he lacked in size and strength. On the contrary, Jacob was a big boned brawny sort well adapted to the challenges facing a farmer. Both men were getting along in years but at the same time each had much more to give.

Zelig was a gifted scientist in the early years of his career, too much to waste in the decaying intellectual climate of Europe in 1938. With good contacts in the United States Rene hatched a plan by which Zelig and the other four could immigrate quickly and quietly to the US. The United States was welcoming bright scientists to their expanding nuclear and aviation research programs. People like the famous rocket scientist, Werner Von Braun, were among the many who ended up in the US.

Jacob did not want to leave the only land he had known and would not consider going with Zelig and his family. However, all were increasingly concerned over his safety if he stayed in Germany, as they watch the anti-Semitic wave fester around them. Since Jacob's wife had died many years ago, Rene suggested that the two men combine their efforts at his farm in Switzerland. The solutions on the surface were simple and made sense. However, the emotional implications were enormous. It was particularly distressing that they may be separated for a long time, possibly forever. Thus, the agonizing decision the family had to make. Tonight they had made that decision.

Time was critical. Any delay and Zelig and his family might be denied permission to leave the country. Some of the rumors they had heard were of people put in that position. They had to act swiftly.

2. FIVE DAYS LATER

To draw the least attention Zelig and his family left for Jacob's leaving most of their belongings behind. As they traveled their baggage looked like what you would take on a long weekend vacation which was their story if asked. However, this was not a vacation. Zelig and Sarah were afraid that they appeared nervous which would arouse suspicion if stopped by authorities. That caused even more apprehension. Almost ready to explode inside they saw the worst ahead on the road, a checkpoint. Since the road they were traveling took them toward Austria, travelers were scrutinized more closely, especially if they might be trying to smuggle valuables out of the country.

The "stop" may have only been a few minutes but it seemed an hour. The guards looked all through the car and luggage and asked both Zelig and Sarah about their travel plans. When asked about their destination Zelig answered Jacob's farm and when they would return. The agent seemed to recognize the name and place. The checkpoint had been setup about 10 miles from the farm and it was entirely possible the agent was from around there and knew of Jacob. A moment later he waved them on. Zelig and Sarah did not speak for several minutes. They were too traumatized to speak. Even upon arrival at Jacob's both were still pale, sweating and shaken. An uneasy and tearful night was spent by all.

The next day Rene was to meet them at Jacob's farm and the first phase of their relocation plan was to take place. He must have left home well before dawn because he arrived late morning. Quite an accomplishment considering he was driving an old farm truck and had to maneuver the rugged countryside from Switzerland, through a sliver of Austria and then into Germany.

This was the first time six year old Isaac had seen Rene and little Isaac seemed to be fascinated by the unusual appearance of the diminutive man. Rene was certainly bigger than Isaac but from a child's perspective he was nowhere as big as the adults he spent all his time looking up to. Isaac may have been wondering if Rene was another child.

Time was precious and much had to be done before undertaking the arduous and risky trip to Switzerland. The adults moved quickly to load a few furniture items and then shifted to the bundles of hay from the barn. As they moved the hay, paper wrapped bundles were revealed. Amongst them was a box which Jacob opened and carefully removed the contents. From Isaac's vantage point, out from under the feet of the quickly moving adults, he could only see that the contents were further wrapped in paper. He caught a glimpse of something that looked like an egg. The rest of the contents looked like notebooks of some sort. From Jacob's gestures it was clear that he wanted Zelig to take that box.

Then Zelig, Jacob and Rene carefully unwrapped one of the many paper wrapped packages. It contained a stack of papers, just sheets of paper. The men examined a few pages intently for a several minutes, shook their heads and then placed them in the box with the egg-like objects. Once the box has been securely tied up with twine, they took the wrapping that had been around the stack of papers and placed the oil-cloth wrapped parcel inside and tied it with twine. It was set aside from the rest of the unopened paper bundles. To little Isaac what the adults were doing made no sense at his age. However, he did comprehend one aspect of the process; the last parcel they wrapped was special because he knew his grandpa Jacob had made the contents. It was Limburger cheese. Jacob always kept it in oil-cloth packages that were tight enough to contain most of the ...." fragrance."

The remaining wrapped packages were carefully inserted under the hay bundles on the wagon and could not be seen. The last package loaded was the one with the cheese. Curiously, it was placed so that most of it was visible, that is, not hidden by the straw but quite visible in the sun. It was as if the plan was to have the packages discovered. And what border crossing agent wouldn't want to probe into or look under a load of hay?

The ruse they decided to employ was that Rene was there to buy some cheese so that he could start a Limburger cheese making operation on his farm. While there and since he had room on the truck he purchased some odds and ends and hay from Jacob, a common practice among farmers. The hay was needed to cover the other wrapped packages. In rural areas like these, farmers engaged in small commerce across the border although not legal it was too insignificant to draw attention from their respective governments. Besides, the locals knew the hidden paths from one side to the other which would be impossible to restrict. Jacob and Sarah would go along to help Rene since he clearly needed physical assistance. Little Isaac was just along for the ride, if anyone asked. However, when the job was done, no one would return. Since Zelig was looked upon as the breadwinner in the family, his presence in the group going to Switzerland would draw more attention. Thus it was part of the escape plan that they would split up, with Sarah and her son accompanying Jacob and Rene. Zelig would return to Munich. If he encountered a checkpoint his story was he was going back to finish the term while his wife and son remained at the farm. He would then rejoin them in a few days. They were hoping that information about his termination would not yet be available at checkpoints.

Rene had a plan to get all five Institute colleagues out of Germany for a scientific conference in Paris. It was a scheduled annual event usually attended by several members of the Institute. Only this year five of the faculty that could not go would be replaced by his special group of five. Two of the five who could not go had recently died, two more had retired and the last had transferred to an institution that does not send delegates to the conference. Once again they were betting that the flow of information would be slow, incomplete or even missing altogether at checkpoints.

It was a difficult moment for Zelig, Sarah and Jacob. Little Isaac knew nothing of the plan but had a deep feeling of uncertainty and clung to Sarah as the family group tearfully embraced each other. Yielding to compassionate urgings of Rene that time was precious, they finally parted. Rene was seated on what could be described as a contrived booster seat in his truck where the pedals were rigged so he could control them, Sarah in the middle holding Isaac and Jacob on the right. As they drove off they yelled messages of love to each other. As the truck began to disappear over a small hill, Zelig ran to higher ground to prolong his view of the vanishing truck. Even at that distance, he saw hand waves and returned them. He even imagined he still heard voices from time to time even after the truck was out of site.

Zelig now deeply and openly wept as he dropped to kneel in the warm golden grass on the hill still looking at the now empty road.

It may have only been minutes or it could have been an hour before Zelig began to collect his thoughts. He realized that he had to regained his composure and focus on the tasks ahead of him. He needed to negotiate an uncertain path to his own freedom and ultimate reunion with his family. The immediate task was to get back to Munich. Since he had traveled light there was little to take back, only the addition of the box containing some old journals, some individually wrapped white objects and the stack of papers added to the box.

Zelig was not fortunate that day. The same checkpoint they had encountered a few days earlier was still there. In fact the ranking agent was the same as before. He immediately asked in his most intimidating manner, "Where are your wife and son?" Zelig responded as calmly as he could, "Oh they decided to stay on at Grandpa's farm. I have to get back to the Institute to finish out the term for a few days and then I will rejoin them." The agent seemed satisfied.

In the meantime a second man was examining the contents of the trunk, a satchel and a box.

The checkpoint was along an isolated part of the road. It was rather high and open location making it easy to observe anyone trying to skirt the checkpoint by going around it. A small table sat along the roadside where the agents could place packages to be opened and examined. The subordinate agent had removed the box, placed it there and opened it. He took one of the sheets to examine more closely. Puzzled by what he saw, he walked to the driver side where Zelig was being quizzed. The agent showed his superior. When Zelig saw their puzzled looks he glanced at the paper they were holding. In horror he realized that they had opened the box. He had expected they would ask what was in it before opening it and at least give him a chance to explain the contents. He had a perfectly plausible explanation.

Sudden moves and outburst were verboten, but Zelig could not contain himself. He bolted from the car to the back where the trunk lid was open and the box sat wide open on the table nearby. His whole body winced with pain, as he saw the last page of paper driven out of the box by a relentless wind. He quickly looked about. The pages were almost out of sight, driven rapidly away from him. In less than a minute they were all gone. None had settled to the ground. They were all airborne seeming to accelerate their movement as they were carried to levels of higher wind velocity.

Zelig was numb and angry. Although the true nature of the papers was unknown, they were priceless from the stand point of having been relics of the distance past and somehow awaiting the discovery of their purpose for existence. He turned to face the agent who had carelessly opened the box and let the contents escape. Zelig would now deliver the explanation for the box and its contents. However, the anger he felt would give depth to his voice and explanation that would shake both of the agents. In a firm, measured and authoritative voice, "You *must* know the new Chancellor of the Munich Science Institute, Herr Hermann Mueller." Both men did a small head jerk and looked directly at Zelig. It was a clear by their response that they knew the man. The previous Chancellor had been suddenly and forcefully replaced by "someone more in tune with the new order agenda." Zelig continued now with an edge in his voice, "Herr Mueller has ordered the collection of all documents, journals and artifacts from past notable scientists and teachers from the Institute. He wants to create the greatest collection of scientific thought in all of Europe."

The agents listened carefully and attentively as Zelig kicked it up a couple of notches and addressed the underling eye to eye, "Herr Mueller specifically identified my grandfather's works to be part of that collection. I knew my father had some of his journals and so I am delivering these materials to the institute." Almost shouting, "And you, Dummkopf, have just let valuable papers blow off with the wind!"

In a daring move Zelig snatched the one remaining sheet from the hands of the underling. A deafening silence followed. Zelig continued his glare while inside he quaked wondering if he had greatly over played the part and would suffer the consequences. The silence was broken by the superior agent. He turned to the underling and began berating for his stupid actions and the trouble it could mean for both of them if Mueller heard of their blunder. He ordered him to collect as many sheets as he could (of course, it was too late because the papers were all long gone) but he ordered the underling to do it anyway. When he realized the futility of his command he ordered the box retied and put back in the trunk. The superior agent then did something Zelig never expected, he apologized profusely and added "We will look for the papers and if any are found they will be returned to your father, Jacob, I know of him."

Zelig did not speak but nodded an acknowledgement of the man's statements. With the box secure and the one remaining sheet still clutched in his hand, he resumed his trip back to Munich, relieved to have survived, sort of, the encounter at the checkpoint. Now he had the added worry that sheets may really be found and attempts to give them to Jacob at the abandoned farm would tip off the authorities.

3. MOVING THEIR CHEESE

Near the border between Germany and Austria the group of would-be cheese makers encountered a check point. It was a secondary sort of crossing on a less traveled road. Security here was just a formality and not taken as seriously as checkpoints at major crossings. Here the clientele are typically locals with family on both sides of the border. The guards on either side were likely to be cousins. However, since Rene and company were going on to Switzerland and he and the rest were not locals, they were given a good look.

The senior boarder guard who was standing on the driver's side was about to ask Rene for an explanation for a load of hay being hauled from Germany, across a strip of Austria to Switzerland, when he spotted a paper wrapped package protruding from the hay. He stopped short of asking his question and raised some hay to reveal more packages. He motioned the agent on the other side to do the same. As that agent poked his way around the truck, he indicated finding more of the same. Now the lead agent had a different question and since the situation looked like a smuggling attempt his demeanor became serious.

"What are you hiding under the hay?" he said accusatively. Rene gave a quick laugh and answered, "Nothing," as he chuckled in between, "Its cheese. I am starting up cheese making operation at my farm and this is what I need to get into operation. The hay is just to protect it from the heat of the sun." The agent did not appear convinced and skeptically said, "With all that cheese I would say you are smuggling it out of the country to sell and to avoid a tariff."

Rene wanted to answer that if he really wanted to do that he would have a lot more cheese and do a better job of hiding it for all the trouble it would be worth. Although it was a realistic answer, it would not remove the doubt in the agents mind. Instead he had a different answer.

"When you start a new cheese making facility for this type of cheese, you smear cheese all over the walls and ceiling and everything to get a good load of the spores, bacteria, enzymes or whatever is responsible for making the basic cheese curds cure into the desired product. You do it only at the start and this cheese is for that purpose."

The agent really looked skeptical now but glanced to the agent on the other side of the cab; he was nodding "yes." Still not convinced he demanded, "show me the cheese, open it up!" The agent on the far side stifled a laugh and shook his head "no." The lead agent either did not see him shake his head "no" or chose to ignore his silent warning. Rene jumped out of the cab with the enthusiasm of a proud parent preparing to show off his first born child. As Rene quickly removed the outer wrapper talking as he did, "This is one of the finest cultures I have encountered anywhere in these parts." Rene began removing the inner covering which had served well to conceal the true............. "fragrance."

Of course, Rene had chosen the one package that was exposed and had been receiving the heat of the sun all day long. As he completed the unwrapping to reveal the creamy white (now a runny consistency) he rapidly moved the package up under the nose of the agent so he could further appreciate its bouquet. The reaction was swift and dramatic. The agent turned and ran gasping for air. He fanned the air in front of his face in an attempt to get rid of the smell, no luck; the odor had almost instantly permeated his clothes and his surroundings. On the other side of the truck the other agent was laughing uncontrollably. He had been raised on a dairy farm and was familiar with soft ripening cheese that has been in the sun.

In a sympathetic gesture Rene said, "Oh, I'm sorry, I did not realize that package had been exposed to the heat of the sun. Here, let me open another so you can sample it. It really is a great cheese. It tastes much different than it smells." The agent wanted no part of it and from his safe distance away from the truck; he urgently waved them on all the while trying to get the stench out of his nose.

As Rene, Jacob and Sarah looked back they could see the two agents, one still laughing and the other waving the air in front of his face.

The relatively short trip across Austria was uneventful. At the Austrian/Switzerland crossing they were stopped again. However, this time it was a social event. Rene knew most of the agents on both sides so the group paused for a social visit. Drinking at this remote crossing was common since they had little else to do and travelers often were carrying beverages they had purchased elsewhere and shared them with the agents to "grease the skids." The agents hauled out two bottles of a fine French wine they had in a cache and all except little Isaac drank a toast.

The agents had no idea that Jacob and Sarah had something really significant to toast.

Not long after the group arrived safely and securely at Rene's farm in Switzerland.

4. WHAT DAY IS IT?

Zelig's mind was in turmoil the whole trip back to Munich. The story he had told about Herr Mueller collecting journals and the like had been a fabrication. In reality Herr Mueller may have had such plans but if anything it would be for book burning. What would happen if word got back to Mueller? At least he figured he could count on the two agents at the checkpoint not telling without implicating themselves in lost governmental treasures, the sheets of paper wafting about the countryside. What of his wife and son? Did they safely make it to Switzerland? If not, word could reach Munich and foil his plans of escape. But if that happened, how could he go through with his plan to leave the country. How would he know for certain what worked and what didn't. His consolation was that anything in the past associated with Rene had worked out well. However, this was the first time the plans were for escaping a country.

It would be another day and a half before Zelig and the four other professors were to board a train to Paris. There would be two very critical moments, boarding in Munich and crossing from Germany to France. In Munich the risk was higher, being closer to the Institute where the names on their identifying papers might be recognized by people who knew the real people. It was too late now to change his mind. Shortly he would be out of a job, his family had already left and Rene was nowhere near to help.

The necessary papers, tickets and instructions had been prepared and arranged for by Rene and left with a trusted contact who was a cobbler. Traffic in and out of his storefront would be a typical occurrence and, since people don't repair their shoes on a regular basis, strange faces coming and going would also be normal.

After a sleepless night Zelig returned to the Institute to perform his normal teaching duties. Although no formal announcement had been made about the dismissals, it was evident, that morning in class, that more had heard the news. When Zelig walked into the room the conversations all stopped. Their expressions were empty. He could not tell if they were shocked and hurt or angry and despising. His lecture was hollow and lifeless. Gone was the excitement. His soul had been drained from his body. The whole place was cold and gloomy. When he asked for questions there was complete silence. Figuring there could be no worse retribution, he dismissed the class very early.

With two more classes that day, Zelig had to remain. He could have left feigning sickness, but felt he needed to avoid drawing attention and potentially spoiling his plans the next day. Tomorrow he would not be in class. By the time of his first class the following day he would be at the Germany/France border. Not wanting to experience the cold stares and whispering behind his back he retreated to his office, a small but quiet and private place. There he sat; his face in his hands for most of day. He was in a state of despair punctuated by moments of joy when he would think of being reunited with Sarah and little Isaac.

He dismissed his last class early and arrived at the cobblers shop by mid-afternoon. He thought holding the tickets and paperwork in his hands would provide some extra boost that he needed to go forward.

Arriving at the shop he glanced in the front window to see if anyone else was there. Seeing only the cobbler, he went in. He produced a claim ticket provided to him by Rene. The cobbler looked at it carefully and then asked, "And the name?" Zelig answered with the last name of the person he was to impersonate. At his response the cobbler's face relaxed and he faintly smiled. Turning away to the back of the shop he retrieved a sack with some shoes in it. "Here you are, as good as new. Since you prepaid, nothing is owed." He smiled again. Zelig saw a face with a caring smile, not unlike Rene. He smiled back, "Thank you very much. I appreciate the fine workmanship." No doubt Zelig wanted to say more but another customer had come in and heaping a lot of praise on a cobbler might seem suspicious.

Zelig tucked the sack under his arm and headed for his apartment. He anxiously wanted to open it to see the documents which would lead to his freedom, but again it might look suspicious to be examining repaired shoes in public. Once in the door of the family apartment, he retrieved the shoe sack. To keep the documents from being crushed and wrinkled, the cobbler had wrapped them with paper on a stiff piece of cardboard and used a spacer between the shoes. *Very thorough and very clever,* Zelig thought. He carefully unwrapped the documents. There they were, train tickets to Paris and back, notification of a hotel reservation, registration for the scientific conference and a passport with his new name, Hermann Welmonn. The tickets were real, the hotel was real, the conference was too. The passport looked very authentic and even had been stamped a year earlier when the other Professor Welmonn made the same trip to the scientific conference in Paris. For the first time in several days he felt confident that the plan was going to succeed. He studied them carefully, first one, then another. Somewhere in that process he fell asleep.

It was night when he suddenly awoke. He was still in the chair and had no idea what time it was or even worse, what day. A chill ran down his back when he thought he may have slept a whole day and missed his train. A clock revealed that it was 4 am but what day? He had no radio. No way to check. Who would you dare call at this time of day? If this was just the next day coming up he would follow the plan and in a few hours show up at the train station.

Once there a glance at a newspaper would tell whether he would be on plan or scrambling to come up with a new one.

As he walked toward the train station Zelig felt self-conscious. He comforted himself saying that it was silly in that few people are up at this time and have enough trouble seeing themselves in a mirror let alone looking at someone else. Anxious to catch a glimpse of a newspaper he hurried more as he approached the train station. At last he saw a paper. It was left over from the day before, issue not resolved. Nearby was another, *YES!* he exclaimed internally. It was the right day.

Since he was early it was still a half hour before he could board the train. That turned out for the good. In that time he could slowdown, catch his breath and establish the composure of a scholar going off to a conference to learn from other scientists. As he waited, he looked about hoping to spot the other four who shared the same clandestine plan. There were enough people standing about that Zelig concluded they could be there but not visible to him. He was not about to raise suspicion by milling about the all but stationary group looking for his cohorts. What if he found one? What then? Strike up a conversation? Not likely. He quietly prayed that none of the others had been found out because it could mean his plans were known to the authorities as well.

After what seemed like hours, a conductor appeared at the mid-train doors and the travelers began boarding. He quickly checked each ticket to be sure no one was getting on the wrong train. Zelig was relieved that it had been just a cursory screening as he stood mid-car deciding whether to go left or right in the still quite vacant car. He decided to go right and selected a seat near the end of the car on the north side. His decision was based upon the fact that the last seat was already taken by an elderly lady; the north side would not be in the sun so he would be less noticeable on that side; and he could see most of the rest of the people in the car, at least the backs of their heads.

To avoid having a seat mate he had placed his suitcase on the floor and his briefcase on the aisle seat. As the car continued to fill, he planted his face in the daily newspaper he had purchased upon arrival at the station. He only folded it away when the train began to move. Now everyone would be seated and facing away from him, an undesired chance recognition averted.

He observed that about half of the seats were occupied with a mixture of single travelers, small families and couples. Still early in the day the car was quiet, even the children. Zelig's view of the backs of their heads yielded nothing for which to be concerned. That done, he turned to view the diminishing cityscape and now the countryside. *How beautiful the dew touched fields looked in the early morning sunlight. How peaceful. How is it possible that a place like this could be the land in which a small (but growing) misguided group of radicals was creating such misery?* Zelig thought to himself. Mile after mile his brain churned as he sought answers. Only one came, *escape, escape far away.* As wide spread as the wave of persecution, even France, his destination today, was not entirely safe.

Zelig's thoughts were abruptly interrupted and his body stiffened when saw the conductor enter the car. He was accompanied by an armed guard. Zelig did not recognize the uniform as regular German military. The pair slowly worked toward Zelig as the conductor now not only examined the ticket but the personal papers as well. Words were spoken, probably questions and answers, but Zelig was too far away to discern. Occasionally the conductor showed the guard something in the papers. So far the guard had nodded yes. As they drew closer to where Zelig was sitting, an even colder chill ran down his back when he could now clearly see the insignia on the guard's uniform. It was the dreaded swastika, symbol of the Nazis.

Now Zelig could feel his body turning numb, his palms were sweating. His diaphragm was shivering which would make it impossible to speak without giving away his intense fear. The day before he had rehearsed saying his clandestine name, Hermann Welmonn, but in his state it would sound false, he feared. He was so transfixed on his plight that he did not notice that the conductor and guard had worked their way up to him.

"What is your name?" Zelig stared blankly ahead. "What is your name?" exclaimed the conductor. The startled Zelig snapped back to reality with a lurch of his body as he turned to see the conductor leering down at him. Somehow down deep inside he mustered up a response suitable to a well-educated and intelligent professor going to a scientific conference. In a kind and gentle voice he said, "Oh, I'm so sorry I was deep in thought. I am Hermann Welmonn." Years of teaching had prepared him for most any situation but nothing compared to this. Nevertheless externally, he sounded confident and assured; internally he was quivering jelly.

Mechanically the conductor said, "Let me see your papers." His neutral manner indicated that Zelig and not aroused any suspicions.

"Where are you going?" For just a split second, Zelig wanted to give a smart-ass answer, *Look! Can't you read? You have my ticket and papers describing where I am going!* But given the circumstances, he did not dare. Once again in his best professorial voice, "I am to attend *La Conférence Scientifique International* in Paris." He pulled out his best French pronunciation for the name of the conference.

The conductor held the papers so that the guard could see them. The guard showed no emotion as he looked at Zelig's papers, then at Zelig, back to the papers and then Zelig again. Then the guard pointed to the papers and nodded to the conductor. He nodded back. No doubt they had an understanding of what was required because no words had been exchanged.

"Where do you work?" asked the conductor. As before Zelig gave a very convincing response, "At the Scientific Institute in Munich."

After a pause that seemed to take forever, the guard nodded to the conductor. This time the conductor handed Zelig his papers and the duo went to the next passenger. Zelig knew he had reason to feel relieved, but his body was not buying it. Many hours remained before the train would cross over into France and a lot could happen during that time.

As luck would have it the gentle weaving of the train, the subtle clicking of the wheels on the track and the pleasant countryside lulled Zelig into a shallow sleep. It was punctuated periodically by stops at small villages to take on and discharge passengers. This would wake Zelig long enough to survey the situation and then back to his quasi awake state. Although not completely aware of the amount of time that had passed, Zelig knew he must have been traveling three or four hours. Not terribly familiar with the route, he could only have an approximate idea of their location. He was aware that at the last stop in Germany, there would be another sweep of the passengers. This time he expected an even more thorough examination. Within the hour the train slowed to make another stop. By now most of the passengers in his car had detrained. At this stop, a few more left but no one got on. The doors closed by someone on the platform which had been the procedure throughout the trip. In a few moments the train would begin rolling gently after an initial tug as the hitches between the cars took up the slack.

The train did not move as expected by Zelig. His body grew tense once again and his stomach tied itself in a knot, the conductor and the same guard were once again working their way in his direction. With few passengers it took little time for them to reach his seat. This time Zelig was not preoccupied. However, he may have given the duo a surprised look when the conductor said, "What is your name?"

The look on the conductors face and demeanor was as if he had never laid eyes on Zelig before. Once again for a brief moment Zelig was tempted to make a wise-crack like having short memories. Just as fast he stifled the thought. Since the question was the same and the responses before had been satisfactory, he was a little more relaxed as he answered the same questions as before. Even the examination of his papers had been a carbon copy moment.

"Do you know Herr Schirtzinger? "asked the conductor.

The question hit Zelig's brain like being hit in the head with a ball bat. 'Schirtzinger?' 'Schirtzinger?' *He did not have a clue. But why was he being asked? Was it a trick?* His mind was seething. Zelig asked politely for the conductor to repeat the name?

"Schirtzinger," was the retort. "Do you know Fredrick Schirtzinger?" his voice easily heard by the rest of the passengers. "He works at the same institute that you do." The conductor's voice taking on tone of suspicion. Zelig was dumbfounded, should he lie and possibly fall into some trap or say yes and fall into still another trap. While he stewed the conductor and guard kept conferring behind Zelig's paper which they still held.

"He is going to the same meeting in Paris, you are both from the same institute in Paris, you are both scientists............ AND YOU DON'T KNOW HIM? HE IS ON THE SAME CAR AND

32

YOU ARE NOT SEATED TOGETHER, YOU WORK
TOGETHER AND YOU DON'T KNOW HIM?"

The conductor's voice rang through the car like someone had hit a
steel girder with a sledgehammer. Zelig was shaken like never
before. His eyes darted about in his head as he frantically tried to
come up with an answer. He began to stammer.

"Well, I ….. I…. that is ……. He must be …… ," in a desperate
attempt to find a solution he looked around the car. There they
were, the few remaining passengers, the backs of their heads not
wanting to get involved. Zelig tried again, "This fellow I ………"
then Zelig's eyes met with the eyes of another passenger at the
other end of the car. The man had turned his head back quickly but
it was enough. Zelig recognized him as one of his group making
their escape through Paris. Zelig was a very bright man and quick
on his feet, in an instant he turned and confidently addresses the
conductor and guard.

"Zingy! You mean Zingy! Zingy Schirtzinger! We never use his
last name." Zelig's excited response was also loud, loud enough
for Herr Schirtzinger to hear the nickname he had just acquired.
Zingy caught on quickly and turned in his seat toward Zelig. Zingy
knew his new nickname but not Zelig's so he chose his words
carefully, "I didn't see you sitting back there."

"Well, I did not see you get on either, I just guessed that you had
boarded another car." Both men bantered back and forth hoping to
distract the conductor and the guard. It worked. Zelig moved up to
joined his colleague for the remainder of the trip.

A few minutes later as the train slowly left the station Zelig and
Zingy could see the guard on the platform. Both breathed a sigh of

relief. Their first action was to look at each other's papers to get their respective aliases correct if questioned again.

There was no stop at the border since no town existed on the border. The next time the train stopped would be in France. There were no signs visible to the passengers so when they actually crossed was difficult to tell. However, Zingy knew how to tell. When they reach the *sauts de mouton* (literally, "sheep jumps) they would definitely be in France.*

The train slowed its pace and began a long turn, the cars ahead could now be seen out of the left side windows. In a moment their car was rocking from side to side and additional track noise could be heard. Zelig frowned as he tried to imagine what could be going wrong. Zingy smiled a broad smile to Zelig, "It's the *sauts de mouton*, we are definitely in France now."

Zelig's frown faded to be replaced by his own broad grin. Now both added gushers of tears to their smiles.

*In the First World War, the provinces of Alsace and Lorraine formed part of the German Empire, and during this time their rail lines were converted to right-hand running. When the provinces were returned to France in 1919, right hand running was left in place. To cope with the change from left hand to right hand running at places where there was no necessity to stop for a border crossing, a number of flyovers or *sauts de mouton* (literally, "sheep jumps") were installed whose sole purpose was to take one running line over the top of another in the opposite direction.

5. YOUNG, SMART AND AMBITIOUS

Laura Anne Olson would soon graduate from college with a double major in math and science. The twenty-one-year-old wanted to be a teacher. There were many indications, to this point, that Laura would be an excellent teacher. Even as early as middle school, her interactions with younger children exemplified her willingness and talents for helping others learn while having fun in the process. Like the rest of us idealists just starting out, she dreamed of how her career would unfold as she met the challenges the future would bring. And like us, what came to pass for Laura Olson would turn out to be completely unexpected and very different from those dreams. But she was a level-headed, well-grounded young woman; she knew that expectations could be at odds with reality.

Laura had a very creative imagination. It was one of the attributes that made her a good teacher candidate. When Laura taught a new concept, rather than continuing to hammer away in the same fashion without success, she would change approaches several times until she found the combination that worked. Often the new approach was quite innovative.

Despite her own dreams and ambitions, Laura also realized that many factors outside of her control would influence her future: other people's dreams, aspirations and agendas; chance; timing. Of these, "chance" was the only factor over which she felt some sense of control. As her mother, who was also a teacher, was fond of saying, "Chance favors the prepared mind." It was her way of urging Laura, in those earlier years, to adopt a philosophy encompassing as much education and variety of experiences as possible. It worked. Laura's education and experiences, even before entering college, were much broader than most of her classmates.

One specific result of her keen imagination and quest for knowledge was a high level of awareness of the events going on around her. As a consequence, she often found herself playing amateur detective (quietly and to herself) as she tried to piece together the clues she observed and draw conclusions about the events transpiring around her. Indeed, it was "play" to her. She never took it seriously, but just enjoyed the activity the way someone else might enjoy solving a crossword puzzle.

As for Laura's future: in the months after graduation, she did meet others whom she had not anticipated meeting; she had experiences she never expected. No surprise there: again, she knew that would be the case. But what her education and wide range of experiences could never have prepared her for, and what she could not have dreamed about, was the magnitude and the nature of change she was soon to experience.

6. FINAL DAYS OF COLLEGE

Laura's trip from her apartment to campus amounted to a short walk to the bus stop, a twenty-five minute bus ride and then a ten-minute walk to her first classroom. Most of the time, especially on the bus, her mind was occupied with a variety of random thoughts: her plans for the day; yesterday's significant news; the weather; shopping she wanted to do; how to solve the world's problems. Any subject was fair game. Seldom was anything resolved, but the time helped her put the issues, problems, and topics in perspective as they related to her personal goals and plans. What could she and what should she do, as an individual, to help the rest of humankind? As usual, this morning as she got off the bus, her gaze fell upon the various headlines at the newsstand by her stop.

Typically, Laura was greeted with murder, mayhem and war. *Oh! What a waste!* she thought, and not for the first time. As she read, a wave of despair would overtake her. *It's usually the women and children who suffer the most from the shortsighted and misguided leaders in the world. And it goes on and on without stopping! What can ever be done to stop the needless suffering?* She would continue to fret and stew for the remainder of her walk to campus.

By the time she was in sight of the science lecture hall, Laura, full of determination, would have resolved to do what she could as a teacher to make a difference. After all, by now she had some very specific ideas of how to be a really good teacher.

The reports of American kids (especially girls) falling behind in math and science emboldened her even more. Her own experiences with less than enthusiastic, ill-prepared teachers only drove her to look for better solutions. She had seen even the most motivated and well-prepared teachers hampered by the endless trivial school procedures. *No, sir,* she thought as she strode confidently across campus, she was not going to let that happen.

Laura was determined to make science come to life for her students. They would not spend endless hours in a classroom; they would participate in the world of science all around them.

When she reached the lecture and demonstration hall, Laura's train of thought would be interrupted. She would come back to the present and begin greeting her many friends who were already in the hall.

"Make a difference as a teacher" was Laura's mantra, and the commute to class was her period of meditation.

At times, it had seemed like graduation was light years away. But in a few days she would receive her diploma and soon start on her *own* curriculum–a curriculum she could never have imagined.

7. MATH, THE LANGUAGE OF SCIENCE

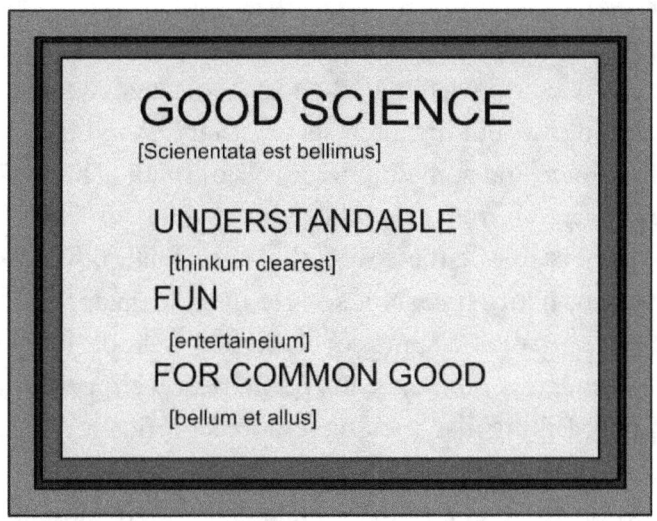

Leffler's "Good Science" poster

As Laura arrived in class each day, she always greeted her many friends. The result being that it usually took a few minutes for her to get seated. Today once she was settled, Laura glanced once again at the "Good Science" poster Professor Leffler had posted near the front of the lecture hall. She chuckled to herself, noting again the faux Latin he had included to help his students remember the message. His class had certainly lived up to those standards, especially the first two subheadings, she thought to herself. Continuing to look about, she remembered the first time she had been in this fine old lecture hall with its ornate wood trim and beautiful stained glass windows. She remembered the many mind changing moments she experienced when Professor Wes L. Leffler ("L" is for Lafayette) explained and demonstrated Physics concepts that until then were mysterious to her. It was an undergraduate class for science teachers. His talent for involving the students, rather than just lecturing to them, was extraordinary.

Excellent demonstrations and humor were tools that Leffler used quite well. Now, sadly, it was coming to end. Laura took her seat next to her friend, JJ.

JJ, who was a few years older than Laura, had been her friend since her sophomore year. He was in graduate school finishing up his degree in Anthropology, but his interests went far beyond that field. He loved all science and some higher levels of math. Thus, his elective choices placed him in several of Laura's classes. The fine arts were no stranger to JJ either. With that combination, you might expect a stuffy or nerdy type. Not so. He liked team sports and played baseball, football and some soccer in high school. In college, because of academic demands, his participation slipped to the odd pick-up game. Biking also took on a more significant role. JJ was a very well rounded individual. Laura was drawn to those qualities, but since both were committed to launching their careers, they had little time for romance. A strong but strictly platonic friendship had sprung up between them.

Today was like any other day in a Leffler class: it promised some challenging aspects, factual stuff, and, as ever, fun. After some housekeeping announcements by a student assistant, Professor Leffler introduced a video. He told his students the video was about the repression of critical thinking. They were about to see a segment from the movie "Galileo," and this would not be the fun part of today's class. The quick, plain and simple truth was that the religious leaders of the time were telling Galileo that his science was wrong and to cease and desist the writing and teaching of it, or suffer dire consequences. It was a chilling video clip.

At the end of the video segment, professor Leffler continued his comments. "This was a portrayal of Galileo's oppression and is factually based," he said. "It is a good example of the repression of science by groups, governments or individuals with agendas of control and greed. In some cases, it was the result of stupidity or

40

even mental illness. Whatever the source of repression, good science will typically break free and thrive until the next wave of repression. During these repressed periods, scientists .....,"he paused and looked directly at Laura and some other students he knew to be math double majors "..... by the way, I am not leaving out mathematicians. I include them with the scientists, since the two go hand in hand ....scientists have gone to great lengths to protect revolutionary ideas, research journals, science apparatus and other artifacts."

"An example close to our time was a family of German scientists by the name of Wallerstein. Over several generations, this family risked much to protect a collection that amounts to centuries of protected scientific information. Just prior to WWII, the Wallersteins recognized the signs of unrest and repression coming at the hands of the Nazis and as a result they moved many times. In the process their scientific treasures appeared to have been lost. Or were they? Some say they just did a better job of hiding and protecting the cache. What made their story noteworthy are the persistent rumors that the information contained in the collection is EXTREMELY valuable. The rumors don't say what is so valuable about the information, only that its value is immense and has worldwide significance. So, I suppose that tells us we should invest in Wallerstein rather than, say, the stock market."

This time his attempt at humor drew only a few chuckles from the class. Undaunted, he continued. "The other point I would like to make is that even during periods of 'free or unfettered science,' a good scientist must still be on guard against the misuse of science. History gives us countless examples of people using good science to justify unnecessary war, terrorism and all sorts of crimes against humanity. Please remember this as you go out in the world and embark on your career paths." His point about 'unnecessary war' really resonated with Laura.

He gestured toward the poster Laura had admired when she arrived. "Good Science also means using science for the common good. With that, let's move on to today's demonstration."

There was a short pause while a student assistant brought out some demonstration equipment. During that time, Professor Leffler brought up a pair of equations on the big screen. Everyone in the class recognized them as the equations for momentum and kinetic energy; they studied them in various Physics classes. Now on the desk in front of him was a classic demo: colliding balls.

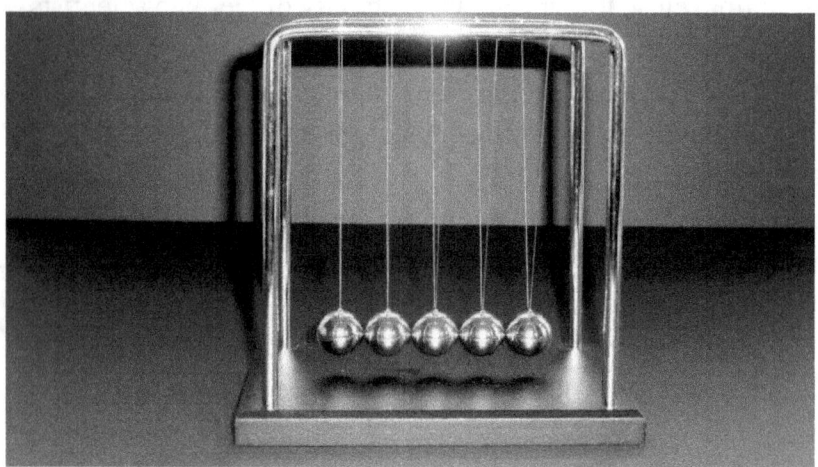

COLLIDING BALLS

"You have seen this many, many times before, but, before I demonstrate, I want to reiterate the wonderful marriage between math and science and urge you to be sure to use it with your students. Now before you can teach someone else, you need to remember that as these objects swing about they have--?" He waited for the class to finish the sentence. "Kinetic energy and momentum," someone called out.

"Exactly," Leffler confirmed. "And by now you probably recognize the equations on the screen and they are?" Leffler paused again for a response. Collectively they answered, "Kinetic energy and momentum equations."

"If I pull back two balls from one end and let them go, what will happen? Will one ball at the other end move a lot? Or will two balls move? Or will all the balls move? Maybe some other combination? Do you remember?"

After a pause, students called out various answers, but no one answer predominated.

"Just as I thought!" Leffler cried. "You have forgotten. Well, here's the deal: you do not have to remember the outcome. Using those two equations, you can accurately predict the actual motion that will result by solving both equations simultaneously. You do remember solving simultaneous equations in math? Right? Give it a try."

Leffler's tone was slightly chiding for not remembering, but after all that's why they were in school, to be reminded of what was important.

The screen background color switched to a rich blue color, the music from Jeopardy began to play and in a voice meant to sound like Alex Trebeck, Professor Leffler said, "Students, you will have three minutes to come up with your answer."

A few laughs followed, as Leffler's wit struck again. The music played on while the students put their math skills to the test. Some looked perplexed while others set out immediately to complete the task. With some help from their peers, those who initially stalled now knew what to do.

When the music stopped, Professor Leffler announced, "Time is up. What is your answer?"

Collectively the class responded with a variety of forms to the answer, but essentially they all came up with the right answer: two balls will move off together at the other end. He then pulled two to the side and released them; as predicted, two at the other end swung off. Until friction took its toll, the balls click-clacked back and forth, repeating the same cycles of motion over and over again: first one way, then back in the opposite direction.

"Isn't that beautiful?" he asked with a beaming smile.

He repeated the process a few more times by pulling back three then four balls, but required they make the calculation for each case before the demo. For each case, as the students applied the equations, the correct outcome was predicted.

If you would like to view this demonstration go to thefinesociety.com, select VIDEOS and view Video Demonstration #1.

Once again the professor repeated, "Isn't that beautiful? This is why we say that math is the language for science. Any time we can describe real events in mathematical equations, we have a handle we can grab and make the science work for us. Be sure to instill that in your students"

The class collectively nodded their understanding and their faces reflected a sense of satisfaction over their accomplishment.

"Now I have another reason for repeating the last demonstration. I want to relate it to basic *quantum mechanics*." He took great care to enunciate the phrase loudly and clearly, eliciting a few grumbles and disparaging comments from his students.

Up to this point in their academic careers, the students had only learned about quantum mechanics as a concept. Most were satisfied with that level of understanding because delving further meant much more sophisticated math, from which most undergraduates shied away.

Quantum mechanics is such a strange world compared to our daily existence that intuition and common experience are of little value to those who study it. To Laura's fellow students, "quantum mechanics" might as well have been a synonym for "hard work." But Professor Leffler knew what he was doing. It was a reaction he was expecting.

"Not wild about quantum mechanics?" he asked. "In that case, forget that I mentioned it at all. Put the subject out of your mind and let's just move on."

Most of his students were visibly relieved, but a few knew that his style was not to dismiss a topic off-hand. A few suspected some sort of 'gotcha'--maybe not immediately, but probably later in the session.

While he had been talking, Herb, the lab assistant had replaced the colliding balls demo with a very similar set, except this equipment only had two balls. In addition there was a white dot on each ball. He also set up a video camera on a tripod that pointed at the equipment; the camera was attached to a laptop.

If you would like to view this demonstration go to thefinesociety.com, select VIDEOS and view Video Demonstration #2.

Laura knew of Herb and recognized the demo he was setting up on the desk. She ran across him working on the demo a few weeks earlier. When she asked him why the camera, computer and sophisticated software for just some colliding balls, he responded saying, "Leffler requires all his grad assistants do this one as part of their studies. For some reason he attaches a lot of significance to it, but I'm not sure why."

Being the curious person she was, Laura watched intently for quite some time as Herb worked on the demo. She wondered if she could figure out what was so important.

Thus, today when Herb began setting up the apparatus in her class this day, she already knew **what** was going to happen but she still did not know the **why**. She remembered that the demo very clearly showed that when the two balls were caused to collide with each other that only a few combinations resulted in meaningful results. He called them **modes** and used words like **stable**, **harmonious** and **well-behaved** to further describe them. "Stable modes," was the terminology used most of the time. He also showed some modes that were un-stable, non-harmonius and not well-behaved. It was easy to tell them apart; the stable modes of motion looked like they could go on and on and on, where the unstable modes of motion died down to nothing very quickly. That's all there was to it. It took a lot of work but it all boiled down to this, modes of motion that could sustain themselves and ones that could not. Like human efforts, if we all work together, our efforts will have an effect. If we works at odds with each other ciaos results and nothing is accomplished.

During the demo both Professor Leffler and Herb asked questions of the class which required them to make predictions as to the outcomes. Laura held back since she had prior knowledge and felt it would be unfair to her peers. However, on one question in particular, the class was stumped. Laura knew the correct answer but not because Herb had previously told her. At the time she had figured out the correct answer. The only difference here was now she was repeating her answer. For that reason she felt justified in offering her prediction and the explanation.

Leffler did his usual pause to let the others think about Laura's answer and explanation and then with exuberance, "Great job Ms. Olson," Leffler said. "I particularly like your point that the equations are still valid. The more times our description, in this case the equations, agrees with the behavior, the more convinced we can be that we have the right description, or equations."

JJ did not hear the questions or the responses because he was completely absorbed in his own thought processes. Laura had noticed the telltale signs: his head bobbed slightly; his pencil moved above his notes; his lips formed silent words. JJ was oblivious to the activities around him.

This was not unusual for him. He was a "concept" type. He would listen intently for long periods of time, absorbing information and sorting it out until a clear picture emerged in his mind. Typically, he was right on the money. Often, he was way ahead of the class— even Laura. More than once his professors were amazed at the depth and thoroughness of his understanding.

Laura noticed that JJ came back to the present when he heard Professor Leffler begin to speak again. Her friend had a smile on his face. Laura noticed that too.

"Tomorrow we'll take this a few steps further," Leffler was saying, in a manner that recalled Julius Sumner Miller, a physics teacher from the past. "I believe you'll be amazed at the result,"

The "Julius" quote garnered a few chuckles from the students, who were familiar with Sumner Miller from the miracle of video. As they began to pack up their belongings Leffler called above the din,

"Oh, don't forget, tomorrow we have an outdoor field trip, so dress accordingly."

JJ and a very curious Laura left together. As they walked out of the building she asked, "Well, what did you figure out?"

Without hesitation he began.

"Herb and Leffler said that these two balls, set into motion without friction, would have only three sustainable motions. And we saw that demonstrated in the analysis. They also said that if you try to force them into other behaviors, those motions will shift to one of the three or some combination of the three or die out; their analysis supported that."

Laura nodded.

"Well," JJ went on, "I think Leffler's plan for tomorrow is to extend that behavior to any two objects, no matter their size, that interact with each other. In fact, I think he will infer that this happens to particles at the atomic level. What's more, I think he will expand it to more than two objects interacting."

Laura could see he was on a roll, so she did not interrupt.

"And last, he'll bring up quantum physics again, because even with the little exposure I have had to the subject, I remember one of the main premises: 'Only certain modes, motions or states can exist.'"

With that, JJ stopped and looked at Laura to gauge her reaction. She had followed him every step of the way and understood.

"I think you could be right," she said. "The way he let go of the quantum physics comment early in the session was just too easy."

There was a pause as each pondered the matter further. Then Laura spoke excitedly.

"The neat part of this, if it's true, is that I thoroughly understood this stuff. If it is quantum behavior, Leffler will have done it again. He will have taken a tough subject and brought it down to an understandable level. The little exposure I've had in the past to quantum theory was anything but understandable."

No one who had ever taken Leffler's classes would argue with her on that point. The professor was well known as a world-class expert in the art of science demonstrations and relatable, cogent explanations. Most high school and some collegiate teachers had at least one of his books for reference purposes.

Laura and JJ needed to keep their conversation brief; she had another class soon and he had an appointment with his program advisor. As they began to move in opposite directions, JJ asked a quick question.

"How's the job search coming?"

He knew she was anxious to find work this summer, even before school started in the fall. Laura's financial situation was even more precarious than most college students. Her father died during her sophomore year of college, and money had been tight ever since. His early death was unexpected and his public relations business was based solely on his expertise, so with his passing, the money dried up quickly. Like a lot of small businesses, much of the family resources were tied up in the business. Laura and her mother carefully charted a course that would take her through the remainder of her undergraduate degree, but she would need to start making money as soon as possible.

The expression on her face gave JJ the answer even before she said, "Nothing yet."

He gave her an encouraging look and said, "Something will turn up. You're too good a catch to be passed over."

She smiled gratefully and they parted company.

As JJ walked to his appointment, he thought about his friendship with Laura. They both lost parents within a few months of each other. JJ's mother had died of lung cancer. It had been devastating. JJ was an only child; now he was completely alone. His father had died in an auto accident when JJ was in junior high.

After his father died, JJ's mother, along with her two sisters, had made JJ their cause. This young man was going to succeed no matter what. They provided what money they could and the encouragement to keep him away from gangs, drugs and mediocrity. He fully appreciated their efforts and it paid off. He was about to graduate with a Masters degree in Anthropology. Most of his relatives had not graduated from high school.

Laura missed several days of school when her father died. When she returned, JJ knew before she spoke a word that something terrible had happened. JJ found that comforting Laura in the weeks that followed her father's death comforted him as well. That sad time became the cornerstone of their friendship. They began to heal by telling each other stories about their parents. It started with a few tears, but as time went by these moments were characterized by fond, repairing laughter.

8. THE NEXT MORNING

At 6:05, the bedside clock radio clicked on, waking Laura to classical music, as it had every weekday for as long as she could remember. She set her alarm for the odd time in order to avoid the announcements that occurred at the beginning of the morning program. It wasn't the announcer who bothered Laura; she simply liked music to be the first thing she heard each day. It made for a smoother transition into consciousness. Today she awoke after a restless night riddled with anxious dreams over not finding work. Thus she was more tired than usual and the soft musical transition was even more important. As her preparations for the day--bathing, dressing and eating breakfast—proceeded, she found herself distracted by more thoughts about work, or her lack thereof. She hoped to find work teaching summer school, but those classes were less numerous, and finding a position had been hard. So far, she'd had no luck. She toyed with filling in with bartending or waitressing, but she had friends who had taken such work periodically and the stories they told about some of the customers and incidences were enough to convince Laura that the bar/restaurant world should be kept as a last resort.

She continued to mull over the job search on her way to class that morning. However, one action item came of all the worrying: she decided to make another visit to the teacher placement office that afternoon. She made regular, but unscheduled, visits to be certain that everything was in order with her credentials and applications. In the past that office had made serious errors that initially set back her search. She wanted to make sure she was not denied a job because of a clerical error.

JJ was in his seat when she arrived at the hall. The usual greeting with friends ensued and ended with Laura taking a seat next to JJ.

He noticed a little makeup under her eyes—it was easy to spot since she rarely wore any. Typically she wore lip-gloss, but that was the extent of it.

"Have a rough night?" asked JJ.

Surprised, Laura asked, "Does it show?" She realized he must have spotted the makeup she applied to distract from the dark circles beneath her eyes.

She went on to describe the sleepless night she'd spent worrying about never finding a job. JJ was in the process of reassuring her when Leffler started the class.

"Since we have a field trip, I'm going to move right along this morning. I'd like to pick up where we left off yesterday with the colliding balls demonstration. To save time I won't recap the findings, but you can review them for yourself in your notes or go online to see the demonstrations and results again. Today I have replaced the two balls with two pendulums."

On the demo table were two pendulums that looked identical. They were about a foot apart and connected at their midpoint by a spring.

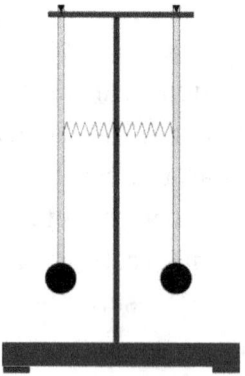

Two linked pendulums

"This apparatus is essentially the same as the colliding balls, except the pendulums do not collide directly," Leffler explained. "However, they do 'collide' with each other through the spring."

As he spoke he started the pendulums much like he had in the previous day's colliding ball demonstration.

If you would like to view this demonstration go to thefinesociety.com, select VIDEOS and view Video Demonstration #3.

"As you can see, these two exhibit the same modes of behavior as the colliding balls. What's different is the 'collision' using the spring lets us examine the interactions in more detail. To save time, here's Herb to summarize his work with these pendulums."

Leffler gestured to Herb to take over.

"I did the same type of analysis using the camera, PC and software," Herb explained. "In short, the results were *identical*. These two pendulums exhibited the *same stable modes* as the balls. When I tried to force other modes, the motions decayed (as physicists say it), or in the vernacular, 'changed' to the stable modes. The two pendulums have *three* stable modes."

Herb injected a bit of humor here, pronouncing the distinction between "decay" and "changed" "in a snobby voice. The students chuckled.

With that, Herb stopped. Leffler stayed silent as well. The pause was for emphasis and the students knew it. They muttered, "Just like yesterday," and, "Yes," and they nodded their heads. It was clear to Laura why Leffler had omitted the review of the previous day's work. This demo effectively accomplished the same thing.

In the background, Herb had been setting up an additional apparatus. With a cue from Leffler, Herb began to assemble it on the demonstration table. As his assistant worked, Leffler explained.

"As you can see, Herb is setting up a third identical pendulum in line with the other two; it is connected by the same kind of spring. As you might have guessed, our next step is to set these into various motions and observe the results.

As Leffler often did he tinkered with the apparatus before having Herb get into it with both feet. It was Leffler's way of "telling 'em what he's going to tell ya."

If you would like to view this demonstration go to thefinesociety.com, select VIDEOS and view Video Demonstration #4.

Okay. Herb, take it away."

Herb stepped up to address the class. His results were flashed on the overhead screen.

"The results in this experiment were very similar," he began. "That is, these three pendulums have a definite number of stable motions, or stable modes, as we have also called them.

If I tried to force other motions, they would revert to the stable ones. But there is one difference: the number of stable modes. Three pendulums have *five* stable motions. I continued the process of adding coupled pendulums and observed the same type of results. Please note that I have not been using the word *harmonious* as I did with the two ball analysis. That has only been to save time and words. These motions were harmonious as well. I could have been saying *stable harmonious modes*. Herb paused a moment for emphasis and then continued, "This table summarizes the results adding more linked pendulums."

He gestured to the table on the screen:

Number of coupled pendulums	2	3	4	5
Number of stable modes	3	5	9	17

Now that Herb had finished the introduction, Leffler picked up the presentation.

"As you look at Herb's table it is not hard to imagine that had he kept adding pendulums, the number of stable motions would continue at an accelerated pace. That is, the number of stable harmonious modes would grow larger faster than the number of linked pendulums. That would be true, but his analysis took a tremendous amount of time and effort just to get to five coupled devices. However, others have already done the work, confirming that increasing the number of pendulums does indeed yield a geometrically increasing rate of stable motions."

Leffler inserted an educational pause for emphasis and then continued.

"The next part will be done in your imaginations, so wake up those brain cells. Clearly, these pendulums are free to move in essentially one dimension, back and forth. Now picture a group of pendulums on a table connected by springs, like this illustration."

Leffler brought up a sketch on the overhead.

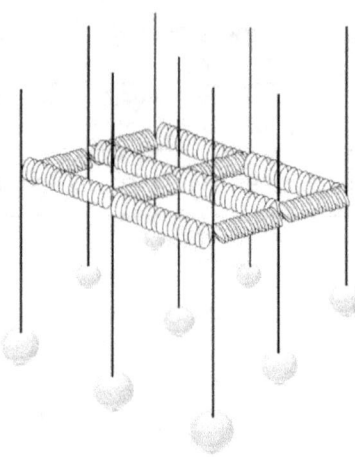

Pendulums connected in two dimensions

"Now you see that any individual pendulum can move in two dimensions. They could be set into motion in any number of ways, and the motions can then be observed by a grad assistant."

Everyone looked at Herb, who was shaking his head as if to say, "no way, not me, man." By now the class realized the horrendous challenge that it would pose for Herb and saw the humor in Leffler's comment. The students laughed.

"Good news, Herb," Leffler announced. "It has already been done—well, at least on a small scale."

Good natured as ever, Herb mopped his brow in a gesture of relief and won another chuckle from the crowd.

"The result," Leffler finished, "is that the number of *stable harmonious motions* or *modes* increases even faster than the one-dimensional pendulum examples."

Leffler paused, and then posed a question to the class.

"Does anyone have any idea where I'm headed with this?"

Laura could feel the adrenalin begin to flow as she remembered JJ's prediction from the day before. She glanced at him to see if he was going to respond. Their eyes met. Each knew what the other was thinking. It was JJ's prediction, so she felt he should be the one to answer. But JJ gestured that she should answer. Laura declined and urged her friend to respond. After a little more urging from her, JJ finally raised his hand to be recognized.

Leffler called on him. The professor's expression suggested that he was expecting the correct answer.

"I would expect that the next example would be a three dimensional array of pendulums all connected by springs," JJ began. "That some grad student"--he pointed to Herb and laughter erupted--"would be given the task of setting the pendulums into various motions and observing the results. So… the results would be similar, except that the number of stable motions would be even greater."

Leffler looked about the class; Laura was shaking her head "yes" in agreement and smiling, as were most of the rest of the class.

The class waited for the professor to comment on JJ's answer. Instead, Leffler asked another question.

"JJ, if this is so, what would be my point of showing you all of this stuff?"

JJ replied immediately.

"I think you're gonna tell us that this behavior can be applied to all sorts of things, especially tiny particles like atoms, subatomic particles and the stuff of which they are made."

Now smiling, Leffler replied, "You said 'this behavior.' Do you have a name for 'this behavior'?"

JJ paused, then clearly made up his mind to go with his gut.

"I have a pretty good guess, I think—like: quantum behavior, quantum mechanics, quantum physics or some similar name," he said.

By now the rest of the class was on board. There was buzz in the room as they murmured to each other about what they now understood. Leffler had dismissed the troublesome term quantum mechanics earlier and yet went on to show how easy it is to understand the basic concept of it. It was an "aha" moment: things clicked; the dots connected; the clouds had cleared.

Laura gave JJ another high five. She beamed with pride for her friend and the insight he had demonstrated.

"Well done JJ," Leffler said.

Once the excitement died down, Leffler resumed.

"Here are some other important parts of these trials that we have not yet covered. I won't be presenting you with proof for these next few comments. However, they are *very* important in quantum physics, so write 'em down. Since we won't be demonstrating these, you will just have to use your imagination again and trust me. First, as the number of pendulums objects or particles (use whatever term you want) increases, the *total kinetic energy* of the group increases. That is reasonable because each moving object has kinetic energy and every extended or compressed spring has potential energy. So, the larger the aggregation of moving stuff, the more energy it collectively has. The second and last point is this: the larger the aggregation, the more stable it is."

But he'd lost them again. Laura could see puzzled looks on the faces around her and knew she wore such an expression herself.

"Let me explain."

Of course, Leffler knew he needed to clarify his point.

"Consider two lines of pendulums. In one there are three pendulums and in the other, three hundred. For the sake of simplicity, both lines are swinging in unison. Now you grab hold of the end pendulum and force it to move opposite of what it had been doing. In doing so, you are acting as an outside force here acting on objects in stable motion. Using your imagination, tell me how you expect the rest of the pendulums in the line to behave."

After thinking for a few moments, Laura raised her hand. Leffler gave her a nod to proceed. "If I understand the circumstances you have described, I think the efforts on the end pendulum would upset the normal stable group motion. I couldn't guess what the patterns would be, but I think you could safely say that the longer chain would take longer to become disturbed."

"Well put Laura," replied Leffler. He restated Laura's assessment in his own words, and went on to question a few students at random, verifying that they understood.

"Let me wrap it up with a hypothetical example," the professor continued. "Assume that an electron is really a collection of a vast number of little particles moving about and interacting with other electrons (i.e. other groups of little particles moving in harmony with each other) in some unbelievably complex but stable harmonic gyrations. There's that word harmonic again," as he did a theatrical 'aside.' After a short pause, "Then, like the pendulum in the group of three hundred other pendulums, an electron could become unstable if acted upon by some outside force." He paused for a moment then restated it once more. "Well, guess what? In our universe an electron is not alone and it does have a finite lifetime. It does not last forever. You can look it up. The half-life is very long indeed, but the fact that there is a half-life supports the notion that an electron is made up of a lot of small moving stuff that could eventually be destabilized by forces from......., other particles. Let's just leave it there for now."

"Before we leave this topic, I want to show you a picture of some old apparatus. Drawings can be found that date back centuries; this photograph is reported to be from the Wallerstein collection of scientific apparatus. I thought you might like to see this picture. It's not the apparatus we just demonstrated. Ours is stark, just the basics."

Coupled Antique Pendulums

Comparing the picture of the antique pendulums and the apparatus on Leffler's desk, she understood his "stark" comment. The old ones were ornately decorated with lines and curves, many of which suggested symbols of some sort. However, Laura did not recognize any ones with which she was familiar. They had a well-crafted look. Leffler's equipment was made with simple metal bars with a weight at the end and holes along its length to connect the springs. His apparatus had served its purpose without all the fancy trapping, but it was still nice to see that science of the past was rich in artistic touches. *They don't make them like that anymore,* she thought to herself with a wry smile.

Leffler continued, "I've seen centuries-old journals with sketches of apparatus like this. Do you suppose scientists of long ago were thinking about quantum theories? Your guess is as good as mine, but nevertheless, it's an intriguing idea. Oh, and here is another thought to tuck in your brain to consider relative to what you have observed here. Consider words like; *standing waves* and *resonance*.

After another pause for emphasis, he announced, "Last item today and also related to standing waves. Do you remember the demonstrations we did with musical instruments? The organ pipes? The tabletop water wave demos?" Heads nodded around the room—it was a memorable unit, especially for music lovers. "Keep those demonstrations in mind when we go on today's field trip. Everyone meet in the parking lot in 15 minutes to board a bus to Montrose Beach. If you prefer using your own transportation, meet us there and just look for the University Bus. ATTENDANCE WILL BE TAKEN" he yelled with a smile as the students had already started leaving. The attendance check was a tongue-in-cheek comment, because no one ever wanted to miss Professor Leffler's field trips. Some were legendary.

About forty-five minutes later, all were gathered at the bus at Montrose Beach. Leffler motioned to the class to follow him: looking like a modern day Pied Piper, with his mop of grey hair dancing about as a result of his almost skipping walking motion. The grey hair seemed a contradiction to his youthful physical appearance and behavior. As a result, Laura noted to herself that his chronological age, probably 60s, did not match is behavioral age, maybe 20s. She resolved to follow his example when she finds herself at that later in life situation.

A few yards north of the parking lot, he stopped. At this part of the park the ground was quite high above the water and there was a sharp drop-off; Leffler led the class here and cautioned them not to fall in (a requirement these days in this litigious climate). Unlike other parts of the lakefront, the land was high above the water level. Huge blocks of concrete formed a wall to hold the earth. There was no beach at this location and water waves crashed right into the block wall. It looked like a manmade cliff about twenty feet high.   While the class stood there listening, the occasional extra-large rogue wave struck the stones and produced a plume of water, spraying the class. Being good-natured college kids, most of them loved it.

However, one young lady asked a question in a rather abrupt tone: "Why are we here?" Her inflection revealed a slight irritation with the dampening sprays. "What does the lake have to do with anything?"

Leffler nodded and said "I'll get right to the point. Look at those waves. See them coming in AT AN ANGLE, hitting the stone wall and bouncing back in that direction? That's the same behavior we saw in the water wave demos back in class earlier this term." Leffler had raised his voice to emphasize the 'at an angle' part of his statement. After a few moments all the students recognized the pattern of reflection and indicated agreement. "Well, this is just a giant ripple tank," Leffler explained. "Now, I'd like you to make some observations. Notice, if you will, the height of the crest and depth of the trough."

The group watched a few moments and then agreed that the height from the crest (the high point) to the trough (the low point) was about a foot. Naturally, a more precise value was difficult because the waves were moving and their observations were made from several feet above.

Leffler continued, "Please also note the angle at which the wave approaches the wall and the angle of the wave as it reflects back from the wall."

Someone yelled out, "The incoming angle looks like the reflected angle, like in the lab." "Exactly," Leffler confirmed and continued, "Now follow me."

They walked about 100 yards farther north. At that point the shear wall made a different angle to the incoming waves. Now the waves were headed straight at the wall and bouncing straight back. The students were getting sprayed more frequently too. Leffler directed their attention: "Look at the waves just a few feet in front of the wall." He said no more and waited. The students craned their necks and leaned over the edge to get a better look.

In less than a minute, a student pointed at the water a few feet in front of the wall and said, "Hey, that wave isn't moving toward *or* away from the wall. The crest and trough just keep going up and down in place." The others looked again and one by one they saw it too.

"And what is that wave doing?" asked Leffler.

Mumblings of "standing wave," "just standing," "not moving," etc…, came from the class.

"Exactly," Leffler confirmed. "At this angle the reflected wave meets the incoming wave head-on. An incoming wave combines with a reflected wave of the same shape and the result is a *standing wave*."

Leffler paused to let this explanation sink in. Then he asked, "Do you see anything else?"

Laura was one of the first to respond and then the rest chimed in. They had noticed that the crest and trough of the standing wave were respectively higher and deeper, maybe by three feet, more than the crests and troughs of the waves around it.

Laura took the lead and explained, "Since the height of the standing wave is higher than the individual waves that make it, the water must be moving faster to rise to a higher level... that would mean more energy. The standing wave has more energy."

"Absolutely right. Remember, that's what we observed with the tuning fork, the flute, an organ pipe and most musical instruments. Standing waves are louder or more energetic than their individual wave components. Broadcasters know about this effect as well...but that explanation will have to wait for a different class," Leffler smiled self-deprecatingly. His enthusiasm for the subject was taking him off track. Returning to the subject at hand, he concluded, "These are all examples of quantum behavior on a grand scale. The standing wave that you see is the unique product of the incoming and reflected waves. If the incoming and reflected were different, the resulting standing wave would differ as well." He paused for the educational moment.

Now facing the lake, the students on his right, Leffler continued in a contemplative tone, "Isn't it nice, too, that nature provided us with tools like the giant ripple tank of Lake Michigan, just down the street from our classroom?" He smiled. "Now imagine an observer in ancient times standing near a cliff like this one, overlooking the water. Such a person must have observed the same thing eons before our more sophisticated apparatus. Do you suppose that observer had thoughts of quantum mechanics? We can only guess. As you go about your teaching careers, take every opportunity to point out the science in the natural world. It will be worth it."

Herb, the lab assistant always nearby and ready to spring into action when called, sensed from Leffler's philosophically sounding voice that he was ready to wrap up the session.

"Professor.............," Herb tentatively spoke as he held up his hand holding some papers. Leffler's head jerked slightly as if being wakened from a dream and he looked at Herb, "Oh, yes, I almost forgot. Herb has a handout that lists a few websites that may be of interest to you. A lot of scientists, students and amateur scientists are placing demonstrations on sites like YouTube. Herb has compiled a list of sites with demos that reinforce the well behaved, harmonic and sustainable motions between objects that interact with each other. You know, the stuff we just studied. You will see lots of variety on the same theme. Now there is no guarantee these will all be there if you go to look. Internet content can vary from day to day as you are probably aware. If you do experience trouble finding some, just do your own search for coupled pendulums, water waves, standing waves or whatever. Some are very clever as well as entertaining."

Leffler wrapped up the field trip saying, "As you go about your life, look for these and other basic behaviors in action. I think you'll be surprised by the number of times they appear. Look for science everywhere." As he spoke the phrase—"look for science everywhere"—several students joined in a chorus, providing clear evidence that they had heard their professor say this before, and listened. Leffler smiled and sent them back to the bus, calling out, that's it for the day. See you later."

9. NO JOB YET, WHAT AM I GOING TO DO?

After the class field trip Laura planned to return to the University's teacher placement office but not before some fun. It was the perfect day for college students in the spring: soaking up some sun; playing a little Frisbee; walking in the new spring flora; enjoying camaraderie with JJ and her friends. It all temporarily helped her stop worrying about finding a job.

By two pm a significant number of classmates had drifted away and Laura needed to visit the placement office, so she said her goodbyes. JJ had joined a group for a pickup softball game, so she and a few girlfriends jumped on the Sheridan Road bus and headed back together.

At the placement office she asked to see her file. Laura wanted to be sure all her credentials were still in order. When she began the process some months ago, someone misplaced her initial filings. Laura passed several weeks in gnawing, frustrated anxiety before the registrar pinpointed the error and corrected it. She'd had to start the process all over again; precious time had been lost. After the second filing she began receiving inexplicable invitations to consider physical education and coaching positions. Once again someone made a mistake at the placement office: she was registered as a physical education major. As before valuable time had been lost. The discovery caused her adrenalin to spike and it was all she could do to maintain her normally well composed demeanor. To be sure, she remained in the office until the error had been corrected. As soon as she was satisfied the correction had been made, she left the placement office that day and headed straight for her apartment. Almost anyone else would have popped the lids off of a few adult beverages to restore calm. Not Laura, she used alcohol in moderation for meals or celebrations. Instead she whipped out her bicycle and took a long ride along the lakeshore trail to work out the stress. Thankfully today was different. All her documents were in the right place. In fact now she had been able to look back on that incident and laugh about it. However, she still hadn't received any leads for science teaching jobs for the summer term.

As she left the office she looked over the bulletin board outside the door. In this electronic communication era, the board was something of a relic. However, some job postings still made it to the old-fashioned corkboard. Being a thorough person, Laura always checked the board.

'*The same old suspects*,' she thought to herself as she looked under fliers pinned on top of other pages. Then she saw one she had not seen before. It was on the bottom, buried under many overlapping sheets. How had she missed it? The notice was for a summer class with Chicago City Schools teaching science and math.

"Wow! Right up my alley! How did I miss this one?"

Laura lost no time calling the number on the form. In a matter of minutes she had an appointment for the next day. The rest of the day and ensuing night, she fought to keep her excitement in check. Just in case it didn't go well, she decided not to tell JJ or her mother about the interview. That way she could wallow alone in disappointment and wouldn't have to drag anyone else in with her.

The next morning Laura hustled to the City Schools administrative office, her credentials in hand. They were already on file with the school district, but who knows where? It pays to be prepared. When she arrived for the interview an assistant welcomed her and handed her a detailed description of the class to be taught. There was one fact the bulletin board flier had omitted: this would be an ELL class. In her nervousness, Laura drew a momentary blank: what did that mean? Then she remembered that "ELL" stands for English Language Learner. Each student in this summer program would have a native language other than English. They were not academically bad students, but needed additional help with physical science and math concepts. Since science often has terminology not found in day-to-day life, the students' ordinary language proficiency was not sufficient for their science classes. A teen from a foreign country would, no doubt, be able to order a pizza in English long before being able to explain acceleration of a falling object.

"No problem," she thought to herself. Part of her preparation to become a teacher had been an ed. course that contained a unit on handling ELL in a science/math environment. It was only two days in length but had provided a good framework upon which to build a program suited for the situation's specific needs. In addition she knew she was an inventive sort and would likely be able to conjure up some suitable learning experiences. Laura was confident she could meet the challenge.

The assistant escorted her to the office where the interview would take place. It was very plain, no pictures on the wall. The only decoration, if you wanted to call it that, were some framed certificates. From where she sat in an old well-worn wooden chair, she could not make out what they said. The desk was painted grey-brown. She thought to herself, if she was in a prison meeting the warden, it would probably look like this.

In a moment the interviewer arrived in a rush and quickly identified herself as what sounded like "Ms. Smurf." Laura started to ask her to repeat the name, but before she could, Ms.

68

Smurf, was off and running. She looked like Ms. Hathaway from the Beverly Hillbillies and she was clearly in a hurry. The few questions asked were rapid fire, like a machine gun. As Laura responded, Ms. Smurf frequently cut her off as she continued with the next question.

At the end of the short barrage of questions, Ms. Smurf said, "Do you have any questions?" Laura paused a moment to prioritize her thoughts and just as she began to ask her first question, Ms. Smurf started again. "Your paperwork is excellent and your preparation is perfect for the assignment. You have the position." Laura was stunned. Inside of five minutes she had the job. The whole session had been a whirlwind. While Laura was mulling over what had just happened, Ms. Smurf continued talking at a rapid pace about the school system in general. It was almost as if she was monopolizing the floor to keep Laura from speaking. Then it dawned on Laura, "She is trying to sweep the ELL part under the rug - talk fast and hope I won't notice."

One of Laura's habits was to 'needle' a person she mistrusted - like the cat that plays with the mouse before the kill. She had no patience for con artists, false personalities, social climbers, inflated egos; the list goes on. Ms. Smurf, or whatever her name, was quickly becoming one of them. So, at her first opportunity Laura interjected, in a deliberate and assertive voice, "I see the job description your assistant gave me this morning involves ELL students. The ad at the placement office didn't mention that. Can you please tell me more about that?" Ms. Smurf became agitated and started flipping through the papers on her desk. "If you are looking for the ELL description, it is at the end of the job outline" Laura said, as she partially rose from her chair to point to the document.

Ms. Smurf studied the papers for a moment and then, in a flippant manner, answered, "Oh, that?" her voice almost a laugh. "We include that in all our class descriptions, since we have such a diverse student body. You need not worry about it at all." As Ms. Smurf spoke, she rose from her chair and appeared to be getting ready to leave the room. Her answer had not convinced Laura. She guessed Ms. Smurf was desperate to fill the position at this late hour and probably had lots of candidates bolt when they understood the true nature of the assignment.

Laura wanted to pursue the point with further questions designed to make Ms. Smurf more uncomfortable, but decided against it. She reminded herself that a job was at stake. Laura reluctantly stifled the urge. Instead she decided to turn on the charm and make sure Ms. Smurf knew she was well qualified and welcomed the special opportunity.

"I hope no one shied away from this class because of ELL. Challenges make you a better teacher. If it happens to be more challenging, then you'll learn more," Laura said confidently. In response to Laura's statements Ms. Smurf now had a look of genuine understanding and amazement. It was if she had just experienced a breath of fresh air. Her personality changed. Gone was the fast and superficial talking. Laura guessed that the sudden change was the result of filling the teaching slot with someone who cared. No doubt Smurf had been under the gun to fill it.

With the mood shift Laura decided to resolve the interviewer's last name and politely asked, "For my notes, could you please tell me how you spell your last name?" Ms. whatever-her-name gave Laura a puzzled look." In a moment Laura knew why. "S M I T H," she said, spelling out her last name." Laura sheepishly realized that the woman had a speech impediment.

On that somewhat awkward note, the two of them moved on to the task of entering Laura into the school database.

Laura spent the rest of the morning filling out forms and providing her life story. The bus ride home from downtown was over the same potholed streets, but for some reason on the return trip the bus seemed to glide smoothly above the ground for her.

10. THAT EVENING

Laura made two calls that evening: a lengthy one to her mother and one to JJ. Both recipients of those calls were delighted to hear Laura's news. Teaching was challenging enough, but with the added twist of foreign language, it would even more so. Both JJ and her mom assured her that if anyone could do it, she could. A personal visit to her mother at this moment would have been better, but Laura had too tasks to finish that evening. With the welcome addition of preparations for her new job, time was running short. She promised to visit on the weekend.

11. LARABEE SCHOOL

A few weeks later with graduation behind her, Laura found herself heading to her new school to set up her classroom. She had been so busy with graduation that she had not yet visited the Larabee building. Having been a lifelong resident of the north Chicago, she was familiar enough with the area that she was certain she could easily find it.

As the bus approached Larabee School, Laura almost completely missed seeing the building. She had been looking for a more modern-looking school, like the one she had attended in Skokie. This building looked like it was built circa 1905 and should have been demolished long ago. She checked her paperwork, which only confirmed that she had come to the right place. Carved in stone at the top of the building was the name, "Larabee School." The well weathered words were hard to see at first, no doubt the results of Chicago's weather assaults over these many years. The rest of the stone and brick work showed similar signs of wear. All the steps were deeply worn into concaved shapes, obviously due to a lot of youthful shoes over the years. The window glass was mostly intact due to the rusty heavy duty wire mesh covering. A few small holes, possibly from a gun, could be seen. Wire mesh couldn't help there. The only green on the grounds were weeds and even they looked like they had struggled.

She headed for what was most likely the main entrance. It was locked. After walking all the way around the building, trying every door she could see, and finding them all locked, she gave up and called Central Administration, using the new smart phone that her mother had given her for graduation. She had to describe the problem multiple times as she got passed around to several people. The last person she spoke to assured her that, if it was the address shown on her data sheet, she had to be at the right building. Sarcastically, he added that these buildings don't move around from year to year. Obviously he had missed the point. She found the building but could not get inside. In a grumbling tone said, "Lady, just go back and bang the hell out of the doors, somebody has to be there." She did just that, pounding vigorously at every door until her fists were sore and she felt ridiculous. She was quite irritated and on the verge of smashing a window to get in, when she remembered that breaking in can also be accomplished without "breaking." Calling upon the amateur detective inside her, she noticed that the locks on the doors were old and worn. Looking through the glass in the doors, she could see chains connecting the two handles. She decided to check every door. At least one door just might be secured without the chain.

'Aha, the door just off the playground, at the back of the building was not chained on the inside,' she observed producing a slight feeling of victory. Next a credit card inserted in the jamb to leverage the latch opened it right up. *'Yes! A good amateur detective is hard to beat,* as Laura internally congratulated herself.'

The inside of the building was a mess and smelled like an old cafeteria. Trash was everywhere; probably the result of a locker cleanout at the end of the last school year. She found her room on the second floor with the number provided in her information packet. The door was locked. Through the grimy window, she could see that the room was a wreck. Papers were strewn everywhere; desks were upturned and scattered about.' *It probably hadn't been touched since the last day of class,'* she surmised. Concerns about her new job mounted and began to stir in her mind.

74

Her information packet explained that a box of teacher supplies would be provided, as well as textbooks. She could see some equipment in cupboards around the room, but there were no boxes in sight that might hold the materials she would need. The lock on this door was relatively new and her attempts to open it failed. She had no choice, but to try Central Administration again. She was dreading the prospect.

Laura started dialing her phone as she made her way along the hallway and down the stairs toward the door she had entered, hoping to get a better signal. As she got closer to the door, faint sounds like distant voices could be heard from the staircase leading to the lower floor. She stopped dialing and decided to investigate. After all, the chain was off on the door she had entered. Someone else may be in the building - maybe the principal. On the lower floor she followed the sounds through a cafeteria that smelled of spoiled food.

She found a small set of stairs at the back of the cafeteria that led to a lower level; probably a basement. Her stomach now felt queasy, as she was reminded of horror movies she had watched with JJ. It occurred to her that a principal would not likely have a basement office. By now the sounds were clearly recognizable as voices, yet words were still indiscernible. Maybe it was the principal talking to a custodian, Laura thought practically. Cautiously, she tiptoed down the poorly lit steps. At the bottom, a few feet away, she saw an open door. The sounds clearly came from there. She moved closer until she could make out the voices.

She moved closer until she could see part of a desk around the corner and a person sitting at the desk. Then she heard shouting: "OH YES! YES! MORE! MORE!" She knew instantly it was not the principal talking to the custodian. Moving quickly to get a full view of the desk, yet keeping a safe distance, she saw a scene that repulsed her.

Seated at the desk was a fat man dressed in matching grey work clothes with the school district logo on the shirt. He was drinking one of those super-sized beverages and eating a double burger sandwich which looked half eaten; however the remaining portion was larger than most uneaten Whoppers. Until he had become aware of Laura's presence, his gaze had been transfixed on some papers on his desk from the Social Security Administration that were covered with glossy grease blotches, probably from his monster sandwich. She could see "Social Security Administration" at the top in large print. The computer on the top of his desk displayed an adult video. "What a multi-tasker," she thought to herself. Laura now had a good idea why the building was locked and not cleaned.

Seeing Laura, the man was clearly stunned and agitated. His speech was rambling and confused as he mumbled some lame explanation of what he was doing, all the while trying to hide the movie. In desperation he grabbed the computer's power plug at eye level on the wall and yanked it out of the socket. He pushed back from his desk, and further away from Laura. From his demeanor, Laura concluded he was probably not a threat and quickly decided to play this to her advantage.

The room was hot and stifling with no air circulation, Laura's heart was pounding from the adrenalin release triggered by the situation. Because of all that she could feel her face and probably her whole body turning red. She began to sweat profusely. The babbling man was red in the face and sweating too. Laura reached deep inside herself and found the strength to put aside the physical problems for the moment and concentrate on her next move. She decided to take the upper hand.

"Are you the custodian?" she asked with all the authority in her voice that she could muster.

"Yes, ma'am" came a sheepish reply. Her ploy worked. He was clearly going to be submissive, so she continued her offense, sounding like a female drill sergeant. She had experienced enough difficulties for one day with the locked doors and filthy building. It was time for her to play the 'adult movie card.' She continued, "Mister! A school is no place for crap like that" as she thrust her arm toward the now blank screen shaking her finger in a menacing manner. He blinked and squirmed in his chair like a little kid being severely admonished by his mother. "I'm going to get Security and HR out here and …." He interrupted her and again sounding like the little boy as he shook his head from side to side, "No! No! You can't do that." Stammering " I, I, I….I'm about to retire. Please, No!"

Laura waited a while before responding. She then decided to get something out of this for the school, her impending class and compensation for the hassles she had endured earlier.

"I'm to start teaching a class here tomorrow and this place is filthy. I'm also looking for the supplies from Central Administration that are supposed to be in my room. I had to pick the lock to get in!! I want this ALL taken care of by seven am tomorrow. Do you understand me? Otherwise…….," she stopped without finishing the sentence. "Yes, Ma'am," came his sheepish reply. "I'll take care of it. I really will."

When she left the building, her heart was still pounding. As she reached the outside she took a deep breath. It felt great to be out of the stifling hot building, with those awful smells wafting from the cafeteria.

As with stressful situations in the past, Laura needed to vent. She thought about a good work out. A bike ride would be perfect; but, it was too hot today. She decided on a nice swim in Lake Michigan. After an hour and a half of laps, Laura left the North Avenue Beach cooled off, refreshed and, most of all, stress free. That evening she treated herself to one of her favorite meals - a delicious homemade salad topped with grilled salmon. The swim and the food had restored her strength and assured a good night's sleep.

The next day was the first day of classes. She would finally be meeting her students. Laura came in early to set up the few things she had brought from home. Upon arriving at Larabee School, she immediately noticed that the outside door was unlocked; the halls were swept; her room was unlocked; the trash was removed; the desks were set neatly in rows; two boxes were set on a table; and the chalkboard was clean. The whole place still smelled like the old cafeteria, but, after all, Rome wasn't built in a day.

'Okay, this is much better,' she thought. Her tirade yesterday had worked.

The smaller of the two boxes contained dry erasers, white-board markers and various teacher supplies. The Central Office had missed the fact that this old building had chalkboards. She needed chalk, not markers. But compared with yesterday's issues, this was a small problem indeed. The big box held science books. They were old and tattered just like the building, she mused. Then she started looking through one of the books. There were just words! Page after page was crammed with words. There were very few illustrations to balance out all those words. How was she going to teach science to a class of students who were just learning English, using books that were full of just words – especially, English words? She needed more pictures and illustrations. Now <u>this</u> was a big problem!

By now she could hear students approaching. They must have figured out which door was unlocked. Kids are good at finding unlocked doors. Over the next half hour they arrived. There was a pair of Asian twin boys, one boy who spoke Spanish, a few from the Middle East, and the rest, well, she had no idea. The last student in the door had "loner" written all over his face. His clothes were all black. His dark brown hair was shot through with spiked orange streaks. He carried a black backpack and sat as far back in the corner as he could. Laura decided that she would make no attempt, this first day, to assign any seating. The students could sit where they wished.

She began introductions by pointing to herself and saying, "Ms. Olson." Then one by one she pointed to each, hoping they would speak their own names. They understood. "No language problem there," she decided. Next, she alternated between speaking simple everyday English words and writing them on the chalkboard. Words like "food," "lunch," "home" and "TV." Each time, she looked and listened for reactions. Heads nodding "yes" predominated, along with hand gestures that mimed the activity.

Her first conclusion was they all had a fair, but limited, command of ordinary words. For example, counting to ten in English was within everyone's grasp. However, most couldn't count beyond ten. Common words, like "TV" and "food" and names for popular computer games were equally well understood by all. "Pizza" was the winner, hands down. However, when Laura mentioned "kinetic energy," she saw a room full of blank faces. She decided her first task would be to introduce the English words associated with science and math.

Laura was prepared to conduct one-on-one interviews with each student so that she could assess specific needs for each. Even with a small class, she determined it would take most of the day to complete and she needed something to occupy the rest during the interviews. From her experience as a teen helping with younger kids, she remembered a few non-verbal activities, such as nail puzzles. She had saved them, along with a couple Rubik's cubes and "BB" games, since childhood. BB games, where the object was to get all the BB's to come to rest in little indentations where the buttons on the clown suit would be. Often these had been prizes in kid's meals at fast food restaurants. They were great brain teasers and provided a wide range of challenges to the individual, plus, operation was obvious, no words were needed. In the event that someone had not seen a nail puzzle before, she held up one set that were coupled together. Then she turned her back for a moment and revealed the nails un-coupled. That's all it took.

With puzzles in hand the class became engrossed in the various tasks and remained so for the duration of that day's session. Their complete absorption, well, all except the kid in the back, told Laura that these were bright kids with curious minds.

As she met with each student Laura compiled a list of words, symbols and numbers they had trouble verbalizing, recognizing or writing. These lists would be the basis for her lesson plans for the near term.

She had started her individual conferences in the front of the room, so the loner dressed in black back in the corner of the room was the last student she talked to. Laura had to ask his name because one student was absent and she was left with two names on her roster, but just one student. She asked his name, but he did not acknowledge her. She concluded that he was not

80

hearing impaired, because his body language changed as she asked which one he was. Could his English language skills be so poor that he cannot understand even the most basic words? He had a laptop that he had been engaged with all during this initial session. Laura changed positions slightly so she could see the screen. He had what looked like a game on the screen and there were English words on it. Laura was careful not to visibly react to what she saw. She concluded that he did understand English but had chosen to stonewall her.

Laura had learned during her student teaching days that, with reluctant or unresponsive kids, like this one, it was best to maintain a pleasant demeanor, never display anger or frustration and never let on when discovering a chink in their armor. If a student is being non-responsive, it may be that they are doing it to get a reaction from the other person. It was a juvenile game, but, then, he was a juvenile. Laura would have to be the adult. Still, question after patient question resulted in nothing.

Casting about for a subject, she took a closer look at his laptop and noticed the manufacturer, model and some stickers indicating its processor, memory and video cards: Core i7, 16 GB DDR3 and HD 5870. She recognized enough to know this kid had a loaded machine. "Wow! That's one screaming piece of gear!" Laura said excitedly. She caught him off guard. Before he realized it, he had looked up at Laura and uttered a brief but revealing, "yeah." It was by no means exuberant; but, rather the halfhearted response common in teens with an attitude. Laura did not hear any trace of a foreign accent in that one word, although its brevity made it hard to tell anything about the kid. His body winced when he realized he had been tricked; he regretted saying anything. Laura was careful not to react to him and chose to end her efforts for the day. It was a small victory for her, but a victory nonetheless.

She had been so consumed with her own situation that it was not until she was leaving the building that she realized hers was the only class that had met there that day. She had seen no other students, teachers or administrators roaming about the building. "That is extremely odd," she thought to herself. "Maybe they had been there somewhere, but just not up on the second floor. Maybe they had the first class off-site." Whatever the explanation, she found it extremely irregular and hoped it was not a sign of things to come. She was not the superstitious type. Nevertheless, she found these strange circumstances unsettling.

12. JJ, LET'S CELEBRATE

Later that evening, Laura got a phone call.

"Hey, Laura, it's JJ." (As if she would not recognize his voice.) "Let's go celebrate your first day teaching and my new assignment."

"Sounds good! Wait—what new assignment?" she asked.

"Well, it is not exactly new; but instead of being an intern at the museum, I'm now an associate curator. Same job, different title and a little more pay," he replied.

"That's fantastic, I'd love to celebrate. But 'celebrate' might not be exactly the right word for my situation just yet…" she responded.

"Why?"

"I'll tell you over dinner."

They made plans to meet at their favorite jazz club on Hubbard Street: good food and great sounds.

They were early, so the band had not yet started. Most of the conversation revolved around the trials and tribulations of Laura's new assignment. She told him about Central Administration ineptness, the old building, the locked doors, the mess, the custodian and his problem, the inadequate books, the broken or missing equipment and the interesting collection of students. Her tone was very serious, her brow wrinkled and her body looked tense. In a sympathetic voice JJ offered, "I agree that that custodian has a serious problem. Retiring from such a

83

prestigious position as head of physical operations at Larabee School at this time and trying to live on social security is risky." JJ's dry humor had the desired effect. Laura paused and smiled saying, "You men are all alike." His humor elicited the desired effect. She realized just how stressed she was. From that point she was more relaxed and upbeat. This was not the first time that JJ, with just a one-liner had been able to lighten Laura's mood. He was very good for her in that respect.

"I need to come up with some strategies, and fast! I also have one student who is reclusive and I have no idea what will work with him." After much discussion, they both agreed that taking lots of field trips should be at the top of Laura's list of teaching strategies. After all, Laura believed strongly that students should learn about the world of science all around them as participants in the world, and not just while sitting indoors at their desk. Fieldtrips would fit the bill perfectly and Chicago had some of the best facilities in the world; all of them not that far away from Larabee School.

It made complete sense to both of them because, as children, they had each enjoyed numerous field trips to the Museum of Science and Industry, the Field Museum and the Adler Planetarium. These had all been fun and memorable experiences not to mention educational. Both recalled specific concepts they had learned at an age when they were not yet able to read. "And, of course, there were the field trips that we took in Professor Leffler's class," Laura said as she and JJ smiled and began to laugh at the memories they had. She continued, "That guy was very, very clever. Remember the time we were supposed to go to the Adler and the bus driver got it wrong and dropped us off at the Field Museum. It was raining and the driver took off right away leaving us stranded at the wrong building. So, to get in out of the rain, we all ran into the Field Museum. Leffler had a specific lesson planned for the planetarium and, rather than abandoning it, he led us around the exhibits at the Field and delivered his lecture using those exhibits as substitutes."

JJ was smiling the entire time, obviously remembering some of the absurd yet funny juxtapositions of stuffed animals being used to explain astronomy. "Oh! I remember one that brought down the house. The whole class came unglued and talked about it for weeks. Remember the life size stuffed musk ox exhibit? Leffler was standing with his back to the exhibit. Right behind him and just over his shoulder was the rear end of a huge stuffed ox. He looked at his notes and then asked the class "As you travel out from the sun, what planet is next after Saturn?" Normally someone would have given the answer immediately, but today was different. After looking over the class with a somewhat bewildered look on his face because no one had an answer, he turned slightly toward the exhibit and pointed to the posterior of the big stuffed ox, whose tail was raised slightly. Then classmate Jay Waning yelled, 'Uranus!' and the whole place went wild," said JJ, laughing so hard he could hardly finish the story. Laura howled too. The two continued telling each other funny stories for another half hour or so.

"Oh, there is something else I meant to tell you," said Laura. "I seem to have the only class meeting in the building. Other than my students, I did not see another soul all day. I know summer classes are fewer in number, but to be the only one is unusual, right?"

"I've got to agree with you," replied JJ. Maybe some other classes will start tomorrow," he offered.

"Yeah, I would think the district would at least require an administrator; not that I feel like I need one. It just seems strange…Well, that's enough of my day, how about you? Tell me what is happening with your job!"

Just as JJ started to describe his new assignment, the band began to play. The sound filled the room, making conversation impossible. They smiled at each other, tacitly agreeing they would "save it for later," as they sat back and absorbed the great sounds.

13. DAY THREE

It was the district's policy to require written parent permission slips for a field trip. To save time and effort for everyone, Laura put a range of dates on the student form. The range corresponded to the summer session. Thus, she avoided the delays inherent in getting forms back for each field trip. It was probably against policy, but when policy conflicted with education, education won, in Laura's mind. She was determined to teach in spite of the district failing to provide her the proper resources. She was not going to allow the lack of a piece of paper to get in the way. While the permission slips might present a hurdle, Central Administration had, perhaps unknowingly, aided her plans by including CTA and museum passes in her teacher kit.

Circulating about the room, she handed out the permission slips. When she came to the recalcitrant one, she also showed him her class roster with two names not checked off. "I'm sure you will understand that I am responsible for submitting an accurate accounting of who is in my class. Would you just check off your name?" Laura stated in a firm but kind manner. Reluctantly, he made a mark beside one of the names. She couldn't say whether what she had said swayed him to comply or whether he complied merely to get her to go away. It didn't matter; she knew now that he was 'L Watkins.' The roster had only provided the initial for the first name, but that would do for now.

Progress, albeit small, is being made, she thought to herself. Now that she knew his name, she could request more information from the administration about her mystery student.

Days earlier, when Laura moved into her room, very little in the way of functioning science apparatus could be found. There were only pieces and broken parts. She did manage to find meter sticks on top of the wall cupboards. They were lying in fifty years of dust and many were broken. A few had been re-purposed into crude swords using pieces of other, broken sticks and masking tape. She surmised that in their last official (or perhaps unsanctioned) use in the classroom, the students had conducted a mock battle of some sort. There were only six unbroken meter sticks. On one side there were 100 centimeter markings and each centimeter was subdivided into 10 units, or millimeters. The other side was in inches and fractions of inches. The markings were well worn and some difficult to read, but a sharp eye could discern where the missing graduations had been located. Today she had a plan for the sticks.

She had the class arrange their desks in a semicircle. Even L. Watkins reluctantly moved to a position just behind the group. His hanging-back body language was clearly expressing his reluctance to participate. Laura placed the sticks on the desks with the centimeter markings facing up, retaining one for herself. Without explanation she pointed the '1' centimeter symbol and said 'one' out loud. She gestured with her hands and asked them to repeat. All responded immediately, except the kid in black. He just sat there looking painfully bored. Next she pointed to '2' and once again the students responded in unison: "Two." She pointed to 3, 4, 5, 6, 7, 8, 9, and 10. The results were flawless. She could hear accents but the numbers had all been immediately recognized. Next she pointed to 11. A few hesitated but finally got it out. As the process continued success diminished quickly. In the 20s and higher, results were sporadic.

Their first task was defined. With the meter sticks Laura had them count to 50 while looking at the symbols on the sticks. As they progressed, she pointed at random and asked for their response. As students caught on, she divided them into pairs and had them continue the process. Later, for variety, she had them count floor tiles in the hallways and lockers. The "Count" from Sesame Street would have been proud. By the end of class that day all of Laura's students could speak, write and recognize the numbers 1 through 50 in English.

That is, all of the students except L. Watkins. He retreated to his corner with his laptop when she divided them into groups. She let it go for now, but watched his eyes shift rapidly as he looked at the screen. At the same time, his fingers moved about the keyboard, moving so quickly they might not even be touching the keys. Whatever he was doing, he was doing it with great intensity. She figured it had to be a computer game.

14. DAY FOUR

Today, the students would be out of the classroom visiting the Adler Planetarium, which had lots of interesting visuals. Laura believed the images would stimulate the students' imaginations even though they didn't have extensive mastery over math and science concepts. Remarkably, everyone had turned in their permission slips. Some signatures looked suspicious, but Laura was hardly trained in handwriting authentication, so it was "off we go to learn." They only had to walk a few blocks to the bus that would take them to catch the EL train, after which, one more bus would drop them at their destination. When the first student got on the bus and inserted the CTA pass in the reader, "Not Valid" popped up on the screen. He tried it again, and it was still rejected. A second student tried his pass; it was "Not Valid." A third… you guessed it. None of the passes worked.

"Good old Central Administration did it again!" Laura said sarcastically to herself. Not able to board the bus, they headed back toward the school. As they passed a small park, Laura spotted a merry-go-round and thought she could squeeze in a "centripetal force" demo, but the ride was so rusted that it hardly moved, even with virtually every student pushing. "So much for that idea," Laura verbalized.

Slightly disheartened, the group wandered back to Larabee School. Laura hauled out the meter sticks. For the next hour they worked on number recognition, writing, and pronunciation. This time they reached 100. They knew the drill and progressed nicely. Laura wasn't surprised: her students were not challenged learners; their only obstacle was the language barrier.

After a lunch on the school's barren playground, the class returned to their classroom and Laura brought out the meter sticks again. Laura then led them down to the sidewalk near the side of the building where a chain link fence surrounded the school. This fence separated the playground from the public street. She put down a meter stick on the sidewalk so that one end lined up with the starting point of the fence. She looked at the stick and said "one". Without moving the first, she laid another meter stick on the sidewalk so that it was an extension of the first. She then said "two." Next she handed another meter stick to Nik, one of the twin boys from Thailand,. He guessed what she wanted and laid his stick in line with the other two, and with a slight accent said "three." With youthful exuberance, every student (except Watkins) took their meter sticks and proceeded down the sidewalk, counting out loud as a group in English. It was a long block. Laura had selected it for that reason. Close to the next cross street they reached 100 meters. Laura pulled a piece of sidewalk chalk out of her pocket and handed it to Hammu, a tall, thin boy from Cairo. She had developed a method combining gestures with minimal words and it had quickly become a game for her students; they loved it. Hammu quickly understood what she was asking and, smiling proudly, marked the 100-meter point.

Her students probably thought that she was just reinforcing the counting process in English. Indeed she was, but there was more. She looked at her watch and, using very few words, gestured for those with watches to note the time. When satisfied that everyone had observed the current time, she positioned herself as if she wanted to run a race in the direction back toward the school. She looked at her watch again. They did likewise and they all began to walk briskly, almost jogging in the direction from which they had come.

When she arrived back where the fence began, Laura stopped and looked at her watch, as did the students. The consensus was that it took about 40 seconds. Next she took the chalk, got on one knee and wrote out on the sidewalk

$$100 \text{ meters} / 40 \text{ sec} =$$

She was banking on them recognizing a division problem; they did so instantly. Quickly Nuk, Nik's twin brother, brought out his cell phone to access a calculator app. Other students followed suit and the group soon verified that the answer was 2.5. They all cheered.

Laura waited a moment and asked, "Two-point-five what?" It was the group's turn to pause; they were not sure what she wanted. Laura repeated it again. "Two-point-five what?"

Finally, one of the twins (she still could not always tell them apart) shyly said, "2.5 meters per second?" She smiled; he smiled. The other students nodded that they got it, but seemed unsure of her point. Sensing this, Laura spotted a school speed limit sign. She pointed and said, "Twenty what?"

Once again, her question was greeted with puzzled looks. Then a hesitant Budru, the other middle-eastern boy from a remote village in Iraq ventured, "Twenty meters per second?"

Laura gave him an encouraging look but accompanied it with a *mezza mezza* wave of her hand.

Budru looked puzzled and looked back at the sign again. He glanced at street and the cars traveling there. Then his eyebrows lifted as if he had remembered an important bit of information. "Twenty MILES per hour?" Budru offered. Laura gave him the thumbs up. Classmates did high fives and made congratulatory comments for the correct response.

Jose Jimenez was near the curb where a motorcycle was parked. He walked over to it and, with excitement, pointed at the speedometer and said, with a Spanish accent, "mile per hour." "Right" Laura answered enthusiastically. The students had picked up on the fact that she was interested in the 'units' associated with the numbers.

Nik grabbed a meter stick and turned it over to the feet and inches side. With the chalk, he quickly marked off six one-foot intervals. Then he stood up, looked at his watch and mimed a foot race along the marks. Almost at the same time, three other students yelled out "feet per second." Surprised and very pleased with the student's initiative Laura joined in the high-fives, adding her own exclamations of congratulations. In math, Laura knew that getting numerical answers was usually easy, but also realized that students often do not pay much attention to the units associated with the numbers. She wanted to make sure that they made that association and could use it to their advantage. It did not take long for her to realize that her multilingual class caught on quickly. The students continued talking among themselves, giving examples they knew, like 186,000 miles per second for the speed of light.

After a few minutes, using some of the examples she had just heard her students exchange, Laura posed several questions that sounded like the previous ones, yet were slightly different: "Two point five meters per second is what? Twenty miles per hour is what?" Finally, one of the students said "speed." Laura shook her head 'yes' and smiled broadly. Then she took the chalk and added the word speed after the equal sign.

100 meters / 40 sec = 2.5 m/sec

Most of the students were already familiar with the word "speed," but may not have formally associated it with a specific calculation. Laura added another word, "velocity."

$$100 \text{ meters} / 40 \text{ sec} = 2.5 \text{ m/sec} = \text{speed} = \text{velocity}$$

Technically, the definition of velocity encompasses both speed and direction, while speed, on the other hand, just addresses "how fast." However, Laura decided she would deal with that distinction later. For now she just wanted to introduce the word and its relationship to speed. As she had suspected, "velocity" was a new word for them. She spent a few minutes reinforcing the spelling, pronunciation and concept.

In a very short time, days in fact, Laura had established a solid core of English words and numbers used in science, related them to key mathematical processes and reinforced them through real life experiences. Laura realized that the targeted topics she had obtained from her student interviews that first day were paying off, evidenced by their rapid success. For example some students recognized numbers expressed in numerical form, but did not recognize the written form, like 11 and eleven. Others recognized the numerical form but could not speak the value in English. Processes like division were understood when she used the symbol but they did not recognize the written or spoken word 'division.' These and many other combinations resulted from her interviews. Future exercises she devised and interactions with students would continue to target these points. Her students had already learned many of these concepts in their home schools in their native language and system of notation; so the key process would be one of simple translation.

An event that day really caught her attention. As the class returned to the building, Laura saw L. Watkins talking to

Hammu. She could barely hear their conversation, but was able to make out bits and pieces. They were introducing themselves to each other. Watkins told Hammu that his first name was "L." Hammu smiled, commenting that it was "a cool name, man." Laura now confirmed her mystery student's first name. Being a single letter, it only added to the non-conformist persona of this kid. However, Laura believed that being your own person was important and it would take more than unusual nomenclature to bother her.

Before dismissing the class, she asked that the transit passes be placed on her desk. She planned to take them back to Central Administration and get a piece of someone's hide. One by one they dropped off the invalid CTA passes and filed out of the room. L was the last to leave. Laura watched from the classroom doorway as he walked away, wondering what it was going to take to break into his shell.

When all her students were out of sight, she went to her desk to gather her things. But when she reached for the pile of CTA passes, she discovered that they were gone. She looked beneath the desk and under it, but they had simply disappeared. Who had taken them? Had her mystery student stolen a stack of invalid, worthless train passes? She laughed to herself, thinking maybe the thief was just trying to save a Central Administrator from the wrath of Laura Olson. She had had enough for one day, however, and chose to head home for the night.

15. DAY FIVE

In the absence of valid CTA passes, Laura had worked up some lesson plans that used skateboards and a camera. She knew she could rely on at least two kids to bring a skateboard to school on any given day and remembered Nik and Nuk taking both snapshots and high-definition video with their fancy digital cameras always carried in their backpacks. Her plan B would be a fun outdoor activity until she could sort out the CTA pass problem.

The class assembled as always. Laura greeted each eager and friendly face as they filed through the classroom door. And, was it her imagination or did L appear less standoffish today? She approached her desk to start class and noticed the pile of CTA passes exactly where she had last seen them the day before. A handwritten note was on top: it read, "VALID." Astonished, she looked up at the class and then down at the passes several times "Does anyone know where these came from?" The students only offered shrugs and no admissions of involvement.

Did it matter where they came from? she thought to herself. It only took a moment for her to decide that the answer was, *no*. She shrugged and announced to the class: "If these are valid, we'll have a field trip, if not, we'll come back here and carry on with Plan B." She held up the passes and they were off to the bus stop. To her relief, the passes worked flawlessly.

The Adler experience was a perfect choice. It had an enormous number of visuals and interactive displays, and a celestial show with fabulous music and special effects. It was 'crowd-pleasing stuff.' The written explanations on the exhibits favored more commonly used words, so the students' so-called "street and restaurant" English was sufficient to understand most of the exhibits. Laura helped them with the more technical terms. In a lot of cases she knew she would be providing a better explanation in an upcoming class, so she answered their questions with a simple, "Later." Seeing the vastness and enormity of our universe is a mind-expanding experience for anyone and it certainly had that effect on her class today.

Much to Laura's pleasure and surprise, L seemed to have forgotten to be withdrawn, sullen and speechless during the visit to the planetarium. He didn't go so far as to smile or laugh, but he was fully engaged with most of the exhibits. His lips moved as he read; he murmured softly; his eyes following the action carefully. It was a behavior that Laura had observed many times before when L was in the back of the classroom working on his computer. He even helped some of the language challenged students with the vocabulary and concepts. Laura still couldn't tell whether he spoke with an accent and he seemed to know an awful lot about what they were looking at. She noticed that exhibits involving math received L's greatest attention. The exhibit showing equal area sectors swept out by a planet in an elliptical orbit around the sun really had his attention. He ran that one at least a half dozen times and Laura could see a faint smile at the conclusion of each demonstration cycle.

She also observed that when speed, velocity, units of measurement, division, distance, time and numbers were part of the information presented, the members would point and discuss, repeat verbally, shake their heads 'yes,' smile and say, 'O-Kaaaay' in a variety of accents. This was another good sign of ongoing learning.

16. DAY SIX, THE NEXT MONDAY

Laura spent her weekend going over her notes and evaluating the activities she had put together for her students. Based upon those findings she devised her lesson plans for the next few days. There was no time left for anything else. Such was the life of a beginning teacher.

Even after a weekend, the students were still excited about the planetarium field trip. They wanted to know when and where the next trip would be. A few asked if they would return to the Adler. Laura assured them that there would be a repeat trip. L entered the room and took his usual seat in the back. His sullen demeanor was back. The engagement that Laura had observed at the planetarium was gone.

Ah ha! she thought to herself, *boredom.*

Over the weekend, she had mulled over the situation with L. He appeared to be very bright; he showed an interest in math and had exhibited no English language problems at the planetarium. She had decided that if he showed up on Monday like his old self, she could conclude that he was just really bored.

Although not a participant, on the day everyone was having fun out on the sidewalk with the meter sticks, L had been paying attention. Today was going to be the next installment of "sidewalk science," so Laura expected to see the blank stare disappear once they were outside.

Once all her students were accounted for, Laura herded them to a CTA bus stop. Destination: the lakefront, where the weather was sunny and pleasant. Laura and JJ often rode their bicycles along Lake Michigan, so she knew of some park streets that would be perfect for today's activity. They were likely to have little, if any, traffic. From the spot where the bus deposited them near Lake Shore Drive on the park side, it was just a short hike to the place Laura had in mind. In minutes they arrived in a big parking lot about one hundred yards from the lake. The road leading into the lot passed over a bridge. From the high point on the bridge's pavement, about eight feet above the parking lot, the slope was long and steady. That would be perfect for Laura's purposes. The lot was also at the end of a dead-end street, thus further ensuring little traffic.

Even before she could give instructions, the skateboarders among her students had seen the slope and were running over to it. She let them skate for a few minutes while the other students watched, then called them all together to explain the drill. The object was to record the motion of a skateboard going down the hill and analyze the motion.

After listening to Laura's instructions, they took their meter sticks and drew one-foot chalk marks from the top of the hill to the bottom, where it leveled out. The resulting track measured about forty feet. Laura instructed Nik and Nuk to set up one of their high tech cameras on a tripod off to the side of the hill. They carefully adjusted the camera position so that it could record the entire hill and every chalk mark on it.

The camera had the capability of taking still photos at regular intervals and placing all the shots in one image. It was set to take a picture once every second. Jose stood on his board at the top of the hill, waiting for the signal. His eyes glued to the monitor, Nik yelled, "GO." After a few false starts, the camera and the skateboarder were in sync and they managed a successful take.

It was hard to see the video on the camera's viewfinder without holding it up to your face. As the camera was passed around, the students saw the skateboard and rider, Jose, several times in the same shot at various positions on the slope. Jose had been clowning to the camera and each shot revealed another crazy expression. Jose didn't appear to be making much progress at the beginning of the series, but the space between his locations on the ramp increased as he went downhill. That was no surprise to anyone. Clearly he was going faster and faster. The next hour went something like this; roller board down the hill then some of the math related to the motion, roller board in crazy positions followed by some of the science involved, roller board down the hill trying to hit classmates, then a dose of the appropriate math and science. It looked like ciaos, but Laura's leading questions and pavement chalk talk led the students through the lessons about <u>acceleration</u> that she wanted them to absorb that day.

The concept of acceleration can be difficult for some, but her masterful handling of the lesson fully established the concept in their minds and the playful experience with the skateboards further cemented this knowledge. Laura hoped that they would remember this lesson for a long time. Seeing how easily they mastered the concept of acceleration, Laura decided to stretch the session just a bit.

"You concluded that your boards had what sort of acceleration?" she asked.

"Constant acceleration," chanted the all-male chorus.

"What caused the constant acceleration?"

Almost as fast they yelled, "Gravity."

Laura gave them one of her looks that implied, "You are right, but a better or more complete answer is still out there." There were no takers, just silence and puzzled looks.

L had one of his disdainful looks, it said, "Look idiots! It's as plain as the nose on your face." He could no longer hold back, and in a know-it-all tone, "The constant FORCE of GRAVITY causes the CONSTANT ACCELERATION."

Overlooking the tone of the delivery, Laura thanked L for his correct response. The rest of the class took note of the point and shrugged off the delivery.

The outing had been successful and, for that, Laura was quite pleased. It was time to head back to Larabee. On the bus ride she contemplated her next lesson.

By now she was convinced that they were equipped to tackle some harder stuff. Laura decided that working their way through the Museum of Science and Industry would serve that purpose very well.

17. JJ CALLING

The phone rang just as Laura finished the dinner dishes—one dinner plate, a fork and a water glass. While tonight's dinner was a less-than-glamorous frozen stir fry chicken with rice entree, at least it was low in calories, somewhat nutritious and relatively tasty. Often she resorted to such fare since cooking for one often seemed like a hassle. Also, the time she saved would be available for working on lesson plans.

Since she was creating the activities based on student progress, with special language considerations, she could not rely on standard course materials, nor plan very far in advance. Even before taking on this, her first and unique assignment, she had committed to putting extra time into her classroom preparations. Her plan was to continually update her lesson plans from year to year. She would even pitch the old set of notes and create new ones if necessary. Laura had endured too many classes where some old professor plodded through his lessons, using notes that were yellowed, tattered and likely written decades earlier. Her preparations took a lot of time in the evenings and on the weekends and she was fine with that.

Laura glanced at her caller ID and smiled.

"Hi JJ," she answered.

"Hey, how's it going? I haven't talked to you since last week. How's school?"

"Well, I just love it," Laura told him. "It's been a challenge, but that's actually been part of the fun. These kids are smart-- they've picked up the necessary vocabulary and concepts quickly. I'm ready to ratchet up the difficulty level with some more museum exercises."

"How's the introverted one doing? Any cracks in his shell?"

"You know, I think at least one of his problems may be boredom. I've seen signs of intelligence and on a few occasions, he even looked like he was ready to participate in the lesson. On our beach outing, he actually answered a question out loud that I had asked the group. He has talked to other students. In fact, I overheard one conversation where he said his first name was 'L.'"

"L? Like the letter L?"

"Sure, why not <u>JJ</u>?" joked Laura.

"And what's this beach outing?" JJ teased. "I can see the headline now: "TEACHER FROLICKS ON THE BEACH WITH EAGER YOUNG BOYS"

"Right, wise guy," Laura responded in mock-indignation.

"It really was a breakthrough session, though," she went on. "I'll give you more details later, but we used a skateboard to demonstrate acceleration. They really got it and had loads of fun at the same time. We went to a bridge near the beach to conduct the trials."

"I stand corrected, and would love to hear more about the acceleration demo," replied JJ.

There was a brief pause as each thought about what to talk about next. Laura spoke first.

"By the way, I called downtown to Central Administration again for L's records, but so far, no response. The summer session will probably be over before I hear back."

"Maybe your principal can help," JJ commented.

"I have never seen a principal or administrator of any kind in that building," she said, laughing. "But you know what? It doesn't really bother me. In fact, it is kind of nice having the run of the place."

"I thought for sure you'd see someone else by now," puzzled JJ. "Maybe tight budgets have something to do with it. Oh well."

He wanted to bring up the question of liability, but that would lead to a lot of speculation and he knew her evening time was precious, so decided not to pursue it.

"Well now tell me what's new in your world?" Laura prompted, putting the ball in JJ's court. "Anything significant? Fun? Reprehensible?"

JJ did not respond immediately as he decided which topic to pick.

"Well," he began, his voice cautious.

She waited while he paused again.

"Well," JJ repeated.

"Yes, JJ," Laura teased. "I know. You mentioned that before. What is it?"

"I got another ticket," said JJ apologetically.

"Oh no!" Laura cried. "What for? Speeding?"

"Yep. The same old problem. It was on the new I-355 connector. As you've seen, traffic is still very light there. No one was around and I was thinking of something else and the next thing I knew I got up to eighty-five, or at least that's what the officer said. I didn't even look at my speedometer because when I saw the flashing lights coming, I assumed he was going to an emergency up ahead. So I pulled over and slowed down. When he did the same, I knew."

"JJ, how many is this for you?" Laura scolded.

"Four," JJ responded humbly.

"You simply must get control of this. Your insurance will skyrocket. You may lose your license and--" but she stopped there, realizing she had said it all before and it had made little impact on his bad habits.

There was a long break until Laura broke the silence.

"Why not try something new?" she suggested. "Pick some object that you could safely mount or put up on the dashboard. Something that would not ordinarily be seen there. Put it there as a reminder not to speed."

"That's a great idea. How about a couple of fuzzy dice hanging from the rearview mirror?" he said jokingly.

"Very funny. You can do better than that," she said in a serious tone.

Knowing that she really had his best interests at heart, JJ grew serious too.

"I will do it and make it work," he said. "I promise."

They bid each other goodnight and promised to get together soon, but did not specify when.

18. LET'S PUT IT TO WORK

As she had mentioned to JJ, Laura felt the group was ready to take on the more complex exhibits at the Museum of Science and Industry. She was already quite familiar with its layout, but had gone back on recent weekends to map out specific displays that fit her plans. She gave each student a packet of information including instructions detailing the exhibits, keywords and concepts to explore, as well as a list of questions designed to lead them in the right direction. The students had their own notes from previous activities, key words and definitions. They would visit each exhibit and work independently to complete the defined tasks. Laura wandered around, making herself available for assistance. With travel time, these activities would consume the whole day.

After lunch at the museum the group adjourned to the beach nearby for some unstructured fun. The students rode their skateboards, played catch and threw Frisbees. Nik and Nuk liked to play chess. Small groups would wander out of Laura's earshot and talk about who-knows-what. She couldn't always hear what they said, but the frequent eruptions of laughter did reach her ears. She suspected jokes were the topic - the kind no one intended a teacher to hear. Laura liked to read and indulged herself with a few chapters from her current novel.

After this respite, it was back to the museum to revisit each display in order. Now they worked as a group, discussing among themselves the objectives, concepts, and lessons learned. In these sessions they worked out the rough places where the students' understanding was uneven. Laura acted as a facilitator during this phase. Once there was agreement, someone was selected by the group to summarize what the class learned at each exhibit. Laura learned long ago that one of the best ways to cement a thought in one's own head was by explaining it to someone else. In most instances, the "spokeskid" got it right. In a few cases Laura stepped in and helped with the wrap-up.

She established this process early so her students knew what to expect as they toured the museum.

19. MORE OF THE SAME

Over the following days and weeks, Laura and her students continued their field trips, gobbling up science and math. The Museum of Science and Industry was not the only venue. Laura introduced circular motion, centripetal and centrifugal forces on the flying chairs and Ferris wheel at Navy Pier. When it was time to learn about gravity, mass, the speed of light, and elliptical and circular motion, they visited the Adler Planetarium.

Most of their learning took place away from Larabee, but one activity at the school was particularly memorable. The twins were questioning the value for the constant acceleration of an object due to gravity (32 ft. /sec/sec or 9.8 m/sec/sec); they wanted to verify that scientists of the past had determined the correct number. It was clearly a tongue-in-cheek effort, since Nik and Nuk giggled and laughed as they made their proposal to Laura. She was a good sport and was willing to let learning come from most any situation, success or failure.

Under her watchful eye, the students set up the test. They would use the fancy camera, taking a series of still photos, as objects were dropped out of one of Larabee's third-story classroom windows. The camera would capture the motion of the objects as they fell to the ground. The tricky part was measuring the distance down the wall. They would need hash marks to accurately determine the precise height of the object as it fell. Marking distance on the pavement for their skateboard experiment had been easy. But, safely and accurately chalking the wall of a three-story building was an altogether different challenge. The students suggested climbing on top of each other's shoulders and even hanging someone out of a window to

109

reach the higher spots on the wall. Laura emphatically vetoed those proposals.

Then it was suggested that they measure a few bricks to see how many it took to make a foot. They would simply need to count the bricks in the high-resolution picture to determine their measurements.

Laura approved that plan and watched like a proud mother as her kids set up, executed and analyzed the experiment. It was like watching monkeys play as they scurried about, no two of them going in the same direction at the same time. With their youth, came seemingly endless energy of motion. Even in her tender years, Laura was beginning to see the contrasts that age presents.

In the end, the students calculated an average acceleration of 31 ft. /sec/sec. With tongues still in their cheeks, they argued with Laura that they had established a new standard value that surpassed all previous scientific determinations.

It was hard to believe that at this time, about halfway through the summer session, these were the same young people she had interviewed that first day. Her students had made such progress, and in such a short time.

All of her students, that is, except L. He was still not participating. However, he was at least spending more of his time observing the activities of the rest of the class rather than being totally absorbed with his laptop alone. As the class sought answers and formulated conclusions to the various activities, L gestured with his hands and tossed his head to himself, as if to say, *These amateurs just don't get it.* Often she thought that L was going to just let loose and say, *Move over and let me show you how it's done.*

Occasionally, she got the odd word out of him, but that was all. His demeanor was either bored or insolent. However, she remembered that, at the museums, he seemed most engaged with exhibits involving math. His facial expressions were more relaxed and he appeared totally absorbed.

"Somehow I need to capitalize on that," she thought.

20. WALTER STEIN, SCIENCE TOYS

As she sat at her desk at the end of another successful day, Laura reflected that even though they were only in junior high, her students were demonstrating some capabilities associated with college level science—particularly physics and mechanics. She remembered some of the demonstrations Professor Leffler had done and thought her students might be ready to tackle some of them.

She thought she would start with the colliding balls demo illustrating kinetic and momentum equations. That would be perfect, but, Larabee had no such equipment. The needed equipment at the museum was out of service. She thought about asking Professor Leffler if she could borrow his apparatus. A glance at the clock reminded her it was time to go. She put aside the question for the moment.

That afternoon she decided to forego the bus and walk home. It was a perfect day for a walk. After a day on their feet teaching school and roaming through museums, most people might think a walk would be the last thing they would want to do. But Laura was different. She knew that brisk walking was different than museum ambling and it would be stimulating. *Besides*, she told herself, *I can always opt out of the walk part of the way home and catch the bus.*

Her inner detective was on duty that afternoon. As she walked, she made observations and then guessed at their significance.

A tricycle near the front door: children live there.

A house with beautiful flowers in the window box: someone lives there who loves plants and doesn't travel far from home for long periods of time. Window box plants need to be watered more frequently than plants in the ground.

A house with nice, but very tall, grass: they might be taking a summer vacation.

In an unfamiliar residential neighborhood several blocks from the school, she passed a small store. It was not until she was right in front of the store that she could she see the sign in the window: "Science Toys." She stopped dead in her tracks and looked at the window. It was full of toys and gadgets, but low inside illumination kept her from seeing deeper into the store. In the corner of the window near the door was the proprietor's name: Walter Stein. Next to that, a cardboard sign read "OPEN," Below that someone had handwritten 'your mind.'

"OPEN your mind," indeed. She had to go in.

The place was filled from floor to ceiling with all kinds of amazing science apparatus. Some she recognized. A lot was old, but she could see a few new toys scattered about. Their newness was made obvious by their shiny plastic construction. She was experiencing the equivalent of a chocolate lover in a candy store—a science and math teacher's candy store. After a few moments of pure wonder, some of Laura's awe began to wear off and she noticed how old the store looked, and how old it smelled. It was dusty and musty. Just when she began to think that perhaps the "Open" sign was a mistake, a figure approached from the back of the store.

"May I help you?" a man said in a friendly voice.

For a moment she thought he looked familiar. He appeared to be in his seventies; his thin grey hair was not quite all in place. He was not a tall man, and he wore half-frame reading glasses. He had a pencil behind one ear and was wearing an apron.

*Mr. Hoo*per, she thought in astonishment. *This man could be Mr. Hooper from Sesame Street!* Having been a huge fan of the beloved television show when she was a child, Laura was immediately and thoroughly charmed.

She returned the man's smile and briefly explained her situation at Larabee.

"This is absolutely astounding," she exclaimed. "Your science toy store is well stocked and here in a neighborhood not at all far from my school!"

She repeated this point several times over the next few minutes, as she continued to fill him in on the details of her position at Larabee. She found him to be an excellent listener.

When he could get a word in edgewise, the friendly old man began an explanation of his own.

"When I opened this store many years ago," he said, "a school was right across the street where that playground is, and there were several more schools around here too. Many of those schools have since been torn down. I chose the location to be central to them—look where that got me."

He smiled ruefully, but Laura didn't detect any bitterness in the expression.

"By the way," he finished, "I'm the owner. My name's Walter Stein."

"I'm Laura Olson. It's nice to meet you, Mr. Stein."

"Nice to meet you too, Miss Olson," Stein said, smiling. "And please call me Walter. Over the years I have helped many a teacher. I can especially appreciate the difficulty you face --the language barrier and lack of equipment together make for quite an obstacle. I'll tell you what I think: the fact that you are relying on more visual things is an excellent approach. Do you have a specific need at this time?"

"Yes, I do. I'm trying to integrate some math and science to show how important the two are to each other."

"Do they do algebra yet?" he asked.

"Yes, and a few do quite well. I suspect that one of them knows more math than he is willing to admit" she responded.

"Do they understand kinetic energy and momentum?"

"Yes--quite well, in fact. I was trying to come up with--"

Walter's expression stopped her. His face lit up with an expression that, had he been a little kid, would be translated as: "Oh goody!"

With excitement, Walter had moved away from her and she thought he might not be able to hear her continue her response. Having cut off her explanation rather abruptly, Laura spent a moment tucking her silky brown hair behind her ears. She didn't know whether to follow him or not, so she craned her neck to see what he was doing. Walter had hurried to one side of the store, where he pointed to a piece of equipment.

"Now," he called, "here is a classic. It does a beautiful job of tying real behavior with math."

Walter pointed to a colliding ball set on a counter next to him.

"That's it!" Laura exclaimed. "That's what I'm looking for."

In a moment, however, reality set in and her excitement level dropped as she asked how much it cost.

"It retails for $299," Walter was saying.

Laura swallowed hard, her excitement crushed. She had no budget from the school district and certainly she could not personally afford it... Walter's price quote was met with deafening silence.

But then Walter broke the silence.

"You can borrow it," he said.

She jerked her head upward in surprise. Then as his statement soaked in, Laura beamed.

"Any equipment in my store can be used for free on a trial basis," he explained.

"Oh, that would be wonderful!" Laura cried, her level of excitement racing back to the top.

As Walter packed the equipment for her, the two spoke briefly about some of the other items in the store and Walter made a few comments about helping other teachers in situations similar to Laura's.

"Wait a minute," he exclaimed at one point. "Larabee? You said Larabee?"

Laura nodded.

 "But I thought that school had been demolished," he had a puzzled look on his brow.

"No, it's still there."

Laura spared him the detail that hers was the only class meeting in the building. Package in hand, she went happily on her way. Her feet did not hurt a bit.

Strange coincidence? Probably.

Wonderful coincidence? Absolutely.

21. BACK AT LARABEE

The next day, Laura was still excited as she prepared the class for the colliding ball activity. In much the same way Professor Leffler had done, she asked her students to predict the outcome of pulling one ball to the side and releasing it to hit the others.

"What do you think will happen?"

A flood of guesses came forth: all would move; the one ball would bounce back; they would all move together …

"Interesting possibilities," Laura cut in, "but only one can be correct. We can do the demo and find the answer that way. But there is another very clever way to find out. By simultaneously solving kinetic energy and momentum equations, you will be able to tell what the colliding balls will do. The solution to the equations will predict the outcome."

The students had used both the kinetic energy and momentum equations before with real objects, but not at the same time. They weren't exactly sure what to do. Introducing a new concept with a challenge had become one of Laura's favorite teaching tools, reasoning that stewing a bit over the procedure would be good for her students.

Her hunch was right. Heads nodded "no," hand gestures suggested, "I have no idea," and she saw some very puzzled looks. Finally Jose spoke up.

"What is simultaneously?" he asked.

Laura was prepared for the fact that this word had not been part of their English vocabulary. On another part of the chalkboard, she wrote two simple equations and turned to the class to explain. But before she could speak, something unexpected happened. From the back corner of the room, L spoke.

"Only the one on the opposite end will move," he said flatly.

Laura was astonished. Naturally, as the instructor, she knew the correct answer—but L had come up with it so quickly. For a moment, Laura and the rest of the class were speechless: L seldom spoke out loud.

His classmates thought he was just offering his guess of the outcome. Laura was not sure about that, because she knew that L's answer was correct. She wondered whether it could have just been a lucky guess. Not wanting to sidetrack the lesson for the rest of the class, she hid her astonishment as well as she could and returned to her chalkboard example.

It took about fifteen minutes to get everyone on board with the meaning of "simultaneous solutions." It took another half hour for them to apply the process to the kinetic energy and momentum equations. Finally, they reached a consensus. They calculated that the ball on the far end would move and the rest would remain motionless, just as L had predicted forty-five minutes earlier.

Laura did the demonstration and the predicted result occurred. In their usual fashion, the class (except L) cheered and high-fived each other; having just witnessed the wonderful connection between math and the real world. In their excitement, the students forgot that L had correctly predicted the outcome.

After the commotion died down, Laura resumed.

"Now, there is always the chance that I picked the one situation where the equations and reality agree. Using <u>good science</u>, we need to test further. Can we accurately predict what will happen for different conditions?" she asked. "For example, what if I pull two balls to the side and release them? What will hap—"

"The two on the far side will move off together and the rest will remain motionless."

L had interrupted again, his voice dripping with condescension. He was slouched in his chair at the back of the room, as usual. His subtext was clear: *This is so easy. What's taking you dolts so long?*

This time the class was not so quick to dismiss his prediction. They turned around in their seats to look at him. L didn't make eye contact with any of them; having returned his attention to his laptop. Nonetheless, the class could still see the disdain on his face. Jose grumbled something that expressed his displeasure at being demeaned by "some punk kid." Jose's neighbors nodded, rolled their eyes, wrinkled their mouths and turned back around.

With Laura acting as a coach, they once again set about applying the equations to the new situation. More than once Laura heard comments like, "This can't be done" and "No way." When that happened, she came to their aid and assured them it *was* possible. Then rather than just telling them what was wrong, she gave them another question to answer, one that she knew they would likely get right. That answer would provide the information they needed to solve the original problem. The process was one of discovery, which always results in better learning. After twenty minutes, one of the students, Nik, solved the problem and just inside three quarters of an hour everyone had accomplished the task. Nevertheless, it had taken far longer than it had taken L.

Now that she knew each individual had the correct solution, Laura addressed the group.

"Well, what do you predict if I pull two balls off to the side and release them?" she asked.

"The calculations say two should swing," Nik and Nuk responded in perfect unison—a situation not uncommon with twins.

The rest of the class nodded in agreement. Then Nuk added, "Just like L said before."

As Nuk spoke, he looked back at L, who was slumped in his seat and looking as bored as ever. Jose did not look back, but muttered something that was obviously not congratulatory.

Acknowledging the students' prediction, Laura pulled two balls to the left and released them. The two on the right swung out to the right. Cheers erupted from the class, expressing victory as a result of the anguish endured a few minutes earlier when they wrestled with the math.

As everyone else celebrated, Laura was gazing curiously at L; the rest of the class turned around to see this usually silent and withdrawn person inherit center stage. But L did not react to the stares. He just sat there, slouched in his chair looking out the window with a smirk on his face.

Laura repeated the exercise two more times with different initial conditions and each time L gave the answer immediately, with his, now familiar, condescending tone. By now the class was

121

anticipating his responses; but without the grumblings and looks of disdain; they simply set about performing their calculations and after several minutes, they confirmed L's prognostication.

Laura then confirmed their predictions, using the colliding balls. That was the desired outcome she had set out in her lesson plans, and Laura was pleased that it had worked. The students were pleased as well.

But, then there was L. Either he had seen it all before, maybe on the web like Leffler mentioned, and remembered the outcomes, he was an extremely lucky guesser, or Laura was right about his math skills. Whatever the case, she felt a sense of accomplishment in that, however reluctantly, L was interacting with her, paying attention and participating with the class. Granted, his manner was still abrupt and cold, but this new behavior was a welcome improvement.

Not a day had gone by that Laura hadn't tried, in her kind yet relentless style, to engage L in a dialogue, but with no avail. Now, however, she had been able to pry open, just a little, the door to his recalcitrant mind, and that made her feel good.

We'll just keep working exercises of this type, she said, smiling to herself as she wrapped up this lesson.

22. TAKE IT UP A NOTCH

At the end of the school day, Laura paid a visit to Walter's store to return the demonstration equipment and tell him about her success. He was impressed by Laura's story and let her know that he agreed with the wisdom of her approach. She should continue to present L with challenging problems. The catch would be to offer activities suitable for the rest of the class while still meeting L's more complex needs.

"Let me make a suggestion for your next step," Walter offered.

Laura nodded, with a hunch that she had an idea where he was leading.

"Are you familiar with pendulums linked by springs?" he asked.

Yes! she thought, as she imagined a pull-down "Cha ching" with her right hand.

She answered Walter in a more controlled fashion.

"Why yes," she said. "It's quite fresh in my mind since it was one of Professor Leffler's—I mean, my favorite professor's—recent demonstrations."

Walter led Laura to another part of the store, past piles of old and strange-looking equipment. The store was dark and it was often difficult to tell where one piece of apparatus ended and another began. Walter stopped and pointed to a shelf above their heads.

Laura squinted at the object on the shelf. When her eyes focused, she gasped and whispered to herself, "O...M...G," followed by silence as her mind raced with questions. *"Is this the same? How did he get it? Is this for real?"*

Noticing her silence and the intense look on her face, Walter asked, "Is anything wrong?"

Barely regaining her composure, Laura spoke haltingly as she tried to answer.

"These pendulums…they look just like….something I saw in an old picture… in my professor's class." She paused and managed to smile apologetically at Walter.

He looked startled by her dramatic reaction, so she made an effort to reign in her astonishment.

"My professor," she went on in a much steadier voice, "had some sketches of these pendulums. They were supposedly very old and were part of a valuable scientific collection… A collection with so much significance that its contents have been guarded for centuries… so it cannot fall into the… hands of the… wrong people."

As she finished her explanation, her voice had lost much of its steadiness.

Walter looked a bit dismayed at her answer. He seemed to be having trouble understanding her response. After a moment, he smiled kindly.

"That is a very interesting story," he said. "I'd like to know more about what your professor has to say on that subject."

He turned away from Laura and reached for a nearby ladder to lift the apparatus down from the shelf. Laura studied the intricate details on the pieces as he handed her the equipment. As far as she could tell, they matched what she remembered seeing in Leffler's picture. Stepping down from the ladder, Walter began to explain.

"I don't know anything about an ancient science group," he said, his back to Laura. "I got these years ago when I first started selling equipment to schools. Some young whippersnapper wanted all the latest and greatest equipment in his college physics lab and asked me to take the old stuff in trade. I did. That was probably forty years ago; I still have this set and a few other pieces as well. As it turns out, it is better made and still works like new. His new stuff was probably trashed years ago."

Laura was still a bit puzzled. Walter's answer seemed plausible but he sounded rather coy. She couldn't help feeling that he had deliberately left out significant details.

Walter went on.

"Anyway, if what you are telling me is true about the value of this stuff, I better hide it all, get some more insurance and add another lock to the door," he said light-heartedly.

Was he dodging the issue? Laura sensed it was a soft put-off but since he was the generous soul providing her with equipment, she did not want to risk alienating him by pursuing it now. It was then she realized that her amateur sleuth muse had taken over. She needed to put the genie back in the bottle. After all, what were the odds of finding legendary scientific treasures in a dusty old store on the near-north side of Chicago? *Back in the bottle*, she said to herself. *There are more immediate issues to deal with.* She and Walter needed to start working out the details

125

of her classroom demonstration. She turned her attention to the devices as Walter began to explain.

"I chose this because it dovetails nicely with the colliding ball demo and you can link up two for the regular class, and let L work with a larger set."

"That's a great idea," Laura responded.

Ten minutes later, she set off with the apparatus and a few notes. Walter had supplied her with the equations and operational information.

The next day she set up two pendulums linked by a spring. She gave each student a sheet with the kinetic and momentum equations, which were the same as the equations for the colliding balls. They worked through the calculations and did a trial. The results matched those of the colliding balls. The only difference was that the pendulums linked by a spring let the observer see the interchange in slow motion. From the back of the room, L watched quietly, but with his same disinterested expression.

Laura instructed the class to work through the cases they had performed with the colliding balls. They could do this without her direct supervision, so she shifted her attention to L.

On a table near his desk, she set up three pendulums linked by two springs. She gave L the handwritten equations that Walter provided. L would use the equations to predict the resulting motions of the linked pendulums. In other words, Laura was asking L to perform what Herb, the graduate assistant, had done for Professor Leffler. Even for a talented graduate student this was no simple task. For someone who hadn't even reached high school, it might be impossible. Laura knew it was a stretch, but had a hunch about L, so she set it up.

23. YOU CAN'T BE SERIOUS

To get him started, Laura planned to do a trial first and let L observe the resulting complex motions. Then, she would show how the equations supported the complex patterns observed for that trial. Finally, she would turn him loose to repeat the process for the remaining cases.

Before Laura began the demonstration, L studied the page of equations intently. Laura set the pendulums into motion and what looked like chaos ensued. Eventually, though, definite patterns could be observed and they repeated time and time again—just as they had when Herb had done it—until all motion finally died out due to friction.

L watched the motions intently. When they were all but gone, he looked once again at the equations and blurted out, "The equation's wrong."

Laura let out a disbelieving, "*What?*"

"It doesn't work," L insisted.

She asked him for an explanation, but L only repeated his initial assessment: "The equation is wrong."

Finally, he pointed to a plus sign between two terms of one of the equations.

"This one," he said. "This sign can't be positive. These equations do not predict what we saw."

Laura was caught off guard by L's insistence, and by the fact that he had spoken with such conviction.

128

"How do you know that sign is wrong?" she asked sincerely.

"It just is! I know it. It has to be minus!" he insisted in his abrupt manner.

She looked at the sheet again, hoping to remember some detail from Leffler's class that would explain the problem. Herb had presented lots of equations, far too many to allow her to remember a detail like that.

"I'll check on this and get back to you," Laura said as she slowly turned away to resume her work with the rest of the class.

She hardly had the words out of her mouth, when L returned his attention to his laptop.

Meanwhile, the two-pendulum demonstration was working beautifully for the remainder of the class. During the brief time she had spent with L, the other students had solved the equations and compared their results to the behavior of the apparatus. All had turned out as planned and their comments indicated that they understood the lesson. "Thank goodness," Laura thought. She needed to see success. She liked closure.

Back in his corner, L plugged his equations into his laptop, using a program that made stick-figure animations. After about a half hour, he motioned for Laura to come to his desk. She had no idea what L had in mind, but the fact that he called her back was a new victory. He pointed to his laptop and started the program. In a moment she saw stick-figure animations mimicking the pendulum demonstrations perfectly. It was very impressive, to say the least, Laura thought. It looked like Herb's work, only much clearer. Laura was pleasantly surprised to see the pendulum demonstration. She had assumed that he was always doing futuristic war games of a demonic or antisocial nature.

L stopped the animation and clicked on the window where he had entered the equations. He pointed to a particular minus sign and changed it to a plus sign so the equation now matched the one she had supplied from Walter. L restarted the animation program. This time, the animated figures moved in ways not at all like the demonstration.

"These equations will not work," L informed her.

Laura was in awe. She was seeing animations on his laptop driven by the equations she had only given him a short time ago. He was doing what Herb said had taken him days to finish. To be absolutely sure of L's accuracy, Laura restarted the pendulums to compare their motion to L's animated display. As before, the correct motion was only achieved when a minus sign was used in the equation driving L's animation.

But Walter's sheets showed a plus, she puzzled. *How can this be?*

Laura's head was spinning. What caused the inconsistent results? And the animated graphics program: where did L get that? What about the skills to deal with simulated motions driven by mathematical expressions? This had not been part of her class. It was not at the museum. She returned to a previous thought: the only time she had ever even seen someone do that kind of thing was when Herb had done it, and he was armed with sophisticated hardware and software. Now, here was a kid with a laptop and no training that Laura knew of, performing graduate-level math without breaking a sweat. He had immediately taken issue with the plus and minus signs supplied by Walter.

The teacher in Laura interrupted her mental turmoil with a positive flash: L had become totally engaged and had spoken several whole sentences with conviction in his voice! Laura had never heard that tone before.

Now, Laura not only had the initial declaration that L had made about the incorrect sign but he had subsequently demonstrated the difference and it all seemed to be supported by the actual demonstration. She didn't have an answer for him; only more questions. She reasoned that standing here and arguing over plus and minus signs would not resolve anything, and she needed to attend to the rest of her students.

"That work you did with the equations and the animation was very impressive," she said, reasoning that a compliment couldn't hurt.

L only nodded his head ever so slightly. He was back to being a mystery

As Laura wrapped up with her other students, she decided Walter would be the best person to help solve the mystery. In a few more minutes, the school day was over. In her empty classroom, Laura sat at her desk reviewing what had transpired with L. She wanted to be sure she had her facts straight when she related the story to Walter. Most of all, she was pleased that more interaction with L had taken place. That brought a smile to her face.

Later that afternoon, Laura stopped by Walter's store. He was surprised when she told him about the equations. Were L's previous correct responses just lucky guesses? Had he manipulated the equations just to simulate the correct display on his laptop? Had both of them overestimated L's mastery of math?

"My copy of the equations and the equipment came directly from my grandfather," Walter said. "They have been around for nearly a century."

Grandfather? The one word question flashed through her head. Walter had told her the equipment came in as a trade. Seemingly unaware of his inconsistent remark, Walter continued to explain that it was unlikely that those who had gone before were incorrect about the equation. He pulled out the old worn notebook that contained the original equations to assure Laura of the viability of his information.

Rifling through the pages until he found what he was looking for, he scrutinized the equation once again to reassure himself. The light was not very good, so he pulled the chain on a nearby lamp. He studied the page and found the formula that L claimed was incorrect. He squinted, adjusted his glasses and tilted the notebook into the light in order to get a better look. Then his expression changed to one of wide-eyed amazement.

The page in question had clearly been handled by many people over the years. It was creased and wrinkled, its markings and handwriting quite faded. One crease in particular cut vertically across the minus sign in question. In dim light, it looked like a plus sign.

"My God," Walter exclaimed, "I incorrectly copied the equation for your demonstration."

Laura took the notebook and could see the mistake. It was supposed to be a minus sign. L had been right.

In the dusty light of the old shop, they both realized the implications of the discovery. L had taken one look at the complex motions of the swinging pendulums and, without having completed advanced high school classes in math, without a supercomputer, and in no time at all, he had evaluated the equations and predicted their outcomes. And he had found a mistake!

Could he be some sort of math savant? What other miraculous math skills did this mysterious young man possess? Excited by the possibilities, Laura and Walter agreed to press ahead with more evaluations of L's capabilities.

"I have, somewhere, a puzzle that we could try," Walter said. "It is entirely different from what we have been doing with the balls and pendulums. It involves a lot of randomly placed, odd looking symbols. I believe it will take an extraordinary mind to sort out what it means."

He moved to a remote corner of the store and rummaged through the boxes and boxes of old documents. As he searched, Laura looked about the store at the enormous collection of strange, old equipment. Feeling a sudden need to inject some levity, she called across the room to Walter.

"You know, Walter, a bunch of this stuff sure looks old enough to be from one of those stashes of secret scientific equipment my professor talked about."

Walter's response came muffled from beneath a stack of boxes, "Do you think so?" He seemed to laugh somewhat nervously.

Laura noted his response, but assumed he must simply be distracted by the search.

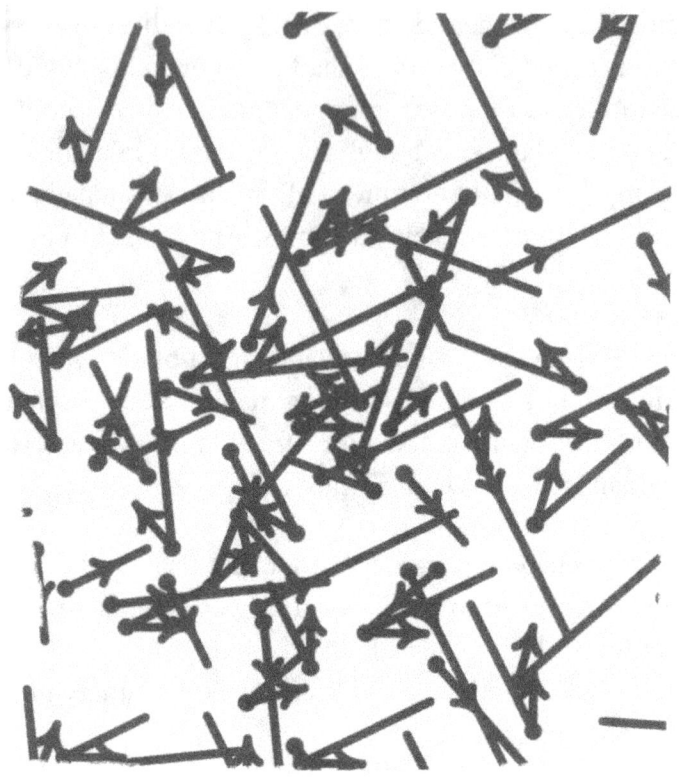

Magnified View of a Section of Walter's Symbol Sheet

"I found it!" called Walter.

Walter produced an old sheet of paper, about eight inches square. Its tattered, frayed appearance and non-standard size gave evidence to its old age. It was covered with small symbols and lines going in all sorts of directions. Some lines were long while others were short; they all seemed randomly placed. There must have been thousands of symbols and lines on the page.

"Since I first laid eyes on this, years ago, I felt there was some sort of mathematical relationship expressed by the symbols," Walter said. "But I never found a plausible explanation. I think it's worth a try to let L take a look at it. With his gift, he might spot something that could help us unravel its meaning."

Laura agreed, but after looking at the page, she felt that, even if L *was* a math savant, he still might be hard-pressed to make sense of the symbols.

24. THE OLD JOURNAL

Laura and Walter discussed the old sheet of symbols for a while. Since neither of them knew what the symbols meant, they would present it to L without any preconditions. No equations came with this one. It was not a demonstration. Both agreed that it was a long shot. But, even if L was not able to reach a definite determination, chances were good that they could use what L discovered as a starting place and take it from there. Just as Laura was preparing to leave his shop, Walter wondered if there might be more pages of symbols where the first one was stashed.

"Wait, while I take a quick look again, to be sure there are no additional pages I might have missed back there."

While she waited, a few yards from where Walter was conducting his extended search, Laura gazed around the room again at all of the old science relics. On the table next to her, she spotted the old journal from which Walter had taken the equations. Remembering Walter's inconsistent statement regarding the source of the equipment, she wondered if the old journal might provide her with some clues to the truth.

She picked it up and began scanning the old writing. They were a mixture of handwriting that she assumed to be German, sketched diagrams, and lots of equations. Looking at one page just inside the front cover, Laura froze. She could just make out the words, "Tagebuch, Isaac Wallerstein" followed by an additional note reading, "FEINE GESELLSCHAFT."

Wallerstein? Wasn't that the name Professor Leffler had mentioned? Could this really be a journal kept by Wallerstein, or another member of the very old, very secret scientific society Leffler had described in class? And what was Walter doing with it? Did he even know what he had? But he must know! Her head was buzzing with questions when Walter returned empty handed, unaware of Laura's discovery. Unable to formulate a coherent question on the subject, Laura decided to say nothing about it for the moment. She thanked Walter for all his help and left his store, her mind still whirling.

She wanted some time to think about her discovery before she asked her new friend any questions, if she asked any at all. If she could believe Leffler (who was, admittedly, prone to hyperbole), the tales of Wallerstein and those associated with him were cloaked in mystery and intrigue. She realized she actually knew very little about the famous scientist, other than what Leffler had mentioned in class. Her imagination kicked in. She wondered if this knowledge could even be dangerous. Despite the warmth of the summer air, Laura shivered.

Wait a minute, she thought. Was she just overreacting? The idea of old secret societies had been the subject of a lot of recent books and movies.

While she traveled back to her apartment and ate dinner—even during her preparations for the next day's class—she was preoccupied by thoughts of the day's events, especially the discovery of the name Wallerstein in the old journal. By the time night fell, Laura was quite tired. The facts, the order of events and their significance became jumbled in her mind. A good night's sleep would help put it all in the proper perspective, so she decided to call it an early night. Just before drifting off, however, a new thought flashed in her mind.

His name is WALTER STEIN, almost WALLERSTEIN.

But, before long Morpheus took over, keeping Laura from mulling that one over any further.

25. NEW PUZZLE

As anticipated, morning brought a clear head and Laura concentrated on the mundane tasks of washing, brushing, dressing, eating, and hurrying to work. She had lots to do today; there was little time to think about ancient, secret science societies. In addition to tackling her regular teaching challenges, she would be meeting with L and presenting him with the sheet of symbols.

Once her class was busy with the day's first assignment, Laura approached L. As usual, he was doing his own thing. His mind was seldom on the same plane as the other students, and, due to his standoffish behavior, no one ever knew what plane that was. Laura had convinced herself that L was some super smart person whose creativity would be stifled if he were forced to go along with the rest of the class. Maybe he was another Einstein. After all, Einstein had trouble in school.

When is that file on L going to get here? Laura wondered. She had been calling Central Administration at least twice a week and still had heard nothing.

"L, would you look at this sheet and tell me if it means anything to you?" Laura asked as she placed Walter's symbols on his desk.

With only the shortest of glances, he looked at the paper; his gaze immediately returning to his laptop to continue whatever he had been doing.

"No," he said, sounding as abrupt and disinterested as ever.

He had outright rejected it, showing no interest whatsoever. Laura was frustrated and disappointed. She had expected him to pore over the symbols, working whatever math magic he had in his teenage head. At the very least, she thought he might have studied the page for a few minutes before making any pronouncement.

Like any good teacher who feels that a student is not living up to his potential, Laura decided not to let it go. At least, she thought, he could explain his refusal in more detail.

"What do you mean, 'no'?" she asked in a non-threatening, but firm, voice. This was a tone good teachers have mastered. It causes students to feel compelled to answer the question.

"Don't have enough processing power," L responded; not looking up from his laptop.

Laura was not sure if he was referring to his computer or his brain and she was determined not to give up.

"What kind of processing power would it take?" she asked. If he meant a bigger and faster processor or more RAM for his laptop, she had friends who could make it happen.

"I'll do it tonight," L answered dismissively.

Laura didn't know what that meant, but for the moment she thought it was probably best to drop the question and regroup. At least she was getting a reaction, as opposed to none at all. The other students needed attention. She spent the remainder of the day looking after the rest of her class.

They were progressing nicely. Their vocabularies were expanding rapidly, and, as a result, the science and math comprehension was moving along at a faster pace. L, on the other hand, spent his day doing who-knows-what on his laptop. Laura even wondered if he was actually secretly absorbing her lessons. Or maybe he knew this stuff already.

26. BURGER AND MUSEUM NIGHT

Laura welcomed JJ's phone call that evening. She needed a break and they had some catching up to do. He still hadn't filled her in on his new job at the museum. JJ had suggested a quick bite at one of his favorite placed, The Billy Goat Tavern below Michigan Avenue. Neither of them typically indulged in double cheeseburgers and fries; often preferring vegetarian and vegan meals. However, they subscribed to the philosophy of taking everything in moderation - including moderation. Besides, what else would one eat at the Billy Goat?

The weather was nice that evening, so he suggested they walk to the Art Institute after dinner to see the new fractal exhibit. Laura remembered hearing briefly about fractals in college, but she definitely needed a refresher course. Tonight could, possibly, revive her memory cells and fill any voids on the subject. Besides, JJ was very excited about the exhibit and he was usually right on the money.

As they devoured their double cheeseburgers and fries and downed a couple of beers, JJ told Laura that he was loving his work at the museum and was not even bothered by the low pay. His title was Associate Curator; though he was responsible for many of the menial tasks at the museum. He explained that there were lots of opportunities ahead but "you've got to pay your dues."

"It will get better with time and, since I'm young, I have lots of that," JJ concluded.

 There was a long pause. Laura expected JJ to say more about his job, but now he had that "far away" expression on his face. He chewed his food slowly, distracted by something. He gazed at the French fries in front of him. Laura recognized the pattern and waited patiently, knowing that some of his best insights followed moments like this. Eventually, JJ blinked his eyes and shook his head back to the present.

"Sorry about that," he said and continued eating.

Laura also continued to eat, fully expecting him to explain what had been occupying his thoughts earlier. After a few minutes had passed, and it was obvious he was not going to explain, Laura prodded him.

"Well, aren't you going to share?" she asked.

JJ had already set his earlier thoughts aside.

"Oh, it was just something silly." And he resumed eating.

But Laura's curiosity was too much. Even his silly stuff was worth hearing, as far as she was concerned.

"Come on, tell me," she wheedled, mimicking a child wanting to know a secret.

"Okay, but it really is silly," he prefaced. "I imagined uncovering some ancient secret treasure at the museum that leads to wild and crazy adventures, like Indiana Jones. See, wasn't that silly?"

They both enjoyed and good laugh as Laura added, "Well don't be surprised. It could happen, so watch out."

But JJ said nothing more, so she let the moment pass.

They had both turned their attention to a news story on the TV above the bar. The sound was low so it was hard to hear, but they could tell that the story was about the governor of Illinois. It looked like he might be in some trouble.

"I wonder what that was all about?" Laura asked.

"Probably some political shenanigans again," JJ said, shaking his head. "Hey! On a lighter note, how is the new job going?"

"Well, it's fun, and it's a challenge too. I've had several of those great breakthrough moments when you see that expression of joy in a student's face as they understand something for the first time."

Laura's face lit up as she described how her students were progressing. She told JJ about the sidewalk velocity lesson and some of her other successful activities. JJ broke into a smile as she described the kids having fun as they learned, remembering the many times she had professed her belief that education should be a "hands on" experience with applications to everyday life. He was impressed with the inventiveness she showed in devising fun as well as effect learning activities. He felt sure his friend was destined for great accomplishments in education.

Then Laura came to L. She described L's experience with the pendulums and recounted the incident with the minus sign in the equation. JJ was intrigued. He had met his share of seemingly weird people, only to discover that they often had extraordinary talents. JJ said he would like to meet her class and observe L. Laura liked the idea and proposed that he come in as a guest lecturer and talk about the museum.

"These days it's tough to get into a school building unless you have a good reason," Laura began. "But with Larabee, the toughest part is <u>physically</u> getting into the building!"

As she chewed her last bite of 'cheezboygeh', Laura's eyes grew wide as she remembered something she had forgotten to tell JJ. She straightened her back and leaned across the table toward him.

"I can't believe I almost forgot this!" she exclaimed. "You know that antique pendulum set that Walter loaned me?"

JJ nodded. He had leaned toward her in anticipation of what was to be revealed.

"Well, when I picked it up, Walter said he got it as a trade-in from a local physics teacher who was buying all new stuff. But when I returned it, he said it was his grandfather's."

JJ raised his eyebrows and thought a moment.

"Maybe his grandfather was the physics teacher."

"That doesn't fit," Laura objected. "Walter referred to the teacher as 'a young whippersnapper.' That is hardly a description you'd use for your grandfather. And there's more. That journal where the equations were written had the name 'Wallerstein,'—'Isaac Wallerstein'—written where you'd see the name of the book's owner."

JJ knew of Laura's penchant for amateur sleuthing and he had always enjoyed the tales she spun from her observations. The difference here was that this was real to him as well.

"Yes, I remember Leffler talking about the Wallersteins and the rumors about their scientific treasures," he answered.

"That's not all!" Laura went on. "Just below *that* it said, 'FEINE GESELLSCHAFT' or something like that." Laura mangled the German pronunciation, opting to spell it out when JJ looked baffled. "I obviously don't know what that part means, but the name Wallerstein has my mind racing."

JJ had that faraway look again. Obviously, her story had piqued his curiosity. In a moment he looked at Laura and said, "When you think about it, each of these guys, Stein and Leffler, hold pieces of the puzzle. Stein has the book with the name and the apparatus. Leffler has mentioned the name and has a picture of the apparatus. They live and work near each other in somewhat related fields. I'm guessing Stein's a little older than Leffler, so they probably weren't classmates. But, with Walter being the equipment guy….maybe Leffler is the whippersnapper."

JJ glanced at his watch. It was a quarter of seven.

"We'd better hustle," he said. "The exhibit closes at eight." They continued their discussion as they walked to the museum.

27. FRACTAL EXHIBIT

As they left the museum an excited Laura rapidly recounted non-stop her experience. She practically skipped as she walked along beside JJ. Distracted by the exhibit, they had both forgotten the unresolved question of the Wallerstein name.

"That fractal exhibit was fantastic!" she was saying (and not necessarily for the first time, either, JJ might have observed). "Not only did it apply to art… but they showed stuff about science, motion pictures, determining shoreline length… and lots more interesting applications. That last one, shoreline length, seemed like a stretch to me, but then they explained it and I got it. Wow! Powerful stuff."

Laura paused thoughtfully.

"Those mountains you see in movies these days? I bet those are done by a computer using fractals as the basis," she raced on. "OK, so if I had to give a quick description of a fractal I would say this: start with an arrangement of objects and then pack more of the same around the original. Like clones, keep packing them around evenly and a larger structure will result. It'll have the same shape as the original arrangement of objects, except bigger. Keep doing it and the objects get bigger but still have the same basic shape. Crystals are an example of fractals. Whoa. I can't wait to see how to incorporate these in my class."

JJ had thoroughly enjoyed listening to the stream of her consciousness. He smiled, shook his head and even mouthed along with some of her words.

When she finally finished, she looked at JJ and he turned to look directly at her. He was wearing a grin from ear to ear.

147

"I'm glad you liked the exhibit," he said.

As she studied his face, it hit her. She realized that the last few minutes she was a victim of her own excitement and had subjected JJ to her blathering on about the exhibit.

"Sorry she said in a shy, little-girl voice. "I guess I do get carried away. Occasionally."

JJ roared with laughter and then consoled her, "You can get carried away like that any time. It is a truly endearing characteristic."

It was still a gorgeous night, so the couple decided to walk over to one of their favorite Pubs on Rush for a nightcap. It was crowded and noisy inside, but a table was available outside. This suited them well because they like to talk. Their talk this night consisted of a light once-over of the Wallerstein issue. It took just one beer each to reach the point of ending the evening.

JJ walked Laura to the bus stop; and as she rode home, she thought about how well her busy and challenging day had ended, thanks to JJ.

To get a taste of what Laura was so excited about go to thefinesociety.com, select VIDEOS and choose Supplemental Video Demonstrations. From that page view FRACTAL EXAMPLE.

28. L AND THE INTERNET

The inside of L's home resembled an urban commune. He
shared the house with his mother and father, his brother,
stepbrothers and, from time to time, some houseguests. Friends
and family members, usually people unfamiliar to L, poped up
unexpectedly, eating at the dinner table or sleeping on the couch.
The exact mix of residents varied, but one thing remained
constant: the place was decidedly lacking in adult supervision.
The adults provided money and shelter, but little else in the way
of traditional parental guardianship.

Surprisingly, none of L's siblings or stepsiblings hads gotten so
far out of line as to become wards of the Illinois prison system.
That was not to say that they were inherently well behaved.
Rather, they're probably smart enough to stay below the radar.
While school personnel might have had reasons to contact the
parents in the past, none had ever actually met in person with an
adult from that family. At best, guidance counselors and
administrators talked to the mother by phone. Most of the time,
the callers have gone away wondering what on earth the woman
said. Given that setting, L could easily come and go at will.

It was the evening of the day when Laura gave L the sheet of
symbols. In the vanishing light of day, L mounted his bicycle.
He had his ever-present black backpack and its contents were as
follows: a laptop and other gear necessary to gain access when
access was needed. For now, we will leave it at that.

L darted about through streets and alleys, his spiked hair
silhouetted against the dim lights of the evening. His pattern
was that of a boy who was trying to shake off someone who
might be tailing him. In a few minutes, he arrived at his
destination and took a position in a dark recess next to the

building. He and his bike were well hidden in the shadows, but he had a good view of anyone who might pass his way.

L took out his laptop; before booting it up he placed a shield over the screen. Airplane passengers use such devices to prevent other passengers from seeing the contents of their laptops. L used the shield to prevent the screen's light from giving away his presence.

In a few moments, he is logged in to the Larabee School's wireless Internet connection. He inserted a 40-gigabyte memory stick into his computer and began uploading data.

Forty minutes later, L shut his laptop and headed down the street to a seedy-looking video game establishment—a teenager's equivalent of the neighborhood pub. For several hours, he played intently. He didn't have to pay for the games; his scores were so high that bonus tokens coverd all but the initial cost of starting the game. This kid was good.

After his marathon session at the all-night video arcade, L rode his bicycle back to the school and repeated the same process he had followed earlier: apply screen filter; boot up; transfer data to a memory stick. However, this time he was finished in only a few minutes.

He packed up quickly and vanished into the night.

29. DC COM.

At 8:00 p.m., at a secure tele-communications center somewhere in Virginia, a handful of people gazed intently at wall-mounted and desk-top screens. They were monitoring traffic of some sort. The largest screens displayed symbols like CHI, NYC, LA and dozens of other abbreviations, representing routes between major cities all over North America. All the screens displayed maps with multicolored lines and flashing icons. Some graphics were constantly displayed, while other lines and symbols appeared and then disappeared. Green lines reassured the overseers that traffic levels were acceptable; yellow indicated heavy loads; red signaled extreme volume and that intervention was probably needed.

Dick Coburn had worked at the Center since its inception in 1993. He was here when the mission changed many years later. Formerly, the Center served as an observation post, looking for bottlenecks in the country's fledgling data communications networks. Individual network companies could oversee their own networks, but this quasi-governmental group was formed to monitor the interconnection of all of them, the Internet. As a particular networking company handed off data to another company, it had no idea what the other company already had running on its networks. Someone needed to act as a backup traffic cop to prevent bottlenecks from occurring as major Internet backbone companies—companies with names like AT&T, UUNET, Sprint, Level3, Qwest, Cable & Wireless, PSINet –shipped data to each other. The graphics that Dick's group watched were the major trunks, which were like big data pipes, through which these companies' interconnected data travel.

151

Most of the time, redundancies built into the system would automatically reroute traffic to avoid bottlenecks, or worse, the loss of a major data path. For instance, if there was an unresolved bottleneck, the general public might notice slow responses when they try to reach some websites. The bigger the bottleneck, the slower the Internet moves and the more people were affected. In a really bad situation, some websites might be completely unavailable.

In 2001, like almost everything else in the United States, the Center's mission changed. Now its primary responsibility was to watch for any unauthorized access of the major data networks and the devices connected to them. Coburn and his colleagues at the Center were now part of the effort to thwart cyber-terrorists. It was a much more critical mission.

Dick had seen crashes and tie-ups happen for just about every reason you can imagine. So, if you need an answer to a problem, Dick likely would have seen it before.

At 8:13 pm, one of the technicians noticed a lot more traffic on a portion of a network that normally had little traffic at this time of day. However, large companies often used off peak hours to ship vast quantities of data to a backup facility, so events like this weren't unusual. Standard procedure dictated that techs simply take note of the heavy traffic. Records were kept electronically, but humans still like paper and pencils; so hardcopies were always generated for notable events, or "NE's."

This NE was not short in duration; in fact, it had begun to spread among the vast, interconnected sites shown on the screens. One by one, each of the major arteries changed color from green to yellow to red. Watching the screens closely, Dick remained

152

calm and unalarmed; he had seen it all, even events this swift and seemingly alarming.

SETI activities (the Search for Extra-Terrestrial life) often resulted in events like this, but they caused no major problems. To increase the amount of data they could crunch from their receivers, SETI enlisted the support of organizations and individuals who had computer capacity to spare. Available computers were automatically connected to and used by SETI at night when their regular users didn't need them. SETI used the extra capacity to work through data and report the results. All of this was on the up and up, with the participants' full permission and cooperation. The arrangement shrunk the amount of time needed to analyze the data from years to minutes.

The concern here was that the Center could only see that the volume of traffic was increasing; they could not determine the nature of the traffic. By law, they could not intercept the traffic. Even if they were permitted to do so, analyzing the data in real time would require several orders of magnitude more electronic effort than they had at their disposal. The guys over at the CIA could do it, but even they would have to settle for a sample of the traffic: there was far too much data for it to be possible to examine every piece.

So at that moment, Dick and his cohorts had no way of knowing if the traffic was an attack by a rogue software program, an attack by a terrorist organization, or merely a legitimate use of the network. Their job was to look for suspicious patterns; if they found any, it became someone else's job to discern the true nature of the event. If a big communications project was on the horizon, the participants knew to give Dick's group some sort of notice. Otherwise, the Center got its clues from the pattern of communication activities they observed. Dick and his team had a good record of spotting good and evil.

It was 3:17 am and the event was showing no signs of dissipating. This was turning out to be a big and long NE, one that did not quite match Dick's past experiences. He sent e-mails to the operations managers at the three biggest private networks. They confirmed that they had heavy traffic on virtually all of their small segments as well. Usually, they would see a few heavily used trunks, but this time it involved almost all portions of their individual networks. This meant that hundreds of thousands of computers were involved.

"Something is going down," Dick thought.

While Dick had developed friendships with some of the network managers at the big companies, direct communication with them was not always desirable or necessary, especially in the middle of the night. But he was beginning to think that this event might be an exception.

He placed a call to Robert "Stoney" Danville. Danville was the vice president of network operations at Calvert Bank, a worldwide commercial bank with its headquarters in Chicago. Calvert Bank was certainly big enough to cause a large data flood with one of their rare upgrade projects, but they always gave ample notification. The phone rang several times before the VP answered in a voice thick with sleep.

"Stoney, it's Coburn. Sorry to wake you."

By the time Dick had identified himself, Stoney was alert enough to carry on a conversation.

"What's up?" he asked.

"We're seeing indications of high volume traffic on all your virtual networks, all over the country. Are you guys running something big on your system tonight?"

"Not supposed to be. I would know of anything that big, and likely have direct involvement. I'll call my night manager and get back to you."

The line went dead. This was no time for correct phone etiquette, and both men knew it.

Stoney called back in a matter of seconds.

"My guys see the high level of activity too, but they didn't initiate it. They thought it might be a project I approved and forgot to tell them about."

As Stoney was speaking, Dick heard a voice coming from a speakerphone on the other end of the line. Stoney interrupted his conversation with Dick to listen. Dick could hear the other voice clearly.

"We're looking at some of the data coming in and out of a server here," the amplified voice was telling Stoney. "It does not look anything like our typical bank data transfers. We grabbed some of the data and entered it into a spreadsheet; it looks like tables of numbers. Every time we look at a sample, that's what it comes out looking like, only with different numbers each time."

"Keep on it," Dick heard Stoney tell the technicians. "I'll be there in 45 minutes."

There was a pause, and then Stoney said, "Dick, you probably heard that."

"Yes, I did. I'll contact Chase and a few others and suggest they look at their data and tell them what your guys are seeing."

"Alright, I'll call you back again when I get to my operations center and have a first-hand look."

Dick gave his two assistants the numbers to call for a few more executives from big company networks. In each case Dick passed on the suggestion that they sample their data and look at it on a spreadsheet. Within a few minutes the other executives had reported back. Their results were the same as Stoney's technicians' had been: tabular data with changing numbers that did not resemble their typical data transfers.

Around 4:14 am, the traffic began to recede. With all eyes glued to the screens, the observers noticed that the drop-off in volume began at the farthest edges of their displays (the most remote computers in cities on east and west coasts). In a few minutes, the high traffic indicators had shrunk back to about half on the most central parts of the network. The rate of shrinkage was increasing. More and more green routes were popping up. In a matter of seconds, the few remaining high traffic indicators were concentrated in the Midwestern states. The last brief pattern was a cluster of icons and red traffic lines: one in the center and five grouped around it. The one in the center was positioned in Chicago. As if someone was turning out a light, these changed all at once, leaving only healthy-looking green traffic displays across the board. The various network people reported that their systems and computers had returned to normal activities.

The NE was over, but its repercussions were just beginning.

By 6 am, Dick Coburn was on a conference call with his boss, Stoney, Stoney's boss, the technicians from the night before and a representative of TSA, trying to sort out what had happened.

Was this an attack? If so, what kind? Was everyone's concern.

Number crunching was usually not a threat. Preliminary checks indicated that no software or stored data were compromised, deleted or added. What was this event? The answers would be slow to come. A technician who had been looking at the captured data on spreadsheets observed that as time went on, some of the numbers in the table had stopped changing. The spreadsheet looked like a vast matrix of numbers being resolved until a solution was reached.

But to what end? And who had done it? There was going to be a lot of sleep lost by these folks and many other government and security types over this one.

30. PLANNING FRACTAL FIELD TRIP

JJ and Laura were meeting for breakfast at one of their favorite Lincoln Avenue restaurants. It was nothing special to look at, but the food was good and the price was right. The aroma of great food filled the air. They could hear the kitchen's radio giving the latest traffic gridlock report. Both were glad to be sitting down to a nice breakfast together and not sitting behind the wheel.

The original purpose of the meeting was to finalize the details about JJ's "special appearance" in Laura's class. Instead they had decided to take the class to see the fractal exhibit; JJ would come along to provide the expert information. From a bureaucratic standpoint, it was easier to take the class out on a field trip than to get permission to have JJ come into the classroom. Plus, this would be a more casual meeting and a better chance for him to observe her students, especially the ever-intriguing L. Laura also gave him an update on L's latest assignment, the sheet of symbols and the student's ensuing cryptic response.

Field trip details finalized, the conversation drifted to the subject of Walter's apparatus store and Laura's "Wallerstein discovery," or "The WD," as JJ had taken to calling it.

"It's sort of creepy to hear about some old secret science group and then see the name in the journal at Walter's place," she was saying.

"I've thought about what you told me, and I still think it's premature to get too concerned about it. I think there could be alternative explanations," JJ offered reassuringly.

Laura had taken her friend to Walter's store a few days ago. JJ liked Walter (he liked everyone); he preferred to think Walter was just a harmless older gentleman whose memory was failing a little. Walter collected old scientific equipment, so JJ reasoned that the presence of an old scientific journal made sense. He found the "the WD" to be interesting, but not necessarily compelling. Trained as a scientist, JJ would not leap to any conclusions based on one piece of evidence. But neither did he close the door on the possibilities altogether.

"I wouldn't worry," he assured Laura.

They talked in general for a while until breakfast was over, and then headed off for their respective buses and another day of challenges and discoveries.

31. L'S FIRST SHEET OF SYMBOLS - RESULTS

It was a typical day at the Larabee School. Laura prepared her students for the next field trip; then she handed out an activity sheet dealing with uniform circular motion. A sleepier-looking than normal L sat alone in the back corner, as usual.

After setting the rest of the class to their task, Laura turned her attention to L, determined to get a meaningful response from him about the page of symbols. Of course, she thought ruefully, she had no idea what the symbols represented, so it might be difficult to determine what was meaningful.

She approached L's desk, a carefully composed question on her lips. She crouched down so she would be eye-to-eye with her reticent student and opened her mouth to speak.

Without looking at her and without interrupting whatever he was doing on his laptop, L blurted out, "It's a map of objects: where they are and where they are going."

He had taken Laura so off guard that she was speechless as she processed his response.

And what a response it was—not an abrupt "No," as often had been the case with their previous interactions, but a concise answer to the question she hadn't even been allowed to ask. There was almost a tone of excitement to his voice. Plus, the sentence sounded like it made sense. Laura was stunned by his manner, his initiative and his answer.

She stood up to gather her thoughts. *But of course, why didn't I recognize that*, she thought to herself flippantly. After a moment

Laura formulated the next question, *What objects? Where are they?*

L was still focused on his laptop when Laura asked her revised question.

"What objects?" she asked.

"Just some objects," L replied, sounding a little irritated.

She tried again, "What do you mean by 'where they are'?"

"Just <u>where they are</u>," he answered, even more irritated now.

Laura persisted, "Where they are going? Going where?"

"I don't <u>know</u> where they're going. They're just going," L said, throwing up his hands. It was the only time his hands left the keyboard during their conversation.

Laura knew she would only be pressing her luck if she continued her barrage of questions. Besides, for now she could not think of another way to ask them. It was probably best to share the answer with Walter and see what he thought. After all, he was the one who supplied the sheet, so he might be able to shed more light on L's response.

Vowing to fight another day, Laura smiled at L and started for the front of the room. Just as she began to move away, L added, with his eyes still glued to the laptop: "And there are more."

"More objects? Sheets of symbols?" she blurted, turning on her heel to face him once again, hands on her hips, too perplexed to keep the urgency from her voice.

"Both," he answered. But this time his response was calm and matter of fact. Laura was borderline furious. She felt he had been toying with her, but not wanting to give him that satisfaction, she reined in her emotions and decided to push no further, for now. On her way back to her desk, she reconstructed the event.

Indeed, L had given a response, even a plausible-sounding one. But it was not enough to resolve anything regarding the sheet of symbols. Laura sat down at her desk in a haze of bewilderment.

Then, quite suddenly, she froze.

Whoa, Laura. Stop! Wake up girl, she said to herself. *The analysis of the sheet isn't important. Getting through to L is what's important. The sheet of symbols was just a means to that end... how quickly we're distracted.*

With that revelation, she resolved to focus on the communications breakthrough with L and what her next steps should be.

32. FRACTALS AT THE ART INSTITUTE

"Wow—"

"Cool—"

"Neat—"

"All right—"

"Fantastic—"

The comments, interspersed with a few obviously approving expressions in languages unknown to the chaperones, told JJ and Laura that the fractals field trip (the "FFT," as it was known to JJ) was a success.

Nik and Nuk flitted from picture to picture, becoming more animated with each discovery and chattering excitedly to each other. Hammu and Jose were fascinated by a display showing how the concept of fractals had been applied to cellular phones. (Cell phones being such small devices, there is limited space for an antenna. Early cell phones had little antennas that extended beyond the body of the phone, but few are seen these days. That's because inside the phone is a fractal antenna: it has a zigzag shape to increase its length for the appropriate frequency range used by the phone.)

The cell phone display was an especially appropriate exhibit for Hammu and Jose since they were known technology geeks.

L seemed be attentive to the exhibit as well. His was more of deep contemplation, but one could catch glimpses of his expression changing as he studied the various displays. Laura was caught up as well. Maybe the students' enthusiasm was influencing her mood; she was deriving even more pleasure from the exhibit this second time.

JJ had fun interacting with the students as he explained, if needed, what was going on in each exhibit. From a few yards away, Laura could not hear JJ's exchanges with her students, but laughter frequently punctuated the scene. JJ pointed at aspects of the displays, and kids followed his lead. His audience smiled and gazed at the young man with open adoration. She saw Nuk waving for Nik to join them, and the whole sequence began again.

With his outgoing personality, interest in others and a sharp mind, he would make a great teacher, Laura thought fondly as she watched her friend.

It was approaching noon when they finished the special exhibit, having fully examined its offerings. A visit to the food court was definitely in order before the growing teenagers headed back to Larabee. Their choices would lead a nutritionist to despair, but what else is new?

JJ took the lunch break as an opportunity to sit down with L. He hoped to strike up a conversation and get a glimpse into the mind of Laura's enigmatic student.

"Hey Dude, how's the museum for you?" JJ asked as he sat down at L's table. But he might as well have been talking to Lake Michigan. At least the lake made nice wave sounds and looked good, JJ thought.

L had not responded. Not a sound. Not a flinch. He didn't even blink. JJ was prepared for what might happen, so he was not put off. He was ready with another question, this time a more specific one: "I noticed you spent a lot of time at the fractal geometry of the marsh shoreline in Rehoboth Bay exhibit. Anything special there?"

"High D," L quickly answered in a monotone voice and deadpan expression.

JJ jerked his head up slightly, and his eyelids snapped up. He froze in that position while he considered L's answer. A typical boy L's age might say that the pictures were pretty or the patterns would make a nice t-shirt design. A typical person of his age would not be able to discuss D values. That was a concept difficult for most educated adults to grasp.

JJ was even more convinced that this kid was bright. Very bright. He could now appreciate why Laura though L was smart but extremely bored. JJ tried a few more questions about the D values, but L had nothing more to say.

Observing from a few feet away and taking pity on her friend, Laura approached the table. Assuming L would have it in his ever-present backpack, she suggested that he show the symbol sheet to JJ. Proving her assumption correct, L produced the sheet and without speaking, plopped it down on the table.

JJ picked up the tattered page and looked at it at great length.. Laura expected JJ to turn back to L and quiz him about what he had discovered about the symbols and what L thought they represented. But JJ remained transfixed by the document for so long that Laura decided to ask the question on her friend's behalf.

L repeated his response of a few days earlier in the same uninterested manner: "It shows objects, where they are and where they are going."

Glancing up from the paper, JJ finally focused enough to ask for more detail from L. When no elaboration was forthcoming, JJ's gaze and attention drifted back to the sheet of symbols, and he seemed once again oblivious to his companions.

Laura recognized JJ's behavior: she had seen it before in Leffler's class when they were being led into quantum mechanics. Now he was hot on the trail of something, but what? She had no idea.

Lunch was over and it was time to return to school. As they exited the museum, JJ and Laura slowed down so they would be out of earshot of the rest of the group.

"I'm sorry for being so distracted earlier, but I'm sure I've seen sheets like that before. I have a vague memory that they are quite old with a hint of importance. I just can't remember where I saw them."

"Oh, my. That's intriguing," Laura said, drawing out her words as she shifted into her amateur sleuth mode. In a moment she added, "Okay, we now have a new piece to add to the WD: you think you have seen more sheets like L's."

The conversation broke off there because both had been distracted enough not to notice that students were already boarding the bus. Laura began to run toward the bus, JJ beside her. He had been shirking his exercise routine lately—as they ran, he breathlessly called, "Let's have dinner tonight so we can talk more. I'll call later."

Showing no signs of being short of breath, Laura called back over her shoulder. "Sure. Love to."

33. JJ AND HIS SHEETS

Louie's Pizza was like most of JJ's and Laura's culinary haunts: local; homey; handy; cheap; delicious. The fact that they served a dynamite veggie pizza was a welcome bonus. Laura arrived a few minutes before JJ. She watched him as he entered and could tell right away that he was excited.

He hadn't even fully settled himself into the booth before he started a conversation about the symbols. She was not surprised. This was typical JJ: when he became engrossed in a subject, he would not give up until he resolved the question or issue. And to say that the sheet of symbols engrossed him would be quite an understatement.

"Laura, that sheet's origin is thousands of years B.C.! I mean, that particular sheet isn't <u>that</u> old, but it's likely one of many copies done over the years. They're rumored to represent some…"

Before JJ continued, he looked around to see how close they were to the other patrons. The booths on either side of theirs were occupied. The pair could hear most of what their neighbors said when they spoke at normal conversation levels. So JJ leaned forward, as did Laura, and in almost a whisper he said, "Like, deep secrets of the universe." He looked around again to see if anyone had reacted. No one appeared to have heard his mysterious pronouncement.

Now who's concerned about ancient science history? Laura thought. *Did I really hear JJ say what I think he said?* Her mind ran down the short list: Eric Von Daniken's "Ancient Astronauts"; Dan Brown's "DaVinci Code." However, JJ was not one to get carried away with that kind of conspiracy theory, so she decided not to poo-poo anything, yet.

"You said, they are rumored to represent secrets,'" she responded. "But L only showed you one sheet of symbols. What makes you think there is more than one?"

"Well, I finally remembered. When I was a summer intern at the Field Museum a few years ago, I was given a lot of mundane tasks, like moving boxes and crates back in the storage warehouse."

An excited JJ went on to give details about museum collections and all the stuff they have that you never see, and how it can take a curator years to figure out what they do have.

"Sometimes a whole collection of some period or other will arrive and be placed in storage for years before anyone gets around to examining and cataloguing the materials," he told her.

The waiter came, and JJ stopped his story.

"Your usual?" the waiter asked.

Laura and JJ looked at each other and nodded agreement and then looked up at the waiter and nodded again. No words were wasted. The simple nods had confirmed: a large onion, black olive and pepperoni pizza with half mushrooms and half sausage (no veggie pizza today); two Italian salads with Italian dressing (blue cheese crumbles on one); and a pitcher of Old Style right away. The waiter was not one to waste words either; without acknowledgment, he left the table. He was back with the beer in a flash.

Laura and JJ resumed their positions.

"OK," JJ continued, taking a sip of his beer. "So this one time, I had to move an old crate that was starting to fall apart."

He paused to lick his lips, smile and utter an appreciative word for the beer.

"We weren't supposed to open anything, but this one's contents started falling out as soon as I tried to move it. It was full of old packages containing sheets a lot like L's. My supervisor saw what happened and was quick to caution me to be very careful. He said he heard the stuff might have, like, great scientific value."

Since starting his job at the museum, JJ had perfected an impression of his somewhat pretentious supervisors. He delivered this last phrase in that classic persona, almost causing Laura to choke on her beer as she broke up in laughter at the impression.

"So he told me the rumors he had heard. The packages and sheets didn't have any recognizable text or illustrations on them, so I wasn't very impressed at the time. So I put them back, wrapped up the crate with duct tape, moved it and, honestly, forgot all about them. Until today."

JJ opened his briefcase, which he was rarely seen without, and produced about a half dozen old sheets that looked very much like the one Laura had obtained from Walter Stein. Laura's eyes widened as she paged though to re-examine each one again and again.

"I can't believe this!" she said. "They look a lot like Walter's sheet." She lowered her voice. "How did you get these out of the museum?"

"Well, technically I should have signed them out; but that could take weeks to give all the required justifications to all the required people. Besides, most of the procedures are geared for long periods of time for research purposes. I plan to return them soon."

"Good rationalization there JJ old boy," Laura answered in her imitation cockney accent. JJ laughed. Laura could do a pretty good imitation herself.

"This is only a sample," JJ continued. "There are crates of these in the basement of the museum. From what I saw, they all looked pretty much the same—just a lot of packages wrapped in paper tied up with twine. I assume the rest contained more sheets"

"I wonder if L would be able to detect a difference." Laura began to smile and continued. "With these additional sheets, he certainly would have enough to unlock… the secrets of the universe."

They both broke out into laughter. Their mirth wasn't directed at L, but at the absurd notion that the sheets could actually be so important.

The pizza and beer was soon gone and their stomachs were pleasantly full. They shared a lot of laughs about other subjects, and dinner was over.

"Don't forget to give L the secrets to the universe tomorrow," JJ called back to Laura as they headed to their respective apartments.

What a guy, he might be a good catch, when the time comes, Laura thought as she giggled her way down the sidewalk. (A little beer typically made her giggle.)

She could be Mrs. Right, JJ was thinking at the same moment, as he walked in the other direction.

34. L SEES THE NEW OLD SHEETS

During class the next day, Laura found a good moment to get over to L for a few minutes of interaction. Perhaps it was more like a few seconds of interaction, but as they say, who's counting? She handed him the tattered sheets from JJ. L seemed excited, like he was seeing an old friend. For a few moments, he looked back and forth between the pages.

"I'll get back to you tomorrow," he said.

Satisfied, she turned to go back to the front of the room. *That was significant*! she thought. *His tone was borderline pleasant; it was a complete sentence; and he looked at me as he spoke. I'll settle for that today.* Now her inner voice became somewhat dramatic. *Was his shell cracking? Were the walls coming down? Yes! Yes! These strange sheets, with their cryptic symbols, had they caused a ray of light to pierce the night of L's existence?*

She halted the mental drama and looked about to see if her students had noticed. Laura was concerned that she may have revealed her inner drama with sweeps of her arm or drawing the back of her hand across her forehead in conjunction with the scene she was playing. No one looked the wiser.

Whew, that was close, she thought gleefully. Very encouraged and very happy, she went back to attending to the needs of the rest of the class, wondering why these old sheets held such a fascination for L.

It was about 8 pm when Dick Coburn's team noticed a building of traffic unlike the patterns they observed on a typical night. The increased traffic was fast building to a high level like the previous NE, which they had yet to figure out. Like before, the traffic built to gigantic proportions with computers in all quadrants, within their view, streaming tons of data. This time they were ready, and the subordinate networks and big user companies were brought on-board very quickly.

The technicians saw the same kind of number matrices and behaviors as before, as they randomly pulled data off the devices at their respective ends. Like before, the table values were changing, but would resolve to a particular set of values in the table. Then a new set of changing numbers would appear and do the same as before. They were still only able to sample some of the data, since so many computers and network segments were involved. It was probably a good assumption that the stuff they could not see was just more of the same. Hopefully, since more network people were involved, greater amounts of data would be caught. Maybe this time they could deduce what was going on and who was doing it.

The previous event, a few days earlier, had gone on for hours. About 45 minutes into this one, it began to scale back and ended just as abruptly as the first time. So fast, that if you had looked away at the final moments, you would have missed the final cluster of activity centered on Chicago. They did not miss it.

35. EAGER L?

The next day in class turned out to be quite remarkable. L was almost eager to get Laura's attention, like first graders jumping about with hands up, hoping the teacher would call on them for the answer. In L's case, the signs were much more subtle—more like establishing eye contact with her and hinting a smile on his face. Some of the other students had picked up on the subtle signs, but were completely unaware of the special project L had been given.

When she arrived at his desk, he directed her to view his laptop. L had his stick-figure animation program running. It was the same program he had used earlier to demonstrate the pendulums and equations with the incorrect plus sign between the terms. For a moment, she flashed back to the day she first saw what he could do with his brain and laptop and wondered how it was possible that he had acquired the skills to do what he did. *Uncanny*, she thought.

L's display showed a group of little circles or balls—it was hard to tell on a flat screen. Since the animation program was intended for simple objects, great detail was unimportant. She could see sixteen little objects. With a tap on the touch pad, the objects went into motion. They moved as if they were connected by little springs. The motions were fairly simple: some moved from side to side; others appeared to bounce up and down. A few had circular or elliptical motions.

By now, the class had noticed the two of them hovering over L's laptop and began to gather around as well. The rhythmic oscillation of little spheres dancing about the screen was a captivating sight. The students pronounced the images to be "cool" and "awesome," then asked, "What is it?"

Budru, the class skeptic, finally said, "*So?*" With a tone that really conveyed, "So what?" In response to their skepticism, L began to explain his efforts in a voice that was poised and confident. It was if he had multiple personalities and a new person just came out. Laura was shocked. A moment ago she had seen L look up at the gathering and address them in a way she had never observed from him: borderline pleasant. Her chin dropped and her arms went limp at her sides as she gazed in amazement at the unfolding scene.

L continued; he was now holding one of the sheets of symbols.

"These sheets show the objects," he said. "Where they are, which way they are going and how fast they are moving." He pointed to an object on the screen and then to a particular symbol on one of the pages. He did this for a few more objects on the screen and on the sheets until everyone got the association.

"These six sheets represent the same objects, but at different times. Like snapshots, but with symbols instead. Notice that this object first goes left, then right in the animation. If you look at the next sheet this part of the symbol has changed and points in another direction."

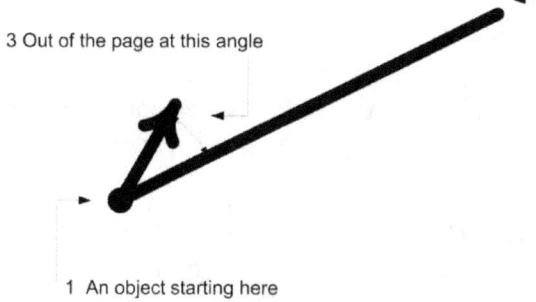

3 Out of the page at this angle

2 ending up here in time T

1 An object starting here

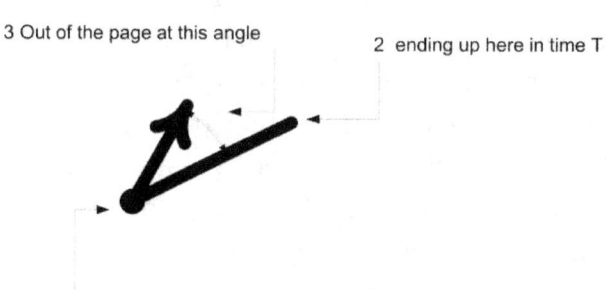

3 Out of the page at this angle

2 ending up here in time T

1 An object starting here

Two objects shown during time T. In the upper illustration the line is longer so it is moving faster than the lower one

The angle between the line and the arrow indicates the direction of motion. As shown the angle is below the line, so the motion is angled by that amount OUT of the plane of the page

To further illustrate his logic, L pulled a piece of paper out of his backpack showing step-by-step how he had interpreted the symbols. His diagrams and explanations were for just two examples, but Laura quickly imagined that all of the rest of the symbols would have similar explanations. Indeed, she could see that L had more similar sheets haphazardly stuffed into his backpack.

L continued with his explanation for all the rest of the symbols.

"So, your animation is based on the symbols on those sheets?" asked one of the students.

"Exactly," L responded. There was a collective groan of disappointment. A few students asked, "Is that all?"

"My older brother does stuff like that on his computer all the time," said Hammu. "He doesn't need pages of symbols."

The class had missed the point completely since they were not aware of the origin of the symbol sheets. Their interest waning, the rest of the students wandered back to their seats. However, Laura was quite taken by L's interpretation of the symbols. Somehow, he had picked up on clues presented by the symbols on the page and come up with his interpretation of what they meant. Plus, the explanation was simple, which is often the deciding factor when determining the best answer to a puzzle. Aside from that, she had just witnessed a behavior that until now had been bottled up inside the taciturn boy. It was truly amazing. Now the task would be to keep this new L in the fore and lose the old one. To reinforce L's new behavior, she quickly and gently reprimanded his classmates for their lack of enthusiasm. She would not want their negative comments to push him back into his shell.

36. WALTER GETS EXCITED

She called JJ after school to describe the day's events. When she finished, they decided they needed and wanted to talk to Walter. Walter was the one who had triggered the process with his sheet of symbols. With the addition of more sheets from the museum and L's seemingly plausible explanation, they wanted answers. They called the always-cordial Walter, and the meeting was on for late afternoon. They found him in his favorite chair near the front of the shop, reading a dusty old science book. From here he could keep a watchful eye on those who entered. Some pre-teens and teens had visited in the past with less than honorable intentions.

Walter welcomed them, and they retired to the back of the store where there were more chairs. Over the usual green tea that Walter graciously supplied, Laura began to describe the results of L's latest test. She told Walter how L at first seemed uninterested but that by the next morning told her that the symbols represented moving objects.

"I was surprised that one day he didn't care and the next day he had an analysis. I'm not sure, but his shell may be cracking," she said. "Then a few days later, when I gave him the other sheets of symbols to study, he came back with—"

Walter leaped from his chair. He was so excited that he couldn't speak. He sputtered and stammered, unable to articulate the one most important question out of what must have been a tremendous number of questions.

"Who? What? How many? Where?" he sputtered. Alarmed by this uncharacteristic outburst, Laura and JJ managed to persuade the old man to resume his seat and take a few deep breaths.

Finally he was able to say, "What other sheets?"

Shooting a bug-eyed glance at Laura, JJ stepped in and patiently explained that he had recognized the symbols L showed him and "borrowed" a few more from the museum. His story was long and detailed—probably too long and too detailed, but the extra time gave Walter a chance to calm down.

"I am amazed and excited," the old man informed them, as if they had not noticed. "I did not know that those sheets still existed."

"Still existed?" JJ and Laura exclaimed in unison. Now it was their turn to become excited.

"Yes, I knew of them. But supposedly they were permanently lost in the years just before the Second World War, when the Nazis confiscated all they could get their hands on," answered Walter, his voice expressing despair.

Laura and JJ looked at each other. Their glances said, *Oops, Walter has spilled a whole barrel of beans and now he will have to level with us. This is also more information for the WD.*

"Since collecting old and antique science equipment is my hobby," Walter said, "I have seen lots of old books, journals and publications of all sorts, which talk of such scientific artifacts. I feel very fortunate to have been able to obtain one such sheet and now you tell me of a large collection right here in Chicago. That's why I'm excited."

His explanation seemed plausible enough to Laura and JJ. For now, they would not pursue the question of Walter's possible deeper involvement. Laura resumed the briefing. She described how L said that the additional sheets also describe objects, where they are and where they are going. At this, Walter became excited again. Laura was worried. "A man his age should not get worked up like this," she thought. "It could result in a stroke or heart attack." Once again, she and JJ offered some calming words to Walter, who agreed to curb his intensity a few degrees.

After regaining his composure, Walter explained in a calmer voice that in all his research on the subject, he had never seen it suggested that the symbols represented objects in motion. For centuries, there was a consensus among scholars that the symbols represented words; countless experts had tried to decipher the symbols to no avail.

"Moving objects rather than words? This is a huge shift in interpretation, How old is this kid?" finished Walter. "Probably fourteen," Laura answered. "Somehow," Laura mused, "that mind of his worked out some equations that could demonstrate those motions with his stick-figure animation program."

She peered at Walter's face. He looked like he could not breathe. His eyes were darting about. His hands trembled. His mouth was open but nothing came out. Was it time to call an ambulance? Laura caught JJ's eye to see if he shared her concern. His raised brow told her that he too was concerned. The two of them walked a few paces away to confer semi-privately.

"What do you think, JJ? Should we get medical help?" "I'm afraid he could have a heart attack or stroke."

They looked back at Walter's face. It was pale, yet he had red blotches on his cheeks. They turned once again toward each other. JJ spoke first.

"I think…" But he stopped abruptly when Walter spoke. "I'll be all right in a minute," he said, then pointed to the desk across the room, "In the left drawer…"

Laura quickly went to the desk and opened the left drawer. It was stuffed with odds and ends, but she spotted a container marked with an Rx symbol, half hidden under some paper. *That's got to be what he wanted*, she concluded. She snatched up the vial and handed it Walter. He nodded his head and placed one of the pills in his mouth.

"Do you need water?" she asked. Walter shook his head. Laura and JJ assumed the pill was nitroglycerin, which is commonly used to treat heart ailments. Within seconds, Walter's color returned to normal and he appeared more relaxed.

"Do we need to get you to a doctor? A hospital?" asked Laura. In soft voice Walter replied, "No. That won't be necessary. I've had this before............with the medication I'll be fine in a few minutes." "Well, you just rest," Laura said. "JJ and I will be right here."

They sat quietly for several minutes as Walter's appearance and breathing continued to normalize.

Walter broke the silence. "Equations?" he asked in a soft voice.

Laura and JJ looked at each other, wondering if they should answer at the risk of upsetting him again. Laura decided to take a delicate approach.

"Equations," she answered softly, and waited. Walter looked like he was thinking. "Tell me more," he said calmly.

Laura hesitated, glancing at JJ for reassurance. Then she began speaking cautiously, ready to stop at the first sign of trouble. "He used them to generate those stick-figure animations. Remember the pendulum demonstrations? You supplied the apparatus and equations and L used the equations to generate the animation. I guess he created similar equations for the group of objects."

She stopped. Walter was getting restless, and she worried about raising his stress level. After a few fidgets, Walter forced himself to speak calmly and deliberately.

"You must be aware of the gravity of his accomplishment. It was enough to come up with the new interpretation of what the symbols meant, but to come up with the equations that replicate the motion is positively astounding." As he spoke, excitement crept back into his voice. He paused a minute to calm down again. Laura and JJ sat on the edge of their chairs intent on his words and his physical condition.

Taking a steadying breath, Walter resumed. "You may remember from the pendulum demonstrations that as you increase the number of pendulums linked by springs one at a time, the number of equations that describe their stable modes go up geometrically."

JJ and Laura nodded.

"In this case, for the number of objects he had on just one sheet," Walter paused with a visible effort to keep his voice from rising. "The number of equations needed to describe the resulting motions will increase exponentially as well. For the number of objects he had, I can only guess it would take thousands of equations to describe the motions. Sharp minds, aided by powerful computers, find it nearly impossible to create equations for even a <u>small</u> number of objects connected by springs. I don't see how it was possible…" His voice trailed off as he found himself starting to get excited.

In a minute he recovered to say, "If it is true that L has found a way to develop equations for this phenomenon, then this is a monumental accomplishment by the lad."

Laura and JJ nodded as he spoke. Having recently seen Leffler and Herb cover the same subject, they were able to follow along as Walter explained the significance of L's endeavors.

It had been close to an hour since Walter's heart episode, and by now he appeared to be normal.

"Walter, do you want one of us to stay with you for a while?" asked Laura. "Oh no, that's not necessary. Once I get one of these episodes under control, I'm all right. I'll be fine," he said, sounding more like his jovial self. "Well, if you need anything, call me!" came a mothering response from Laura.

Just as Laura and JJ were ready to leave, Walter asked, "I'd like to meet L. Could you somehow arrange that?" "I'll see what I can do," Laura answered, and they all said their goodbyes.

37. A LITTLE WALK AND TALK

The pair walked in silence for a few blocks, each deep in thought.

"I don't mind telling you *that* was quite an experience for me!" JJ said at last. Laura looked at him, knowing that he was about to elaborate.

"Before the meeting, when you told me what L had done, I was impressed. But after seeing Walter's reaction, well I... You don't react like he did unless it is really important. Now, it may only be important in his mind, but still....I, mean...I was getting pretty worked up, too. Partially due to Walter's heart acting up, but also what was being said..."

"I thought you looked a little tense, big guy. But I knew you could handle it." Laura smiled and gave him a playful elbow in the ribs.

It had been a stressful and emotionally draining meeting, but Laura found energy out of nowhere. Much to JJ's surprise, she said, "It's still early. Let's get a drink, huddle in a corner and discuss WD. We have juicy data to add to the mix now."
"You're on." JJ smiled; it was his turn to elbow Laura.

Sometime later (She had waited a few days so that Walter had some time to recuperate) in a series of subsequent phone discussions between Laura and Walter (which JJ listened into from Laura's end), Walter insisted that the meeting with L needed to be independent of the rest of the class.

"This stuff may be too important to be on the street," Walter warned rather dramatically, inspiring JJ to whisper about 'the secrets of the universe.' She smiled at JJ's high jinx, but she could tell they both felt uneasy about the significance Walter was placing on the whole affair.

Since Laura normally only saw L in class, the tricky part would be arranging a meeting with L, herself, Walter and JJ, without compromising her obligations as his teacher. That would be difficult. How would L react to Walter, a new outsider to him? Would L openly discuss his findings with a stranger? Worse yet, was there a chance of spooking him back into his shell? Perhaps they could arrange a "chance" meeting of the players? Since they all admitted to being poor actors (not to mention the ethical grey area they found themselves in when hatching a plan to trick a fourteen-year-old boy), the "chance meeting" idea was trashed. Instead, Laura would take a straightforward approach; she would simply ask L if he would like to meet at Walter's. Walter and JJ agreed it was probably the best way after all.

The next day in class, Laura planned to find a moment when she and L could speak privately. The moment arrived as the day began—L came in earlier than normal. The rest of the students weren't all there yet, and those in the room were gathered around Budru's desk up in front. Laura moved quickly to intercept L.

Before she could speak, L asked, "Where did you get the sheets?" Laura stifled the question on her lips and thought a moment. "Well, the last ones came from JJ—you know him," she said. "The first one came from a very interesting old gentleman who runs a science toy store. Would you like to meet him?" "Sure," L answered, and it was still in a pleasant tone. "Halleluiah," Laura thought. "Not only does that solve the problem, but I'm talking to a new L. All our scheming was just a bunch of tempest in a tea kettle."

The meeting was set for next Thursday, after school at 4 pm.

38. L MEETS WALTER

On Thursday, Laura and L walked in silence to Walter's store. Was it Laura's imagination, or was the boy hurrying to their destination? When they arrived, he followed her inside and back to the table in the back, moving with more intention and animation than she'd ever seen in him. He roamed around the shop, examining certain objects before moving on to the next. Laura thought he looked the way she had felt when she first saw Walter's collection: L's eyes were alight with barely-concealed curiosity. She resolved to put Walter's shop on her Field Trip List.

JJ arrived, and L greeted him with an almost-friendly nod. Laura tried not to show how flabbergasted she was by her student's behavior. It was true that he had barely spoken, but the energy he exhibited was, to say the least, in stark contrast to his regular slouching demeanor.

Once they were gathered at the table in the back, Laura suggested that L explain what he had accomplished with the sheets of symbols. Much to everyone's surprise, L began his explanation without hesitation and in a comfortable and knowledgeable tone. He was thorough and to the point.

Laura was stunned by the night and day transformation in his personality. It was a moment of discovery for her: he might not know how to deal with social situations, but when he dealt with technical matters, he appeared to be in his element. Simply stepping into the shop had made a dramatic difference in his demeanor.

"When I looked at the sheet," L was explaining, "I saw that the symbols were all made up of lines and arrows. There are so

188

many, they cover almost every square inch of the page. The symbols all looked similar, but they had differences, too. For one thing, the arrows pointed in many different directions. Sometimes the arrows were on one side of the line, and in other cases, they were on the other side."

L had placed a sheet of symbols on the table and pointed out each of these features as he described them. Walter, JJ and Laura gave him their undivided attention.

"Also notice that the arrows, or caret-shaped signs, are all the same size," he continued. "But the lines associated with them are not. Look at this one," L pointed to one of the symbols. "See how the line without the caret is very short? Then look at this one: the line extends almost halfway across the page. The rest of the lines are in between in length, and they're going every which way."

L paused to let them study the sheet; they examined the various combinations on the page, verifying his observations.

"Taken individually, I had the feeling that each combination of arrows and lines was too simple in its structure to convey much information, like a word or even a letter or number. So I took a guess that the symbols were describing the position, or the motion of something—like maybe there was an object associated with each symbol."

"I can see the logic in that," said Walter as Laura and JJ nodded knowingly.

"OK. So imagine a camera pointed at a group of, say…at a group of marbles. Imagine these marbles are all moving in different directions, at different speeds. Also, the camera shutter is set to be left open longer than normal. Everybody understand the set up?"

Laura, JJ and Walter nodded: so far, they understood.

"OK," L went on. "Now we take the picture. Since the marbles are moving when the camera clicks, the developed picture will show a blurred path for each marble. The marbles that are moving fast will have long blurs and the slow-moving ones will have shorter blurs. Do you see how this relates to the page of symbols?"

Three sets of eyes stared blankly at Laura's young student from beneath furrowed brows. JJ even grunted with the effort it took him to make the connection.

And then, it was like someone had turned on a light. To everyone in the group, it became obvious that this was, indeed, a very plausible explanation of the symbols.

Now their thought processes shifted into high gear.

JJ's face lit up, as if he had solved part of the mystery. "The photo would only be two dimensional, but the *arrow* associated with the line tells us additional information about the object's motion."

"Exactly" responded L.

Laura picked it up from there. "So the direction of the arrow tells us which way the object is moving? That doesn't seem to fit, because the object must be moving in the direction of the blurred path, but the arrow points off to the side at some angle."

"That is exactly what I thought the first time I saw these symbols," L answered. "Then I added one more item to the mix: 'In' and 'Out.'"

His audience looked puzzled.

"Into the page or out of the page?" Walter asked after a moment.

"Exactly," said L. "The objects are going in all directions; a few may be moving in the plane of the picture, but most will have components of motion either in or out of the page. Look at the symbols again and look at the arrow's relationship to the line."

The trio studied the page for a few minutes, and then Laura spotted something. "About half of the arrows are on one side of the line and the rest on the other."

"Bingo," L responded. "The angle the arrow makes with the line tells how angled into or out of the page the object's path will be. If it is on one side, that means it's coming out of the page. If it's on the other side, it's going into the page. The arrow head indicates which direction along the line the object is moving."

Laura, JJ and Walter continued to examine the sheet on the table, applying L's elegant logic to symbol after symbol. Giddy with new comprehension, they started warning each other to duck because an object was coming at them.

It was all so simple.

"Why had this interpretation escaped all those great minds of the past?" Walter wondered out loud. Laura, too, was letting it soak in. Her science studies had taught her time and again that the simplest explanation was almost always the one most likely to be correct.

191

"Tell me what the markings around the edge mean?" JJ asked. There was another group of simpler symbols on the outer margins of the page, and JJ pointed at these.

"When I saw" [In a jarring moment that reminded everyone that L was still an awkward adolescent, L just pointed at JJ] "his sheets, I guessed that they might have something to do with the numbering of the pages. As you examine them, you see that they are similar, but each is just slightly different from the previous one."

L showed the group what he meant while they looked at the short stack of pages.

"Assuming these are in order," he continued, "let me take two pages in order and hold them up to a light."

With the edges all lined up, L pointed out how the trails from one sheet began where the other had left off.

"So," he explained, "the sheets appear to be like several still camera shots of the same objects. When you combine the plots of several sheets, you can track the movement of individual objects. Here, I'll show you with my stick-figure animation."

L tapped a few keys, and little round objects on his screen began moving. Some moved left and right, others up and down—they moved diagonally, in circles, elliptically and in even more complex motions. It was just like the group had imagined a few minutes before, when they learned how to interpret the symbols.

"Fantastic!" exclaimed Walter. "How did you do that?"

"Equations," L answered simply.

"Oh, yes," said Walter. "Laura had mentioned them before. Could I see them?"

"No problem."

With a few clicks, the laptop's screen filled with equations. Walter and Laura recognized them immediately as similar to those used to describe periodic motions in the pendulums demonstration. For just the handful of objects on the laptop, there were pages and pages of equations. Several days earlier, Walter had predicted to Laura and JJ, there would be voluminous equations.

Laura, Walter and JJ were now more convinced than ever that L's work was legitimate and not some kind of faked animation. They shifted their questions to the issue of power: how could L work all those equations using just his laptop?

L explained that he had developed algorithms that combined many of the equations, making the solution and manipulations quicker and easier. The three adults once again found themselves in dumbfound silence trying to comprehend what this fourteen-year-old kid was telling and showing them. A withdrawn, enigmatic youth, L might have accomplished in a few weeks what scientists and mathematicians had struggled with for years.

And where did he get the knowledge? Certainly not in ordinary schools—at best, their focus was limited to the most rudimentary education; in the worst cases, it was all they could do to keep the peace. *Did L learn this stuff from the Internet? Maybe,* Laura thought. He did spend most of his time looking at that laptop screen. *Could it be pure intuition? How much of this ingenious demonstration might just be pure, natural talent? And if talent was the answer*, thought Laura, then it was scary to think that a mere youth could have such a gift.

L sat waiting for more questions, but it was clear that Walter, Laura and JJ had seen enough to keep their heads swimming for the near term.

Signaling that the session would be coming to a close, Walter asked, "One last question. What, if any, other computer resources did you use?" Walter was certain that the number crunching required in L's work was far beyond the capacity of a single computer. "I have access to other resources," L answered cryptically, and left it at that. Laura and JJ's similar follow-up questions were met with the same tight-lipped reticence.

The three adults felt a little disconcerted that L didn't provide them with a more detailed answer. With the question of resources hanging in the air, L now seemed less at ease and said he must go. He packed up his laptop, slung his backpack onto his shoulder, and was out the door in just a few minutes.

With L being less than candid about how he actually did the analysis, JJ, Laura and Walter felt uneasy as they pondered his inadequate response. It was Walter who finally broke the contemplative silence.

"That was amazing, truly amazing," he remarked, shaking his head. "There's a fellow I know very well; I'd like to get him in here to look at this boy's work. His name is Leroy Shire; he is a brilliant mathematician, engineer and all-around computer whiz."

Walter went on to describe how, as a young man in the late 1950's, Shire had worked at Argonne Labs doing the math calculations associated with the design and construction of something called the Zero Gradient Synchrocyclotron, or ZGS. Both Laura and JJ frowned; they hadn't heard of the ZGS. Walter saw the reaction and laughed.

"I can see that you two are too young to remember," he said. "It is—or I should say *was*—a particle accelerator. When the much bigger and higher-energy accelerator at Fermi Labs opened up in the seventies, its usefulness was diminished. It's been gone for years now."

"That was in the very, very early days of computers. Those guys did most their math manually. You can bet it took a good math brain to deal with that stuff," he concluded neatly.

Although no one really had any official capacity, Laura and JJ gave their approval of Leroy Shire.

"I'm not sure what he's doing today," Walter said as he dialed the phone. "He's retired and likes to work in community theatres. I think he still dabbles in music composition…"

He didn't get an answer at Leroy's, so Walter called another friend to see if he could help locate Shire.

"Nick, how are you? Walter Stein here."

Walter explained he wanted to reach Leroy and they conversed for a while. After a few minutes, the call seemed to be winding down.

"Thanks for reminding me about the Society meeting," Walter said, causing Laura's ears to perk up. "I'll see you next Tuesday at the D & W." He wrote something on his calendar. Laura recognized the abbreviated reference to the Devon and Western

195

diner. She didn't intend to be nosey, but could clearly see that Walter had written "FS" in his calendar on the space for the coming Tuesday.

FS, she thought. *S for Society… Is the S for Society? Then what is the F for?* She was playing her amateur detective game once again. *Inquiring minds want to know.*

39. LEROY SHIRE

Leroy called back later that evening after Laura and JJ had gone home; Walter explained the situation. Walter was right: Leroy was involved with a production of *Oliver* with one of the local amateur theatre groups, doing some directing, singing and scenery.

"Time is a little tight as you can imagine, but I'll make some time for a sharp young mind," said Leroy. "I could meet later in the day on Friday."

Walter replied, "That would work. I'll contact Laura to see if she can set it up."

"Does she know anything about the Society?" asked Leroy.

Walter answered, "No, however, I think she would make a good member. We can discuss that at next Tuesday's meeting. You going to be there?"

Leroy replied, "I'll squeeze it in around rehearsals. You know if this kid is good, the Society will need to discuss bringing him in."

"I agree," responded Walter.

Walter called Laura and she agreed to approach L about meeting Leroy. In class the next day, Laura asked L about sharing his analysis with a mathematician, Leroy Shire. He seemed a bit reluctant. Laura was not sure what had put him off, but suspected it might have something to do with the line of questioning that had ended their last interview.

Questions lingered, like how did he take the graphical representations, the sheets with their myriad symbols, and convert them to data? According to L's theory, he would have to have several parameters for orientation of the line in three dimensions, as well as the direction of motion on that line and the time for the events to take place, not to mention going from sheet to sheet. Then once he had the data, he'd need a program to deal with it. Lastly, he would need the processing power to do it all. His laptop's processing power would not even be a drop in a barrel. It all added up to one big unknown, and it was bugging them. As unsettling as it was not to have those answers, no one entertained any notions of not going ahead. Sometimes a good scientist has to be a little scared.

In any case, Walter had supplied her with some background information on Leroy so that she could put a real face to Leroy's name for L. She emphasized his non-professional activities (amateur theatre, composer and tuba player among them), hoping to add some human characteristics to Leroy's image. As Laura shared Leroy's background information, L's apprehension faded and he agreed to meet Leroy to make his presentation again. Since Laura knew nothing of L's background, she could only guess what he found to his liking.

When L and Laura arrived at Walter's on Friday afternoon, Walter was in the back talking on the phone. She could not make out the subject of the conversation. As she and L waited for him, Laura once again looked about at all the old equipment she had seen many times before. She was always amazed at the size of the collection; this time her gaze fell on a calendar. It was a familiar one—the one Walter had written 'FS' on during her previous visit. She could not help but notice several other FS entries over several months; each was associated with the name

198

of a restaurant. She recognized most of them. They were good, but not exceptional restaurants.

Then it clicked.

During a previous visit, Laura had spotted the note in Isaac Wallerstein's journal reading "Feine Gesellschaft." She had later looked it up to find that the German phrase "Feine Gesellschaft" translates to "Fine Society" in English. "FS": Fine Society. It fit. Laura's mind raced as she considered what this new piece of evidence meant for the WD (Wallerstein discovery, in case you forgot).

Her frantic thoughts were interrupted when Walter, having finished his call, entered the room. She closed her eyes and promised herself she wouldn't forget to tell JJ about this new WD development, and turned her focus to the task at hand.

Walter was just greeting L and Laura when Leroy Shire arrived. Leroy was in his mid-seventies. He wore a brown corduroy jacket, a matching hat, coordinating pants and comfortable walking shoes. He was the kind of man whose look and demeanor immediately set a person at ease. Introductions were made and Leroy wasted no further time. He turned his attention to L.

"Well, young man, I understand that you may have some rather interesting math to show me."

Leroy's rehearsal started in less than two hours and he still had some prep to do beforehand. However, his manner was not rushed, so no one would have known that the gracious gentleman was in a hurry.

"I would very much like to see what has impressed these folks so much," he said. He smiled pleasantly. In a few short moments, Leroy Shire had succeeded in putting everyone thoroughly at ease.

As he had before, L produced the sheets and explained how he had managed to interpret the symbols. He went on to describe how he had come up with the equations that fit the motions of the small set of objects.

"Their movements looked like the objects were interacting with each other. Like the pendulums linked together with springs, except in all directions. So I used the same basic idea for writing equations to describe their motions. The only difference was, unlike the pendulums (which were in a line), these objects are moving and interacting in 3D."

Leroy nodded that he understood then asked to see his work. If L really had come up the equations to describe the motion, Leroy would be able to tell if they were valid. Anticipating the pages of sophisticated equations, Leroy frowned. He thought of the still-unread notes left by his conscientious stage director and the lines of dialogue he still had to memorize; with a sea of complicated equations to wade through, Leroy would be hard-pressed to finish his theatrical obligations in time for rehearsal.

L complied with his request and produced a pile of pages. Leroy looked intently at page after page of L's work. After twenty minutes of mumbling to himself and punching keys on his scientific calculator, Leroy looked up with bleary eyes.

"Young man, that is very good work," he announced.

Walter and Laura somehow managed to hide their elated expressions.

"I understand that you have animated your results, yes?" Leroy asked.

"Yes," said L, promptly switching his laptop's display to show the demonstration.

There they were: a group of big dots moving rhythmically back and forth, up and down, in circles, in ellipses; some moving a little; others moving a lot. As time passed, the patterns of movement shifted; those that had been moving to the left and right were now moving in another direction. Similar shifts occurred for the other objects. Eventually the earlier motions returned, only to start the same sequence of motions as before.

"That is a lot of complex motion for that laptop," Leroy said. "I would not expect a laptop to be able to deal with all those equations."

"It doesn't," L responded. "I devised some algorithms that compress the resulting actions of all the equations into a few statements. I use those statements to generate the animation. See, I noticed that the motions are basically the same. They just shift from object to object with time. So I only need to deal with the shifts, and that's a far smaller set of instructions."

L pulled up another single page of more equations, those produced by the algorithms he had devised to shortcut the number of equations required. As Leroy looked over this new set of equations and compared them to the larger set, he muttered, scratched on a note pad, and pointed to the screen, following the flow of terms in the equations with his index finger. This continued for about fifteen minutes, at which time he pushed back his chair, looking dazed.

"Amazing," he exclaimed. "Truly amazing… And the result is so simple— it is quite elegant."

As he spoke, his voice became louder and more excited.

"This is really quite a piece of genius," he said, vigorously shaking L's hand.

Laura and Walter were excited by Leroy's excitement. By now, time had expired for Leroy and he had to get to his rehearsal. He didn't have time to discuss his findings in detail with Laura, L and Walter.

That evening, around 11:00, after his rehearsal, Leroy made a call to Walter.

"Sorry to call so late, but we need to talk about this kid, L. There is too much to explain at this late hour, so I would propose we get together over lunch tomorrow. What do you think?"

"Of course," replied Walter. "Can you meet me at the Dempster Deli at noon? My rehearsal is nearby and that will save me some time, okay?"

"I'll be there," responded Walter.

40. WOW! WHAT A MIND!

Leroy walked over from rehearsal and arrived just as Walter got off the Skokie Swift. It was just a short walk to a great lunch from there. Once situated in the Deli, Leroy jumped in with both feet. He had obviously been impressed with L's accomplishments.

"This looks big, and I think there could be a lot more to come of it," began Leroy, "especially the fact that more symbol sheets have been discovered. You didn't tell me that part."

Walter nodded in agreement and said, "Yes, I'm sorry—I forgot to tell you about JJ."

"Who's JJ?" asked Leroy.

"I'll have to fill you in later if we have time," Walter said apologetically.

"Well anyway, here's what I see," Leroy said. "First, let's take his new interpretation of those sheets. As far as I know, that is the first time this theory has been proposed. In any of the old journals we have, I have not seen this interpretation. You have probably been over the documents more than I. Do you agree?"

Walter nodded agreement again.

"Absolutely nothing has hinted at this interpretation. Most scholars were looking for words. Secondly," Leroy continued, "L has somehow figured out how to efficiently translate the symbols into equations. What he showed us would take an army of mathematicians, and a lot of computer power, to complete. It would still take weeks. Finally—and this may be a really big breakthrough—are the algorithms he devised that shrink all those equations into a few very manageable ones that he uses for the animation. I'm not sure what all this means, but my gut feeling… this is going somewhere."

Walter nodded, scratching his chin.

"Who has been involved with this kid?" asked Leroy.

"Laura Olson, his teacher whom you met yesterday," Walter responded. "Her friend JJ, too. He is with the Field Museum and supplied the new sheets."

"Well, I think we need them all in the Society, so that we can work more freely and openly with them" said Leroy. "After all, if they knew the purpose of our group, I'm sure they would be very willing to participate. They would also better understand our concern to keep information like this under wraps."

Walter asked, "Do you think it is that big, Leroy?"

"It could be."

"Okay, then let's bring it up to the rest of the Society at next Tuesday's meeting."

Both then agreed that the members needed to be alerted that something big would be on the agenda. Walter would do the calling since Leroy was very busy with his production.

"I'll use our special phrase, 'a big fish fry' in my calls," Walter said.

This made sense for another reason: the D & W was known for good fried fish. To the Society members, a big fish fry was a code phrase indicating that something important was going to be discussed, and they should be sure to attend. Before they parted, Leroy added, "I'll call one of our sentinels to see what background information is available. We need to be sure the prospective members can be trusted."

"Good idea," responded Walter. "Let me suggest you include Leffler, since I think he is likely to have had some contact with Laura."

Leroy acknowledged the suggestion and the men parted company.

41. MORE PUZZLE PIECES

The next day, Laura stopped by Walter's store. He was on the phone and gestured for her to get comfortable while he finished his conversation. She could hear him clearly; he made no effort to keep his voice down.

"So, I hope you can make the meeting next Tuesday at D and W's," he was saying. "It's going to be a big fish fry. I'll see you then. Goodbye." He hung up.

"I've just got one more quick call to make," he called to Laura. "Are you okay to wait?"

Laura smiled and waved him away. She would do her usual browsing of the store.

The next call was a quick one. She could tell by the flow of his words that Walter was talking to an answering machine. Having moved farther to the front of the store, Laura could just make out the words "D and W's," "big fish fry" and "Tuesday."

Unable to tamp down her inner detective, she wondered if "Fine Society" might refer to a fine <u>dining</u> society. But the restaurants they chose hardly qualified as "fine" in the traditional, fancy sense of the word. Laura finally concluded that this must be a tongue-in-cheek reference to fine dining. She chuckled to herself at the subtle humor and another elegant solution by amateur detective Laura Olson. Still, there was the Feine Gesellschaft reference in the old German journal. How did that fit into the WD puzzle?

Laura had stopped by Walter's store to discuss Leroy's evaluation. But Walter did not mention anything to her about his meeting with Leroy at the Deli. If she knew of the meeting, then she would expect to hear his suggestions for the next action to be taken. There was an action item, and that was taking up her potential membership as well as JJ and L's, at the next Society meeting. However, he could not tell her of those plans. Instead, he put her off by saying that because of Leroy's current involvement with the musical, they had not been able to discuss it further. It was a white lie and she did not appear to be suspicious. Since there was no feedback for her, the two of them talked in general for a few more minutes, and then she excused herself.

42. D&W DINING

Since it was a weeknight, D&Ws was not very busy. This made it easier for the Fine Society to gather, as a group, away from the rest of the patrons. Of course, Walter and Leroy were there. In addition, Nick, a chemist and metallurgist, Carl, a retired physics teacher, and Megan, a biologist, were in attendance. One other belonged, but lived too far away to attend regularly, five was a typical turnout. Most were in the 50 to 60 year range, but Megan was much younger. A common thread among members was the tenure of their friendship. Often, the relationship stretched back to college years.

Nick had a small metal products company on the north side that specialized in small jobs for precision (read lucrative) metal products. He, like the rest, was an avid science fan.

Carl, the retired physics teacher, loved to make the most fantastic model airplanes, cars, ships and you name it. They were so realistic you would expect them to work right down to the finest detail. Of course, he too loved science.

Megan used her talents in a genetics research firm in Evanston. Physics and math were not her strong suits, but she had a great mind and understood conceptually a lot of the physical sciences. She also was very interested in the interaction of genetics and behavior.

If an outsider were to eavesdrop on the group when they met, nothing would be heard that even hinted at a secret society. They talked to each other about interesting scientific or technical topics that might be related to their own backgrounds. They told stories and jokes, usually related to science. They went to see and experience science wherever it was.

Eventually, Leroy and Walter directed the conversation to the trio of persons who might be of interest to the group. At no time did Walter or Leroy reveal the potential candidates full names, or anything that could be used to specifically identify Laura, JJ and L. Even their accomplishments were described in euphemisms. "One of them has a new approach to an old classic physics demonstration. Walter and I thought the group would like to see it. One of the others has access to lots of documents of interest to science historians. The third party is an out-of-the-box thinker and a resourceful science teacher." This was how the discussion continued, as questions were asked and answers given. During this part of their discussion, Megan asked if anyone had contacted a sentinel and if so, what details did they have.

"Yes, I have some input from Leffler," Leroy answered.

A few heads bobbed approvingly. "Wes usually has very good information," Nick commented. "I'm glad he is involved."

Leroy went on to tell the group what Leffler knew.

"He gave her very high marks both academically and personally. Nothing in the records he had access to would indicate any negatives regarding her suitability. She has a record of service to others all the way back to her childhood; a hard worker and deep thinker who often came up with the out-of-the-box solution."

A few comments expressing satisfaction were made. Leroy resumed.

"There's more—a bonus. Coincidentally, the other adult candidate has been in a few of Wes's courses as well; his record is spotless, which is remarkable considering the potential for problems as a young man."

Leroy continued with a thumbnail sketch of JJ's childhood. His father was military and his mom an accomplished jazz singer. They lived near Hyde Park, but not in the expensive areas. To keep JJ away from undesirable influences, like gangs, his parents made sure to fill his spare time with museum trips, youth activities, church groups, and special classes. They scrimped and scraped to send him to a military school in western Indiana that would be far away from bad influences.

When JJ was a young teen, his father died in an automobile accident and money became even tighter. However, two of his mother's childless sisters chipped in what they could to keep him in school. As a result, he knew the meaning of sacrifice and had developed a strong sense of gratitude for the blessings bestowed upon on him. He worked hard at everything to be sure he became the best he could be for his mother and aunts. JJ managed to avoid the pitfalls that have ruined countless lives for so many young males on the south side.

"Regarding the kid," Leroy concluded, "Wes could only come up with a sketchy file for the name; it said he was 'intellectually challenged' so it really couldn't be the one we met with. At this time I have nothing further."

The lack of information on L didn't appear to worry the group. Kids may have attitudes but are too young to have baggage.

Since Walter and Leroy were trusted colleagues and they did not raise any flags, the positive responses from the group would have been expected. For the members, feeding the mind with fresh science was just as important as feeding the face; they all agreed that these candidates sounded like good additions. When it was time for a decision, those present gave nods, gestures and words of approval without hesitation. Leroy announced once the decision had been reached,

"I know this is short notice, but I think it warrants a quick turnaround. Could we meet next Tuesday? I'll be done with the play over the weekend."

The group did not meet on a rigid schedule, but managed to gather about once every four to six weeks. Leroy's request for another meeting so soon was a clue to the extraordinary circumstances.

"Let's gather at the usual time at ...." Nick paused a moment to select a venue. "...........At Spiro's on Halsted."

"Fine," Walter agreed. "After that, we can come to my shop to see the young man's demonstration."

Everyone agreed and the meeting came to a close.

43. NEW HORIZONS

Walter called Laura to explain that a group of science-minded friends of his would like to get a look at L's accomplishments and extend an invitation to her and JJ.

He also asked if she would extend the invitation to L and arrange for his transportation. She accepted his invitation and agreed to help and offered that, in her opinion, L would not have any difficulty clearing the event with his family.

He probably won't even lay eyes on his parents before then, she thought cynically. It was just a brief phone call since the subject matter, L's presentation, was familiar and Walter sounded hurried, maybe to inform the others.

Laura's excitement began to build. The idea that she was going to attend a dinner and session with Walter's scientific cronies conjured up pleasant and scary thoughts. Because of the reference she saw in Isaac Wallerstein's old notes about the Fine Society, mystery and intrigue were chief among those thoughts. She couldn't help but laugh, too, remembering that she had thought the group's name meant fine eating society and the restaurants chosen were far from Haute Cuisine. Whatever, she thought, hanging around with other science buffs couldn't hurt. Who knew? This could usher in a new chapter in her life, and she had never shied away from change.

The following day, Laura arrived at Larabee a few minutes before the students were due. On her desk was a sealed envelope addressed to her from Central Administration. Stamped across the front of the envelope was the rather daunting word, "CONFIDENTIAL."

The custodian, of whom Laura only saw glimpses on occasion, must have delivered it. As she expected, the envelope was the long overdue file she had requested on L. It was a letter to her from an administrator she did not know. The letter was brief and contained some very disturbing words. In part it read, "The long delay was due to the fact that L. Watkins was assigned to the wrong class. He suffers from greatly diminished intellectual capacity and was to attend class this summer in a special education class. Somehow his assignment was improperly coded and assigned to your class. Upon receipt of this letter please contact us immediately so that he can be reprocessed and placed in the appropriate remedial class."

DIMINISHED INTELLECTUAL CAPACITY! REMEDIAL CLASS! I DON'T THINK SO, Laura fumed at the thought. *What moron could have come to that conclusion?* She stewed and groused about this matter until the class began to arrive. Before anyone could observe her with the letter, she stuffed it and its envelope in her big teacher's bag.

She greeted the students as usual, all the while thinking about the letter. "I wish now I had not been so insistent about a response from the administration. I wish that letter had not come." Then it hit her. The letter was here when she arrived. No one saw her with it. No one saw her read it. It could have been lost or delivered to the wrong place. The term was almost over, and it would take more time than that to get him reassigned. Why bother? Smiling, she said to herself, *What letter?*

By now, L was getting used to the idea of making presentations and seemed to enjoy the company of adults much more than his peers.

"No problem," he said when Laura broached the subject of the meeting.

A rush of positive emotion enveloped her as a result of the exchange. Here she stood, having an intelligent exchange with a young man who now appeared poised and intelligent, when just a few weeks earlier he might have been the world's next teenaged serial something. Her persistence had paid off. And to think that some person or persons in the school district concluded he was intellectually deficient. Laura still was savoring her success when she called Walter later in the day to say that the meeting was 'on'.

The next day, Walter called JJ at the Museum and extended an invitation to him. He also explained that Laura and L were being asked to attend. JJ said he would be honored and accepted the invitation. *Maybe this will allay some of the concerns Laura has expressed and answer some of her questions about Walter's friends and the rumors of a secret society. Or it could result in more questions,* JJ mused after hanging up the phone.

44. ARRIVING AT SPIROS

Laura had eaten at Spiros before. "Great food," she remembered.

As she and L approached the restaurant, Nick arrived. One-by-one over the next few minutes, the rest of the members arrived. It was only of slight significance to her, but Laura had noticed that all, except she and L, had come in alone and at slightly different times. *It's like people trying to make it difficult for anyone trying to observe the movements of the participants, STOP IT,* she said to herself, *enough of the mystery novel thoughts.*

The meal was good as usual. The price was also very reasonable and that made it even more worthwhile. There were several retirees in the Society; leave it to them to find a great meal at a reasonable price.

The conversation over the meal was light and revolved around science and technology. No surprise there. Laura, JJ and L fit right in. Shortly after they finished their meal, Leroy announced, "Well, I have work to do, so I'll see you later."

He did not mention regrouping at Walter's.

That's odd, she thought.

Others agreed and began leaving the restaurant. Walter's place was a few miles north and east of Spiros. As they left, Laura expected those who had arrived on public transportation to board the same bus and travel together. However, only a few got on her bus; and they even sat apart. At the transfer point, they did not get off. She also noted, at the restaurant, that the rest who did not board her bus walked off in other directions.

Are these folks lost? she thought.

L and Laura arrived at Walter's, and within a few minutes everyone else arrived, coming in one-by-one. *How strange, Did they all have errands to run?* she thought. Laura might have had stranger thoughts had she seen Megan Reed, the biologist, hang back at the restaurant and, when no one was looking, put three water glasses in plastic bags and stuff them in her backpack. The glasses she took belonged to Laura, L and JJ.

45. THE SOCIETY AT WALTER'S FOR A DEMO

Regarding the group members' staggered arrivals, Laura wanted an answer regarding this peculiar behavior. But that had to wait until another time. The meeting was about to begin. The backroom of the shop was the only place that could accommodate the group, and it was crowded. Most found a stool, chair or box on which to perch. Leroy took the lead and summarized what he had observed in his previous session with L. He figured this would save time by focusing the group's attention on the important points. L began and inside of fifteen minutes had covered his topics, shown the equations, explained the algorithms and their resulting equations and demonstrated his animations. Occasionally, Leroy would jump in and point out and re-emphasize some of the remarkable sets of equations that L had constructed. All were very impressed.

When it was over, Carl Niles, the retired physics teacher, recognized the significance of what L had done. Nick, the chemist, had a pretty good idea as well, since his background had not just been limited to chemistry. Megan Reed, the biologist, felt impressed by association. If Carl, Leroy, Walter and Nick were impressed, she knew it would deserve her support as well.

"Let me understand, you did this for just a few symbols?" asked Carl.

"Yes," replied L.

"Do you plan to include more in another run?" Carl asked.

"I could."

"That would be interesting," stated Carl. Walter, Leroy and Nick concurred.

Next, JJ asked a question.

"I understood the part where you explained your interpretation of an individual symbol, but how did you get from an individual symbol to capture the data from a bunch of symbols on the sheets?"

So far, L had not revealed that part of his work, and Walter and Leroy, who had seen this before, had not asked. Walter and Leroy looked at each other with a look of astonishment.

How had we missed that question? their faces said.

"I scanned the sheets as graphics," L answered. "Then, with a program I had previously written to parse data, I used it to read the page of symbols that had been scanned into memory. As it read the page, the output was compared to virtual objects I had created to represent the line, the line with an arrow, the angle between line and on and on. When it got a match, all the associated data points for that symbol were recorded as one object. Once I had scanned all the pages, I had a mathematical description of the objects. The description included where it was, where it will end up and how fast it was going. Next, I selected which ones I wanted and fed them to my program that gives me equations describing their motion. Finally, the equations are used to drive the animation program. It's that simple."

"I'm glad I asked," said JJ with a somewhat bewildered look on his face.

The others appeared overwhelmed, too. Leroy, the most knowledgeable mathematician present, was shaking his head in amazement.

"I thought I was impressed before," he said, "But that just blew me away… Fantastic, just fantastic."

"Well, I must say, young man, that you have made a significant accomplishment and deserve volumes of credit," Nick seemed to be searching for appropriate superlatives for the unique work.

"You will no doubt have a great future in math and science," Megan added.

Laura was silent, but she felt proud. After all, this was one of her students; she had helped bring him out of his shell.

The Society members had been careful not to reveal the true purpose of the evening. As far as the young guests were concerned, they were a group of people with a healthy interest in science and math. While that was true, the group had another motive: they needed to examine L's accomplishments and decide whether to offer membership to the trio.

"I want to thank you again, L, for that enjoyable and enlightening demonstration," Leroy said, his tone implying that the evening was wrapping up. "Good luck to you." He turned to Walter.

"Will you take the lead in planning our next get-together, Walter?"

"Certainly," replied Walter, and the meeting ended.

The request by Leroy to Walter sounded like it had nothing to do with what had transpired that evening. However, it was understood by the Society that Walter would be calling them to hear their feedback from the evening's session. The Fine Society had a habit of speaking in code. As they had done before, each member left Walter's place separately.

Laura was left wondering again.

46. WALTER, LAURA AND THE ZOO?

The next day, Walter polled all of the attendees. The results were unanimous: to extend invitations to all three to join the Fine Society. In particular, when Walter called Megan, the one who took the drinking glasses, she gave her wholehearted support and added, "And they all passed my test," after which she and Walter chuckled.

One thing that might stand out in this situation was the inclusion of a teenager in this group of adults. To the group it was of little concern, since the precedent had been set several years ago, when they invited Megan, who had been working on a significant genetics project, to join the group. She was still in high school at the time. However, this event was noteworthy for one reason. As far back as any of the members could recall, this was the first time that three people had been proposed for membership at the same time.

It was a sunny Saturday morning, and Laura was having a late breakfast while reading a book. WFMT, was playing Ravel's *Daphnis and Chloe Suite* softly in the background. The phone interrupted this peaceful scene.

It was Walter, asking if they could discuss L at some length. Laura wondered what Walter wanted to discuss. If it had been an item requiring a short answer, the phone call would suffice. That not being the case, she concluded it was a topic that needed to be dealt with face to face. She decided to wait until the two of them met. Being such a nice day, they agreed to meet at the Lincoln Park Zoo Conservatory at 2:00 that afternoon.

From the Conservatory, Laura and Walter walked a short distance to a nearby pond that had a bench under a shade tree.

The day was warm, but being that close to Lake Michigan, provided a nice breeze. It was a gorgeous setting.

The conversation began with talk, in general, about the events of the last several days and how his science friends had been thoroughly impressed with L's accomplishments. Then he began a lengthy and detailed description of the group. He told Laura that they were a loosely knit group of people, with a deep and sincere love of good science; they were dedicated to its promotion and preservation. Laura noted that much of what he had said so far sounded very "Lefflerian." Walter went on to tell how, over the years as a science equipment salesman, he had established friendships among notable teachers and bright students who shared these goals. He then briefly described how each of the people she had met had become part of the group.

Then it was time for the big disclosure.

"Our group is called the Fine Society. It had its beginnings many, many years ago. Numerous groups that had the same mission preceded us. Curious people wonder if it refers to fine dining or wine or maybe art, and we don't discourage those conceptions; it aids in helping us maintain a low profile. In fact, we nurture those impressions to a certain extent. For instance, you may have noticed that our meetings usually take place in restaurants."

Laura nodded.

"The real meaning refers to an old theory which has been ridiculed by many. Those who espouse the theory have been treated as nutcases or worse, especially in ancient times. The theory is quite simple and assumes that the entire universe is made up of some very, very fine uniform particles that attract

222

each other. So, according to the theory, what we call outer space or even a vacuum still has this material in it. The particles are simply too small to detect. This stuff would be even smaller than the matter the String Theory folks talk about. At times in the past, it has been called 'ether,' especially when trying to explain light and radio transmission. Another strong point in its favor is that it embraces both Newtonian and Quantum physics. Our theory accounts for both and in fact makes it easier to tie them together. That takes a while, so I'll save that one for later."

Walter paused and looked carefully at Laura to see if her eyes had glazed over yet. Nothing of the sort, she was turned sideways looking at Walter and appeared transfixed on his every word.

Laura was spellbound as she processed his words. These were some of the rumors she had heard regarding the secret science societies, and a lot of the clues of the WD were coming together. She felt a chill of excitement run down her spine.

Sensing she was still with him, Walter continued.

"Another important aspect is that these tiny particles are moving and that their motions are in harmony with all the other particles around them." In his last statement Laura got the hint of the tie-in to Quantum physics. "We cannot say with certainty that the fine structure exists," Walter continued. "But we believe that it could, and as good scientists, we contend that it is a plausible idea until its proven wrong."

"As I said before, the roots of the Society go way back. As I'm sure you already know, over the centuries there have been repeated instances of 'good science' being plowed under, beaten back or restricted by some dogma of the day. Some religions, governments or misguided groups have, for a variety of reasons, stifled the good science. So this drove those who would have enlightened the world to keep hidden and secret that which they believed could be the truth. They were waiting for a better day to come, when their ideas would be embraced."

Laura recalled again the specific examples that Professor Leffler had shared with the class: the Catholic Church censured Galileo; Copernicus, Newton and countless others.

"We currently believe that the world in general is still not ready," Walter continued. "There are lots of enlightened people, and we continue to look for them to help us nurture and protect the science that could be misused.

"I came to be involved because my father and grandfather were keepers of some ancient documents that had been passed to them from generations before."

"Isaac Wallerstein?" Laura interrupted.

"Why yes, but how did you know of my grandfather?" Walter asked with surprise.

"My science history professor talked about him, and when you and I were looking at one of your old journals, I saw his name. The book was inscribed, 'Isaac Wallerstein, feine Gesellschaft.'"

"Then you knew all about the Fine Society?"

"Not exactly, I only suspected some connection, but had no understanding of the Society and its purpose. I did wonder once about your name," she added with a smile. "Walter Stein seemed so close to Wallerstein."

"You are correct!" answered Walter. Then he continued in a more serious tone, "I changed it as a young man, because of what my family had been through. Actually, we had another name, Welmonn, for a brief period. It was so my father could slip out of Germany. Once free, we went back to Wallerstein."

"My father, Zelig, immigrated to the US with other German scientists just before World War ll. He worked on many secret government projects related to the war. When the war was over, he continued to work for the government. He had top-secret clearance, and they used him on sensitive research. He was based out in New Mexico. We never knew exactly what he did, but there is one thing I will never forget."

Walter took a deep breath, as if he was about to relate some horrific event.

"My father came home one night and told our family a tale that we could not believe. Not far from his lab, something crashed into the desert that day. The military security folks saw it happen and quickly went to investigate. Lots of aircraft were secretly being tested in the region, so an ill-fated aircraft test was suspected. They called in the Air Force. However, when they arrived, they did not recognize the wreckage. It was not like any aircraft they had ever seen. What was left was pretty much all debris and had little discernible structure.

Since my father's secret lab was nearby, security assumed it was something the lab was doing. Dad and several others were rushed to the scene. Debris was scattered everywhere, and signs of some sort of flying craft were found, or at least that was their initial interpretation of what they saw. There were lots of shiny pieces of material that resembled metal foil, like aluminum foil. But to the touch, it was silky and quite supple. As my father wandered about the site looking for clues, he kept finding the silvery material; and just out of curiosity, he put some in his pocket to examine back at the lab."

Laura was completely captivated by his story. She was so astounded that she felt numb all over. Like her mind had lost contact with her body. *'Am I really hearing this, or is this a dream?'* she wondered.

"My father did not see them," Walter paused and looked as if he had second thoughts about what he was about to say and now with more stress in his voice, "But others, supposedly present that day, said they saw little people, or parts of them, scattered about. The military secured the area and Dad went back to his office several hours later. No one knew what they had seen that day and figured that it would be a hot topic for a while. Naturally, the part about little men caught the newspapers' attention. I'm sure, even these days, you have heard the stories."

Laura nodded slowly, as if she was still absorbing the astounding revelation.

"Well, the next day, my father and the rest of the scientists who had been out at the site were brought into a meeting room where the head of the lab, all his underlings and several serious-looking military brass had gathered. They were told that the official explanation was that a weather balloon had crashed, period! They were instructed not to talk to anyone, ever, about the incident. They were to refer all questions that anyone would ask to an office they designated. There were to be absolutely no further discussions of it at the lab or outside the lab, even with families. From that time on, the press could only get the official version and everyone else clammed up."

As he described how distressed his father was, Laura noticed that Walter was growing quite tense and shaking every now and then. His voice became more stressed; he squinted and seemed to be reliving a deep-seated traumatic event from the past.

"The way in which the incident was handled smacked of the heavy-handedness our family had witnessed in Germany leading up to WWII. What made it worse was that for most of the rest my father's adult life, men from some governmental agency occasionally visited our family and asked a lot of questions. Dad was always shaken by the experiences. Sometimes we saw a car parked near our house for hours on end. One or two men would sit there, reading the paper and killing time. They hardly bothered to hide it when we caught them looking in the direction of our house."

Walter's tone shifted to a louder and determined tone, "I vowed that I wouldn't let them do that to my life. When I left for college, I changed my name from Isaac Wallerstein to Walter Stein in case they wanted to be sure the rest of the family 'stayed in line.'"

"That is incredible," breathed Laura. "What a stressful situation, especially for a child."

Now more relaxed and normal sounding, Walter answered, "Yes, but getting away to college broke the chain. I went on to have a fun and fulfilling career in science equipment sales. A lot of the people you have met have been in my life for many years, so it has been great after all."

Then, almost whispering and in a sort of taunting voice, he said, "It's almost humorous now, but for all the years my dad was under surveillance, I don't think those guys ever knew he had a piece of the debris. In fact, I don't think they ever knew about all the scientific journals and artifacts that were passed down by the family. After all, our collection could very well contain stuff a government might want to suppress."

Walter chuckled out loud before continuing.

"So, our group is quite cautious about our activities. Until now, we have had few scientific breakthroughs to become concerned about protecting. It's not as though we have ever experienced any efforts to monitor or thwart our mission, but we still take precautions."

"I knew it!" Laura muttered. "I mean, like what precautions do you take?"

"Well, like coded phrases. For example 'a big fish fry' means it's important. And we take extra effort to arrive for meetings and leave them individually. Individuals attract less attention than groups. Besides, if anyone were tailing us in a car, he would have trouble following individuals going in all different directions." Walter took a breath and added sheepishly, "The slight bit of intrigue is even a little fun."

Laura was relieved to hear the explanations for the strange behavior she had observed. At last, some of her questions had answers.

Having bared the Fine Society's soul, Walter got around to officially inviting Laura to become a member.

"There are no dues or initiation," he explained. "You can participate as much and as long as you wish. Incidentally, we intend to ask L and JJ as well. All we would ask is no matter what you decide that you keep our secrets."

Laura paused to be sure Walter was finished and then responded,

"It would be a wonderful opportunity to be involved with such a talented and interesting group. I have a temporary teaching assignment, so I'm not sure where I'll be six months from now, but yes! Yes! I would." At that moment, she experienced another pleasant chill down her spine. She also thought that being part of such a well-connected group might help her chances of landing a good teaching job in the fall. As for the risks of being part of a secret group, Laura was not worried: she was young and had at least some of the feelings of invincibility characteristic in young people. She was also dying to ask if he had the shiny material.

"Walter," she began, "what about the silvery material? Is it still around? Has..."

"Oh sure. Now there's an interesting story there," he broke in, anticipating her question. "Remember a few minutes ago I said we had some breakthroughs? Well, Nick, one of our members, analyzed it and found it was related to carbon nanotubes. And as you may know, scientists have only recently developed nanotubes. We even figured out how to replicate the stuff, but so far we haven't a clue of what to do with it. As you can guess, we are not about to reveal what we know to the world—and that's a story for later.

"One last thing," he added. "Would you set up a meeting for me with L, yourself and at least one of his parents? Since he is a minor, I believe it would be better that way."

229

Laura agreed. They shook hands and parted.

Her mind was in a whirl as she returned to her apartment. Although the Fine Society members she had encountered were low-key and casual, what they were dabbling in was far from ordinary. The silvery cloth especially fascinated her, as well as the fact that they had it in the first place, had analyzed it and even made some. That was not insignificant. And she was invited to join. *Who would have imagined this a few months ago?* she marveled to herself.

47. WALTER, JJ AND L

"JJ, this is Walter Stein. I don't know if you have talked to Laura this afternoon, but I would like to discuss in person some future activities that could involve you, L and Laura."

In his always-friendly style, JJ answered.

"No, I haven't talked to Laura. I've been out most of the day. How soon?"

"Do you have any time left today?"

"I have some office work at the Museum I need to finish this afternoon; I should be done by five-thirty. How much time do you need?"

"Under an hour should be plenty."

JJ agreed.

"To save you time," suggested Walter, "What if I meet you down there, near your office?"

"That's fine," JJ said. "Make it the north side entrance, closest to the Shedd Aquarium. That will be cooler, and we'll have a nice breeze off the lake."

They met at the appointed place and time and walked along the long finger of land that leads to the Adler Planetarium. As they strolled, they spoke idly of the beautiful Lake and skyline views. After walking for a few minutes, they found a place to sit outside the Adler Planetarium. There was a magnificent view, and they sat taking it in for a few moments.

Then Walter began his pitch to JJ; he bared the Society's soul as he had done with Laura. After hearing the older man out, JJ agreed. Their meeting was basically a carbon copy of the meeting with Laura, involving feelings of excitement, surprise over the silvery fabric story and the mystery that deepened with Walter's revelations. Nonetheless, JJ was ready and willing to join.

On the outside, JJ was the picture of clam and composure. Inside, his mind was a whirling dervish. He could not wait to sit down with Laura and talk about it.

In the meeting with L and Laura, no parent showed. Laura was skeptical that L had even asked his parents to attend. However, the relationship between parent and child was one of those grey areas as far as she was concerned, and Laura had elected not to interfere. Walter skipped a lot of what he had shared with JJ and Laura. Not that he wanted to hide anything, but Walter was not sure all of it would be relevant for L. In time, L would come to learn more, but for now, just knowing that the society existed to promote good science would do.

By now, L had met the membership and found them non-threatening; and the fact that his teacher and her friend, JJ, with whom he also felt comfortable were joining the group, added to his decision. Having access to more science and math puzzles definitely intrigued him. In addition, he was beginning to enjoy the challenges. His usual diet of laptop games and video arcade activities was beginning to lose its excitement. L enthusiastically agreed to participate.

Laura was also pleased that L had shown even more civility than in the past. His verbal exchanges with adults were still awkward at times, but that could be due to the lack of practice. Laura speculated that his problem all along may have been that the education system was trying to shove a smart round peg into a mediocre square hole.

48. ALL ABOARD

Carl Niles and Leroy Shire thought carefully about what the next step in the analysis of the symbol sheets should be. L had used only a small portion of the available data and they were curious about what a larger sampling would yield. During L's demonstration, when they had a chance to look at the sheets more closely, each noticed other symbols on the page that were different from the ones L had used. There were only a few of the other symbols; and L had chosen the ones that made up the bulk of the collection, but Carl and Leroy were still curious.

Also, according to JJ, there was still an enormous cache of sheets at the museum. What could these contain? Would it be more of the same or altogether different symbols?

They asked JJ if they could examine the documents at the museum. Since the opening of many crates was involved, the process could not be done unofficially. JJ now needed to involve the museum's upper management.

Management's concern was not to deny access to potentially valuable information, but to safeguard the documents from being lost or damaged. They were sheets of very old, somewhat delicate paper. There was also the question of keeping the pages in order in case that was important.

Permission was ultimately granted on the condition that JJ was responsible for safeguarding the materials. The documents would be examined in his presence and only in the museum. To facilitate the effort, the museum made a small, secure, private work area available for the group to use. L's school schedule made a coordinated effort difficult, so the museum agreed to let them photocopy sheets if they needed to make the information available to L outside the museum. The management was unaware that JJ had loaned a few pages to L for use outside the museum.

Next, Leroy contacted Laura and asked to be put in touch with L. A few hours later, L called back and Leroy outlined the actions they would take at the museum to obtain more data. "We'll photocopy the stuff so we can get sheets to you to work on after school" explained Leroy.

"What about a scanner?" L asked. "Using a scanner takes the same effort as copying. Then you can load the data directly on a memory stick for me. That's what I've done for the other sheets."

Leroy told Carl about L's suggestion, and both slapped their foreheads. Of course, that made more sense. A PC and a scanner would work nicely.

"I guess we were not thinking outside the box," Carl told Leroy. "Old habits, I suppose."

Turning back to the phone, Leroy continued, "Great idea L, we'll do that. While I've got you on the phone, can we figure out a way that Carl and I can contact you? Calling Laura to call you so you can call us…It's not ideal—"

L interrupted. "Text me," he said simply.

"Text you?" Leroy paused, befuddled. "Oh, text <u>message</u> you…"

"You do text, don't you?" replied L, in a tone that suggested he had one up on these seniors.

Without directly answering L's question, Leroy replied, "Carl and I will, uh…We'll go ahead and set that up. Thanks for the input. We're looking forward to working with you on this project."

They said the obligatory goodbyes, and the call was over.

"We need to talk to someone and get set up for texting," Leroy informed Carl.

"What's 'texting'?" asked Carl.

49. BOXES AND BOXES AT THE MUSEUM

A few days later, Carl and Leroy borrowed a PC and scanner from Nick and brought it into their small workspace in the museum basement. Also, after an hour-long tutorial with a very patient Laura, they were now able to send and receive text messages on their cell phones. JJ helped them retrieve a few boxes of the old cryptic sheets from the storage area, and they got to work.

They were wrapped in paper and bound with twine, each containing about 80 to 100 sheets. The aged outer wrappings had a few recognizable markings. They appeared to be labels written in German, which translated meant "'Cheese' with circa 1938 dates." The contents were most decidedly not cheese, so Carl and Leroy concluded that the label was probably an attempt to divert attention from the contents of the bundles.

In good museum archivist form, Leroy, Carl and JJ wore gloves to handle the material, opened the bundles carefully, studied the papers carefully and took copious notes. They even took note of the specific way the wrapping had been applied and the orientation of the sheets in the wrapping. They needed all the clues they could find, since they were still not exactly sure what they had. L's interpretation was quite compelling, but it was still preliminary.

Painstakingly examining each sheet, the group noted that the papers all contained the same kinds of symbols as those given to L a few weeks earlier. But the three men also noticed single or small groups of markings that they hadn't seen on any of the previous sheets. Occasionally, they would encounter a sheet that bore very little resemblance to the rest. Because the order of the pages might be important, they were careful not to mix any up.

They began to notice patterns among the markings, and developed some working explanations. For instance, one of the markings that appeared near the edge of each page seemed to be a pagination code. Another seemed to indicate to which bundle it belonged.

In his original presentation, L had suggested that the markings might be page indicators. The symbols the three men took to be bundle-indicators varied widely: they ranged from simple, almost rudimentary shapes to extremely complex, intricate forms. They assumed the simplest symbol, which resembled an arrow, must be the marker for the first bundle.

The marking that they assumed represented a page number also went through various iterations, but from bundle to bundle, the same markings appeared over and over. These assumptions also made sense when they looked at all the bundles as they removed them from the crating. They appeared to be in order according to the bundle marking: they went from simple to more complex.

Going with that theory, they decided that the scanning should begin with the simplest bundle marking.

After many hours of examination of hundreds of pages, they hadn't found any new symbols or markings. Carl suggested that it was time to start scanning. Even with their very good and fast equipment, the scanning would take days. They all agreed that it would be a big task. As each sheet and bundle was scanned, they saved the results on the hard-drive and on a memory stick, just the way L had "texted" them to do it.

50. L, DO YOUR THING, AGAIN

It had taken Carl and Leroy about a week to complete the process. By the end, both of them looked at the thumb-sized, sixteen gigabyte memory stick and marveled that all of their efforts were in there.

"This is incredible! This thing is only about the size of a domino," observed Leroy.

For now, their work was done and it was time to hand off the data to L. Leroy had a preproduction meeting soon (His theatre troop was putting on "Memories Are Made Of This" in October), so it fell to Carl to make the delivery to L.

As the men parted, Leroy yelled to Carl, "Don't drop it down a sewer drain or step on it! Hey! Check to see if your pants pockets have any holes."

Carl chuckled. Of course it was a joke. They were not dummies. The data had also been backed up on their PC and another memory stick.

It was near the end of the school day when Carl arrived at Larabee. Having been a physics teacher in the suburbs, he was curious about the educational setting and classroom environment that fostered L's progress.

This building looks like it should be condemned, he thought as he circled the building looking for a way in. It took a few minutes to find an unlocked door; as Carl entered, a very heavy man slowly approached the door. Carl paused to hold the door open and in the time it took, Carl guessed the man was a custodian. An unkind thought entered Carl's head: *This guy probably doesn't maintain a very tidy building.*

Laura's class was a pleasant contrast to the decrepit exterior. It was buzzing with activity. Rather than just sitting with noses in books or daydreaming while some dry teacher rambled on, Laura's students stood at the chalkboard writing solutions to math problems and worked with apparatus, albeit worn and outdated.

Good education can occur anywhere, Carl thought.

Laura took Carl over to L, and Carl filled the kid in about their data-capturing efforts at the museum.

"When do you think you will have some results?" asked Carl, expecting that it would take at least a week for L to perform the calculations.

"By tomorrow," L replied, taking Carl by complete surprise.

"How will you be able to deal with all that data so quickly?"

In the past, L had had little to say when asked about his methods. This time was no exception. While the meeting had ended on a friendly basis, Carl went away with an uneasy feeling. These solutions were not trivial; as a trained scientist, Carl was fully aware of that fact.

How could some kid with a laptop crunch that gargantuan amount of data so quickly? he wondered. *Well, maybe he'll do it, maybe he won't. I guess I'll find out tomorrow.*

51. ANOTHER NIGHT RIDE

By now L's evening visits to the side of the school building were almost becoming routine. He knew that even though he had several orders of magnitude more data to crunch this time, it would be a piece of cake. In his previous sessions, he produced algorithms that considerably shortened the analysis process. Now he could simply dump the new instructions into the computers so they would be able to do more calculating in less time. L estimated that a couple of hours would be sufficient, even for this immense amount of data.

52. WE'LL BE READY, THIS TIME

Dick Coburn and his team had taken quite a verbal beating for their failure to track down the rogue user. If it happened again, they planned to be ready. The clues indicated that Chicago was the scene of the crime. So far, each time the NE had taken place, the last cluster of computers to stop crunching numbers was located in the Midwest; it fed to a point in Chicago. It had happened so fast on previous occasions that they could not react fast enough. In case it happened again, Dick had arranged to have more eyes and equipment available to focus on the Chicago traffic the next time. They planned to capture a lot of data, especially in the Midwest and Chicago.

For L, the session was going as planned. He got on the network, dumped the instructions and sent out the data. The computers, with their new instructions, quickly crunched the vast amount of data, summarized the results and reported back upstream, where a few computers in the Midwest combined the results into compact and efficient algorithms. These results then returned to a server in Chicago.

L dumped the results to his laptop. It was now merely a fraction of the data he sent out at the beginning of the night. But the equations he received were powerful indeed. At 9:45 pm, he was finished. The whole process took less than two hours.

The last piece of information Dick's team caught was the dump to a server in Chicago. From their vantage point on the network they could not "see" L's laptop, but they identified the server. Getting the answer they needed was just a matter of locating the server that received the final data and looking at its internal records.

The process began immediately.

53. THE GUYS IN SUITS AND DARK GLASSES

Back at Dick Coburn's office outside Washington D.C., the pertinent facts were being readied, along with the required boilerplate to submit a request for a warrant. The warrant would allow its bearers to gain access to a server owned by Tendom Networks and operated for the Chicago City Schools. The warrant provided for the seizure of equipment and associated data files, as well as any responsible person or persons discovered at any unspecified locations that might have been connected to the server during the time of the event.

Dick was on the phone with Stoney, thanking him for calling in the favors around Chicago that had made the operation successful. Without Stoney's contacts providing the level of data network coverage Dick's team needed, they would not have been able to locate the server in question. The server was not part of the bank's vast network, but Stoney had experts on his staff who proved invaluable in nailing the specific device.

"I owe you for this one, Stoney," Dick was saying. "This has been a pain in my ass for several weeks now. If I didn't come up with something soon, I'd probably be demoted or even out looking for a new job."

"That's alright" replied Stoney. "You never know when and who is going to find themselves in a pickle. Glad I could help."

"By the way, if you ever get out this way again, I have a lot of new places to visit." Stoney was careful not to say pubs or bars in case a governmental minion was monitoring the call. Their past pub escapades had been notable, to say the least.

244

The regional FBI office in Chicago was designated as the point of contact; the local agents would execute the warrant and investigate. As the warrant specified, they would have the authority to detain anyone they found who might be complicit in the event. Recent government budget freezes had caused veteran agents to take early retirement, so the remaining skeleton staffs were overworked, their load being heavy with administrative activities (paperwork). They were a mix of rookies, a few very competent and seasoned agents, and a handful of hangers-on who should have been fired years ago. Like most bureaucratic institutions, the latter category seemed to outnumber the former two.

When the orders with the warrant were sent to the Chicago bureau, two rookies and one of the hangers-on got the assignment. Time was short, and these were the only agents available. Since it might involve a breach of national security, and since the true nature of the problem was not known, the orders required only that the agents find the server and establish who had been connected to it during the specified time span. If the agents found such an individual, that person was to be detained.

However, due to the sensitivity of the problem and its potential national security implications, someone outside of the Chicago office would ask the questions. The FBI team did not know the full nature of the crime, only that they were to find the following: a server; the computer or computers connected to the server; and the person or persons involved.

54. AGENTS ARRIVE AT TENDOM NETWORKS

The trio from the FBI arrived unannounced at Tendom Networks around 10 A.M. The company's offices were located in a light industrial business park on Chicago's southwest side, in one of several non-descript buildings obviously constructed in the 1970's. The receptionist was a piece of work. She chewed her gum like it needed to be tamed; her lipstick was piled ten layers thick and much too bright for this time of day. A plus-size woman dressed in a petite woman's clothes, she did not get excited when the men announced they were from the FBI. Nonchalantly she called the operations manager.

"He'll be right out," she announced in a distinctively 'Chicaga' accent, and went back to demolishing her gum.

The operations manager promptly appeared, smoothing down his thinning hair and adjusting his outdated glasses. He introduced himself as Nate Jennings.

"May I help you?" he asked.

The lead agent, Dolan Newport, was not conservatively dressed, trim, polite and precise—what you might expect from an FBI agent. He was the antithesis: he wore a tattered, ill-fitting suit scattered with cigarette burns, old shoes much in need of heels, and his demeanor resembled a pit-bull's. He produced the warrant and explained, unpleasantly, why he was there.

Jennings responded with calm cooperation; he acted as if this was a common occurrence. Newport asked to see the unit; Jennings complied, ushering the agents to the appropriate server, which was located in a large equipment room. There were several long rows of metal racks crammed with electronics.

Green, orange and red lights glowed or flashed from the machines. The cooling fans in the devices produced the only noise in the room, a whirring din that the agents quickly tuned out. A few computer terminals with a monitor, keyboard and mouse were tucked in among the machines. There were no chairs except at the terminal sites, so the agents stood.

"These are secure units," Jennings said. "In order to see the data, we need to set up a telnet session from a terminal. No one can just physically hook up a keyboard to it and get access to the server's traffic records. The problem is that only the client has the level of access needed to reach the data you require. I need to get someone with that authority from the school district to access the files. It may take a while to get someone out here. I can log in, but only at a maintenance level, and that's not going to do you any good."

"Get somebody here as fast as you can," Newport demanded impatiently.

To Newport's dismay, it was almost four hours later before a technician from the school district arrived at Tendom Networks. He was a geeky young man named Walt Lewis, with the personality of a mud wall and clothes to match.

Newport, very agitated by the delay, showed Lewis the warrant. The young man had scraggly stubble for facial hair and was wearing a grungy shirt with expletives prominently displayed across the front and back. Newport gave no indication that he even noticed, but the two rookies did.

Agent Bererra leaned close to Agent Nowak and whispered, "He must be pretty smart to hold a job and dress like that."

Nowak nodded agreement while the technician examined the server.

"So what do you want me to do?" he asked in a bored voice. (Lewis and Newport were perfect for each other. Both exuded "I don't give a rat's…," attitudes.)

Lewis began typing to login at a nearby terminal while Newport grumbled an explanation. In just moments, Newport saw the screen fill with what looked to him like scrolling pages of gibberish.

"It's gonna take me a while to set some filters to eliminate all the 'keep alives;' ya know, handshakes, so that the two devices still know they are connected and stuff like that," Lewis explained, further baffling his audience. While he typed, he filled the time with commentary about how network devices send messages that he called "packets."

"Even at night when little business is conducted, there will be lots of packets exchanged by the devices to move files off for storage, back up files, install new software, stuff like that."

The agents quietly waited, wondering if the tech could get the job done any faster if he talked less. Each time Lewis activated a new filter, the same type of junk filled the screen, but there were fewer pages each time.

"What time is the event?" he asked.

Newport answered him.

About ten more minutes had passed when Lewis announced that he might have found what they were looking for.

Newport, Jennings and the other FBI agents quickly gathered closer to the terminal.

"Here are a whole bunch of data packets around nine-forty-five that night," Lewis said. "If I had to make a quick guess," he continued, "based on the typical data packet size and the number of packets, I'd think we're looking at about ten gig of data."

Newport remembered being told that the guys from Stoney Danville's team had estimated the last dump to this server was about nine or ten gigabytes.

"This is looking good," Newport said. "Where is the device that data was sent to?"

Walt Lewis changed the view so he could see the header in one of the packet frames and read out a series of digits and decimal points.

"It's a router," he added. "Not surprising, because a router is what you will see between buildings."

"Can you tell what computer or computers are on that router?" asked Newport.

"No, at least not directly."

"Where is the router?"

"I don't know," Lewis answered

"Well, how in the hell do we find out?" shouted Newport. It seemed to him as if every breakthrough they had made was met by a roadblock.

Wanting to calm the situation quickly, Nate Jennings stepped in.

"I have the network layout showing the locations, types of equipment and their IP addresses," he volunteered. "We can locate it by IP address on the map."

He hurriedly stepped out of the server room and returned in a few minutes with a large blueprint, which he unrolled and spread out on a conference table at the end of the equipment room. The map looked like an airplane plant that had been flattened onto a page. The operations center was in the center of the page. Nate pointed to it.

"We're here."

From the OPS Center dozens of lines radiated outward to dozens of points labeled "Node 1," "Node 2," etc... At each node, dozens of lines radiated out, each line terminating on points labeled with the names of buildings or street addresses.

"Out here, where these lines end, each router is indicated by a little triangle symbol," Jennings explained. "Written nearby are the IP addresses used by that router."

"Hope this is up-to-date," Lewis said, inspecting the blueprint. "Equipment gets moved and changed without updating these."

The technician's smirk only strengthened Agent Newport suspicions that these guys were dragging their feet and making comments like the last one just to needle him. Why? Because the geeks knew the agents would be lost without them.

The ops manager and the agents poured over the map looking for the specific IP address, but it was not an easy task. Each of the hundreds of routers can have several IP addresses, and the layout had been reworked so many times that the network numbering scheme did not follow a logical progression. After a few false identifications, Jennings spotted it.

"Here it is," he said. "Larabee Elementary."

"Where is that?" Newport demanded. "Never mind, I can get it from my office as we go. Let's roll."

As the trio rushed for the door, Lewis called out after them.

"What are you going to do when you get there?"

Newport paused, sensing it was a loaded question.

"What do you mean?"

"Well, all you're going to find is a black box with some wires attached and a few blinking lights. It's not going to tell you anything," the tech said with yet another smirk.

"Alright! I've had it. Give it to me straight and quick or I have you guys hauled in for obstruction of justice."

Newport was livid; this was taking far too much time. Lewis' last smirk had put the agent over the edge. Jennings realized it and started giving instructions with an air of heretofore-unseen efficiency.

"Look, here's what we need to do next. We can access the router from here and look at its logs." Jennings offered in an effort to placate Newport. Still stone-faced with rage, Newport slowly shook his head, realizing more delays were likely.

"Like we logged into this server right here, we can do the same thing over the network using telnet. The only thing I need to do is—" he paused here, glancing at Newport before continuing in an apologetic tone, "—call someone in the router group to get access." That did mean more delay, but the agents could tell the manager was telling the truth.

"In most networking situations," Jennings added while he dialed the phone, "technicians have to be properly trained and certified to handle the routers. We're not exactly a part of that group, but I have a buddy who is authorized, and he would probably trust us enough to provide a login and password. Since logins can have different permission levels, he can give us authorization to look, but not change anything."

On the other end of the line, his buddy agreed and provided a temporary login and password. Moments later, Lewis had logged into the router at Larabee School.

While he was navigating the screen, Lewis provided more background.

"Since this device is out at the end of a network, its communication log requires less memory. But that means the person configuring the router originally might have configured the memory to roll over if the memory gets full. If too much time lapses between the events you're looking for, the record may be gone when you go in and look."

Lewis was trying to prepare the agents for the fact that they might not find what they came to see. Newport took it as more needling and gave the tech a disparaging look. It was the middle of the afternoon. He couldn't believe he'd been cooped up in this building since the morning, and he wanted to throttle the little geek.

But they had caught a break. In a few more seconds, Lewis spotted the data traffic log, which indicated a great deal of activity; it was probably several gigabytes, and it all appeared in just a short time span from the evening before. The memory had not been erased. One column in the log listed the MAC address (Machine Access Control) of the receiving machine.

"Okay, here's the MAC address."

The address combined numbers, letters and punctuation marks; the tech wrote it down for the agents.

"It is unique" Lewis explained. "Unlike an IP address, which can be changed, the MAC address belongs forever to the machine. If you find a machine with that MAC address, then you'll have what you're looking for."

The trio was out the door in a flash.

When the door had slammed behind the FBI agents, Lewis turned to Jennings and asked, "I wonder if those guys know enough to be able to locate the machine's MAC address?"

With the school address supplied by their office, rookie Jose Bererra, punched it into the car's GPS. The trio arrived at Larabee about twenty minutes later at the school in their unmarked brown sedan.

55. AGENTS GO TO SCHOOL

By now, the school day was about over. Since the school looked so dilapidated, the agents' first impression was that they were at the wrong building. There were no signs of children or activity of any kind. After trying many doors and finding them all locked, the agents were ready to call the office for "information support." (That's double speak for "Need more details," or "Are you sure?")

"This looks like another wild goose chase," Newport steamed while mumbling expletives and yanking on the chained doors. "This damned derelict place is empty! Just as Newport was about place a call to headquarters and rant at someone there, Nowak radioed that he had found an open door. Agent Bererra scrambled to join Nowak. Newport tried to run, but in his less than stellar physical condition it was more of a fast shuffle. Even at that he arrived panting. The agents climbed several steps to reach the door. Once inside, there were more steps leading both up and down.

"So if you go down," Nowak mused aloud, "is that to the first floor or basement? Do the steps up go to the first or second floor?"

"Knock it off Nowak. Just search the damn building!" Newport blurted, following up with more mumbled expletives.

Nowak was right to raise the question. Law enforcement officers are taught to notice such details so that if backup is called for, they can give explicit instructions. In a school setting like this, the possibility of needing backup seemed rather remote, but these days one never knew for sure what could be lurking in a derelict building like this one. Nowak was going by the book, something Newport quit doing long ago.

Newport gestured that he'd go up and that Bererra and Nowak would check the lower floors. The first step was to search all the rooms. They didn't expect to find the router upstairs; it was more likely to be in the basement in an equipment closet. But before they tracked down the equipment, the agents wanted to look for people. In a situation like this one, people—not routers—were the threat they must evaluate.

The big old school had thick walls and, unless the door was open or a class happened to be making a lot of noise (imagine that), you might not realize a room was occupied until you got very close. After a few minutes, as Newport carefully peered around another doorway, he spotted his prey and grinned wickedly. He pressed his mouth to the mike on his lapel and whispered, "Get up here."

Laura's door was closed. Through its window, Newport could see the class. He observed a teacher walking around helping students. Some students worked alone; a few in groups worked together with pieces of science apparatus; one student in the back, quite isolated from the rest, intently worked on a laptop. Since the school was in an urban area, Newport imagined that some of the students, maybe even the teacher, might be packing heat. He imagined that they might also have drugs in their backpacks. In fact, he imagined, the whole class might be a front for drug peddling. He realized that the teacher, who was young and attractive, was obviously a drug pusher in disguise. Or maybe, he thought, she really was a teacher, and just used the drug money to supplement her paltry, new-teacher income. And this appeared to be a perfect setup, what with the obvious variety of cultures represented by the kids.

His wild (and inaccurate) imagination had Newport in a frenzy. He was still lightheaded from his recent unaccustomed physical exertion—rushing to keep up with the rookies had taken its toll.

"*Where are those idiots!*" he thought frantically, wondering what was taking them so long to join him. The building smelled, his feet hurt and it was hot. Newport's face was crimson, and sweat gushed from every pore. If a human could explode, he would surely do so. At last, agents Bererra and Nowak arrived.

Larabee's windows were relics of another era. They had huge old sashes that opened down at the top and up from the bottom. Today, a decent, but borderline hot breeze drifted through the room. Trees outside tossed gently, and the drone of a lawn mower could be heard in the distance over the quiet sounds of a well-run classroom. The students worked in groups on the day's assignments; Laura circulated, acting as facilitator; L sat quietly at his desk in the back of the room, doing whatever L did.

Suddenly, three men burst in through the doorway.

"FBI! DON'T MOVE!" Newport bellowed, his eyes wide and full of an alarming zeal. His right hand was tucked inside his coat, as if he were ready to draw a gun. He looked rabid as he gazed around the room. He was panting and dripping sweat.

Teacher and students alike were frozen in place, speechless, unable to think. For a moment, they remained this way, staring in alarm at the aggressive men who had just interrupted their school day. Laura felt panic. But then her mind started working again; she tried to sort out what was happening.

A bomb! she thought. *They must be here because of a bomb threat!*

Her heart pounded as adrenaline kicked in.

"What—" Laura tried to get out a question but none materialized before agent Newport interrupted her.

"WHAT ARE YOU DOING HERE?" he demanded.

She was puzzled by his question and, naturally, gave him a puzzled look. She expected a pronouncement from him, but had gotten a question instead.

Isn't it obvious? The thoughts in her mind raced, baffled by the man's hostility and question. *This is a school building...it's daytime...on a weekday...these are young people in a classroom... with adult supervision...*

She took a deep breath and tried to collect herself before answering. Still, her voice shook and she spoke haltingly.

"This... is... a... math.... science.... class," she stammered, still trying to make sense of the situation.

"WHAT KIND OF SCIENCE?" asked the agent in his harsh, angry voice.

"This is a—" she began, her voice approaching its normal tenor, "—this is a class for students who need extra help because of language issues."

Laura saw the agents look around at her students. She knew they were taking note of the various apparent nationalities in the room and wondered what possible reason they thought she could have for lying about the classroom's demographics in the first place.

"WHAT TIME IS CLASS OVER?" the agent demanded.

"We are usually finishing about now," Laura informed him.

"DO YOU HAVE NIGHT CLASSES?"

"No, this is a junior high."

Laura had let an edge creep into her voice. By now, he should have realized her students were teenagers and would not be attending school at night.

What planet is he from? she thought.

"IS THERE ANYONE ELSE IN THE BUILDING? DOES ANYONE ELSE USE THIS BUILDING?" The agent shot out the pair of questions without waiting for her reply.

Laura took another deep breath, trying now to keep her temper in check for the sake of the students. During the interrogation, Laura glanced at the youngsters to see how they were faring. They were not saying a word. They shrugged, raised their eyebrows and shook their heads, reacting quietly to the evolving situation. They looked worried, but not quite frightened—they could see that Laura had it under control. Even L, who seldom showed any emotion beyond disdain or impatience, watched the interview with a furrowed brow.

"We are the only class in this building. Since it is summer school, fewer classes are held," Laura informed the agent.

The agent, who had finally identified himself as one Dalton Newport, continued interrogating Laura. Each of his questions was more stupid than the last. Through it all, he never mentioned why the FBI had paid this most unwelcome

258

visit. Laura answered the questions dutifully, even supplying her driver's license when he asked for it. Knowing her students were watching closely, she tried to show respect for the agent, but the man's bullying behavior caused a few of Laura's answers to come out with a bit of a sarcastic, impatient edge. By now Nik and Nuk were making faces, rolling their eyes and gesturing in response to questions they readily recognized as stupid and foolish. They laughed openly (as only adolescent boys can do) at the specter of Newport melting into a puddle of sweat.

Meanwhile, Agent Bererra, feeling uncomfortable with Newport's multiple breaches of protocol, moved around to gaze through the outside windows. He could see the steps they had used to enter the school and in a moment, he spotted a man coming toward the building. The man moved slowly—his extreme weight obviously made walking difficult. He was headed toward the steps. Bererra gestured to Newport to take a look. Newport spotted him just as the man entered the building and signaled for the younger agent to investigate. Bererra quickly left the room.

Laura and her students, still unsettled by the FBI presence, watched the pantomime with detached curiosity. None of them knew what the agents had seen or what the gesturing was about. They watched the younger agent exit the room and then grew alarmed as Newport shifted his attention to L.

"Any computers in use in your class, Miss Olson?" Newport's question was directed at Laura, but his eyes never wavered from L's desk.

The students and Laura remained silent. She followed the agent's gaze and noticed that L's ever-present laptop was not in front of him. L had slipped it into his backpack. Newport was staring at L as if he was trying to read his mind. L, a young master of the poker face, gave no clues.

"Do you have a computer?" Now the agent's question was directed at L.

"Yes," he nodded, his eyes expressing displeasure.

"Where is it?"

L paused as if he was thinking whether to answer or not. Then he grimaced irritably and pointed to his backpack.

"Why is it in your backpack? It was on your desk earlier." The agent's tone was like an attorney cross-examining a defendant.

"I was done," L said matter-of-factly, not at all disturbed by Newport's accusatory tone.

"Were you hoping I would not notice it?"

"I was hoping to save some time; the school day ended several minutes ago and I have a bus to catch," L replied with a measure of impatience. It was a lie; he rode his bike.

Unmoved, Newport demanded, "Get it out and power it up!"

With a look that said, "You'll be sorry you made me miss my bus," L reached for his backpack.

Laura was by now outraged by the way they were being treated; she did not liking the tone of the agent and he still had not told them why he was there.

"Wait a minute!" she commanded with all the authority she could muster. "You need a warrant!"

Newport grudgingly produced a document from his pocket and handed it to her. As she read, he verbally summarized the section that referred to finding a computer with the specific MAC address they were looking for, and explained that if he found it, he was to retain as evidence the computer and anyone associated with it.

Laura found the section and read and re-read the document, looking for a way to avoid further invasion of their right to due process. Operating on a hunch she said,

"You can't search a minor's possessions without his parents being present."

Newport did not react immediately, which gave Laura a chance to think, too. Had she been naïve about L and his laptop? She remembered Walter and others wondering how he managed to do what he did with only a laptop. She felt a wave of doubt, followed by a cold and gripping fear that the agents might actually have a reason to be here. The silence was broken by Newport.

"Look," he said. "We are not here to look at files. We only want to see the MAC address. That's like asking for a name. It's as simple as 'What is your name?' That's all. We have the right to do that. We don't need a parent to ask for a name."

After several minutes, it was evident to her that they wouldn't back down; the warrant was clear. Laura's doubts were now getting the best of her. If L really had done something wrong, there was little she could do to help him at this point. She felt shattered that all that had been accomplished to break L out of his shell might soon be for naught. Reluctantly, she nodded to L to go ahead.

56. DOWN IN THE BASEMENT

Agent Bererra, looking for the portly man who had entered the building, had taken several minutes to find him as he systematically checked each room on the lower floors. As it turned out, the man was in the basement, which was reached by the separate stairway in the rear of the cafeteria. It had been a long time since its use, but there was no mistaking the smell of institutional food as the agent passed through the dingy old cafeteria.

Bererra's thorough search had given the custodian time to reach his office and power up his computer. The office consisted of an old beat-up desk with a bare light bulb dangling overhead, power panels on the walls, a computer on the desk and an assortment of seldom-used cleaning tools. The desk was around a corner from the door, which was semi-permanently wired open.

By now it was clear to the rookie that this guy must be the custodian. Judging from what Bererra had seen as he moved about the building, the custodian did little work.

How could he with all that fat? agent Bererra wondered.

As the agent approached, he could hear sounds. Since the custodian was around the corner from the door, Bererra could not yet see him. Listening more carefully, the agent heard sounds much like Laura had heard on her first day at Larabee: "Oh baby! Yes! Yes! Yes! You know what I like!"

The rookie was getting an education, but clearly it was not the kind this school had intended.

263

Bererra rounded the corner to see the custodian seated at the desk, eyes glued to the images on the screen, pleasure sounds of his own emanating from his mouth. The agent glanced at the screen (in case he needed to testify at a trial), cleared his throat and identified himself as an FBI agent. Realizing the agent had caught him doing something that was most definitely illegal, the custodian started cursing and swearing, mostly at himself, for getting caught a second time. The agent took a long look at the screen again (just wanting to be sure that he had all the "facts") while he waited for the custodian's mutterings to subside.

Bererra was just about to arrest the custodian when he remembered the content of the warrant. The warrant stipulated that they were searching for a particular computer and people associated with it. This guy would be implicated only if his computer's MAC address matched the one specified in the warrant—not because of what he was doing with the computer. By now, the custodian was acting quite humble as he continued to mumble about how stupid he had been. Bererra decided the custodian's bulk made him a low flight risk. Besides, the big man had made no move to leave; the agent could keep an eye on his suspect and work on the computer at the same time.

Bererra took control of the keyboard. With the adult movie still streaming, he opened the "network connections" window to look at the computer's MAC address. He typed a few more keystrokes and opened a few windows, and there it was. He called Newport on his radio.

Back in the classroom, L had booted his machine and opened the network connections window. He followed the same sequence Bererra had used in the basement. Newport was squinting at the laptop's MAC address when his radio beeped with an incoming message from Jose.

He interrupted his own matching process to read the MAC address in the warrant to the rookie downstairs.

"Say it again," Bererra requested.

Slowly and deliberately, Newport read off the letters and numbers.

"I've got a match down here," an excited Bererra replied.

Realizing that L's MAC address could not match the one in the warrant if the one downstairs did, Newport immediately abandoned the classroom, closely followed by Nowak. The agents were out of the room as fast as they had arrived.

When the agents were gone, Laura and the class were abuzz with what had just transpired. She was concerned for the students and worried about any repercussions that might result from the ugly event. What would the parents think when they hear? To whom did she need to report this? She led a quick group discussion and then spoke briefly with each student. She concluded that they were okay, for now.

Nik happened to be walking near the outside windows when he saw something.

"Come see, come see quick!" he yelled and jestured.

They all rushed to the window in time to see the agents, the custodian and his computer leaving the building. One of the agents had brought the car around to the asphalt playground behind the building; they were all getting into the car. Laura recognized the custodian from the beginning of the term. It was after that incident that her room was always clean and the door unlocked. What had this guy done to get the attention of the

FBI? Had they somehow found out what he was doing with school property? Would that be a federal offense?

Emotionally, she was drained. The stress of the raid brought her up to a level she had never before experienced. She slumped into her chair, trying to regain control of her rampant thoughts. She knew that some thorough decompression was in order. Then another, more pleasant thought came to mind: It wasn't L they were after. For the moment, her concerns about his possible wrongdoing vanished.

That brought a much-needed smile and a sigh of relief. However, she still needed to vent.

57. WE'VE GOT TO TALK

When the class left, Laura called JJ at the Museum.

"Could you come over to my place after work? I need a level head," she said with an urgent tone.

She needed someone who would think clearly and not let emotions get involved. Laura was normally unflappable, but this event had been a challenge for her. Over the phone, she did not tell JJ what was bothering her, and he didn't ask. JJ knew that if she wanted him there, it was important; he didn't need an explanation.

"You bet," he replied. "I'll be there. How about five-thirty—okay?"

"Yes, that's fine. Thanks."

Knowing that JJ would be there soon to console her, she already experience some relief.

Laura hadn't asked if he had plans for the evening, so her assumption was he would only be there for about an hour. It was too early for dinner, but was just about the right time of day for cocktails. Laura was not a regular cocktail drinker, but she thought a glass of spirits would help take the edge off. JJ arrived exactly when he said he would. He was always punctual.

She called it a cocktail hour, but it was really wine they liked to drink. Laura put out one of their longtime favorite snacks: Vienna sausages cut into bite sized chunks and heated on a grilling pan for a few minutes. Along with that, they liked rye bagels. These too were heated and cut into bite sized pieces.

When JJ arrived, he pulled a small bouquet of flowers from behind his back. It brought a smile to Laura's face. When the aroma of the sausages and bagels reached his nose, his smile widened. In a few minutes, they were sipping pinot noir and munching the snacks.

JJ waited until Laura brought up what was troubling her. Laura was much calmer by now; having JJ there added to the effect. She began her recount of the day's events, speaking evenly and objectively, almost like a newscaster. But when the angry, fearful or frustrating events came up, she had trouble disguising her emotions. JJ waited to hear the whole story before offering any opinions or advice.

"How did the kids handle it?" he asked and took a sip of wine.

Laura had taken a bite of her rye bagel and tried to answer with nods and hand waving but none conveyed the proper meaning. A hard swallow followed by a sip of wine, and she was ready.

"I am amazed at those kids. Sure we all were terrorized at the beginning, but I couldn't believe how quickly they started noticing the stupidity of the lead agent, that Newport guy. They were kind of mimicking him, and I know they were saying stuff, making fun of him. When it was all over, I held a meeting to see how they were coping. They really just brushed it off—the way only teenagers can do."

She paused, remembering, before going on.

"At one point, I noticed that L had a worried look on his face. It got me to thinking he may have done something wrong. That really upset me. But to answer your question, I think they're okay. Obviously, I plan to follow up with them to be sure there were no delayed reactions."

She took a deep, steadying breath.

"I guess what really bothers me is the way they just left—they didn't even offer a simple 'sorry' as they walked out," she said. She closed her eyes, leaning her head against the back of the couch and sighing heavily.

"Now I'm worried about the Fine Society members," she continued. "How will they feel if news of this gets into the press? They shun publicity, and now here would be two of their brand new members implicated in a porn raid at a school!" She had lost control of her feelings as her voice rose. The concern over what the Fine Society members would think seemed to be the trigger. JJ felt it was time to offer whatever he could.

"Laura," JJ interrupted, with a sympathetic smile. Then he mustered his best Oprahish-voice, "Calm yourself, girl!"

"Well, obviously, we had nothing to do with it," Laura responded, not yet ready to see humor in the absurd situation. "But the press could get it wrong, or try to sensationalize the event."

JJ placed his hand on her knee; if his Oprah impression couldn't inspire a smile, he thought, they were going to need more wine.

"How is this even possible?" Laura went on, her voice rising. "I mean, that kid just made a significant change in his life and at the same exact moment, a totally unrelated event put it all in jeopardy!"

"Here is my take on the situation," JJ said gently. "First, chalk up the agent's poor conduct to shortcomings in his training or a basic personality deficiency or—I don't know, some other personal problems. These FBI guys are supposed to be a cut above, so I would guess his poor handling of the situation may be an isolated problem. Based on the way he treated you, it's pretty obvious that he's got some issues. Now, if you lodge a complaint with the FBI, you may or may not get satisfaction. If you get an apology, it most likely wouldn't even come from those agents. It would probably be someone whose job it is to smooth ruffled feathers. Would you even want that?"

Laura, her mouth again full of bagel and sausage, shook her head: she was too mad to accept a bureaucratic apology.

"Right, so there's no real benefit there. Even if the agents personally apologized, there's no doubt a superior forced it. Again, it's not much of a victory and you might risk future retribution, depending on their personalities."

At Laura's look of alarm, JJ smiled to indicate the retribution angle was very unlikely.

"I think you should direct your skills and attention to the kids" he went on. "Make sure they're okay. Make it a lesson in life. Your time is worth more than trying to reform FBI agents. You're doing a wonderful job with your class, Laura. Keep that good work going and don't let this ridiculous incident distract you."

She smiled for the first time since seeing the bouquet of flowers.

"I agree that it does seem unlikely for these events to happen at the same time; and I have no idea how to explain it, other than to say it's just an unusual pairing of unrelated events. I mean, if they hadn't arrested the custodian, I have to say I'd wonder if L had been up to something shady."

Laura, still feeling disloyal about her own briefly held suspicions, looked horrified that JJ would suspect her young student. Before she could lay into him, JJ continued.

"Come on! You have to admit the kid is a little weird! I don't think he's a criminal or anything, but he still hasn't told us how he's been getting all that computing power..." He raised his eyebrows and looked her dead in the eye.

"But they weren't there for him, JJ!" she protested. "They took the custodian!"

"Right," he answered. "They took the custodian. I'm not saying this insane FBI raid had anything to do with L—anything at all!" he trailed off for a moment, then added distractedly, "I still want to know how he solved those problems, though..."

Greeted with Laura's mutinous look, JJ wisely got the subject back on track.

"OK. I do think that Walter will get worked up—just because of his family's experiences, though. The others will probably think it's strange, too; but they won't draw negative conclusions, Laura. Your involvement with the Society is not in jeopardy. Actually, you might want to have a discussion with your class about talking to the media. I'm not suggesting they withhold information—not in any way am I suggesting that. I'm just suggesting you warn them to be careful not to provide anything but facts. No opinions, hunches or subjective stuff."

They had been talking for an hour and had made their way through most of the sausages; they'd even put a bit of a dent in the wine bottle. JJ sensed Laura was feeling better now that she had talked about the problems and planned some definite actions.

"OK," he exclaimed, rubbing his hands over his face. "The more you think about it, the harder it will be to get a good night's sleep. I know you. I'll tell you what; let's have a diversion."

Laura smiled her encouragement.

"We'll walk down to Grant Park," he proposed. "The Grant Park Orchestra is performing tonight, and I had been thinking of going by myself."

Laura looked doubtful—a concert sounded nice, but it had been a long day.

"It's an all-Mozart program," JJ offered, knowing it would be frosting on the cake.

"Wonderful idea!" Laura responded. Any trace of reluctance had vanished. Mozart was one of her favorite composers.

On the walk downtown, she expressed her agreement with JJ's assessment; she resolved anew to concentrate on her class's well-being.

"I will treat it as a challenge to a new life problem," she declared happily.

Laura liked to have closure for her problems; the session with JJ and the concert did the trick. She slept pretty well, too.

58. THE DAY AFTER THE RAID

Kids are pretty resilient, Laura concluded after the next day's class. The students had only brought up a few comments and questions about the events of the day before. No one seemed as troubled and concerned as she had been. However, Laura was always thoughtful and prepared; she considered that a bad reaction might be delayed and manifest itself at some future time. She would be watchful and ready.

As JJ had suggested, she led a brief discussion with the students about the media. She gave them suggestions about what they should do if the media came around. She found that the class was already quite savvy on the subject. They had not personally had to deal with aggressive journalists, but examples like the sensational newspapers at the grocery checkout lane had provided an educational experience for them. They already knew about how the media exaggerated details, misquoted sources and took things out of context in order to guarantee a sensation.

When Laura visited Walter after school, however, it was a different story. He was troubled about the close brush with the FBI and particularly disturbed when Laura described agent Newport's demeanor. It was too close to what his family had endured after the incident in New Mexico. Laura thought he was verging on paranoia when he suggested that the raid and subsequent taking of the custodian was merely a cover to get close to Laura and L.

"Maybe they somehow knew he made a significant scientific find and this was a way to get information without tipping us off," Walter worried. "Plus, there is no way to know their intentions; we can't just go ask them."

Laura agreed it was possible that the agents had a hidden agenda.

"We will have to be very cautious," he warned. "The Society members have developed many diversionary procedures; I'll teach the three of you about the ones we use."

Laura had already observed a few of their secretive tactics, and Walter had touched on the subject when they discussed joining the Society. At the time, she had felt the extra caution was a little over the top, but now she found herself reconsidering that assessment.

59. OUT IN THE BURBS

Carl Niles and his wife, Helen, were having lunch in the kitchen as they had done every day since his retirement. Carl was at the table going through the mail as Helen prepared lunch. In the background, the noon news had started on TV.

"In our lead story today: a Chicago City Schools employee was taken into custody by the FBI in connection with an alleged nationwide pornography ring. The employee, Devoid Williams, was apprehended at the Larabee School yesterday afternoon."

Carl looked up to see the picture of the man and then another shot of the school.

"Helen, look at this," Carl said. "That's the school I visited a few days ago, where Laura teaches — and there's that fat man I told you about."

The image switched to a woman standing in front of the school, holding a microphone. She related the story of Devoid's alleged involvement with porn over the school's Internet connection.

"Well, I'll be," said Carl. "I wonder if Laura knows anything about this."

Over the course of the day, the rest of the Fine Society heard the story. That prompted a flurry of phone calls among the members. Once they heard Laura's version of the story, they concluded it was just a rare and bizarre coincidence. Still quite worried, Walter reminded the members that they needed to be cautious. He also offered his conjecture that it had been a ruse to get closer to L. The rest of the society knew of Walter's troubled past and understood his level of concern, but none believed that the FBI had any interest in L. To help alleviate his stress, everyone pledged to exercise extreme caution. It helped Walter--- some.

60. THE CLUB

At the next meeting, held at the Club house, a faux name for Nick's factory, the group discussed the raid once again. All the same facts, consequences and fears were rehashed. In the end, the Society members agreed that some additional precautions should be taken. The school would be off-limits for the Fine Society with the exception of Laura and L. If an exchange of information were to take place between a member and L or Laura, it would be at another venue. Since Walter had become re-sensitized, his store was ruled out as well, at least for the short term. That left public places like restaurants (their favorite) and the Club. Restaurants would be okay for discussions, but presentations and demonstrations would need to be done at the Club.

Nick Worthington owned a small metallurgical company specializing in one-of-a-kind and commissioned projects. His facility was located on Ravenswood Avenue near Lawrence Avenue, one of several unassuming small businesses amid a cluster of similar buildings. Built in the late '60s and not since updated, they all needed some serious cosmetic attention. Like Nick, the businesses around him did not rely on walk-in customers to stay afloat, so the buildings remained unattractive but serviceable. The office was convenient for most of the Society members, so they met there on occasion. They affectionately named it the Club, as if it was a swanky retreat, although it was far from that.

The group's next meeting was to be held at the Club. L was scheduled to give the Society members a first look at what he had accomplished with the data Carl and Leroy scanned from the myriad sheets of symbols.

61. L HAS A MEETING WITH TRUTH

The night of the FBI invasion, L found himself doing a lot of deep thinking. He thought about who he was, what he wanted to be, and the new friends he had made that summer. Kids in general feel invincible, and L was no exception. But that day, he had come very close to reality—too close for comfort. He thought the FBI had him nailed; when Newport wanted to see his MAC address, L thought it was over. He was shocked, but didn't show it (because he never did), when the numbers Newport read over his radio to the rookie did not match his laptop's address. When the rookie in the basement said he had a match, L was totally confused. Then he saw the custodian being led away, and it clicked. He knew he had somehow dodged a bullet.

Later, L surmised that both he and the custodian had been downloading data at the same time. The custodian came to work in the afternoon, so a regular shift would put him in the building at night. Due to the amount of data each was dealing with, the number of frames of data would be enormous. Whoever looked at the router log had only seen a series of frames belonging to the custodian. Had that person continued to look, L's MAC address would have shown up as well. If that was the case, he may not be completely off the hook yet.

What if someone saved the router's log? I could still get caught, he thought.

The time had come for L to evaluate what he wanted to do with his life. Being in juvenile detention or worse, jail, scared him. Part of what drove him into his shell was bullying. There would be bullies in a detention home. Years earlier in L's young life, it became obvious to a couple of kids in his old neighborhood that

279

L was smart—very smart. Those kids verbally and physically bullied L so badly that he resorted to sealing himself off from the outside world. Even when his family relocated to Chicago some years ago, the shell remained. He now realized how much Laura's attempts to bring him out of his shell had enriched his isolated life. Before, he was just doing geeky stuff like playing games and learning how to hack into computers. That was worthless mischief, and it was to the detriment of his parents, teachers, what few friends he had, and anyone else with whom he had contact. Now he was experiencing Laura's kind and purposeful support and direction, which his parents had never supplied. He liked meeting the Society members and interacting with them.

Give that up? he thought. *Not worth it.*

L vowed that he would change.

62. JJ, REALLY BIG DAY

It was Saturday morning. In JJ's apartment, the smell of fresh coffee and toast mingled in the air with the smooth voice of Johnny Hartman. Hartman was one of JJ's favorite vocalists since his mom knew Johnny from her days as a jazz singer on Chicago's south side. As a teenager, she had idolized his voice and singing style. When Hartman died at much too early an age, JJ's mother had been crushed. When she married Jack Hartman, a career pilot in the Navy but no relation to the singer, they decided if they had a son, he would be named Johnny in his honor.

Today, Johnny Hartman's namesake, JJ, would experience the Fine Society at work. At the demonstration at Walter's shop a few weeks ago, the members had limited themselves to hands-off observation. Today, the group had a more active agenda planned: they would dig deeply into L's findings, and who knew what they would find? Today might be a banner day for the Fine Society. JJ knew the members were experts in the field, and the way they talked about L's equations, animations and the unique interpretation of the symbols had him wondering just how important their discoveries might be.

JJ set off to accompany Laura and L to the Club.

63. NEW MEMBERS' FIRST MEETING

Laura, JJ and L got off the CTA bus at Lawrence and Ravenswood and walked a few blocks to Nick's factory, the Club. Since this was their first visit, the Society had eased the travel protocol and allowed the three of them to travel together; they didn't want anyone to get lost.

When JJ rang the bell, Nick unlocked the door and offered the new members a warm welcome. From the small reception area, they moved through Nick's factory to an interior conference room upstairs, where the rest of the Society had already gathered. JJ, Laura and L greeted the members and then Nick introduced them to a man they hadn't seen before.

"I would like you to meet Dieter Kreiling," Nick said. "He's an old friend and member of the group. He lives way out in Ladd, IL so he can't make it to every meeting. But I told him about L's discoveries, and he couldn't stay away."

Nick smiled at Dieter and continued his introduction.

"Dieter's field is math and physics. I'd give you more details, but that would take all day."

"I'm glad to be anywhere these days," replied Dieter with a chuckle and a slight German accent.

The group chuckled fondly—Dieter was clearly a welcome presence.

After a few minutes of small talk, Nick called for their attention.

"I'd like to get started in a few more minutes," he began. "Since it's Saturday, I know many of you have other obligations. We should move right along. Go ahead and get a drink and a snack. Helen has once again provided a tray of goodies—thank her for us, Carl—and you're welcome to anything in the cupboard or refrigerator in the breakroom as well."

JJ was delighted to see that Nick maintained plenty of good food in his office, as well as a gourmet coffee machine. There was hot water for tea with an ample supply of green, Oolong, Darjeeling, Earl Grey and other assorted flavors. As he rummaged for a snack, JJ noticed there was even a reverse osmosis water purifier beneath the sink. Clearly, Nick wanted his customers, employees and friends to be comfortable. It was certainly working for JJ, balancing a plate of muffins atop his steaming coffee mug.

Leroy had been working with L at the end of the conference table, getting his laptop set up and linking it to the video projector. Seeing that that everyone was either seated or about ready to be, Leroy spoke. He began by explaining the scanning process he and Carl had followed in the museum. He described the data transfer and the memory stick in detail, so the members, who might not be familiar with the technology, could understand. JJ smiled: a few weeks ago, Leroy hadn't even known what a text message was.

"I presume that L has worked his magic on the new data," Leroy finished. "And that's what we are here to see today. Right?"

L nodded.

JJ could see that L, still just a high-school student, was feeling a little anxious about talking to this group of adults. It seemed like the Society kept bringing in bigger guns for each meeting. (It was safe to assume that Dieter was a particle- or astrophysicist).

The kid stumbled a little at first, but Laura and Leroy helped by filling in words or phrases here and there, and he was soon up and running completely on his own. Not only did L behave and sound much more normal, but he also looked more approachable. The spiked hair was gone. It was by no means a masterpiece of tonsorial work, and the orange-red color streaks were still visible, but this look was geekier and less anti-social. His clothes were different, too. His jeans were still black, but the shirt was short-sleeved, light grey with a subtle but darker abstract design.

"What a transformation," Laura whispered to JJ. He couldn't help but notice that she was radiant when she smiled.

"OK. So," L continued, gathering his thoughts, "you asked to see the application of my algorithms to the new symbol sheets, and also the animation of the results."

He turned his attention to the laptop and began typing.

"First, for comparison, here is what I showed last time, based on just a few data points."

L held up a sample sheet and explained his interpretation, politely directing the tutorial largely to Dieter. Once Dieter had expressed his understanding, L moved on.

"Next I'll show you the animation based on the same few data points."

First he showed the two-dimensional version, with the objects moving back and forth, side to side, in circles and ellipses. It was obvious that each object's motion was being influenced by the objects around it. It looked as if they were all connected by little invisible springs.

"This is like the classic multiple-pendulums demonstration," L explained. "The difference here is that now the motion is not just in a straight line. It's in a plane, as you can see. The equations I showed last time were developed from the motions I derived from the symbol sheets. The animation is a result of the equations. So what you're seeing is what I think the sheets intended to show: the position and motion of some sort of objects."

He paused to let them study the moving objects and the patterns they made before going on.

"Now let me switch to a three-dimensional view. This will let me shift our point of view."

As L typed, the animation froze. The screen went blank momentarily, and then the frozen display reappeared. This time the display had an eyeball icon in the lower left of the screen. L demonstrated as he spoke.

"This new icon, the eyeball, shows the position from which we are observing the array of objects. Notice as I move the icon with the mouse that our view of the array changes." L moved the icon to various places on the screen and the display changed as if we were walking around and looking from different positions.

"Nice," said JJ.

"What is really neat is when I start the animation again and then move around."

L restarted the animation once again. It was the same as before, but now he slowly shifted the viewpoint.

"Wow! That is really neat!" said Laura and she jumped up to point to the screen. "Look here. Notice this one doing an elliptical pattern; a moment ago we only saw it from the edge of its motion, and it looked like an object only moving back and forth in a straight line."

L took a cue from her observation and moved the icon back to its starting point. Then he slowly moved it back and forth so everyone could see what Laura had observed. The motion smoothly progressed from straight line to an ellipse. The reaction from the membership was immediate and positive.

"That's a great tool, L," said Leroy as Carl nodded vigorously beside him.

"Well then you'll like this," said L as he slowly shifted the icon. As he did, the ellipse in question clearly became a circle.

That received an "Ah ha," from Walter, as well as observations from the group that the rest of the objects' motions looked different.

"It only proves that what you think is happening depends upon your perspective," offered Dieter. "The wise person looks from many perspectives and better understands what is happening." He was the group's unofficial and self-appointed sage. Others had sage moments, too, but Dieter seemed to score more often.

"Well put Dieter," said Nick as he reached across the table to shake his hand.

Laura smiled at the group, all the while considering her student. L's delivery was remarkable. Here is a kid who a few months— no, weeks—ago, would hardly speak. Now he was addressing adults and doing very well. His presentation looked even more impressive this time, because of the large screen. She beamed with pride.

L paused to take questions, but everyone was following along. He continued.

"Next I'll repeat the same process for you. But this time I'll use lots more data points."

"How many is lots?" asked Leroy.

L thought for a moment, then answered,"Probably about five-hundred thousand, give or take a few."

"That is definitely lots," Leroy agreed, smiling.

"First, here are the equations. When I applied the algorithms, these resulted."

L showed them several pages of equations.

"I have a question," Leroy interrupted. "That looks like, maybe, three times the number of pages you had with the small sample of points. You said you used hundreds of thousands of points, but there are only a few more pages of equations for all those points. Shouldn't there be hundreds more equations, and hundreds more pages? How is that possible? Shouldn't you have reams of pages instead of just a few?"

"I thought that would happen, too," L agreed. "But, see, the purpose of my algorithms was to simplify the whole mess. It told me that even though I had many more points, the same set of motions was just being repeated over and over. Mind you, there were <u>some</u> new types of motions with the big sample, so the extra equations were needed to account for those. Let's look at the animation, and I think you'll see what I mean."

The picture on the big screen looked like the one he had shown a few minutes earlier, only now the screen was completely filled with moving dots. As before, some went left and right, others up and down, some moved in diagonal patterns or circular patterns, and all varieties of ellipses were represented. All the moving pieces were moving in different ways, yet the entire mass seemed to be always doing so in a harmonious way.

"Oh, by the way," L said, "notice the eyeball icon is gone. Because I am showing so many objects, the animation would slow way down if I had that program running. We could still shift our view if it was running, but it would take a long time. Since my new display is just lots more of what we saw before, you can imagine what it looks like from other directions."

The members gave nods of acceptance.

"However," L added, "any time we want to turn it on we can."

As JJ studied the movements, it became obvious to him that the collective movements of the dots were in harmony. No individual motion seemed to be at odds with motions adjacent to it. The motions looked like they had been carefully choreographed. He was reminded of the pendulums linked together in a line, which had similar complex but harmonic movements.

The behavior of the dots had prompted Leroy, Walter, Carl and Dieter to whisper excitedly in their corner of the room. They gazed at the screen and then huddled together, muttering in voices too low for JJ to hear. JJ could just make out a repeated word: "harmonious."

L had paused his demonstration while the physicists' conference took place, and then Dieter spoke.

"The apparently harmonious motion of the dots in your demonstration is very important in quantum physics," he said. "For that reason your work has piqued our interest. But that can wait until your presentation is over, young man. Sorry for the interruption."

His statement and apology was intended for those in the group whose scientific discipline did not include quantum mechanics. Good-naturedly, several of them looked at Megan.

She understood and smiled a *thank you*.

L resumed his demonstration.

"One thing I have not done so far is turn on trails," he said.

As he looked at the group, it was obvious to him that they didn't know what he meant by "trails."

"Let me explain. So far my demonstration has just shown little objects moving from place to place. It has been up to your eye to see the paths the objects take. If I turn on trails, you will see a faint trail for each particle. The trail will slowly fade."

He turned on the augmentation. Now the circles, ellipses and lines were visible for each of the myriad particles on the screen.

"That is quite impressive," Dieter remarked. "I can now see more clearly how the path of each is influenced by the others. The harmonious movements are even more prominent now."

"I can turn it on any time," L continued. "But for the next part of my demonstration, there will be less clutter if I turn it off."

With the trail effect deactivated, he continued.

"Now I'll change the magnification scale gradually, so that more data points can be seen at any given time. It's like zooming out with a camera. I will be doing that a lot."

The zoom was gradual. As the view changed, the movements of individual points could still be seen, but they appeared smaller and more of them were visible. The harmonic undulation of the whole mass became more noticeable as the scope of the image changed. Groups of particles seemed to be churning and swirling, moving past each other but never colliding. The Society members were mesmerized by the images on the screen. L's voice brought them back to reality.

"I cheated here."

For a moment, the group held its collective breath. Was he going to tell them this whole thing was a hoax?

"Obviously, the objects appear smaller when we zoom out. So rather than have them disappear because of the screen's resolution limits, I forced the animation program to keep the objects at a minimum size, at least until their motions are so small we can't see them move. It's like watching a freighter in

Lake Michigan that is far from shore. It's probably doing twenty knots, but from shore it hardly moves."

L's audience smiled in relief. Leroy and Dieter nodded: they understood what L was talking about.

"The other thing I need to point out is that you're watching a slow motion display of the data," L continued. "If these really were small particles, then their real motions would be entirely too fast for us to see."

This comment was greeted with nods and sounds of understanding from the group. The process of zooming out continued and, as it did, more and more data points could be seen. They were still in motion, but greatly diminished because of the scale. By now the screen looked more like a grey mass, rather than distinguishable dots.

L continued to zoom out in what seemed to be a never-ending process. The grey mass eventually shrank to almost a dot itself.

Walter asked, "Running out of data points?"

"No," L answered simply.

Then in one corner of the screen, another dot appeared. It was roughly the size of the original grey mass. The audience could see both masses moving. As the scale change continued, more dots appeared until the screen was once again filled with dots. The dots moved in patterns that were nearly identical to the patterns of the dots at the smaller scale: circles; ellipses; as well as in lines. These dots were moving in patterns that were clearly harmonic motions, like before at the smaller scale. As L continued to change the scale, the disparate particles multiplied until they once again congealed into a single grey mass. No one said a word as they watched the dots. Each Society member's eyes were transfixed by the images on the screen; their brains were fully engrossed.

Then the display on the screen froze. L did not appear to be alarmed.

"Is your computer locked up?" JJ asked in mild alarm.

"No," responded L. "Now I'm out of data."

With this pause in the action, the group talked among themselves. Those members with backgrounds in quantum- and subatomic particle physics had some ideas about what to make of L's findings, but they were not yet ready to draw any conclusions.

"L, have you run this before?" asked Carl. "And is this what you've seen on previous runs?"

"Just to check," L answered, "I ran about one hundred thousand data points, but I didn't get this far. I can load more data to see where that goes."

The group eagerly agreed that this was the next best step. When L said it would take about twenty minutes to load the data, Leroy called for an intermission, and the members began to cluster into groups.

Leroy, Dieter and Carl were in a corner discussing what they had seen, and Megan Reed came over to join them.

"I know this stuff is right up your alley," she said. "What do you guys think it is?"

"It is too early to tell," Dieter replied, "but the whole of it is very, er, quantum mechanical-looking (to coin a phrase)." Charmingly, he snickered at his own joke before continuing.

"Little pieces moving in harmony with one another—that's what quantum theory is all about. Whether this boy's findings relate to real matter—"he scratched his chin as he thought. "Well, that remains to be seen, doesn't it?"

The others agreed with Dieter.

"Even if this material doesn't lead to something tangible," added Leroy, "one thing's for sure. This kid, er, young man, certainly has demonstrated some fantastic math skills. For that alone, he is an asset."

Laura and JJ had moved over to watch as L loaded and prepared for the next demonstration. The ease with which he manipulated his laptop was remarkable. Thanks to video games, this is a skill found in many of today's youth. What Laura did not know was that L got some help from his genes. His father was a nuclear physicist and mathematician.

It was time to restart the demonstration. L went through the same steps, showing the equations and starting with just a few moving objects, as he had done before. After a few minutes, when it was apparent that not much was different, he spoke.

"I can speed this up and get us to the place where we ended with the last batch of data. Later, we can come back and run slowly through this portion, if you want."

They agreed. L hit the accelerator, and within a few seconds, they were back where they had left off. This time, the screen did not freeze, but continued to display the same evolving patterns as before.

The Society members watched as objects appeared in great numbers, displaying the same types of harmonious motion that had been observed over and over again. Small objects collected to form new, bigger objects. It happened over and over, again and again. The same process continued for twenty minutes as the group members watched, captivated.

Finally, the display stopped. There was one grey circle, surrounded by lighter areas of grey, which then faded off the edges of the screen. The dark grey was a region with the highest density of dots. The lighter grey areas contained fewer dots. Even in the far corners of the screen, where it was basically "white," a few dots were visible.

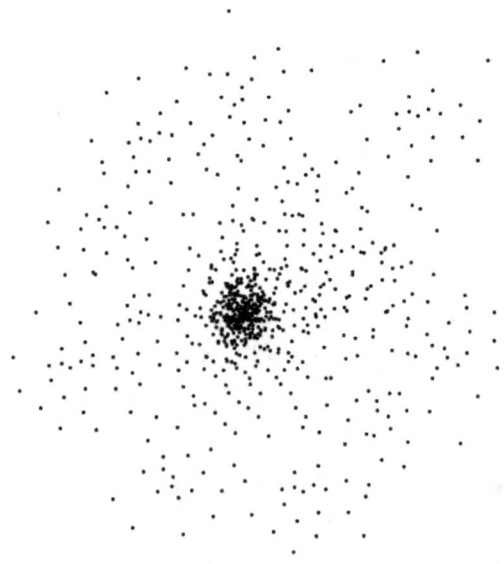

"That's it," L announced. "That is as far as this data takes us."

"WOW!" exclaimed Walter.

A din of excited chatter followed as the group speculated about what they had seen. The free-for-all discussion continued, peppered with the occasional question for L; after he responded, the members would return to their lively discussion.

"From what it looked like to me, you had many millions of data points involved with what you showed us," Dieter observed at one point. "I understand that the algorithms you constructed reduced considerably the effort necessary to deal with them. However, from what I understand of the symbol sheets, the number of points represented by the individual symbols scanned by Carl and Leroy would be far fewer than the number it took to generate the demonstration we just saw. That seems to be inconsistent."

L nodded before he answered.

"When Mr. Shire and Mr. Niles were copying the sheets, they noticed some other unique markings on the edges of each sheet. We already mentioned the bundle and page-number markings. These were, like, extra," he gestured uncomfortably, searching for the words to explain the markings; he took a deep breath and continued.

"They had a form different from rest of the symbols on the sheets. And these markings showed some variations, as well. Mr. Shire and Mr. Niles concluded that these were acting kind of as "ditto" signals, telling us how many times each sheet was supposed to be repeated, and in what direction. You might say it is a sort of shorthand to save the transcribers time—not to mention space and effort. Those folks didn't have copy machines."

The audience snickered and L smiled, gratified. A moment later, though, heads were shaking in confusion—they still didn't quite understand the ditto marks.

"Would one of you like to come up and explain?" L asked.

Leroy and Carl looked at each other.

"You do it Carl," Leroy joked. "You're better looking."

64. CARL, THE SYMBOL PLAYER

Doffing an imaginary hat, Carl conceded and headed to the whiteboard. He drew two symbols that were easily recognized as the sun and moon, with the sun several inches above the moon. Between those symbols he drew a line that resembled the capital letter T, with the T's horizontal bar just beneath the sun. To the right of the sun and moon, Carl drew a small rectangle with lines inside it. The Society members, primed as they were to make such associations, immediately recognized that it represented a page of symbols. To the right of the little page of symbols, another T extended, this one oriented horizontally with the crossbar on the right side. Sometimes the T had crossbars across its body.

"We looked at many, many sheets," Carl began. "But we only really noticed one variable. Sometimes, the T has extra crossbars. The only variable we found was the number of those crossbars. This only occurs in the T that extends from the little symbol-page icon."

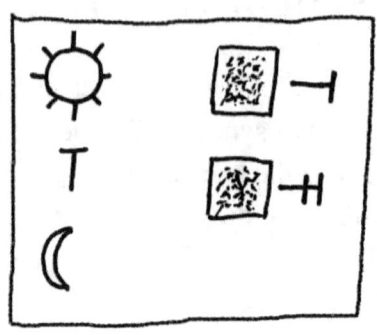

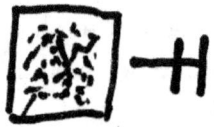

As he spoke, he was drawing a second symbol page icon beneath the first one. When he drew the horizontal T extending from the icon, he added the second crossbar beneath the top crossbar:

"It took us a while, but I think we came up with a good explanation. After seeing L's presentation today, I think Leroy and I got it right."

Carl turned to the whiteboard and gestured toward the various symbols as he talked.

"We think the T that points from the moon symbol to the sun symbol is a kind of instruction," he began. "We think it means to <u>compare</u> the two symbols. After a few false starts using other variables for comparison (like color and the amount of time they appear), we hit on one that seems to work. We think we're supposed to compare the <u>size</u> of the sun to the <u>size</u> of the moon.

298

An obvious choice would be to compare the diameters of these two bodies. We started by making the comparison in a ratio of their diameters."

On the whiteboard, Carl wrote:

$$d_{sun} / d_{moon}$$

"Next we had two choices: the actual sun and moon diameters or their apparent diameters. We know now that the sun is many times larger than the moon, but if these sheets had their origins eons ago, we thought they could only refer to the apparent sizes of the bodies. That would make the moon larger than the sun to an earthbound observer. We cut out various disks from cardboard and held them at arm's length at night looking at a full moon. We did the same for the sun. When we had our disks to a size that just covered them, we used those disks to come up with a ratio. I sure hope the neighbors weren't home when we did this."

The members laughed, picturing two old men squinting at cardboard in the sunlight.

"And don't try this at home," Carl admonished, "especially the sun. We are trained professionals."

His audience kindly rewarded him with more chuckles, but he could sense they might be impatient to hear his findings, so he went on in a more businesslike manner.

"We measured the diameters from the cutouts and compared them," he said. "You and I know the sun is larger than the moon, but to the uneducated observer, the moon looks bigger because it's closer to Earth. The sun to moon ratio was about one to two. But that number didn't set well with us. A multiplier should be an integer, not a fraction."

The group members, mathematicians all, nodded.

"So," Carl concluded, not without drama, "we decided to use the actual measurements."

Scientifically speaking, it was the most obvious step to take, but the less adventurous members of the group shook their heads: the actual measurements of the sun and moon had not been discovered until perhaps centuries after these symbol sheets were created. Laura and JJ glanced at each other: this was more like an episode of "X Files" than it was like any science they had ever learned. JJ was smiling at this fact, while Laura frowned her skeptical-most-skeptical frown.

(Carl saw Laura's frown and smiled rather mysteriously before continuing.)

"Let's think about that choice for a minute," Carl said. "If the rumors are true that these pages hold some fantastic secret, would those who provided them want to have unenlightened people unlocking that secret? Maybe they wanted to be sure we had access to certain information first, information that would prove us worthy to know the secrets of these symbols.

He paused, realizing he might be getting a bit extravagant, and then backtracked slightly.

"I'm not saying this is true, mind you; it's just supposition on my part."

The other members nodded; it was certainly plausible, even if things were getting a bit otherworldly all of a sudden. With the air of a man who's gone too far to turn back (and who knows just a bit more than his skeptical audience does), Carl wrote the commonly accepted diameters on the whiteboard.

SUN: 865,000 mi

MOON: 2,160 mi

SUN/MOON =400.5

"We rounded the ratio to four-hundred," he announced. "(We like nice round numbers like that.) So—we go back to our symbol sheet. The T sign asks us to compare the two things it's connecting. We just needed to know *how* to compare the two things. And what is a ratio but a way to compare two things?"

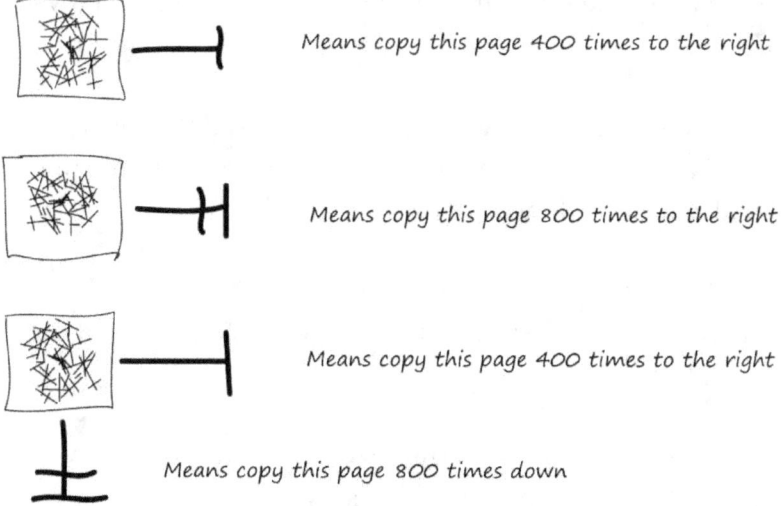

Means copy this page 400 times to the right

Means copy this page 800 times to the right

Means copy this page 400 times to the right

Means copy this page 800 times down

"So we contend that the T meant four hundred," Carl said. "Now look at the icon of the small page of symbols. Sometimes you just see a T next to it. Other times there is a T with one crossbar, and sometimes there are two, three, four, or even more extra crossbars. Again we performed a little trial and error; but pretty quickly, we concluded the T is instructing us to repeat the pattern on this sheet four hundred times in this direction."

Carl drew more T's, some pointed to the right, some to the left, and some were upside-down T's.

"The direction in which the T points," Carl explained, "is the direction in which we're supposed to repeat the pattern. Is this clear?"

The audience nodded, intent on his explanation.

"Next we tackled the crossbar," he continued. "The best explanation we could come up with for the crossbar was that it's another multiplier. A regular T is four hundred; a T with one extra crossbar—that's *two* total crossbars—would be four hundred times the total number of crossbars. So that's how many?"

"Oh!" cried Megan. "That's eight-hundred, right? The number of crossbars tells you the number by which you multiply the original ratio, which was four hundred. Right?"

"Yep," Carl said. "We gave these added instructions to L so he could algorithmize them and use them with his data. And the rest, you know."

Carl's use of the word "algorithmize" drew chuckles; he was famous in the group for his neologisms.

302

"OK," Carl concluded. "So that's how L knew how many times to use each sheet. That's why there seem to be so many more points than there are symbol sheets. Dieter, since you asked originally, I'll answer you: I would say the potential is for billions of points, maybe more. So, what L did was use these multipliers when they appeared on a particular sheet of symbols, to determine how many times to reuse that sheet."

Head shaking and expressions of amazement followed this very plausible explanation.

65. OMG

Dieter Kreiling was not a person to ask silly questions.

"L," he began, "Can you tell us the scale at this time on the screen? How big is the dark grey area?"

The dark grey sphere occupied about one quarter of the screen. Dieter, like the others, had seen a progression of images representing extremely small moving objects building to progressively larger and larger ones. The current image was big on the screen, but in reality, what was its true size? That's what Dieter wanted to know.

"Give me a moment" L said as he looked at various windows on his laptop.

A short time later, L replied, "I would say that its diameter is around two times ten to the power of negative twenty-two meters. Its radius, therefore, is around one times ten to the negative twenty-two meters."

Carl stood and wrote the figure on the whiteboard:

$$1 \times 10^{-22} \ m$$

Megan asked what that meant.

"The center part is quite small, ten to the minus twenty two meters." Carl answered. Seeing that this was too vague for Megan, he elaborated, drawing the numbers on the whiteboard as he went.

"If you have an object one millimeter wide, let's say a pencil lead—"

$$1 \text{ mm}$$

"—that is one-one-thousandth of a meter and is written as—"

$$1/1,000$$

"—The 1,000 in the denominator can be written as 10^3, So now we can write

$$1/10^3$$

or write it with a negative exponent like this. It's the same

$$1 \times 10^{-3}$$

"The 'negative three' is the exponent. Remember exponents? Here, the exponent tells us how many zeros are in the denominator. So you see, ten to the power of negative twenty-two —"

$$1 \times 10^{-22} \text{ m}$$

"—means that there are a *lot* of zeros in the denominator. This is something very small indeed."

Megan's eyes widened. No one spoke, as they anticipated Dieter would have more questions. In a moment, he did.

"Nick, do you have a chemistry and physics handbook about?" asked Dieter.

"Wouldn't be without it," responded Nick.

They were referring to an old reference book that most engineers, mathematicians and scientists bought for college forty and fifty years ago. Some even got the book when they were still in high school. If you purchased one then, you're likely to be still using it today. Most of the data and the math references haven't changed very much. Laura owned one.

It was a fat book with thin pages and very tiny print. Dieter thumbed through the index and found the heading he wanted. But he was having trouble seeing the small print. He turned to Laura and pointed to a place in the text.

"Laura, would you read this section for me?" he asked. "I forgot my reading glasses and can't quite make out the little print."

Laura obliged.

"The classical radius of the electron is two-point-eight times ten to the negative fifteenth power…meters," she recited.

Still at the whiteboard, Carl wrote as Laura read:

$$2.8 \times 10^{-15}$$

"Ten to the negative fifteen?" Dieter repeated, as if to be sure he had heard it correctly.

"Yes," responded Laura, squinting at the book.

Dieter first looked puzzled, and then dejected. He was acting on a hunch that the size of L's particles would turn out to be the same as that of an atomic or subatomic particle, like an electron. Leroy, Carl, and Nick had known where his question was headed; they, too, were disappointed when they heard the answer.

Of course, they had only looked up the data for an electron. There were other possible particles that they could check as well.

Without knowing quite what it was about, Laura sensed the disappointment. The demonstration had raised her expectations that this would lead to a fantastic discovery, and the excitement in Dieter's voice had made her think they were mere moments from an earth-shattering discovery. She shook her head, marveling at how quickly she'd gone from profoundly skeptical to wildly optimistic that everything would reveal itself at once. She looked down at the handbook sheepishly, hoping to hide her disappointment from the group.

Something on the page caught her attention. A few lines farther down the page, she glimpsed a familiar number.

$$\text{``}1 \times 10^{-22} \text{ m''}$$

That was the value L had given for the dimension of the dark mass of particles in the center of his last display. It was still on the screen.

She focused her attention on the surrounding text and read silently.

> *"The classical radius is based upon*
> *an orbital model and in light of*
> *quantum consideration, that radius*
> *would be too big. More current*

*thinking places an upper limit for the
electron radius at 1×10^{-22} meters."*

Then she read it again to see if she had understood the entry. Her eyes had not deceived her. Without fanfare, she began reading aloud to the group with her voice increasing in intensity as she went on. One by one, they asked her to read it again. Each time a few more facial expressions changed from glum to awe as they realized that L's work might actually have revealed the structure of an <u>electron</u>.

"Read that again and again," Nick called gleefully. "I want to be sure I really heard correctly."

Laura complied. But Dieter interrupted, barely able to contain himself

"Does <u>anyone</u> have any reading glasses I can borrow?" he called out, in something of a panic.

Leroy held his glasses out to Dieter, then snatched them back so he, too, could read the entry for himself. One by one the giddy members took turns looking at the text to verify what Laura had read.

After about twenty minutes of jubilation and merriment, the participants calmed down and Dieter rose to speak to the group.

"I know that this looks very promising, and I don't want to be a wet blanket," he began. "But we still need more evidence that this indeed could be the underlying structure of an electron. I know of another quick check we had better do before we get too carried away."

The group dutifully agreed with Dieter, but they did so reluctantly. They knew that good science dictated the double-check, triple-check and more, but the thought that their glorious model might be false was hard to accept.

"From the quantum view," Dieter continued, "everything has a lifetime. For those of you not as familiar with physics, we call it a half-life. It expresses the period of time for half of a sample of material to disappear or change to something else. In general, it is a function of the number of smaller pieces that make up the larger object. We have seen here today a magnificent demonstration of the basis of quantum physics. Basically, all those little wiggling particles that built bigger wiggling particles (that built bigger wiggling particles, and so on)... They all contribute to that lifetime figure. In general, the more stable the behavior of your small pieces, the longer the life of the aggregate object. Other factors play a role as well. But for a good approximation, we can get a reasonable answer just by looking at the number of pieces."

Laura had a good feeling. She knew what he was talking about. It was one of the last subjects in Leffler's class: the demonstration and analysis by Leffler and his graduate assistant, Herb. The analysis showed that as you couple more and more pendulums, not only do you get more stable harmonious modes but the time it takes them to die down increases. Their group motion lasts longer.

"David Maxwell and Eugene Smart came up with a mathematical series that does a good job of approximating the lifetimes of particle systems," Dieter explained. "We can give it a try to see if we're even in the right ballpark. Their work was done many years ago, so it should be in the handbook. Laura, you seem to have the sharpest eyes. Take a look in the index for the math section and see if the 'Maxwell-Smart series' is listed."

Laughter broke out.

"I know, I know, it's hard to take a name like Maxwell-Smart seriously, but it has been proven quite reliable," added Dieter.

"Found it" said Laura.

She handed it to Leroy, who was nearby and still wore his reading glasses. After he spent a few minutes studying the Maxwell-Smart series, Leroy looked up and addressed the eager group.

"This will take a while to evaluate," he said. "Does anyone have a scientific calculator handy? It will take a while to type the equations of the series into the calculator, but once that's done, it won't take long."

Up to this point L had been silent except for his presentation. He had to listen to learn because so far in his education he had missed a lot of science, due to his attitude. Now he was more like a sponge.

"Why not find it online?" L suggested. "I'll bet there's a trusted website that has it available for free. All we would need to do is input the data. I already have the data on my laptop, so dumping into the series would be quick once we find a good site for it."

"Absolutely right," said Leroy.

He turned to Carl, who was close by.

"You know," Leroy whispered, "we need to keep fresh young minds around here to teach us old dogs the new tricks."

The group watched on the big screen as L brought up the web on his laptop. After a few minutes of surfing, he found that the Maxwell-Smart series was available online from the math department at the University of Illinois. That was most certainly a trusted site.

It took longer to set up and dump the data than it did to evaluate the series—a fact that was not lost on the old dogs, who had been educated in pre-computer days (that is, with slide rules). Within moments of finishing the data dump, L received the results and read them aloud:

"Mean lifetime: 4.2 x 10^{+26} years"

Dieter had borrowed Leroy's glasses again. He had the reference book open, his finger on the mean lifetime of an electron. He had been careful not to reveal the value to anyone before getting the response from the U of I server. (The results needed to be verified by independent means. Good science always wants to avoid questionable circumstances.)

He looked back at the reference book and read:

"Mean lifetime of an electron 4.8 x10^{+26} years"

The difference was well within experimental error. The second parameter, mean lifetime, had checked out.

It looks, he thought in awe, *like the Fine Society has stumbled onto something real, something really big and really scary at the same time.*

It was time to share the handbook's answer with the members. Dieter read the line out loud. When he finished, there was a hushed pause; the members mentally compared the two answers.

It did not take long for the bells to ring, the confetti to fly, the champagne corks to pop, the horns to blow, and the people to whoop and dance around. Well, maybe it was not exactly like that, but the Fine Society's exuberance was just as intense as if those things had really happened. They knew that more verification was needed, but the evidence thus far was compelling, to say the least.

They had just seen evidence that their fine-structure model might be the map of an electron. And the Fine Society believed that all matter was based on the same fine structure, so they may have discovered an inroad to investigating other particles. The structures of protons and neutrons were just as much of a mystery, and solving that mystery would be a historic scientific breakthrough. Now that their fine-structure theory had gained strength, maybe they had a chance of figuring out the actual structure of other subatomic particles. It was a mind blowing thought.

By now it was late in the afternoon. No one had anticipated being in the meeting for so long. But no one would have traded that day for anything. As the group wrapped up its momentous session, Leroy took the floor.

"I have no idea where this could lead," he began. "But it could be momentous. If so, we must be extra careful now, to protect this information. It could be devastating to the world in the wrong hands. We must be diligent and use the precautions we have practiced in the past, but with renewed emphasis."

The group wholeheartedly agreed. A glance at Walter's face revealed a very troubled man. He knew all too well what the malcontents of the world could do with knowledge of this sort. The knowledge itself was not the problem. The problem was what it could open the door to.

"I hope we will still have our fun with science," Carl said. "But I must say: we may now be headed in a very challenging direction."

His comment expressed a certain loss of innocence, as well as a hope that they would be able to cope with what might lie ahead.

Finally, the group said its good-byes and began to leave, one at a time. Nick, JJ, Laura and Leroy were the only ones left; they stood together while L packed up his laptop.

"How much of this—the data, equations, algorithms and everything—is backed up somewhere?" asked Nick. Leroy replied, "The raw data is on Nick's PC and an extra memory stick. The analysis, equations and animations are all on L's laptop."

Thinking a moment, Leroy responded, "I see what you're saying. We have only the raw data backed up. We need to safeguard the whole thing."

"I agree," L said. "When I saw a few minutes ago how the half-life and diameter numbers matched up with other independent scientific findings, I realized this is not just some math or animation exercise. This is hot stuff. How and when do we back it up?"

66. A PAUSE FOR PERSPECTIVE

Before we return to our story, let's take stock of what has happened. Over the centuries, scientists were laughed at (or much worse) for suggesting that outer space was anything but a void. Besides the big pieces—galaxies, suns, moons, and asteroids—we know now that there are gasses and dust scattered about the cosmos. By examining the light from distant stars that happens to pass though gas and dust, scientists gathered indirect evidence of the material that makes up outer space. The Fine Society completely embraces these findings. But the Fine Society's beliefs go much further.

The Society believes that everything is made up of very small, very basic, very uniform particles—particles much smaller than even the smallest particles being investigated using giant particle accelerators, of which the new Supercollider particle accelerator is an example. The Fine Society's theoretical particles are smaller than what the String Theory folks theorize, if you have heard of their work. To somewhat oversimplify, the string folks theorize that the basic building blocks of all matter are like teeny tiny little vibrating strings. As in the Fine Society's model, these strings are so extremely small that we are not likely to directly observe them. In fact, the Fine Society members don't expect to ever directly detect these particles' existence.

But that doesn't keep them from thinking about their existence—indeed, nothing could keep the Fine Society from thinking. Stephen Hawking and others think about stuff you cannot see, so why not our group?

And neither did it keep its followers from establishing a name for their theory. They call it the Fine Structure Model or sometimes to be brief, the fine structure.

In turn they use it to explain the behavior of matter. To them, many aspects of science make more sense when viewed through the lens of their model. And in case you wondered, such a theory does not, in fact, put the Fine Society at odds with Newtonian or Quantum Physics. In fact, the Fine Structure Model makes a case for both. The Society contends that its Model helps reconcile Quantum and Newtonian Physics. The presence of fine particles also helps explain the missing or Dark Matter (astrophysicists figure better than 90% of the matter and energy in the universe is unaccounted for).

In the Model, fine particles are uniform and simply attract each other. Their mutual attraction serves as the linkage between them; much like the springs provide that are used to connect pendulums in the demonstrations. Like other scientists the Fine Society members, agree the universe would be filled with all the stuff you and I see. They believe that all the big pieces are made of smaller pieces, and the smaller pieces are made of smaller…you get the idea. Again this is not contrary to what science accepts as truth. The Fine Society members believe that the subatomic particles are made of smaller pieces. That too is not contrary to accepted beliefs. Society members simply differ in their willingness to suggest a base model, The Fine Structure, as a place to begin. In fact, FS members would see what we call the vacuum of outer space, filled with the little stuff. In the "vacuum" part, the little stuff would be like an ocean. The little particles are there, attracting each other but not going anywhere. Incidentally, Fine Society members don't have a clue what the little particles are made of, where they came from and why they attract each other.

Another belief that the Fine Society and other scientists hold is that the behavior of matter that we can observe, like coupled pendulums, are matched, reflected or similar to behaviors of matter we cannot directly observe. For example, in quantum physics the states or modes or motions of the electrons associated with the nucleus of an atom are described as permissible. If you substitute "stable and harmonic" for the word "permissible" you see the agreement immediately.

Now consider an ocean of uniformly distributed little particles. We won't say how, but picture a situation where a small group of particles are pushed from one side so that the particles within the group move closer to their neighbors. Our experience in our world, like working with a couple of magnets, would suggest that now that the particles are closer, the attractive forces between them would cause them to "cluster" together, but not stick together. After all, they are still being tugged on by their other neighbors. Since each particle in the original group was moving, those around it would be moved by the push as well. If the resulting motions were "just right," the particles in the little group could keep on dancing with each other. If by chance the motions were not just right—well, then the dance would be over. We have observed in our world that unless the motions are harmonious, or just right, then the motions will not be sustained. Remember the coupled pendulums?

Now, what would set these particles into motion? How about a Big Bang? That would surely result in gargantuan motions. Then, as the sea of little particles seethe with frantic motions, in time according to our observations, only the just-right motions would remain. And the theory suggests that out of the vast number of particles, stable groups would result—maybe subatomic particles, electrons, protons, neutrons, atoms, molecules and on and on.

Oh, as a reminder: that is essentially Quantum Physics.

And with the results of L's insights regarding the symbol sheets, the Fine Society may actually have some hard evidence to support its theory.

So what could the Fine Society do with this new knowledge regarding the structure of matter? Consider this analogy: Genes play a tremendous role in who and what we are. In recent years, the human genome has been defined in some detail. Now that scientists have this detailed human gene information, they are better able to understand diseases and find new and more focused cures.

The Fine Society might very well be on the verge of understanding the basic construction and behavior of the material that makes up the universe: namely, matter. Armed with that knowledge, the Society could change our world in ways of which we have only dreamed.

We don't know what, if anything, the group will accomplish with this new knowledge. L's interpretation and analysis of the data and his subsequent animation have produced a tantalizing model. With that model, the members of the Fine Society can let their imaginations run wild; they can study the way this information relates to other known scientific principles; they can develop more theories; they can look at the old in a new light.

Or they can do nothing. They could decide to set this knowledge aside to be investigated at another time. They could tuck it away safely hoping for a more sensible world to evolve when the knowledge would most certainly be used for the good of mankind. We can only watch and wait to see what they will do.

And finally, why <u>this</u> group? Why wouldn't a bunch of PhDs have accomplished this already, rather than a loose conglomeration of science-loving people who gather in restaurants to discuss pet theories? They're hobbyists—so why <u>them</u>?

Well, here are some things we know about these "hobbyists" of ours: they seek to protect and promote good science; all are bright and well educated, even if they're not necessarily in the upper echelons of their fields; in many ways they are just ordinary people. Granted, L might be a math savant, but now he seems to have a more normal side as well. Indeed, the Society is stocked with people unlikely to change the course of human history.

Did they start out expecting to find themselves on the brink of what might be one of the greatest scientific breakthroughs ever? No. They were just in the right place at the right time, with the desire to promote good science—nothing more.

Scientific discovery can be funny that way.

67. WHO IS L?

Now where were we? Oh, yes. L asked Nick how they could back up his files......

"The computer that Leroy and Carl used for the scans is over in my office," Nick answered. "It's a spare, and I can keep an eye on it. No one else has access to it, so that should be relatively safe. Plus, a backup copy of the data from the sheets is already in there. It will all be in one convenient place."

Laura and L followed Nick next door to his office. As they entered the office, Laura saw a model airplane on the shelf. The details were exquisite. It looked realistic enough to fly. As she continued her examination of it, she remembered seeing one very similar at Walter's store.

"That is a good looking model plane," she said to Nick.

"Isn't it?" he answered. "Carl makes models that are just phenomenal. They all look like the real thing, except shrunken. He loves to make them, and then he gives them away. Several FS members have them," he finished, raising his eyebrows meaningfully. "Maybe he'll give you one sometime."

She smiled hopefully and continued to examine the flawless model with fascination. Nick and L hovered over the computers, focused on saving the priceless data, but Laura's reaction to the airplane had not gone unnoticed.

While waiting for the data to transfer, Nick peered curiously at the young man.

"L," he began, "what does the 'L' stand for?"

319

L gave one of those disparaging looks one only sees in a teenager who is about to reveal something unpleasant.

"Lawrence" he answered, grimacing and then allowing a small smile.

"Not to your liking?" asked Nick dryly.

"Nope," replied L.

"Why not use 'Larry?'" asked Nick.

"Nope, I don't care for that one either."

Then Nick appeared to have an idea.

"Could you use your middle name?" he asked brightly.

"Livermore?" L asked incredulously.

"Whoa," Laura interrupted, L's revelation, having broken her model-airplane reverie. "Hold on. Your name is Lawrence Livermore Watkins?"

"Yep," was L's only reply.

 "Lawrence Livermore," Nick began. "That's the …"

"Lawrence Livermore Labs, near San Francisco," L finished Nick's sentence and then went on to reveal the rest of the story.

"My Dad worked there when he met my Mom. She was a…like, a flower child from the Bay area. I mean, I'm sure you know they used a lot of weird names back then. I was born here in

Chicago many years later, so I guess maybe they were trying to keep an old memory alive with my name."

Both Nick and Laura had listened intently, especially Laura. For all of her asking, she had gleaned little information from L about his background. Now he was spilling personal information like a bucket with a broken handle and sounding a little sentimental.

"Something has changed!" she thought happily.

L's flood of information stopped when a window popped up on the PC, indicating that the copying was complete. That little icon served as the punctuation to end not only a line of questioning, but a long and very fruitful day.

68. L's FUTURE, LAURA'S NEXT JOB?

The summer term would soon be over. Now that L had begun to blossom, Laura wanted to keep him from being thrust back into a repressive school setting. She knew that would put him at risk of being pushed back into isolation. With that on her mind, she had brainstormed various scenarios, but so far none was particularly realistic or promising. She had also been working on her own plans for the fall. So far, she had not received any responses from her multiple emails to the teacher placement office. Unless she could find a job in the next three weeks, Laura would be forced to work as a substitute teacher in the district. She did not relish that possibility. Since Walter had been around the educational community for a long time, she decided to seek his help.

Laura paid Walter a visit the next Monday on her way home from school. When she arrived, he was in the far reaches at the back of the store, surrounded by old boxes. The disarray added another dose of old-box smell to the place—not that this was a bad thing. On the contrary, it was the kind found in old attics redolent of forgotten treasures. Obviously, Walter was looking for something.

"Walter," Laura said quietly, so as not to startle him (it was clear that he hadn't heard her enter).

"Well, hello, Laura. I've just been going through some old stuff here," he smiled sheepishly, indicating the mess he'd made. "After finding that symbol sheet, I wondered what other forgotten treasures might be in here. What brings you in today? Need a demonstration for your class?"

"No," she replied. Happily, she noticed that he was calm and relaxed today, more like the Walter she first knew. "I have a question," she began, adding reluctantly, "well, I actually have, well…I have two questions, actually."

She knew she was stammering, but she hesitated because the second question was about her job search. Walter smiled kindly and she felt encouraged to go on.

"I'm concerned about L and where he will end up going to school in the fall," she began, this time with a bit more confidence. "I want to do what I can to ensure that he doesn't get into a situation that pushes him back into seclusion. After all, the district thinks he is mentally challenged."

"OK," said Walter. "And what is the other question?"

Laura described her frustration with the teacher placement office. It felt good to talk about her anxiety, and she was grateful that Walter had pressed her on that second question.

After a short pause, Walter answered, "I have your answers, and they are probably the same," he answered, somewhat cryptically.

She gave him her best "are-you-being-serious?" look, but before she could make the obvious reference to Yoda, he finished his thought in a much more concise manner.

"Washington Science and Math."

Laura felt her heart skip a beat. Washington Science and Math was a highly rated and very successful magnet school named for Harold Washington, a former mayor of Chicago.

"Both of you would be a perfect fit for the place," Walter was saying. "Have you heard of it?"

"Yes," Laura answered evenly, reluctant to get her hopes up but already picturing pristine meter sticks and virtuous custodians.

"Well," Walter said, smiling at the gleam in Laura's eye, "the principal there is an old friend of mine. You'd like her. She's a straight shooter and relates well to everyone. Her name's Ramona King," he continued, "and she is a very busy person, by her own design. It can be hard to catch her on a moment's notice, but I bet I can reach her by this time tomorrow. Can you come back then?"

"Deal! I'll drop by tomorrow after school," replied Laura.

The brief conversation had kindled hope in her worried mind. Walter's solutions would be perfect if they came to be. L would do very well in a school that could challenge him, and Laura had dreamed of teaching in a magnet school. She felt very grateful for her chance discovery of the man with the science toys.

Walter resumed his search as Laura walked away.

"Rocks?" he muttered. "Crystals? Eggs? What was that stuff I saw Grandfather showing that strange man?"

Walter was positively grumbling as Laura slowly picked her way around the piles of boxes. She smiled at his distracted monologue.

"I was so young," he was saying as she waved goodbye. "I can't remember."

69. WHAT DID SHE SAY?

The next day, Laura hurried to the shop after school. At the door, she stopped to catch her breath and compose herself, not wanting to look too eager. Also, she needed to be prepared in the event that the news was not good. Walter was in the back of the store again, but this time he heard her enter; he came to the front to greet her right away. He knew she would be anxious to hear his findings, and he was not one to string a person along when the verdict was due.

"Laura," he announced, dispensing altogether with a formal greeting, "Ramona King would like to meet with you."

Laura felt a rush of relief as Walter continued.

"No promises were made, but she seemed quite impressed when I told her how you thought outside the box to build your class out of virtually nothing. Your accomplishments with L got her attention as well," he continued. "She wants to talk to you about a particular class assignment. It's called Science Seminar. And she wants to discuss L as a potential student. Ramona is hard to track down, but if you can make it tomorrow after your class, she will see you. It shouldn't take more than a half-hour to get there by bus. She said that when you get there you might need just to camp out in her waiting room until whatever crisis is going on has been dispatched," he smiled before going on.

"Here is her private number; you will no doubt get her voice mail since she's rarely behind her desk. Just let her know if you plan to be there."

Tears had been welling up in her eyes; she realized from Walter's tone just how proud he was of her, and she realized how much that meant to her.

"Oh, thank you, Walter, I appreciate your help so much."

The understatement inherent in her words was made all the more obvious by the fact that she had thrown her arms around him with affection that was out of character for Laura. Taking a step back, she smiled sheepishly and spoke in a more even voice.

"I have always wanted an opportunity to teach in a magnet school," she said, "but figured that would only happen later in my career."

"Well, it isn't for sure yet," cautioned Walter, blushing with rather fatherly delight. "But if anyone should be teaching there, it's someone like you."

"You said Ms. King also wanted to hear more about L's accomplishments," Laura said in her usual business-like manner. "How should I handle the more sensitive parts? Like, you know, his work leading up to what may be the discovery of an electron?"

"Oh," Walter joked, "that old thing?"

She laughed, and watched as his expression turned more serious.

"Tell her that he was able to decode some symbols," he began. "Say he expressed them as equations and replicated them in stick-figure animation. Those tasks alone would win him admission. Few college students can even do that much. No one outside the Society needs to know how we interpreted the symbols and animation. Besides, we may not be right anyway."

"Do you think I should bring up the incident with the FBI?" Laura asked reluctantly. "You know, in the interest of full disclosure and all that?"

"Laura!" Walter said in a reassuring tone, realizing how worried she must be on that subject. "It is not necessary for you to bring that up. If she brings it up, fine. Because you filed a report with the summer school director, Ramona is well aware of what happened. Like everyone else in the world, she understands that you and L played no part in it."

Happy and relieved, Laura thanked Walter again. And again.

"By the way," she added, "did you ever find what you were looking for yesterday?"

"No, but I haven't given up yet."

"Good luck," she called out, closing the door and floating home.

70. MEETING RAMONA KING

Washington Science and Math Magnet High School was a rehabbed building west of the Loop and south of Madison Street, near Western Avenue. When originally built in the 1930's, the stone and marble structure was a showpiece of beautiful architecture. It fit well with the building designs found in downtown Chicago, but in the intervening years it had become shabby due to neglect and mistreatment. Now it had been outfitted with new interior facilities, so it was once again "lookin' gooood."

One of the features the building had not originally included was a security checkpoint at the entrance. Ms. King's office had alerted security that Laura would be arriving that afternoon, so there were no problems getting into the building. As she passed through the metal detector, Laura thought how sad it was that such an intrusion in this fine old place was necessary.

As anticipated, Ms. King was not in her office when Laura arrived. A student working the front desk greeted her with a smile and asked her to be seated. The smiling young man told Laura that Ms. King was expecting her and would be back soon. Forty-five minutes later, the principal arrived, but Laura was not bothered in the least by the wait.

 Ms. King was middle-aged; dressed professionally and had a kind face that smiled easily. Despite her nervous excitement about the stakes of the interview, Laura felt immediately at ease with Ramona King. She impressed her as a person who would always give you the straight answer, but with a delivery such that you would not blame her if the answer did not go your way—a handy skill to have when you work with kids.

Laura had brought her resume and a small teaching portfolio, but Ms. King never asked to see her credentials. Instead, she engaged Laura in a lively conversation that lasted the better part of an hour. Laura realized that Ms. King steered the conversation toward topics that would give her a better idea of who Laura was and what made her tick. It was probably more effective than a battery of multiple-choice questions and a resume could ever be. Even though she knew Ms. King was well inside her head, Laura did not feel uncomfortable. She felt a willingness to speak freely and openly.

Part of the exchange took place while they toured the building and Ms. King described the facilities. The last stop on the tour was the science department. To Laura's delight, the equipment was up-to-date and appeared functional.

What a contrast to Larabee, Laura thought, unable to keep from grinning.

When she finished describing the science department, Ms. King turned to Laura.

"Would you be interested in teaching a special science class called Science Seminar?" she asked. "We have some students like L, who have capabilities that exceed even our more challenging classroom activities. Students in Science Seminar map out a topic or program of study to pursue independently. The class has a facilitator, and each student also has an advisor from the science department. You would be taking over as the facilitator for Science Seminar. Sound interesting?"

Laura wanted leap and yell "YES! YES! YES!" but she somehow managed to keep her composure.

"Oh, I would love to. That would be wonderful."

Laura wanted to wallow in the pleasure of the moment, but Ms. King had more to say.

"I thought so," Ramona replied, smiling as though she could see Laura's internal gymnastics. She briefly explained the paperwork Laura would have to fill out, and then changed the subject to L.

"This school is here for students like him," she began. "If he is interested, I will support his application. There is a board that screens the applicants, and we also require parental approval. I know it can be a lot of paperwork and hurdles, but I have my ways. We try to remove hurdles wherever we can, and I must say we've gotten pretty good at it over the years."

Ms. King smiled at her wonder-struck new teacher and realized the young woman probably wasn't hearing much of what she said, even though she nodded politely.

"I have a contact at central administration, a very nice person, I might add, who will walk L and his parents through the steps to get an application to the admissions board. We have ways to expedite the process. I also have some unofficial influence with the admissions board, so I feel confident he will get in once he's run the gauntlet. Don't get me wrong; he is not receiving special treatment. He deserves to be here. I just want to be sure the process doesn't deter his entry. I have seen qualified people give up; it has happened in the past."

Ramona King wrapped up the meeting by assuring Laura that she would be a good addition to the school and sent her new employee on her merry way.

Laura left the building and went home, not touching the ground once.

71. SPREADING THE NEWS

Laura would explode if she didn't share the news. She called JJ. When he answered, she launched

"I got it!" she shouted, her words streaming a mile a minute. "I-got-a-job-at-Washington-it's-called-Science-Seminar-can-you-believe-it-JJ?"

He laughed happily, infected by Laura's excitement.

She went on to describe the class and how well it fit with her style of teaching. She raved about Ms. King. In ecstatic terms, Laura described the newly renovated, "fine old school building." She rejoiced at the possibility that L would soon be getting his academic career on the right track.

When Laura finally paused her tirade of joy, JJ congratulated her and suggested he take her out to celebrate.

"Great idea! I'm really in the mood to celebrate!" was her excited reply.

After the call to JJ, she dialed Walter. This time her delivery of the news was more controlled but not enough to keep Walter from sensing her excitement. He was very pleased with the news and confided that he knew all along that she would be perfect for the job.

"I expect that L will do well there now that he seems to have found himself," he said.

Laura agreed and went on to describe, in some detail, her new assignment and the school's facilities. Partway through an overjoyed description of the building, she stopped herself.

"I'll bet you're already familiar with the facilities, aren't you?"

Walter laughed.

"Yes," he said. "But you're so excited—as you should be. I didn't want to stop you."

"Well, I'll spare you for now," Laura said. "But next time I see you, I want to tell you about Ms. K—" Laura cut herself off again, realizing what she had started to say.

"But you already know her, too, don't you?"

Walter laughed again. Laura's excitement was contagious and he was glad to have had a hand in creating it. She regrouped for a moment to regain her thoughts.

"Not to change the subject, but did you ever find what you were looking for?" she asked.

"Yes, as a matter of fact I did. They were all wrapped up in a box, and the label did not match the contents, something I should have realized. I'll show them to you next time you're here."

They said their goodbyes, ending the pleasant conversation. Laura smiled for the rest of the day.

72. CELEBRATION AT NAVY PIER

It was a beautiful early August evening, perfect for a celebration. A rare cool front had come through Chicago earlier in the day, so even for August, it was quite pleasant. Laura and JJ decided to walk to Navy Pier for cocktails and dinner at Charlie's Pub, one of their old favorites. They usually sat in a corner near the windows so they could have a good view of the lake. It had the added benefit of being out of the way of the crowds that came in later in the evening. The two old friends were not in a hurry, so the plan was to sit in their corner and enjoy the sunset. They could take their time and savor all the good things happening in their lives. They had a few brews and good food as the lights on the pier winked on in lieu of the sun.

The conversation centered on Laura's new job until she realized she had been monopolizing the evening. She asked JJ what was new in his world.

"Well," he began, "I decided I'd see if I could locate more of those symbol sheets. I don't know if more even exist, but I can't imagine that my museum has the only ones."

Laura agreed that it was a plausible idea, and JJ continued.

"The tricky part in researching their possible existence is that I have to do it without putting up any flags. See, when you send out an inquiry, anyone who's holding the stuff you're looking for suddenly gets very stingy with information. That's how they drive up the price."

"So what do you do about it?" asked Laura.

"Well, you ask around for an item that's related to the one you want, then that will often get you close to what you're really looking for, and it doesn't tip off the guy who's got what you're really searching for."

"Clever," responded Laura, holding up her beer glass for a toast.

"Yeah, thanks!" JJ said, touching his glass to hers and smiling. "Except the owners know the game, too. But it still works because they don't know which related item you really want.

"Besides," he added, "there are some who play the game better than others."

"And do you play the game well?" Laura asked with a smile.

"I'm new, but you know I'm a quick learner, so time will tell."

He held her gaze for a moment, and then they both looked away. If the light had been a bit brighter, a casual observer might have detected a blush on both their faces.

"Speaking of finding things," Laura injected with a hint of excitement, "Walter said he found what he was looking for"

"What was it?" asked JJ.

"He hasn't yet said exactly, but the last two times I was in there—when he was helping me get hooked up with <u>my new job</u>—" (the happy emphasis brought that radiant smile back to her face as she spoke the words) "—he was looking in old boxes. He said it was related to the symbol sheet he had originally provided for L. The next time I came in he would show 'them' to me."

335

They both shook their heads: they were clueless about what "they" could be. It was JJ's turn to change the subject.

"Hey—remember the field trip to the Art Institute and Fractal exhibit?" he asked.

"Of course I do, JJ. It was very impressive, and very memorable," she added pointedly. "I love to think about it, actually—that it's not only art, but such a useful tool in science and even movies. Why do you ask?"

"I keep replaying those images from last Saturday's Fine Society meeting," JJ answered. "Particularly the 3D animation. As I watched the little objects, and they joined with others like them to form larger units of something, and then those units formed with other units, over and over again—do you know what I mean?"

"Yeah, JJ," responded Laura. "I know what you mean."

"Well, to me it looked like fractals," JJ announced. "The bigger groupings were made up of little groupings like themselves."

Laura paused while she thought about the demonstration.

"You're absolutely right! I hadn't made that connection before, but you're absolutely right!"

"I plan to mention it to the group at our next meeting. Some of them may have already thought of it, and that's okay. But nobody mentioned it at the last meeting."

Always amazed by JJ's perceptions, Laura said, "I think that's a great idea. There are so many sharp minds in that group—I bet somebody will know what to make of your fractals connection."

At the end of a very satisfying meal and with a few empty beer glasses on the table, they sauntered off into the glittering lights of Navy Pier, and then into the lights of Chicago.

My, but they made a nice-looking couple.

73. EGGS FOR DINNER?

Walter arranged to have a conference call with Leroy, Carl and Dieter on the following Sunday. Walter was anxious for the group to see his find.

"I have some new eggs I would like you guys to try," he told them. "How about coming over here Tuesday for dinner, say six o'clock?"

Leroy and Carl agreed to be there, but Dieter could not make the long drive.

"Save an egg or two for me," he said. "I'll try one next time I'm in town."

Everyone laughed; as infrequently as Dieter visited, an egg would not be worth eating by the time he came back to town. However, the laughter was also for the effect: it was a front. They knew Walter was using "egg" as a code word for something else. Double speak had always been their habit, just in case someone else was listening.

Next, Walter called Laura.

"Got a meeting of the Fine Society at my place on Tuesday at 6," he told her. "I have some special eggs, so it should be a rare occasion. Are you available?"

"I wouldn't miss it" she responded.

Walter asked her to pass the word onto L and JJ before they hung up.

Laura had a hunch that this was important; she knew it was unusual to schedule a meeting during the week, and so soon after the big Saturday session. The group had decided not to meet at Walter's store for a while, so whatever he had to show must be very sensitive if he didn't want to take it out of his store.

At school on Monday, Laura told L about Washington High School and the next meeting of the Society. He was excited, which was quite a change for him.

"I still have trouble dealing with the positive change in my life," he told Laura. "It's a good thing, but it's sometimes overwhelming." Laura could see that L was grateful and excited.

"Well, we've both prospered from our experiences this summer," she said. "I've been hired to teach at Washington next year."

"Cool," responded L. "Do you think I'll have you for any classes?"

"Maybe," Laura replied. She described Science Seminar; L seemed to like the idea of the class.

"I'm not sure of all the details yet," she continued, "but you'll learn more when you apply. Plus, from what Ms. King told me, you're totally the kind of student they're looking for."

"Cool," L repeated.

On his way home that afternoon, L's mind was preoccupied with all the new developments in his life. He was thinking about his new school, the next meeting of the Society and the reassuring prospect that Ms. Olson might continue to be one of his teachers, even after the summer class ended. The unfamiliar feeling—was this what people called happiness? His musing distracted him from the task at hand. Unfortunately, the task at hand was riding his bike. At an intersection he had passed through hundreds of times before, L simply didn't see that the light had turned red.

He simply didn't see the truck that was fast approaching the intersection.

And the truck driver simply didn't see the young boy with the black backpack as he darted into the intersection into his path.

L's bicycle was caught up in the undercarriage, and L was all tangled up in the bike. It looked grim. He was not moving; blood seeped from countless wounds. For a few desperate minutes, passersby and the distraught driver tried in vain to get him out from beneath the truck. Sirens approached, and the police and paramedics arrived to attend to the gravely injured boy.

When the EMS personnel finally managed to separate him from the wreckage, they began their assessment of his condition. He was still alive. Their priorities were to stop the blood loss and secure him for transport. He began to stir. Minutes later, L opened his eyes, looking dazed and confused. By the time they reached the hospital, the medical team determined that L had been knocked unconscious, but other than some deep cuts and bruises, he was actually fine. The Doctors said he would make a full recovery. Unfortunately this was not true for his bike or his backpack. The computer in the backpack was completely destroyed.

74. WALTER'S EGGS

As they always did, the members arrived at Tuesday's meeting individually. Everyone except Dieter and L was present. Neither Laura nor anyone else in the group had heard about L's accident since it hadn't made it into the local news. L had not been in school that day, so Laura didn't expect him to come to the Society meeting. Laura assumed he had come down with something simple like a summer cold, but felt uneasy all the same. He had been so excited about the meeting.

"Thanks for coming on short notice," Walter began. "As you know, a few of us had a conference call last week and decided that we should escalate our efforts for the time being. Plus, I have some objects for your discerning eyes to ponder. I don't know what they are or what their origin might be. I do know that they were in the same box as the sheet of symbols, and I have a vague memory as a child of seeing my grandfather show them to a man who was a stranger to me."

Walter opened an old box to reveal individually wrapped, egg-shaped objects. The box contained about a dozen of the objects. Walter partially unwrapped them all. There were ten. He completely unwrapped one and passed it around for the group to examine.

Laura studied the object closely when it came to her. It was the size of a chicken's egg, but unlike a chicken's egg, the rounded ends were the same. Where a chicken's egg has a pointed end and a rounded end, this object had two rounded ends, and they were symmetrical. Laura guessed that the object weighed twice as much as a comparably sized egg. It was ivory in color, and the surface was perfectly smooth, like a billiard ball. If it was old (and it must be, to have belonged to Walter's grandfather), it did not look it.

As the members examined the object, they offered their observations, which were mostly the same as Laura's had been. Then, as Carl was passing it to Leroy, the unthinkable happened.

They dropped the egg.

It sounded like a billiard ball hitting a hard floor; it was not a shattering sound, but the group members cringed and gasped. Laura was the only one seated in a position to see the egg hit the floor. As it hit the floor, she thought she saw a flash inside the object. Leroy quickly bent to retrieve it from the floor, where it wobbled in a promising, hearty-looking way. Leroy examined it closely for a moment. Forever the thespian, he paused dramatically and took a deep breath before speaking.

"Not a crack," he proclaimed. "Not a dent. Not a scratch that I can see!"

Everyone began breathing again. By now, Laura was not sure she had seen a flash. She thought it could have been a momentary reflection of light. For the moment, she decided not to mention it.

"Walter, you say this was with the symbols sheet?" asked Nick.

"Yes," Walter answered. "It may just be coincidental that they were in the same box, but at this time we need to look at everything that could possibly be related."

The group discussed a few possibilities, but nothing seemed to click. They decided to proceed, with the qualification that if anyone came up with an idea regarding the egg, the discussion would resume on the subject.

The second purpose for the meeting was to discuss what to do with L's findings. Leroy had some ideas to share.

"First," he said, "let's assume that what we saw in L's presentation—" Leroy stopped speaking when he realized that L was not there.

"Where is he?" asked Leroy.

Laura told him L had missed class that day.

"I assume he came down with a cold or something," she said. "He was excited about being here tonight. I'm sure he's fine, but I wish he could have made it."

While Laura was talking, Leroy was texting L. She realized she might have created a monster when she ushered Leroy into the world of text messages.

"Well," he said smugly, "we'll see if L's feeling well enough to pick up his phone."

L was not, in fact, feeling well enough to pick up his phone. That is to say, he wouldn't have been up to it if even if his phone had survived the crash. Leroy would wait in vain for a response from the young man. In the meantime, he had some ideas to share with the Society.

"First," Leroy began, "let's assume that what we saw in L's presentation is an example of the Fine Structure Model of matter that we believe in. At the least, I think it's safe to say L's demonstration gave us encouragement for the Fine Structure

Theory. The next question could be this: how do we interact with the Fine Structure? Just looking at the model does little. But suppose that we could devise a test based on the model. If the test predicts a certain result, then we get that result, our theoretical Model is strongly supported. I think that could be our next step."

Leroy was hoping to trigger a discussion about how exactly the Fine Society might go about devising that test.

"Any ideas?" he asked.

But they remained silent. No one had any idea of where to begin. Undaunted, Leroy continued

"Let me illustrate that last point: how can we interact with this model, with an idea," he offered. "Carl, how fast are we moving through space?"

"Well," Carl responded, "that depends upon what frame of reference you're using. If the earth's axis is your reference, then we're moving through space at roughly one thousand miles per hour. That speed is measured at the equator. If you take the sun as your reference, then our movement around the sun adds an additional component of sixty-seven thousand miles per hour. Then if you—"

Chuckling at his friend's elaborate calculations, Leroy interrupted.

"Great answer, Carl. Now, as we sit here, none of us _feels_ like we're moving, do we? Right. We all know the reason for that. If everything around us is doing the same thing that we're doing (in this case, sitting still), we don't notice anything, right? Right."

The group signified they were following him so far.

"Now," he continued, "what I'm about to propose is going to be a big stretch, but stick with me."

Scientists all, the Society members smiled encouragingly. They wouldn't dream of doing anything other than sticking with Leroy at this point.

"The Big Bang," he announced with a flourish (and apropos of nothing, as far as Laura could tell). "We could spend hours—days, maybe—discussing that one alone, but I mention it here just as a jumping-off point. Theoretically, there could still be ripples in the universe that originated in that ancient, tremendous blast. And those ripples would be moving through the Fine Matter that makes up all matter—all matter, <u>including us</u>."

He ran his hands through his hair and comically patted himself down, like he was searching for something in his pockets.

"Do you feel ripples?" he asked in mock surprise. "No? Neither do I," he whispered conspiratorially, winking at Laura.

"And why don't we feel the ripples?" Leroy continued. "It's because, as a ripple comes by, all the matter around us moves with the ripple. The ripple doesn't only move through you. It moves through your shirt and your socks and the chair you're sitting on. It moves through the person sitting next to you; it moves through the chair she's sitting on; it moves through her blue jeans; it moves through her sneakers; it moves through the

345

barrette in her hair; it even moves through the cup of coffee in her hand."

Laura laughed—Leroy had just described almost every item of clothing she wore. She sipped her coffee as he continued.

"And so," he said, "the ripple goes unnoticed. It is like our traveling through space, we are doing the same thing that everything around us is doing, so we don't notice the motion. Everyone with me so far?"

Leroy's theatrical background rendered his last question rather moot. When he was in his element—performing in any capacity—it was hard to look away.

He stepped to a nearby whiteboard and drew a series of dots and arrows. As he spoke, he explained that the dots were objects and the arrows indicated the direction objects moved when a ripple went through them.

"Look at this object," he said, pointing to a dot. "Now, here comes a ripple...and the ripple pushes the object...say...it pushes the object this way."

He drew an arrow pointing to the upper-right hand corner of the board.

"The same ripple would push all my other dots the same way, right? Right."

So far, nothing Leroy had said came as a surprise to his audience. The look that appeared on his face at this moment, however, told them that was about to change.

"Now let's do it again," he said. "But this time imagine the dot is on a miniature turntable. The ripple pushes on the dot and it moves like before. In fact the pieces of the turntable do the same. BUT, because the table is turning, the dot has that motion as well as the motion due to the ripple.

As he spoke, he drew an arrow heading to the bottom left of the board, in the opposite direction of the first arrow.

"Now look at the direction arrow," he said. "This dot is NOT moving in the same direction as the rest of the dots not on the turntable."

He looked around in silence for a moment, then erased the board dramatically and repeated the entire dot-drawing procedure.

He's telling us what he taught us, Laura thought gratefully. *Leroy should have been a teacher.*

Satisfied that everyone had followed him to this point, Leroy continued.

"Now onto the last part of the idea. Imagine an object…for example–" he looked around and saw the egg on the table, "–this egg. Let's use the mysterious egg as an example. Imagine all the little fine particles in this egg. As a ripple comes by, and we see nothing happen because———--------"

He raised his eyebrows, waiting for a response.

"Because the ripple moved everything around us, too," Laura offered.

"Yeah!" Leroy exclaimed. "Now imagine that, like we did in my drawings, we could place this egg on that turntable and strap it

347

down. Then, when the ripple passes and the table turns------------
------."

He held the egg before him on the flat palm of his hand, staring at it intensely (and, it goes without saying, dramatically).

"What would happen to the egg?" he asked.

There was silence, and then Walter answered.

"The egg would have a motion different from its surroundings," he said. "Just like the little dot on the turntable did."

Leroy nodded, and then he waited a long time to let this sink in. Nick was the one who broke the silence.

"That's a great idea," he said. "But how do you propose to make it happen?"

"Oh, my" Leroy responded with a chuckle, "I haven't the foggiest."

The members laughed as if Leroy had suckered them, and he smiled mischievously. After a moment, the laughter died down. Then Leroy's expression became serious and he spoke.

"Think about this," he said. "Without L's model, my idea would make no sense. But now that we have a reasonable model for the structure of matter, it is also reasonable to consider that putting my theory into practice is possible. We only need find the method."

The group gave nods and sounds of approval.

"As I said," Leroy reiterated, "I have no idea how to make happen what I just described. I'm only saying that if it could be done, the object we use would have a different motion than the rest of the matter around it. And if it has a different motion, we could actually watch it happen. We would see it move because it would move relative to our frame of reference. That movement would be what we needed to test the predicted outcome."

Leroy paused again to let them think about it. While the members talked among themselves, Leroy turned to Walter and asked him if he had some specific demo equipment. Walter nodded and the two of them set off to another part of the store. Shortly, they both returned carrying a bicycle wheel, some string and metal poles. Upon seeing the wheel, the members turned their attention to Leroy and Walter. All except Megan recognized the wheel as part of a classic conservation of angular momentum demonstration (you knew that). In that demo, a person is seated on a stool that can freely rotate and is handed a spinning bicycle wheel. It has handles on each side so the victim—er, participant—can easily grasp the spinning wheel.

The participant is then instructed to re-orient the spinning wheel so that the axis of spin is up and down. Depending on the amount of spin, mass of the bicycle wheel and the mass of the participant, the participant immediately begins to spin on the seat. The amount of spin he or she experiences is dependent upon the previously mentioned factors. For the unsuspecting person on the seat, the experience can be quite surprising, even scary. To the observer, it is usually quite amusing.

Neither Leroy nor Walter had produced a stool that could spin. Instead, they were rigging the metal poles on a small demonstration table near the seated membership. The wheel had metal eyelets attached to the axle where the handles would have been. Two poles were stuck into holes in the table and a third was securely clamped between them forming a stable frame. The bicycle wheel was then hung from the upper bar by two pieces of string, each piece tied to the eyelets on either side, and then to the bar above.

Leroy turned to the group, "Some of you are familiar with this setup, others not. Whatever the case I'm going to do the demo, and then I'll have more to say after."

Without delay, Leroy gave the wheel a healthy spin. It wobbled from side to side and swung back and forth like a swing for a few moments. Shortly, these motions died down, and because of the really good bearings in the axle assembly, the only significant motion was the rapidly spinning bicycle wheel. It made little sound as it whirred in place supported by the strings on each side.

In his usual dramatic style, as if he were a magician, Leroy then produced a knife and held it up so that all could clearly see it was a knife, probably a very sharp one. With a slow and deliberate motion, he brought the sharp blade up to one of the strings, stopped and turned his face to the group. He made some devilish faces and inched the blade even closer to the string. Those who were unfamiliar with this demo made gestures and motions indicating they were ready to get out of harm's way if he cut the strings. They were certain a wheel spinning that fast upon hitting the table would be propelled in their direction. Leroy milked the moment as he toyed with those closest to the desk.

Feigning that he was not going to use the knife, he quickly severed one of the strings. The quick motion surprised Megan

Reed as she made an audible gasp and drew her body away from the demo.

But to her amazement, the wheel did not fall. Of course, Leroy had only cut one string; so at least one side was supported. However, the wheel remained almost upright, as if both strings were still attached. Instead, as the wheel continued to spin, it was now also moving around in a circle. It was slowly rotating in a circle around a point where the other string was still attached. Megan was quite impressed and studied the new motion intently.

Gradually, the original spin of the wheel on its axle diminished; and as this happened the wheel tilted downward more and more, until it was just spinning slowly in a horizontal plane. Megan was clearly excited, and like an excited kid experiencing something for the first time, she exuberantly said "do it again."

Without hesitation Leroy tied up the loose side with a piece of string he had already cut and restarted the wheel. Foregoing the theatrics this time, he cut the string; and as before, the wheel appeared to defy gravity by not falling but rather beginning its rotation motion around the other remaining string.

Laura, too, was amazed at the demo and watched the excitement shown by Megan. Laura had seen the demo in Leffler's class, but the result was always mystifying. The mystery was removed once the result was explained in terms of conservation of angular momentum, but seeing it happen was still a surprise.

If you want some assistance picturing Leroy's demo go to thefinesociety.com, select VIDEOS and choose Supplemental Video Demonstrations. From that page

view the BICYCLE WHEEL demo. Like Leroy this guy is funny as well

Leroy then stepped in front of the demo as it ran down in order to secure the attention of all the members. They complied and waited for his next pronouncements.

Speaking very deliberately for emphasis, Leroy said, "Now the purpose of this simple………. I don't plan to explain this demo………… I simply want to make some observations about it…………. First, and quite obvious to all, the force of gravity is pulling down on the spinning wheel……….. But, the strings are holding it up so the wheel just spins in place………..When I cut one string, the force of gravity on that side is no longer offset by the string and the wheel starts to fall on that side as evidenced by the fact that the wheel now tips down a little on that side……….Instead of falling all the way down, however, the wheel begins to move in a circular motion, as if a force was applied to it to drive it in a circle."

Leroy studied their faces, especially Megan and the two new members, to see if any puzzled looks could be found. None found, he went on.

"So we have a force, in this case gravity, a rotating wheel, and now it moves in a new direction relative to us. Isn't that what I proposed earlier when I talked about the little particles on a tiny turntable being pushed on by a wave from the Big Bang? That there would be a resulting motion different from the particles not on the turntable?"

He really let them ponder that one for at least a whole minute. When he did resume, he addressed the three new members directly.

"Let me add something for our newest members. One of the beliefs we hold in addition to the fine structure model is that behaviors that we can directly observe in our macroscopic realm have their counterparts in the microscopic realm. It was expressed very well in the old saying, 'Clues of the unknown are known.'"

Laura looked about to see the older members nodding in agreement. When she looked at JJ. he gave her an "I guess so" look. Laura did not recall hearing the idea put as strongly before but was willing to entertain the concept. After all, they were just theorizing.

Once again, Leroy paused to let it all sink in. Then with mystery and excitement in his voice, he resumed.

"Now think about my little particles on the turntable from this point of view: their movement relative to the ones not on the turntable would be the result of their rotation and force due to the ripple passing through our space. The object's new motion would be a direct result of the ripple."

Leroy's voice rose as he repeated himself in slightly different ways.

"The energy of the ripple would result in an object moving relative to us. The object's motion would be powered by the ripple. We would be personally witnessing movement from kinetic energy left over from the Big Bang."

353

The members stirred and murmured as they realized where Leroy was leading them. Still speaking in a booming stage voice, he continued.

"If the fine particles exist throughout the universe, and the ripples exist throughout the universe, then there is <u>untapped energy available everywhere</u>."

Unable to contain his excitement, Nick jumped in.

"Leroy," he said excitedly, "what you're saying…it might mean—maybe way down the line, but sometime in the foreseeable future—we could power <u>spacecraft</u> without rockets, without the ships having to carry our own fuel."

"Exactly," responded Leroy.

"Could it be adaptable to other activities that require energy," asked Megan, "like electricity generation…heating…cooling…transportation?"

"Exactly," Leroy responded.

While Leroy's presentation had indeed been compelling, the quantum physicists were really the ones who dominated the discussion at this point. JJ, Laura and Megan sat on the sidelines wondering vaguely if they might be witnessing megalomaniacs in action. Where was the scientific basis for what these guys were talking about? It was certainly fun to think about it, but the younger members of the group were definitely lagging a bit behind at this point, and Leroy sensed it.

"Listen, you three," he said, addressing JJ, Laura and Megan. "I know it sounds like we're getting carried away, but bear with us.

When you have a new toehold in the structure of matter, it's hard not to get carried away."

"Oh, certainly," Nick broke in. "You know where we stand on the question of Good Science. This is merely a brainstorming session."

Laura and the others felt better now.

After the reality check, Carl wanted to discuss Leroy's turntable effect. Of the subgroup of physicists, he remained the most skeptical.

"It's a great idea, and the theory sounds reasonable," he said. "But, Leroy, you're talking about taking some sort of action— the 'turntable effect,' as you call it—on an unimaginably small scale."

The others nodded. They understood the task but had no clue how it could be accomplished. The bicycle wheel demo had been easy. But Leroy still sounded upbeat.

"Yes," he said. "I realize the enormity of the task, but once again, we may have a model here that is valid. All we need is a means to make it happen indirectly. What could we do to that egg or some other object up here in our large world that would cause the "turntable" effect down there at the little particle level?"

The Society members spent the better part of the next hour discussing this task, to no avail. They were getting tired, and it was time to go home.

Walter was ready to cap off the session and thank everyone for coming to see the egg when he realized that no one else had offered any ideas that night. Between the egg and Leroy's theory, the entire evening had been consumed.

"Before we wrap it up tonight," he announced, "are there any other ideas to consider?"

There was a long pause, and just as Walter began to close, JJ rather apologetically spoke up.

"Sorry," he began, "I'm new to this and my background is a little slim in these areas, but I have an off-the-wall observation. It's not a theory, just an observation."

"Oh, please go ahead," Walter encouraged. "No idea is insignificant in this group."

"Well," JJ said, with less apology in his voice this time, "in L's animation, as little objects formed bigger objects by grouping with more of the same, it looked to me like…well, like fractals."

There was a period of quiet while the group pondered the term. Sensing that only a few remembered or knew what the term meant, JJ described the exhibit at the Art Institute. Some of the members had seen it, and JJ urged the rest to go visit the exhibit.

"It does a really good job of showing all the practical uses for fractals, as well as the theory behind them," he finished.

"You're right," said Nick. "I hadn't noticed that."

Nick recalled for the group an article in one of his chemistry journals from some years ago that had struck him at the time. The article had explained the process of crystallization. Now it seemed to fit the description of fractals.

The group discussed fractals for a while. Several commented on JJ's astute observation. They agreed that it might even be significant to the matter at hand. It was clearly a point to ponder. As they discussed his contribution, Laura beamed with pride in her friend.

"Go home and think about it," Walter commanded, and he adjourned the meeting.

Walter sent an egg home with Nick.

"Use your chemical genius," he exhorted his friend. "Find out what you can about its composition and structure."

Nick agreed most enthusiastically.

As Laura and JJ prepared to leave the meeting, she said to JJ, "Abners?" JJ realized quickly what she meant and responded, "Abners."

A moment later, she left Walter's and turned north on Sedgwick St. She continued for a few blocks to W. Wisconsin St. and headed for Lincoln Ave. JJ exited south on Sedgwick to W. North Avenue, then east to Wells and then north on Lincoln. When JJ arrived at Abners on Lincoln, Laura was already seated and had two coffees in front of her. Her diversionary route was shorter than JJ's.

Abners was like most of their favorite eateries, good food and priced right. Gordon, the owner, was usually there no matter what time of day you visited. JJ and Laura often joked that he must just live upstairs. This was a place where you could get a great cup of coffee. It was always fresh. It came in an old fashioned brown ceramic cup with a comfortable handle and pleasant shape. You won't find any grande, mega-grande, super-gulp or fancy blends and brews here, just great traditional coffee. Now for pie.......... that was a different story. Although Gordon did not stock all of them at the same time, he usually had several mouthwatering freshly made pies on hand. Laura had ordered only coffee for herself and JJ because he would surely want to mull over tonight's flavors and make his own choice.

It was never easy to make a decision, and tonight was no exception. Eventually, they both made the same choice, graham cracker cherry. Gordon promptly delivered the ample portions, and the pair began savoring the delicious dessert in front of them. After a few bites Laura began,

"I don't need much of an excuse to come here, but tonight I have another reason."

She broke off long enough to have another bite and utter another "uummm" of approval.

 "I wanted to get your take on that session. I mean, when Walter spoke to me in Lincoln Park about joining and mentioned that they draw upon <u>known</u> science to ......" She stopped to "uuummm" another bite.

".....they use known science principles to come up with answers to other scientific questions or issues. I thought he meant something like...... like making better mouse traps."

She waved her fork around as she attempted to come up with a better example.

"Well, you know what I mean. I didn't expect wild stuff like Big-Bang waves and new ways to move things in the universe."

With that, she looked at JJ and awaited his reply. Always the critical thinker, he was less emotional than Laura; but nevertheless, he looked at least concerned.

"I know what you mean. I was not prepared or expecting ideas like that to come up. Now I have heard other scientists conjecture about Big-Bang waves but not in this context. As wild as Leroy's theory was, I go back to the people in the room. They are regular sorts, not prone to doing rash or dangerous things. I don't believe we are in over our heads or in danger of any kind." JJ paused and looked like he was assembling another thought. Laura watched and waited. She was right, JJ began again, "I would think that if we had been in the room when Einstein laid out his special theory of relativity we would have been flabbergasted." Sometimes JJ liked to show a little flair for the theatrical and decided to pretend to be one of the attendees at Einstein's meeting. In a very indignant tone he began,

"Imagine that you had two identical clocks and that one was taken off in a rocket and traveled at some very high speed, then brought back and compared with the other. How could the times be different? That's just preposterous! I've heard enough Martha. We're leaving this place of nonsense."

JJ finished his improvisation with a haughty flip of his head.

Laura's frown had been replaced by a smile and laughter by JJ's antics. "I suppose you are right. Who is Martha?"

"Oh, just a name I pulled out of the air," said JJ now in his normal voice. "Yeh, sure," chided Laura.

359

They continued the conversation a while longer as they consumed the remaining bits of pie and the last sips of coffee. The evening was getting late, and the pair decided to head for home. The edge of the meeting dulled by time and the discussion over dessert, they were much calmer now. Given the late hour, JJ saw her safely to her apartment.

75. L RETURNED TO SCHOOL

By Friday, Laura was ready to dig out L's emergency contact information and start making frantic phone calls. But before she could do that, a bruised, bandaged and limping L appeared in class, about ten minutes late. He was not used to taking a bus and misjudged the time it took.

"What happened to you?" exclaimed Laura.

 L described his accident, including perhaps more gory details than the moment strictly called for. His fellow students were duly impressed; and his teacher seemed ready to faint with anxiety, which gratified him more than he let on.

"My! You're lucky to be alive!" Laura gasped.

She noticed that his ever-present backpack was missing.

"Your backpack?" she inquired.

"It's history," he responded.

"Your laptop?" she asked.

"Smashed, phone too," said L.

She looked at him in dismay and remembered the valuable information on his laptop. How fortunate that they had stayed a little longer to offload his work at Nick's.

L stayed after class that day so Laura could give him a summary of Tuesday's meeting. He was attentive and appeared to understand the concepts in question. He could certainly appreciate the logic of Leroy's ideas, but much like the other members, L had no immediate ideas for the application of either Leroy's or JJ's most recent contributions. He did not appear to be bothered by the far-fetched nature of Leroy's theory.

Maybe it lost something in translation, Laura thought to herself.

76. SUMMER WAS WINDING DOWN

The last day of Laura's summer science class was a mixture of emotions for her. She had grown attached to her little hodgepodge of students, and she felt sure that they had all learned much more than anyone expected them to. It showed in their enthusiasm. She even detected some feelings of reluctance to leave.

"They had fun and they learned something," she reflected. "That's the way science should be."

Professionally, Laura had grown as well. Even the episode with the FBI had taught her a valuable lesson; retribution would have been sweet, but focusing on her students instead would pay better dividends in the end. Her new assignment at Washington was just ahead, and she was most definitely looking forward to the challenge.

At noon on a Friday, JJ called Laura on her cell phone. He planned to leave the museum early and invited her to a Cubs game. She was just finishing her move out of Larabee and felt a sense of completion.

A dog; a brew; the game; a nice day; and JJ. That's a no-brainer, she thought.

"You bet I'll go!"

They had been busy this summer with their new jobs and it had taken its toll on their ballgame attendance.

To save some money as students, they often stopped off before the game to get a bite. Then at the game, one expensive stadium beer and hotdog would hold them for the duration. So Laura and JJ had a habit of exiting the Red Line at Belmont, one stop before Wrigley. Their destination this time was a newcomer to Chicago from Detroit. It specialized in a Detroit-style hot dog, but offered the Chicago version as well. To be sure the place deserved a spot on their list of destinations, JJ and Laura both ordered the Chicago version first. If the new shop got it right, the duo would come back to try the rest of the fare. With their food in hand, they found a corner table and dug in.

What was the verdict? They would be coming back for more.

As they enjoyed their pre-game repast, JJ brought up the subject of L's presentation to the Society.

"You know what I've been thinking about," he began, "is that last part of L's demonstration, where we saw a dark central region surrounded by progressively less dense grey areas."

"OK," she responded. "I'm with you so far."

"OK," he continued, "do you remember that as L further changed the scale, the dark region kept shrinking smaller and smaller until it was just a dot itself? Well, the lighter grey areas had shrunk too, but there were still very light grey areas extending off the screen. To me that indicates that some groups of particles associated with the total group are way out there, but still part of the central grouping.

JJ gestured with his long arms; a passerby would clearly understand that he was describing something far away.

"Probably," Laura confirmed, listening carefully and noting (with some amusement) his waving arms.

364

"Well I wonder," JJ responded, still flapping his arms, "if that stuff moving way out there…if that stuff has anything to do with magnetic or electrical fields?"

Laura looked puzzled, but she was still concentrating.

"If you hook a battery to a copper wire, electrons flow through the wire. Right?" JJ asked.

"Right."

"Then if you take a compass, which responds to magnetic fields, and bring it near the wire that's carrying a current, the needle on the compass deflects from North. Right?"

"Right. And if there is no current in the wire, nothing happens. "

"Well, in L's demonstration, the graphic at the end showed a central core made of particles all packed together, and some thinly spaced ones that could be seen far from the core."

"Is that the graphic where we estimated the size of the central core and found that its radius matched the book value for the radius of the electron?" asked Laura.

"Exactly," replied JJ. "Here is what I think is happening. Some of those too-small-to-detect particles are interacting with little particles that make up the compass needle. After all, if the basic materials of all matter are the same and we believe they all exert attractive forces on each other, then the particles of the wire's electrons and the particles of the compass needle's electrons would exert the same type of forces on each other. This could explain how the interaction can take place even though you and I see that the needle and wire are just near each other, but not touching as we know it."

Then Laura chimed in, voicing her interpretation of what he had just said: "So, in essence you're saying that when I normally explain to my students that the magnetic field produced by the current in the wire and the permanent magnetic field in the compass interact, that it is really the interaction of little particles associated with each? They pull on each other and since the needle can easily move, it moves toward the wire."

"Yes. That's how I would picture it happening," he responded.

Laura thought a while about what she said and what he had explained. Then she smiled.

"It makes a lot of sense," she said. "After all, if down on that basic level, these little particles pull on each other as part of, say…an electron, then they should do the same with other say electrons—electrons from the atoms of the compass needle. Yes, I could believe that. In fact, I can easily see this discussion expanding to other particles beside electrons. It could apply to protons, neutrons and all those subatomic particles. After all, if this is the story of an electron, there could be similar stories for other particles."

"I wholeheartedly agree," JJ replied.

"I realize this whole thing is a lot of speculation," Laura continued. "But at least it's a model for discussion. In time, it may turn out to be true. By the way, have you had any luck locating more symbol sheets? We could really use the ones that explain protons and neutrons."

JJ laughed.

"As a matter of fact," he said, "I do have a few leads…but we better hold that for now. Look at the time."

They quickly finished lunch and dashed off to the Cubs vs. St. Louis game.

The Cubs won. It was a great day.

77. WHATEVER BECAME OF DEVOID?

When Devoid was released by the authorities after weeks of questioning, there was no fanfare, no gaggle of news media. He was free, but most decidedly unemployed. He was still bewildered by the events of the last few weeks. He never fully understood most of the questions they asked him. He knew that his use of the school district's computer was wrong, but how that had anything to do with national security was beyond him. How were his actions related to terrorist's activities? If he didn't know, then how could the FBI know? When they had asked about other terrorists in his family, Devoid felt compelled to mention that his brother had stolen a car back in 1971. But he'd been clean ever since then.

And bringing down the Internet? He barely knew how to log on and get to his favorite sites. Knowing how to hack into the Internet and gain access to thousands of computers around the United States was way beyond his capabilities.

Every branch of government—federal, state, county and city— had taken turns looking for grounds to prosecute Devoid, but they all came up empty-handed. Forensic technicians examined his computer but they could not tie any of his activities to the network fiascos. Only the school district had a case: misuse of school property. They had fired him for that. He was just old enough to retire, though. With his Social Security checks, Devoid's life would go on. No doubt as he spent his retirement years fishing off a pier on Lake Michigan, he would have lots of time to figure out what happened to him during those few weeks at the Larabee School.

78. AGENT NEWPORT

There was no such peace for Newport. Ever since federal prosecutors were unable to bring a case against Devoid, a division manager had been chewing on Agent Dalton Newport's hide.

"You are to be on this case twenty-four seven! I want answers and I want them fast! Failure is not an option!" And so on.

Of course, the division head's hide was being chewed on by his boss, whose hide was being chewed on by his boss…all the way up to the highest echelons of National Security. Newport, an old hand at passing the buck, turned to the rookie Jose Bererra.

"Find that tech who got us into the school router!" Newport ranted. "See if he saved the log file we looked at that day at Tendom Networks. And be quick or you'll be a rookie forever!"

In the beginning, Bererra and Newport did not have all the facts that are now known. They were given very little information to start with. Even now, they don't know the whole story. But now they do know that this case involved national security and had a very high priority level. The current thinking around the agency was that these events had been rehearsals for an even larger event—one that would compromise not only the Internet, but all the equipment attached. Although Newport knew little about the Internet, he knew that this was big and that his future with the agency could be jeopardy.

That meant no screw-ups, or he would end up in Podunk chasing speeders with a beat-up old Dodge. That also meant getting fired and losing most of his retirement benefits; given the current economic slump, jobs would be scarce, and he would end up with a low paying job working security at a Wal-Mart, or as a cop in some small burg. Newport had heard the speech before and knew the meaning, his boss was not kidding.

Bererra called Tendom Networks and found the operations manager, Nate Jennings. Jennings tracked down the smug little tech, Walt Lewis, and Bererra placed a call.

A brief conversation established that Lewis had kept the records the agents needed. Bererra rushed to the district office, struggling to keep himself from running through the halls.

When Bererra arrived at his cubicle, Lewis was examining the file on his monitor. Dispensing with any pleasantries, they got right to business.

"After you called, I started looking over the data," Lewis began. "If I remember right, we were looking for the MAC address of a computer at the site, right?"

"That is correct."

"OK, well, there are lots of entries here and these have the MAC address we gave you guys that day. There are tons of entries with that MAC address, so we all assumed the rest were the same. But, if I scroll way down…"

Lewis held down the arrow key for what seemed to be several minutes and then stopped.

"Here," he said, pointing to the screen. "These log entries have a different MAC address and have about as much data associated as the one before."

Bererra called Newport.

"Get that MAC address and get over to that school!" Newport bellowed into the phone. "I still have a hunch that kid is involved. I don't care if it happened at night. He just looked like the kind of kid who would pull big tricks. Before you get out of there, be sure there aren't more computers involved," Newport added. "And get a copy of the log, dammit!"

Bererra hovered over Lewis as the tech searched for another MAC address. Satisfied that only two computers had used Larabee's connection on the night in question, the rookie agent dashed out of the cubicle, clutching the report in his hand.

Agent Bererra arrived at Larabee School at around noon. A chain-link fence surrounded the whole property. Signs on the fence indicated that it was to be demolished.

No school today, he thought, and called Newport with the news.

"Damn it! Well just hustle your ass downtown to Central Administration and figure out a way to <u>find that kid!</u>"

Newport's voice had grown even more frustrated at the new roadblock.

Jose knew that no one would be available during the lunch hour, so he drove to the Central Administration building and bought a Chicago dog from a nearby cart. When lunch was over, Jose explained to the receptionist what he wanted and she directed him to the correct office. She also pointed out the mustard on his sleeve and right cheek. When the assistant facilities manager returned, Bererra was waiting; and he did not waste any time.

"I'm looking for a student who took a class at Larabee this summer."

"Larabee?" the facilities manager said with an unbelieving look.

"Yes, Larabee."

"You must be mistaken," she replied. "That building was demolished last spring."

"Impossible," Bererra insisted. "I was there this morning and a few weeks ago. I stood in the classroom where this student was in attendance. There was a sign that <u>said</u> "Larabee" on the building."

"Well, I'm afraid I can't help you," the assistant said coldly. "I don't have any records indicating a class there this summer. I only see occupancy until early June and then… that's it. You say it was a math and science class?"

"Yes," Jose responded, "At least, that's what I was told."

"Why don't you try the math and science curriculum coordinator?" she offered reluctantly.

She looked in a directory and made a few calls, clearly eager to have the anxious agent off her hands. Hanging up the phone, she turned to Bererra.

"Ms. Leppert, who is the science curriculum coordinator's assistant, is available," she informed him. "Would you like to talk to her?"

He said 'yes,' and she handed him directions. He thanked her over his shoulder as he hurriedly left her office.

When he entered the next office, he began explaining his request as soon as he was through the door. The woman behind the desk looked a bit surprised at his abruptness but answered him in an even voice.

"Are you sure it was Larabee?" she asked. "I haven't had any classes scheduled there since last spring. In fact, I think the building has been torn down."

A very frustrated agent Bererra told her of his visit and that the building was very much still standing.

"I am completely at a loss to explain this situation. Are you sure it was Larabee?"

If anything, agents are trained to attend to details. The fact that these "assistants" would question his ability to correctly recall a giant sign on a building was driving him up the wall. This frustration was clearly revealed every time he rolled his eyes at the question.

He was redirected twice more, and underwent two carbon copies of the same interview before he hit pay dirt. Everyone insisted that Larabee had been demolished. Everyone he met with was the assistant to someone else. One of them was even an assistant to an assistant.

Do bosses exist here? Is everyone here an assistant? he thought angrily.

The fifth assistant he met introduced herself in a very pleasant manner.

"Hi," she said. "I'm Devoida Williams."

She was in her fifties and was not wearing a wedding band. Her name set alarms off for Bererra, who would not soon forget his experience with Larabee's custodian.

"What an unusual name," he said smoothly. "Do you know a Devoid Williams?"

"Yes," she responded "I have a brother by that name. You know him?"

"Sorta," replied Bererra.

He was distracted by the bizarre coincidence, but explained what he was looking for.

"Yes," Devoida answered. "I know about it. I set it up."

Bererra listened in stunned silence as the woman continued in hushed tones.

"The class was originally scheduled for another building, but my older brother, Devoid, needed his job at that school for a few more months so he could qualify for Social Security. My cousin works in building maintenance and construction, which includes demolition as well. I talked him into switching Larabee with another building that was scheduled to be torn down in September. Then I switched that science class to Larabee. Nobody lost any money or anything—it was an even switch. I just did it to help out my brother. No harm, no foul."

Bererra was speechless at her candor.

"I haven't seen Devoid in a few weeks," she said. "I've been out of town. Have you seen him lately?"

"Not since summer at the school," replied Bererra.

That was all he was going to say on the subject, so he changed it.

"I need the list of students from that class, with contact information," he told her, holding out the warrant for her to inspect.

She gave it a once-over, pretending to understand all the details. Actually, it looked official and that was sufficient for her.

"I can get that information for you," she sweetly replied.

She rummaged around in a filing cabinet and came out with a file. It included the names and ID numbers of everyone in the class, including the teacher.

"If that is all you need, we'll just walk by the copy room on your way out," she said sweetly.

After all the roadblocks he had come across, Devoida Williams had been like an angel to him.

What a difference, compared to her brother, he thought. He made a point of smiling and thanking her sincerely and hurriedly left the building. It was the middle of the afternoon, and fast becoming late afternoon, when Jose Bererra left the Central Administration building, hoping never to return. Breathing deeply of the outside air, he placed a call to Newport. If he had expected his boss to be pleased with his success, he was disappointed.

"You just got that information?" Newport wailed. "What in the Hell have you been doing all day?"

Jose thought a moment and decided not to try to explain what he had been through. He knew how the conversation would go, so he kept silent and treated Newport's question as a rhetorical one. Even if he had decided to reply before he could Newport bellowed back, "Gimmy the numbers!" Bererra obliged.

"Get back to the office and file your report," Newport commanded, and slammed the phone on the cradle.

Newport immediately dialed Laura's number. He wanted her to reveal the identity of the student with the computer. His agent training would have required that he obtain the name on initial contact, but he had failed to do that at Larabee School on that fateful afternoon. His work had been getting sloppy as the years mounted up.

79. A FEW HOURS LATER

Laura was putting away groceries when the phone rang.

It had been several weeks since the end of summer school, and Laura had begun her new assignment at Washington Science and Math Magnet School. As with any new teaching assignment, there were many hills to climb: getting oriented to the processes and procedures; finding equipment and in some cases fixing it; writing lesson plans and setting up the Science Seminar where the students did independent projects. The load was heavy, and virtually all her waking hours were spent on job-related matters. Some nights, she even dreamed about school tasks and how to resolve them. She loved every minute of it! It was a challenge that was right for her. The toll was sleep. She needed more rest but realized that in the short term that might not be possible. Being young, resilient, motivated and in good physical shape, Laura believed she could pull it all together and orchestrate another fine classroom production. Nonetheless, she was beat; her wagon was dragging.

She looked at the caller ID, it was a local call but an unfamiliar number. She decided to answer in case it had something to do with her school.

"This is FBI agent Dalton Newport."

Laura's heart sank. She had hoped never to encounter him again, and now he was calling her. Already exhausted from her work, the thought of talking to him was especially repulsive. *I wish I hadn't picked up.*

He has my phone number, she thought ruefully. *What else does he know about me?*

Newport had not waited for her reply, but was barking orders into her ear.

"I want the name of the student who had the computer," he ordered.

But Laura did not respond immediately; she considered hanging up on him. This happened to him all the time, so Dalton knew how to read the silence.

"Look, I know what you're thinking and I would advise against it," he practically shouted. "This is an investigation regarding national security, and anyone interfering with it can be prosecuted. You were there with the student and the computer when I talked to him. That makes you a material witness."

"But what could you possibly want from a young man like that? How could he be implicated in a security problem?"

She was hoping to deflect Newport's question by asking some of her own.

"I'm not able to discuss that with you, ma'am," came his pat answer.

Laura tried to come up with another delaying tactic.

"Why didn't you ask him his name at the time?" she asked testily.

Newport reacted to the jab as she hoped he would. He exploded in rage, threatening her with everything but excommunication. Laura was actually having fun as she listened to his sputtering and fuming. It was her turn to "play with the mouse." Not a person to succumb to threats, Laura continued to look for ways to dodge the questions and redirect him.

"It won't do you any good to talk to him anyway," she stated. "He had a bicycle accident and his computer was destroyed."

"Oh, sure it was!" Newport scoffed. "Now you're adding lying to an agent to your list of crimes."

"I am not lying!" Laura retorted indignantly. "That is the truth."

"Look! Just give me the name so I can do my job. If the kid is innocent, you've got nothing to be afraid of."

Laura simply ignored this wheedling statement and decided she should address Newport's professionalism, or lack thereof.

"The part that bothers me most," she began, "is how you conducted yourself with a group of innocent kids. You didn't do the law, your office or the FBI any favors that day. Respect for the law is hard enough for many of these kids. You know, I should have filed a complaint with your superiors. Maybe I'll do just that."

"Are you through?" Newport replied, and she was gratified to hear that his tone had softened slightly. "Lady, if you had to put up with what we see and do on a regular basis, you'd understand why I'm a little rough around the edges."

But Laura wasn't buying it.

"Look, you're supposed to be smart enough to be able to tell the difference between criminals and kids," she said.

It was a valiant effort, but the agent was not giving up.

"Give me the name, or I will file a complaint against you," he said. "Every department all the way up to Homeland Security will have your name and number. Even if you are never charged, the depositions, phone calls and questions will make you wish you had answered this one simple question. So I will ask you again: who was the kid with the laptop?"

But Laura had long since grown weary of the pointless exchange with Newport. She knew she was not giving in, and it was becoming obvious to her that he was not going to quit. She hung up on him and then left the phone off the hook. She was fairly certain that he wouldn't find her cell-phone number: Laura was a second user on her mother's cellular account, and she didn't give the number to many people.

She was fuming and wanted to vent, but she thought she might be a little too upset to bother even JJ tonight. She spent the evening eating ice cream and watching mindless TV shows. By the time she went to bed, she had calmed down considerably. Knowing she had done right by L as well as being exhausted, she slept like a baby.

80. STAKEOUT L

Newport's call to Laura had merely been a timesaving measure. Granted, it had turned out to be a futile one, but he didn't dwell on it. Bererra had acquired the students' names and emergency phone numbers. He could use the process of elimination to narrow his search. The agents knew that the kid they wanted was not Asian, so Nik and Nuk were eliminated right away. He and his two agents spent the evening calling the rest of the numbers on the list. It wasn't a long list, and they made short work of it. They were able to talk to Jose, Budru and Hammu and eliminate them because they had accents.

That left L. Watkins.

They also used a reverse phone directory to find his address in case they needed to make a personal visit.

"When do you expect him back?" asked Newport in his usual offensive manner, when he called the Watkins home.

"Oh, I don't know. He just comes and goes as he likes. He is such a sweet kid, don't you think?" L's flower child mother replied. Newport thought she sounded like she had been too close to some strong vapors.

"Would you have him call me when he gets home?" Newport grumbled.

"Okay," came the sing-song answer.

She hung up before he could give the number. He called back, gave it to her and once again got "Okay" in the same voice. Maybe she was high or playing dumb like a fox; he decided not to take any chances. As soon as Bererra returned, Newport sent him to stake out the home and let him know as soon as the kid returned.

At 9:30 pm, the silhouette of a young teen approached the house, walking with a limp. When he reached his front door, the sconce illuminated his face. It was L. Bererra called Newport, and within ten minutes, the senior agent arrived at the Watkins residence. It was a three-story apartment in the Belmont Central neighborhood. The agents went to the door and rang the bell. L opened the inside door. A locked screen door separated the young man from his inquisitors. Newport identified himself and agent Bererra. In case it was necessary, he mentioned the session in the classroom some weeks ago. L did not need the reminder.

"May we come in?" asked Newport. "I have some questions to ask."

He had tried to speak with a sensitive touch, but had no luck. His old style could not be hidden.

"You can ask from right there," L responded coldly.

"I want to see your computer."

"Can't."

"Why not?" the agitated Newport asked.

"Trashed."

"Why?" asked Newport; he was getting fed up with the one-word Q and A.

"Bike accident."

The agents could see black, blue and yellow marks on his face. They noticed bruises on his arms and legs as well.

"This kid's a mess, boss," Bererra muttered, leaning toward Newport so L wouldn't hear him.

"Where and when did you 'trash' your computer?" asked Newport, ignoring Bererra's compassionate warning.

Bererra, meanwhile, was distracted by a fleeting glimpse of himself sifting through a landfill for days on end.

"About two weeks ago in our building dumpster," L responded.

Without a word, Newport looked at Bererra and nodded. Jose knew what it meant: go around back and look in the trash. Bererra hurried away while Newport continued asking questions. He tried to get more out of L or trip him up, but L continued to give the same short answers. Agent Bererra returned in a few minutes, shaking his head

"Completely empty," he said briefly.

Empty-handed the agents reluctantly returned to Newport's car.

"I want you and the other boneheaded rookie, Stan, to set up a daytime and evening watch," Newport said, slamming the car door. "This kid is hiding something. I want to know where he goes and when he goes there."

The next morning at about 7:20, L left home and headed to Washington Magnet, his new school. At the end of the school day, he returned home. Nowak and Bererra traded shifts. Nowak covered days and Bererra stayed on duty until 1 am. There was nothing to report the first or second days.

On the third day of surveillance, the day shift with Nowak went as usual. However, at 6:14 pm L left the house and walked east. Bererra put the car in gear and followed L at a discreet distance. The distance was, in fact, too discreet; L had left the street level and boarded an elevated Red Line train before Bererra could park the car. All he knew was the train was going north.

Newport was livid.

"Next time use your head and your feet!" he roared.

81. MEETING AT NICK'S, PLAN B AND ETC.

L was off to a meeting of the Society at Nick's plant (the Club) and was unaware of the agent's attempt to follow him. Tonight, they skipped the restaurant and went straight to the meeting. There was much to discuss, and they didn't want to waste time on dinner. Carl's wife, Helen, had sent a picnic basket filled with food, so no one was going to go hungry this evening.

Before the meeting, L and Laura caught each other's eyes and moved aside to talk, each clearly with something to say to the other. Although both were now at Washington Magnet, L and Laura did not regularly seen each other. She could have called him, but really wanted to discuss the matter in person. Thus, tonight's meeting was their first opportunity to talk.

L told her about the visit from the FBI. She realized then that Newport had found another way to find his identity. She explained that they had contacted her as well and wanted her to reveal his identity but that she had refused.

"I'm sorry you had to go through that. It's my fault in the first place," he said almost in a whisper. She did not quite understand his statement of fault, but the meeting was about to begin; and her question to clarify that point would need to wait.

The meeting started, and Megan asked to share first.

"I'm the least prepared in this group for the physics, quantum physics, some of the math and other stuff," she began. "But when I hear you physics types explain what you think is happening, or your theories, I have to admit that it makes some sense to me, as a biologist. I guess I just want a plausibility check on this thought that's been going around in my head ever since the first demonstration."

She paused and looked around before she continued.

"As I understand it," she said, "the animation that we believe to represent an electron has a dense core of harmoniously-moving sub-particles. Layers, or regions, of the same stuff surround those sub-particles. But the surrounding layers aren't nearly as dense. Also, a scattering of the basic particles extend way, way out beyond the core, right?"

"Very well put," complimented Carl.

"Further," Megan continued, "these groups of particles are made up of smaller particles doing the same thing, right?"

"Yes," said Carl.

"And someone speculated that all the rest of matter—protons, neutrons, zolons and everything—have similar structures, right?"

"I would agree with all of that," Carl responded, "except for the zolons. I've never heard of those."

"Whatever," she said jokingly.

"So if humans are built of this stuff, then beyond the dense core that we see," she said, gesturing to her torso, "there is even more extending away from us for quite some distance, but it is too fine to detect, right?"

Leroy took the pitch.

"I think it is entirely plausible," he said.

Megan's voice now shifted to a more philosophical tone as she continued.

"I have often thought that some events described as 'paranormal' could actually be attributed to some real but unseen mechanism, which is the result of the part of 'us' extending beyond what we perceive as our bodies. Like having the feeling that someone is staring at you and you turn around to see someone who you did not know was there, looking at you. You know what I mean?"

"Absolutely," answered Leroy.

The rest of the group jumped in, and each had a few examples that they felt could be explained in the same way. Laura and JJ recalled to each other their discussion about the magnetic compass and a copper wire carrying an electric current (before the Cub's game). After several minutes, Nick spoke up.

"I like these ideas, and this is the right forum for discussing them," he said. "However, we have some pressing questions on the table right now, and we should get to those first because time is short. I promise we will get back to those topics." Nick was extremely apologetic for the intervention but he knew how pressing the topic of the night was.

"That's fine," responded Megan. "I'm just glad to be on the same page. I'll be glad to bring this up at some future time." Since the others had joined in the brief discussion, she felt confident that the matter would receive attention at a future meeting. So she was not put off by Nick's request to table the matter.

Leroy took the floor and suggested that Nick start by sharing the results of his tests on the egg.

Nick headed to the screen and turned on the projector, which was attached to his laptop. An image of the egg appeared on the screen.

"Before I begin, let me make a comment to our newest members." Nick had turned so that he could directly address them.

"You will notice from time to time as we make presentations or enter into discussions that we refer to events and processes that are easily observed and commonly occur in our lives. For example, and I am sure you are familiar with this one, we use water waves to help us understand and explain all kinds of other phenomena: resonance of musical instruments; standing waves; optical refraction, e.g. eyeglasses; and on and on, ad nauseum." Chuckles were heard. "Others in science do this as well, but in our group we tend to push the boundaries a little further. That little plaque over there on the wall says it well." Nick pointed to the wall near the coffee station. It read

The clues to the unknown are not unknown.
*ancient, un*known

He wrapped up his comment, "We think that the events, structure and even behavior at the fine structure level are the same those we witness at the much larger level of our existence. Remember Leroy's bicycle wheel demo at our last session?"

It was a rhetorical question; no one would forget that meeting, with Leroy suggesting a way to interact with Big-Bang waves.

"So, we draw upon what we can observe at this level and see if it leads us to a better understanding of what our theoretical fine structure could be doing. It is as simple as that. Okay? Okay." Nick finished his point with a question and immediately answered it himself. He knew they had understood and did not really need a reply.

After pausing to let the point sink in, Nick began his presentation, "At the end of our last meeting, Walter asked me to examine his egg-like object. It won't take long to tell you about what I found. At the last meeting we already examined its external physical properties. What we did not and could not see is that this object has a crystalline structure. It might seem like an odd shape for a crystal, since we normally imagine crystals with jewel-like facets and angular surfaces. Unlike those more common crystals, which are made of the same materials, this is like a ceramic material with a crystalline structure. So what does the basic crystal structure look like? Like this."

He pointed to the egg again.

"As far as I could go in magnification, the basic components are in the shape of this egg, and they repeat over and over again. That JJ brought up fractals last week is a pretty amazing coincidence, since this structure is built the same way fractals are built."

JJ was surprised, and smiled with satisfaction. Maybe he fit in better than he had given himself credit for, he thought. Laura smiled and gave him a thumbs-up sign.

"Now based on L's model," Nick continued, "I think we might be able to assume that this same pattern will repeat all the way down in scale until we reach <u>The Fine Structure</u>." As a joke,

Nick spoke "The Fine Structure" in a booming voice, then looked up as if the pronouncement had come from above. Subtle laughter was heard, his comic point successful.

After checking in with his audience and seeing that they understood, Nick went on.

"The components that make up the egg are quite common and unremarkable," he said. "In other words, there's no exotic stuff from another planet. Silicon is most prevalent, aluminum next, oxygen, nitrogen, carbon and a bunch of trace elements. Again, as I said a moment ago, what makes it quite unique is its structure."

For the next twenty minutes or so, the group asked Nick questions about the methods and procedures he used. After the questions died down, Carl took the floor and hooked his laptop to the projector.

"That was nice work Nick," he said, "especially on short notice; I'm sure you spent some late nights on that effort."

"A few," Nick affirmed. "But it was worth it."

"When Nick told me his results the other day," Carl resumed, "I was reminded of my youth."

Leroy let out a loud moan.

"We'll be here all night," he complained theatrically.

Everyone laughed.

"Okay, I'll keep it short," Carl smiled.

"I talked to Nick earlier this week about his findings," he went on. "When he described this thing as one big crystal, it reminded me of Boy Scouts in the fifties. One of the merit badges was rewarded for creating a crystal radio. You needed a good-sized piece of a specific, naturally-occurring crystal."

He paused, thinking.

"I can't remember the name," he admitted.

"Galena!" shouted Leroy.

"Thanks, Leroy," Carl responded. "Gosh, you're older than you look."

Carl waited while the laughter subsided.

"Then," he resumed, "I thought about all the other uses crystals have had in communication."

He nodded to Leroy, who had some experience as a communications engineer. Leroy nodded and Carl continued.

"Even in modern times, we see it in some gas grills."

"No way!" JJ exclaimed. He considered himself an expert on barbecue, even if he could only afford a second-hand charcoal contraption.

"Yes, way," Carl said, smiling at the younger man's enthusiasm. "Some gas grills use crystals to create a spark. When you deform certain crystals, an electrical potential is produced between two of its surfaces. If the deformation is sufficient, you can get a spark sufficient to ignite a gas grill."

"I know how I'm spending my next paycheck!" JJ called out.

"I can also remember when crystals were used in microphones and headsets," Carl continued over the chuckling crowd. "With the microphone, it's like the gas-lighter example. Sound vibrates the crystal, and the electrical potential is fed to an amplifier. The sound becomes louder."

He snapped his fingers as if to say, "There you have it."

"And," he continued, "there were crystal cartridges for record players as well. The process is actually reversible. For example, in headsets or headphones, the fluctuating voltage from the amp responded to the sound and caused the crystal to vibrate. The vibrations were the same as the voltage fluctuations. To increase the efficiency ……..," "Okay Carl," as Leroy interrupted him. Leroy sensed that the older members already understood the principle and the younger ones were getting lost on the crystal phonograph cartridge example. He felt the gas grill example had been sufficient. Carl was not offended because in the years of being around Leroy he understood it was just his way to say, "We understand."

By now a few Society members thought they had a good idea where Carl was going with this line of thought. Megan was one of them, and she gently interrupted.

"So since this egg is a crystal," she began, "we may be able to interact with it. Distort it and get a voltage? Or apply a voltage and get some movement?"

It was obvious to the physicists in the group that Megan had a good grasp of the concepts involved, even though that was not her strong suit.

"Great catch, Megan. Exactly," responded Carl while Nick and Leroy nodded their support. "That's what the three of us noodled up the other day."

The three men were shaking their heads in amazement at her insight.

"Now, here's another wild thought," Carl announced, then turned and looked at JJ. "Could the motions we observed in L's demonstration carry over to influence the motions at the next level? When we watched L's demo, we kept seeing the moving particles, resulting in bigger groups of moving... groups," he hesitated, searching for a word that seemed to fit. "That process continued over and over until we got to the big group, which turned out to be the electron. Right? Well in my mind I saw that building process as having levels. Sooooooooo, as we went from level to level we saw a similar effect. I have no proof, just a hunch. If it does exist, we could call it a 'fractal effect'?"

JJ and the others looked puzzled. Carl continued as he sought to convey the concept,

"Remember that JJ suggested that the sequence of building bigger and bigger objects from small but similar objects looked like a fractal process." To be sure they understood, Carl restated using slightly different wording,

"We saw in L's demonstration that the motions of the little pieces were the same in the larger aggregations. In fact, the motions were similar as we went up in scale all the way to what we think is an electron. Now here's the kicker, could it be that motions at smaller levels are responsible for motions at higher levels? Or vice versa? Could the motions at each level be linked somehow to each other?"

393

When Carl paused to let this sink in, Laura closed her eyes and pictured L's particles. In her head, she replayed the images she and the others had witnessed. She could not picture the linkage that would result in one level influencing the motion of another, but the concept seemed worth investigating. When Laura opened her eyes, she looked around to see various members looking up from their notes and disengaging themselves from side conversations. Their expressions seemed to say, "It's possible, it could be, maybe, let's give it some consideration." They were all on the same page, and Carl continued.

"If the motions of the smaller particles are influencing the motion of the aggregate groups of particles," he began, "then there may be a way, at our macroscopic level, to know what is happening at the fine-structure level. And vice versa. Now push it one step further: maybe, at our macroscopic level, could we induce motions that would carry all the way down to the fine structure?"

Carl stopped. The room was silent. Everyone had followed the logic and understood it. Now they were letting it soak in. He was suggesting a way to achieve the highly theoretical turntable effect that Leroy had introduced a few weeks ago. Only coming from Carl, it didn't sound quite so theoretical anymore.

L was usually quiet, except when he was making a presentation. He silently and gratefully absorbed the knowledge presented by the more experienced members. Now, however, he had something to contribute.

"I agree with Mr. Niles," he said. "I could argue in favor of a fractal effect. The equations I generated from the symbol sheets describe the motions of the fine-structure particles as they move and interact harmoniously with each other. Well, also remember that the <u>same equations</u> describe the motions of the larger objects—the objects that are made from the groupings of fine-structure particles."

"Oh, yeah," Megan muttered, nodding along with the other members.

"And remember," L continued, "that when these larger groups joined with similar groups, they <u>continued</u> to move in the same harmonious way. <u>And</u>—that process occurred over and over again as the groupings got larger. In every single case, the same equations described the motions."

He was right. The equations had always been the same, whether they dealt with five particles or five billion. To be sure she understood correctly, Laura offered her own restatement.

"So not only is the structure of the particles repetitive, but their <u>behavior</u> could be repetitive, too. The particles share a fractal <u>structure</u> and they share a fractal <u>motion</u> effect."

The others agreed with Laura's version. It was a simple but powerful argument. An enthusiastic discussion began and continued for over an hour as the Society revisited each of the new ideas and how they fit together. Other than the symbol sheets, the rest of the science involved (namely fractals and crystals) was fairly common knowledge to anyone with a scientific background. The members were caught up in a whirlwind of excited speculation, offering only the occasional fragment of explicitly stated evidence.

Laura knew that much of their discussion was based on non-existent science and bordered on wild conjectures. Good Science requires proof! In the case of this new fractal <u>motion</u> theory, proof would be especially difficult to come by; there were so many variables and unknowns. In this case, there were two aspects of the theory that were intriguing: the theory is simple, and it has some support from the science of crystal behavior.

The group's explanations of what they were seeing, and how they sought to interact with the fine matter, were based on simple and understandable concepts. What's difficult about a crystal creating a spark in a gas grill? In science, the simple explanation is often the best explanation, so the fractal theory met the criteria for simplicity.

She also remembered from her education: in scientific endeavors, each step is usually tested and proved before moving forward, changing only one variable at a time. But sometimes it is possible to leap to the end and see if all the assumptions along the way produce the anticipated results. It doesn't always pan out, but if the assumptions and theories were correct, making an educated guess can save a lot of time, effort and money. She also remembered Professor Leffler's ruminations on theoretical science and people like Stephen Hawking who are always dealing with the hypothetical. Indeed, this this is what the Fine Society members were doing.

Having mulled it over in her head, she felt much better knowing that linking a bunch of theories and assumption together is commonly done by physics and math intellects like Hawking.

.

82. NOW ON ANOTHER SUBJECT

The evening was getting long, and when the excited conversation had died down, Nick asked if there were any other items to bring before the Society. Laura was anxious about what she and L were about to bring up; even if it meant prolonging the meeting, she felt it must be done.

"L and I have something to share," she said in a shaky voice. "First, I e-mailed you all about L's bike accident last week. He's healing well, but as you can see, it was a pretty scary run-in."

Everyone nodded and expressed relief that L was OK. He smiled, and then laughed when Nick joked about having backed up the laptop files.

"That was a close one, huh?" L sighed knowingly.

"Sure," Nick responded. "But that brain of yours is impossible to back up. Be careful, would you?"

L looked around the room and was surprised to see genuine relief mingled with worry on the faces around him. He quickly looked away, but not before they saw the blush in his cheeks.

Seeing his embarrassment, Laura continued.

"I know you're all aware of the incident some weeks ago with the FBI at Larabee," she began. "Well, as far as I can tell, it was all about a MAC address. L was the only student in class who had a computer, so he caught the agent's attention. But before they could look at his laptop, they found the custodian in the basement. His address matched, and I thought we'd seen the end of the FBI."

397

Laura was looking at the floor to keep from having to look at Walter. She knew how her story would affect him and dreaded being the bearer of such unwelcome news.

"Well," she reluctantly continued, "a few days ago, the FBI agent, a jerk named Newport, called and wanted to find L and his laptop. I told him it had been damaged beyond repair and thrown away. He insisted—he even threatened to arrest me. I tried everything I could think of to dissuade him from pursuing L. But it didn't work; the agent figured out who L was from some data they obtained from Central Administration. He went to L's home, and L told him the same thing. Needless to say, I'm troubled that he keeps coming back."

She paused, miserable about busting everyone's bubble.

"I thought the group should know about this matter," Laura finished.

Walter knew firsthand the trauma associated with government officials returning time after time to ask the same questions and spy on his family. The news sent a chill down his spine, his hands went clammy. Laura looked at Walter. She saw the stress as well. Everyone else was concerned too; an edgy murmur filled the room. Then Nick took the floor.

"In light of the activities we're pursuing at this time," he said, "prying eyes would not be good. If we're onto something significant, now is not the time to reveal it to anyone—not the government or the public. Even if our efforts come to nothing, someone might try to invent or embellish a story that would make us look bad or foolish. We all know the media is hungry for a story; they'll go to great lengths to stretch, bend and even invent facts. Just picture the tabloids at the supermarket checkout lane."

The membership enthusiastically agreed with him on that point.

"I think it's time for a Plan B," Nick announced. "I volunteer myself to make one."

While JJ, Laura and L looked around blankly, the veteran members nodded sagely.

"I'll pattern it after the one we did 5 years ago," Nick continued. "L, Laura and JJ, I'll catch you up when it's ready." Laura could only guess what was meant by a Plan B, but knowing Nick and the others she felt comfortable for the present.

Leroy took the floor with,

"If we can, despite the FBI issue," he said, "I think we should keep this accelerated schedule of meetings while we have good momentum. A good Plan B should make that possible........
And with that, I suggest we adjourn"

The members nodded agreement. It had been a long and productive meeting, so it was a unanimous decision to end the evening session.

83. BERERRA and NOWAK ON POINT

For several days now, the FBI had been keeping watch over L's house only in the evening. They had determined that during school hours, the odds of an event occurring were small. After all, the big network events had only taken place at night. Canceling the daytime watch also made it possible to double up on coverage in the evening. The past few nights, L had gone to a library once, a convenience store twice, and a video arcade three times. Nothing else. Agents Bererra and Nowak were beginning to think Newport had them chasing a lost cause.

Tonight, however, L stepped out of his house and headed east. The library, video arcade and convenience store were not in that direction. Bererra proceeded on foot, with Nowak in the car following far behind. They maintained visual contact and radio silence, since radio sounds carry in the quiet evening and might tip off the kid. As the agents anticipated, L boarded a northbound Red Line train. It was the same train Bererra had lost him on the week before.

This time Bererra caught the train.

L left the train at Foster and walked to Broadway, then walked south a short distance to a diner. Bererra spotted a convenience store across the street and established his surveillance point there. He also called Nowak and gave him his position. Nowak arrived in a few minutes, and the two agents pretended to be talking sports in the parking lot. In a little more than an hour, L emerged and began to walk north, presumably to Foster and the Red Line to return home.

Bererra was ready to resume following L when another person emerged from the diner. It was a woman. She paused and looked around for a moment and then crossed the street, moving diagonally past them toward their side of the street. Both agents immediately felt as though hers was a familiar face. As she walked the diagonal, which brought her closer to their position, Nowak spoke in amazement.

"That's the teacher at Larabee School," he said.

"You're absolutely right," responded an equally surprised Jose.

The new development caught them off guard. They lost precious time while considering their next actions. As the teacher continued south on Broadway, the agents decided that Nowak would follow her as soon as she was far enough away. But they had failed to notice a bus at a stop near her present location. Before they could act, she had boarded it and was gone. L was gone, too. All they could see was a bus on Foster, pulling away from its stop as a young person with a backpack walked to a seat.

"The boss is really going to be pissed," said Nowak. Bererra did not even respond.

As expected, Newport was livid. Bererra just got to the part out about losing L when Newport interrupted.

"How is it that two agents can't keep a tail on one kid?" he railed.

He proceeded to berate the rookies until he ran out of nasty words, at which point he leaned back in his chair and gazed at the space over his desk, as if fresh new insults were floating there. Bererra seized the opportunity and quickly interjected, "The teacher was there, too."

"What did you say?" growled Newport.

"The teacher from Larabee School came out of the same diner just after the kid."

Newport sat in stunned silence, trying to make sense of the information.

"They must be in this together, whatever it is," he mused, cracking a sinister smile.

"You guys keep your program in place. I'm going to get directly involved." Newport assigned himself to watch Laura, while Nowak and Bererra were to continue their surveillance of L.

84. LIFE GOES ON

Between the more frequent society meetings, life went on as usual for the members.

Laura enjoyed her Science Seminar at Washington.

L was doing well academically and even making some friends.

JJ tended to his assignments at the museum while quietly looking for more symbol sheets.

Carl and Leroy got together during the day at a variety of public venues to discuss ideas. They looked like any number of other retirees discussing the current news. However, these two were discussing quantum physics and a potentially world-changing scientific discovery.

Nick thought every day about the Fine Society's project.

Megan worked every day in her specialty, genetics, busily pushing frontiers.

These days, Walter spent more time looking around to determine if he was being watched. His anxiety level was up a few notches.

In addition, they all had their recent discussions going round and round in their heads as each tried to understand the significance and implications of the new found knowledge.

85. A BIG BREAK

It had been several nights since Newport started watching Laura's place, and to Bererra and Nowak, it seemed like an eternity since they had begun following L. Even Newport, who had been on point for less time, was growing impatient. But he would not be disappointed tonight.

Tonight, the Society skipped the restaurant to save time. The members headed directly to Nick's factory.

"Kid moving, Nowak is on foot," Bererra radioed to Newport.

"DON'T LOSE HIM!" Newport bellowed back over the radio.

In a few minutes, Bererra's radio crackled.

"I'm in pursuit," Newport radioed to the rookies as he watched Laura leave her apartment.

He got out of his car and set out on foot on the opposite side of the street from his quarry. After walking a few blocks, Laura boarded a northbound Sheridan Road bus. Newport waited until the last minute to board and then grabbed a seat at the front. He sat facing the front of the bus. He could not look back to see if she had spotted him. However, if he leaned ever so slightly to his left, he could get a glimpse of her in the bus driver's mirror. She was seated mid-coach and did not appear to see him.

At Lawrence, she disembarked using the middle doors. Newport followed using the front door, but only after waiting until the last second to exit. He quickly moved to the other side of the street. She walked half a block and stopped at a westbound bus stop. There was no bus waiting. He looked east. No bus was in sight. He walked fast, headed east on Lawrence and eventually broke into a jog. (It was not a run. A jog was the best he could do in his condition). A few blocks later, he crossed to the north side of Lawrence and waited at that bus stop. It was a gamble, but if he were already on the bus when Laura boarded it, she would be less likely to notice him. Still wheezing, he boarded the next westbound bus.

It worked.   At the next stop, Laura boarded his bus and didn't even glance in his direction. Minutes later at Ravenswood she got off. At the last moment, so did he. As she headed north on Ravenswood, Newport held back in the shadows. A few blocks down the street, she entered a building.

As a cover, he took a position near the door of a nearby building and lit up a cigarette. He no longer smoked, but it was so common to see a smoker standing outside that he knew no one would give it any thought.

Not more than two minutes later, a young person walked by on the other side of Ravenswood. The figure was headed north and carrying a backpack. Could it be? While Newport studied the passing silhouette, his eye spotted another figure coming up the street. That profile he knew. It was agent Nowak. L entered the building, and Newport crossed over to greet a surprised Nowak. Stan's radio was silenced, so he did not know Newport had left his post at Laura's.

They both now pretended to be smokers, relegated to the outdoors to indulge their vice. Nowak quietly radioed his position to Bererra, and in minutes the three were ensconced in the brown sedan, sorting out details and collecting data. They recorded the building address, the number of people entering and the descriptions of those people.

405

The mood in the car was far from one of triumph. At the least, Bererra had expected Newport to express some kind of relief when they made the connection between the kid and the teacher. Instead, the senior agent seethed with a barely-contained fury that made the rookies extremely uncomfortable. Newport seemed to have some kind of vendetta against these two, and, Bererra reflected, that did not bode well for a guy's career.

86. THE SILVERY STUFF

This meeting was more subdued than recent meetings. All that concerted thinking still hadn't produced fresh ideas, so the Fine Society was stuck in a rut. An hour of general discussion went by, but it only amounted to a rehash of earlier meetings.

Nick suggested they take a break and change the subject. He had prepared a Plan B and suggested they use their time to review it, especially for the benefit of the new members. They reviewed the code language to use in case they felt they could be overheard. Nick also presented the outline for a special meeting, which would only be conducted if it became absolutely necessary. The plan called for very specific equipment and supplies and Nick had carefully drafted assignments detailing which members were responsible for bringing the disparate objects. They worked over Plan B for an hour, until they knew it backward and forward.

The Plan B discussion, with its bizarre ingenuity, invigorated the group. By the time all of their questions were answered, the mood was lighter and livelier than it had been all evening.

As he ambled over to the snack table for another lemon square, Carl thought of a question he'd been meaning to ask Nick.

"Nick," he called over his shoulder, "those electrical conductivity tests you performed—you said the egg behaved like a semiconductor, right?"

"Correct," Nick answered, then added, "Could you get me a muffin while you're up?"

"You bet," Carl answered, perusing the picked-over selection of baked goods. "So on a conduction versus non-conduction scale, which end would this be closest to?"

"Oh, this semi-conductive material is definitely closer to the non-conductive end," Nick answered. "Why do you ask?"

By now, what had started as a casual back-and-forth had caught the attention of the rest of the group. Side conversations had grown quiet as everyone listened to Carl's explanation.

"Well, the crystals I talked about in a previous meeting were closer to the conductive end of the spectrum," he began. "So it was easy to hook up some wires and get results. Remember the grill spark unit and the crystal radio example?"

Everyone indicated remembering.

"I'm wondering about a series of tests," he explained. "We would apply varying voltages to the egg and see if we get a response. The problem with that strategy is that it won't really work well with semiconductors. When the object's a poor conductor, just hooking up wires to its surface doesn't get you very far."

The group members thought for a moment, and then Leroy spoke up.

"Well," he said, "we do this sort of thing in electronic circuits all the time. Semiconductors get hooked up to copper conductors on circuit boards for all kinds of electronics. Been doin' it for years."

"OK," said Carl. "Go on."

"Layering makes the transition between materials gradual," Leroy said. "Imagine a sandwich where the top layer is a conductor. The next layer is less of a conductor, called a semi-conductor. The next is still less of a conductor. We keep layering like this until the last layer almost matches the conductive properties of the substance we want to connect to. In that multilayered substance, the electrical characteristics vary from one side to the other. On the side attached to the copper, the semiconductive stuff is almost as conductive as the copper. On the other face, it's almost as much of an insulator as the semiconductor it touches, and the layers sandwiched in between have gradually mediated the difference in conductivity.

"Hold on there, Quick-Draw McGraw," said Megan, using a line from an old cartoon. "I don't understand what all this layering and semiconductor stuff has to do with the egg? Could someone put this in layperson terms?"

She waited while the "physicists" pondered the question. Leroy answered for the group.

"An excellent question," he said. "We came up with two choices; Carl could explain, and you would understand. It might take an hour." Everyone laughed. "Or I could give a quick reason and see if that suffices." Leroy finished with a theatrical gesture of an outstretched hand palm up in her direction.

"I'll try yours first," Megan said, smiling. "No offense Carl." Carl and the rest laughed.

"Well," began Leroy, sounding like he didn't have his explanation completely ready, "We want to apply an electrical pulse to the egg to see if we can make it…twitch." Twitch sounded like a last minute choice. "Yes, we want to make it twitch. This is oversimplified, but we would hold two wires on the egg; and the wires are connected to a source of electricity, say a battery, for now. The problem is Nick found that the surface is a poor conductor—we would call it a 'semiconductor,' but the 'semi' just means poor."

Leroy was still speaking somewhat deliberately, searching for words.

"Well," he continued, "if you turn on the juice, some electrical current would flow through the egg and around the circuit through the battery. But this egg is so poor a conductor that our current would be almost nonexistent. This next part you'll just have to believe, trust me. If we put little sandwiches of layered material—like the ones we just described—in between the wires and the egg, we get much better flows of electricity."

Leroy stopped and gave Megan a big-teeth grin as he waited her approval.

"Okay, I'll buy that, for now," she said. "But I reserve the right to hear Carl's version when we have a week or two."

All laughed at the good-natured ribbing.

"Nick, can you give us the resistivity or conductivity you measured on the egg?" Carl asked, standing up and heading to the whiteboard. "Either one would do."

"Sure, I've got it right here. Its resistivity is about..." Nick read off the number, which Carl scribbled on the board.

$$6 \times 10^2 \text{ Ohm·m}$$

A protracted discussion followed among Nick, Leroy and Carl. But Nick started to appear distracted. He lost his place in the discussion several times, apologizing only to have it happen again moments later. Something was obviously tugging at his memory cells. He plucked a notebook off the desk and began scribbling in it. The other physicists had stopped trying to include him in their discussion when he let out a loud grumble and turned to Walter, effectively ending the physicists' ramblings.

"Walter," Nick barked, "do you remember that piece of shiny material you gave me years ago to test?" He turned to the other veteran members. "Do you guys remember that?"

They stared at him as if he were crazy. Did they remember the alleged extraterrestrial material Walter's father had taken from an alleged wrecked space ship? Of course they did! Laura and JJ felt the mood shift and glanced at each other: Nick must be talking about the shiny stuff Walter's father had gotten in New Mexico, right? They waited tensely for the reply.

"I don't remember the exact numbers," Nick was saying, "but I do remember that I kept getting strange results from the conductivity tests, and some of them were close to the number up there on the board. One time I would get good conductivity readings and then poor ones. At the time, I chalked it up to an equipment malfunction. I'd done all the other tests I could think of and hadn't really learned anything interesting. Then something else came up—probably business, knowing me—and I never got back to check it again."

"It's a long shot," Carl jumped in, "but that hasn't stopped us before. I recommend you revisit those tests."

Everyone was nodding vigorously: it was difficult to maintain a scientific objectivity in the face of possible extraterrestrial material.

"I'll do them tomorrow—as soon as I can," said Nick. There was an unmistakable tone of urgency in his voice.

87. OUTSIDE IN THE SHADOWS

In the unmarked FBI car parked outside, the agents were developing their own plan of action. The goal was to identify everyone who had entered the building. They already knew L and Laura, so the agents were free to spend this evening identifying the remaining attendees. Since they did not know how many people were already inside, they did not know how many were involved in total.

The Bureau-issued car had an infrared camera as standard equipment. With it, the agents would capture every face as the participants emerged from the building, and identify them later. No flash was required with infrared, so the attendees would be unaware that their pictures had been taken. Newport didn't expect any immediate results from the pictures because none of the participants seemed to him like the type who would have a mug shot on file with the police. However, the department of motor vehicles would hand over driver's license pictures to the FBI with no questions asked. With today's face recognition software, identification could be done in a matter of days.

In case anyone had traveled by car, the agents gathered the plate numbers from cars in the vicinity. Finally, they planned to tail anyone who walked away from the building. They would only be able to follow up to two walkers, though, while the remaining agent stayed behind to take pictures.

Carl was the first member to leave. He walked down Ravenswood toward Lawrence, and Bererra followed him. Once on Lawrence, Carl boarded a westbound bus; so did Jose. About a mile into the ride, Carl exited the bus, walked about two blocks north and got into a car.

"Bingo," Bererra said and copied down the license. "One down."

He radioed Newport with the news.

"That was quick," said a surprised Newport. "Now get on a bus and get back here in case you're needed."

The plan seemed to be working quite well so far, which was a change compared to Newport's other recent efforts.

Walter was next out the door; he walked, too. Newport told Nowak to follow him. After a series of bus and train rides, they ended up at Walter's apartment, which was located above his store.

Laura and L were next, and Newport watched them leave—he knew where to find them. JJ came out next, but without another agent to put on his tail, Newport had to settle for his picture. In a few more minutes, agent Bererra returned. He was just in time to follow Megan. He maintained a safe interval, watching as she took a combination of buses to reach her dwelling, an apartment off McCormick south of Oakton Ave.

When Leroy and Nick came out, Nick locked the door behind them, so Newport figured they were the last to leave. Nick got in his car, and Leroy kept walking. Newport snapped their pictures, He had already recorded Nick's license plate, so he proceeded to follow Leroy on foot. What Newport did not know was that Leroy liked to walk. He walked all the way home.

While Agent Newport was pleased to have made some progress that evening, he was irritated when he realized he would have to walk most of the way back to his car. His feet and legs already hurt, and his car was at least two miles away. Leroy lived in a residential area, so there was no bus. Newport could not get a response on his radio from either rookie; they were following people themselves and had to maintain radio silence. No ride for him. He trudged back to his car, cursing the whole way.

88. LOOKING AT THE DATA

The following day, the three agents looked over the results of the previous night's pictures and data.

"I can't believe this!" Newport ranted. "An actor-composer-retired broadcast engineer-physicist; a retired physics teacher; a stupid kid; a lady science teacher; a curator from a museum; a biologist; and a guy running a metals company! And no rap sheets on any of them? What are these clowns up to? Why do they play all the games with how they come and go? Are they just a bunch of wackos?"

He flopped back in his chair, glaring at the flimsy pile of "evidence" on his desk. The only branch of government that had ever heard of any of these people seemed to be the Bureau of Motor Vehicles.

"They must have something to do with those big network events, but what?" Newport moaned, rubbing a hand over his face.

For half a day, the agents batted around ideas, but they couldn't come up with a single plausible explanation for what brought the disparate group of law-abiding citizens together. And there appeared to be no connection to the big network problem, either. Worst of all, they had no grounds to get warrants for a raid or property seizure.

Then Newport's expression changed abruptly, and he blurted out,

"SLEEPERS! This must be a bunch of sleepers. You would use the least suspicious people to do the most dastardly crime, but what? Somehow we have to get inside to see what is going on."

Nowak and Bererra were amazed by the enthusiasm shown by Newport as they exchanged wide-eyed and raised eyebrow expressions. They could almost hear the wheels turning in his head.

"Nowak, did you find out who owns that building?" asked Newport urgently.

Nowak leafed down through a stack of paper.

"Yes," he answered. "It's owned by Great Lakes Properties in Sheboygan."

"Wisconsin?" asked Newport.

Nowak nodded, thinking *duh*.

"Do you know who the principles are?" asked Newport.

Nowak did not.

"Get on it!" Dolan commanded, but Nowak was already halfway down the hall.

He returned in twenty minutes.

"I have it," Nowak reported, reading from a printout. "Wilamina and Marcy Baumgartner are listed as the owners. They're the widows of two brothers who bought the property in 1988. It's managed by Vogel Property Management, in Sheboygan."

Newport studied his "suspect list": Nicholas Worthington, originally from Columbus, Ohio; metallurgist; graduate of Ohio State.

"You know, I'm willing to bet that Worthington is pretty isolated from the building's owners," he said. "Nowak, find out who owns and runs that Vogel Company."

This time, Nowak was back in ten minutes.

"Richard Fletcher is the owner; according to this, he's originally from around Tomahawk, Wisconsin."

Newport was entertaining a thought, which revolved around Worthington and Fletcher being unknown to each other. He wanted to be sure that neither the owners nor their management company were related to Worthington. Newport was betting that Nick and the owners were not connected, other than through the lease for his business space.

"You guys are going back into the smoke-detector business," a cocky Dolan Newport announced. "Get your facial hair and glasses out and dust them off."

The agents groaned inwardly. It was time for disguises. Nowak did not wear glasses, so he had a clear set to wear, along with a goatee. Bererra normally wore glasses, so he used contacts and pasted on some out-of-date lamb-chop sideburns.

"Don't shave, either. I want those margins around your fake stuff to look real," barked Newport.

Their disguises, along with hats and uniforms adorned with fictitious company names and logos, would keep anyone from recognizing them. Only Laura and L were familiar with their

417

faces, anyway, and the agents planned to visit Nick's company during the school day.

89. DING DONG SMOKE DETECTORS ARE HERE

Bererra and Nowak entered the reception area at Nick's factory. During the day, Nick kept the outside door unlocked for any unanticipated visitors. However, the door to the rest of the facility remained locked. A sign on the counter instructed visitors to ring the bell for service.

Nick appeared shortly and was greeted by the pair of faux installers. Bererra spoke using a slight Hispanic accent.

"I'm Jose from Ace Alarm Company. We have a contract with..." he lifted a page on his clipboard to read, "Vogel Management Company."

Jose paused a moment to watch Nick's expression. He searched his face for clues that he was suspicious of the agents. Nick's expression remained open and polite, so Bererra continued.

"We have a contract to install new smoke detectors in the building," he explained.

"I haven't heard anything about this," Nick replied mildly.

"Well, we have a contract to do a whole bunch of these for Vogel Management; they may have slipped up in notifying you. It's no big deal. We will be in and out in less than an hour," said Bererra, struggling to sound disinterested.

"But we already have smoke detectors. What's wrong with them?" questioned Nick.

"I don't know. I just do what I'm told. I guess it has to do with new OSHA standards and better detectors."

"If this is a bad time, we could come back later?" offered agent Nowak without thinking.

Bererra shot Nowak a scowl that Nick just missed seeing.

Damn, Bererra thought, *Newport would have taken Nowak's head off for that.*

Nick was silent for a moment.

"Are you sure this won't take much time?" he asked. "I have a client coming in an hour and a half."

"No problem, we'll be out of here in a jiffy," responded Jose. Nick nodded a hesitant approval.

Stan and Jose went to their truck to retrieve boxes of smoke detectors and ladders. They installed units in Nick's office, the conference room, a break room, the manufacturing floor and every hallway. They put in a total of eight detectors. Jose was right, it did not take the duo long to do the job. Nick watched their progress, but not too closely.

The manufacturing area had several new detectors and the other areas of the office would just have one. At one point during the installation, the building power went off for a couple of minutes. Nick happened to be watching one of the installers at the time, and the interruption didn't seem to bother him. The other guy must have been out at the truck getting materials for the installation.

When they had finished, Jose asked Nick to sign off on the job, showing that the work was done. At first, Nick resisted on the grounds that he had not asked for the new devices; but the signature box clearly stated that a signature only confirmed that the work was done. And so he signed, asked for a copy, received a copy and watched as the installers drove away. The whole process had taken about an hour.

Thirty minutes after the installers left, Leroy arrived, right on time. Nick was watching the street from his office. When he saw Leroy's car approach, he picked up a box and carried it downstairs and out to Leroy's car. He got to the car just as Leroy was opening the door.

"What's this, a gift?" Leroy asked, as Nick put the box in his back seat.

"Just pretend it's something you were expecting," said Nick.

Leroy, being an amateur actor, picked up on the situation instantly. Anyone watching these two from afar would have sworn they were telling each other jokes. The two men's hand gestures and body movements did not match the real tenor of their conversation. Nick told Leroy about the visit from the "installers." He asked Leroy to scope out the units without letting on that he had any knowledge of their existence.

The two men entered the building and talked at great length about the Cubs, White Sox, Leroy's last production and some mundane project Nick was doing in manufacturing. The conversation took them all around the building, even to the break room, where they bought peanuts from a vending machine. They aligned their conversation to each room they visited—they appeared to be friendly business associates, taking a casual, rather aimless tour of the premises. They concluded their meeting in less than forty-five minutes, and Leroy suggested that they grab lunch. They left in Leroy's car.

Leo and Catherine's Club 13 was one of the Society's old haunts; Leroy and Carl knew most of the other regulars, so they felt like they could talk safely there.

"What made you suspicious of these guys?" inquired Leroy as they slid into a booth.

"Well," Nick began, "for one thing, that cheapskate Richard, the management company owner, would never spring for those detectors. He'd scream all the way to the courtroom. He's kind of a conspiracy theorist—thinks the whole thing, like radon mitigation, is a hoax. He'd argue that the original units were fine and doing their job. And I know he would have called me to see if I had any information to support that position."

Leroy laughed. Nick had often regaled the group with stories of his slightly crazy brother-in-law, Richard Fletcher. When the humor wore off, though, Leroy spoke soberly.

"I believe you're on to something, Nick. For one thing, those new units are powered by transformers that are plugged into regular outlets. Most commercial code requires that a powered unit has to be hard-wired. Anyone can unplug one of your new units, and when that happens, you've got no smoke detectors. Say what you will about OSHA, but they don't let something that obvious slide. Also, I couldn't get close enough, but they looked pretty cheap. The plastic has that yellowed look that old plastic gets with time. I'm pretty sure those smoke detectors have been used before. Did you get any paperwork from them?"

Nick produced the copy he had signed, and both men looked over the document. Nick took out his iPhone and brought up a business phone number and address application. He typed in the phone number. According to the Internet, there was no such

422

company as Ace Alarm Company, at least not with that phone number and address. They checked the data on the paper and tried again with the same result.

"Do you have Google map application?" asked Leroy.

Nick opened it and entered the address. Google's stickpin pointed to a building in a complex belonging to The Chicago Sanitary District. To verify, they tried again and got the same result.

"Something else here smells fishy," Nick said, "and it isn't just the Sanitary Canal."

Both men were familiar with the location and knew that it could not possibly house the offices of Ace Alarm.

"I have an idea," said Leroy. "These may be cameras, microphones or both."

"All you see is the power connection. How would they be getting the pictures and sound?" asked Nick.

"These days, quite a few options exist. Judging from the physical appearance of the units, they're doing it on the cheap. You say all of them are connected to a standard AC outlet? No battery-run units?"

"All have power cords with the little transformers at the plugs," responded Nick.

"One possibility that would be both cheap and easy (as long as you don't have to go very far with the signal) is power-line transmission. That's when the signal is fed over the power connection, and a device nearby picks it up. Did they install any other boxes anywhere?" asked Leroy.

"Not that I'm aware of" responded Nick.

"I think we could figure it out fairly easily. I have some network sniffing software on my laptop. I can test your building power to see if any such carriers are present. They might be trying to piggyback on your building Wi-Fi or your phone system, but I doubt that—it would be more invasive and easy for you to detect. If we're lucky and do find a signal, I have some network protocol software that will determine the type of data being transmitted. Let's go back after lunch, and I'll give it a try. We can swing by my place to pick up a few tools." Nick agreed.

"If someone is monitoring the building, will they be tipped off by your testing?" Nick asked as they headed to the car.

"Not a chance. My software acts only as an observer; no interaction is required," Leroy said with a grin.

Once in the building, Leroy took his laptop to the conference room while Nick went into his office.

"Hey Nick," Leroy yelled down the hall, "ya mind if I plug into your network? I need to see if some important e-mails have come in."

"Help yourself," Nick called back. "You know where to find it."

"Thanks," said Leroy.

He plugged his power adapter into the wall outlet and his network cable into the building LAN. He positioned the laptop at an angle so that if a camera was in the smoke detector, it could not see his screen. The check of Nick's LAN/WiFi combo network was quick. If other devices were using the network's wireless Internet or plugged in directly, his scan of connected devices would reveal them. Only three devices showed up: Nick's computer in his office, Leroy's, and the building router.

Leroy next brought up the software for the scan of the power system. Bingo. This time, he was able to identify nine devices. That would be the eight smoke detectors and probably one receiver somewhere. They could look for the ninth device later. Right now, Leroy wanted to know what kind of information was being transmitted.

Once again, due to the wonders of software, Leroy identified the data packets that were being used. It was a protocol used to carry digitized audio and video over power-line applications. There were several such protocols, but this was one of the cheapest and easiest to implement. It was also low quality. The picture the agents would see could not be very good, and the audio would only be passable. To avoid further degradation, the receiver (the ninth device) would have to be relatively close.

Leroy closed his laptop and invited Nick to take a little stroll. The two men walked around the building, pointing at peeling paint, broken trim and various other features of the structure, all the while discussing, as a ruse, the repairs it needed. Near the power meter for the building, they noticed a rather new-looking metal box. It was so close to the meter that upon further inspection, they saw that it was actually attached to the power meter's mounting ring. Unlike the meter itself and the nearby housings, the ring and box were free of dust, dirt or bird crud. Nice and shiny and new looking.

"Nick, has your power gone off recently?" asked Leroy.

"Now that you mention it," Nick replied, "it did for a couple of minutes while they were installing the equipment. I could see only one of the installers at the time."

Leroy pointed to the bottom of the meter.

"See right here?" he asked. "See that little protrusion of glass with the hole in it? There's supposed to be a wire looping through it to the meter base. If someone tampers with a power meter, they have to break that wire; and the power company will know someone has been messing around…"

He squinted at the area surrounding the meter, then crouched on the ground.

"There it is," he said. "Down there on the ground. See that little piece of wire? This meter has been pulled off its base, and they attached this adapter ring with the box. Then they put the meter back on this new assembly but didn't put back the anti-tamper wire. I'll bet if we look inside, we'll see the box of electronics they're using to pick the data off the power line and retransmit it to a cellular network."

The men got into Leroy's car and drove to a park a few blocks away to talk in private.

"We could do more investigation about where the signals are going and to whom," Leroy said. "But that might tip off whoever is doing this. If we're careful, we may be able to get them to slip up. They already kind of blew it by not faking a new wire seal on the electric meter, and with those old yellowing plastic housings.

"I mean, this is amateur," Leroy scoffed.

"Well, that's why we have our Plan B," said Nick. "Maybe it's time to put Plan B into action?"

"I think you're right. Let's get hold of Carl, Megan and Dieter, since they've done this sort of thing before, and get their input," said Leroy.

As they walked, Nick remembered a topic he wanted to bring up with Leroy.

"Hey, by the way, I took another look at the electrical properties of the shiny stuff."

"Nick!" Leroy exclaimed. "You're waiting until now to tell me this?"

"Yeah, sorry about that," Nick answered sharply. "Something about planting bugs in my office distracted me."

Sheepishly, Leroy patted his friend on the back. That someone had invaded Nick's privacy that very morning, Leroy could probably forgive him for addressing that problem first.

"Anyway," Nick continued, easily mollified, "the outside conducts like copper, and the inside has a high resistivity. In fact, the inside resistivity is about the same as the egg. My meter was fine all the time. I just didn't recognize that I had something completely different between the inner and outer surfaces. How about that!"

"That's amazing!" Leroy exclaimed. "That is phenomenal! That is too weird to be a coincidence! I'm going to have trouble sleeping, thinking about the ramifications."

Leroy continued to express elation as the two men headed back to the car. The grim caution of the morning had given way to an extraordinary sense of possibility, and both men were glad of it.

90. PLAN B IMPLEMENTATION

Nick arranged the next Society meeting at a restaurant they hadn't visited for a while. As he made the calls informing everyone of the meeting, there was no hint of what he and Leroy had discovered. Anyone overhearing the phone calls would have thought they were just arranging a gastronomic treat for their palates.

The restaurant was a funky place called 'How Weird.' It was located on Howard St., and the play-on-words was the owner's idea. While most people thought it was just a bad pun, it had been operating since its start in the 1970s, so maybe the name hadn't hurt.

Over dinner, Nick summarized for the group what he and Leroy had discovered and the events surrounding the smoke detector installation. So as not to be overheard, he spoke in a soft voice; and every few sentences, he would raise his index finger slightly and the group would laugh. The higher he raised his finger, the louder the laughter. It gave the impression of someone telling a joke that wasn't quite fit for public consumption. Everyone who spoke followed the same procedure to hide the true nature of the subject. After a long and hilarious-sounding meal, everyone's assignments were established. Plan B was officially in effect.

91. THE NEXT MEETING

The agents were ready. They had video and audio streaming back to their office. They had a technician monitoring the incoming pictures and sound. There were eight camera and microphone units, but the antiquated system could only record four at a time, so the technician had to switch between units to capture the action. Newport would use his cell phone to tell the technician which video was to be recorded.

He could have obtained a more up-to-date system that recorded more than four units at a time and had much better video and sound quality, but Newport knew this would require a requisition to borrow the equipment from another office. That would require a reason—a legal, official reason—and approval of his boss. He had none.

No, Newport did not have a solid case for this surveillance; this was sort of a rogue mission. He hadn't followed the department rules, which required him to obtain legal authority for his actions. But he barreled ahead, convinced that the twenty-one-year-old schoolteacher and her junior-high student were plotting, with the help of a bunch of retired guys, to bring down the Internet. If Dolan Newport isn't paranoid, he's headed there fast.

Thus, the result of using what equipment they had on hand was that the data they pulled from it was very low quality. The sound was passable, but the pictures had extremely low resolution. The quality was good enough to identify people, but small details could not be seen. Also, if an object in the camera's view moved, you saw a blurry trail. Leroy Shire's assessment of the quality of pictures that the agents were going to get had been absolutely correct.

Newport had a video/audio receiver in his car that used 3G cellular technologies. This enabled the agents in the car to see the images on a monitor connected to a cell phone. They could switch between any of the four views that the technician had selected. This was good technology, but the quality of what would be seen and heard would still be compromised by the old surveillance system.

The agents assumed that if a meeting were going to be held at Nick Worthington's factory, Nick would have to arrive first to open up. Thus, from the early afternoon, Nowak was stationed outside Nick's house. In the event that Nick didn't go home between the work day and the evening's meeting, Bererra would take up a position at Walter's place. If Walter went out, Bererra would alert the others. Newport planned to hang around nearby, but left the real surveillance work to the rookies.

For the Fine Society's next meeting, Nick did stay at the office to prepare things. Although the group had decided not to tamper with the cameras, they needed a place to stage some of their own equipment where they would not be observed. Nick's office would be ideal, but the agents had placed a camera there, too. It was located about seven feet up the wall, near the corner behind his desk. As luck would have it, Nick kept an American flag on a stand beside his desk. The flagpole was about seven-feet tall.

In the late afternoon before the next meeting, Nick pretended to be cleaning his office; dusting; sweeping; and tidying up. As he swept, he moved objects to make it easier to get to the dust bunnies. He moved the flag several feet away from its location and swept there. He then returned the flag to its original position. Only, who could blame him for forgetting what, exactly, that original position was? So what if the flag was now a few inches to the left? Uncle Sam wouldn't care. Would he?

431

The brass eagle on the top of the flag-stand now mostly blocked the FBI's view of Nick's office. The agents couldn't see the doorway, nor could they see Nick's desk or the table along the opposite wall. Their view of Nick's office was now limited to a glimpse of the windowsill, while the rest of the camera frame was dominated by the eagle's posterior, which was displayed quite clearly and prominently. When the technician reported the sequence of events, the agents chalked it up to bad luck.

"We'll still be able to hear them in that room," Newport said confidently.

Bererra watched as a car pulled up in front of Walter's place. The driver looked like Carl Niles. The man went in and emerged with Walter about five minutes later. They loaded a large and somewhat heavy box into the trunk of the car, and placed a few smaller boxes in the back seat. Bererra could tell the boxes were heavy by the way the men moved as they carried them. Stein and Niles climbed into the car and it headed north. As Jose followed, he advised Newport, who was having coffee near Nick's place. In a few minutes, Bererra called Newport again.

"From the route they're taking, I'm guessing they're headed to Worthington's factory," Bererra reported.

"Your hunch is right," responded Newport. "I just saw Megan Reed and Leroy Shire go by. They had boxes, too."

Within twenty minutes, all the members had arrived at Worthington's office, each carrying nondescript packages of varying sizes.

By now, all three agents had gathered in Newport's car. They were watching and listening intently for clues to the group's activities. With all the people and boxes being moved about, the camera images were difficult to make out. Only when there was a pause in motion could images clearly be seen. Voices, too, were difficult to understand. With several conversations going on simultaneously, whole sentences were garbled and lost to the agents. They could clearly identify only occasional individual words.

Most of the activity was taking place in and between Nick's office and the conference room. Of course, the agents could only guess about what was happening in Nick's office—the combination of eagle butt and bad audio left that room shrouded in almost complete mystery. Additionally, the group members were moving all around the building, so the technician was challenged to keep an eye on everything. He was getting frustrated with Newport's constant commands.

"Switch to factory floor," Newport barked constantly, "now the hallway—the conference room! CONFERENCE ROOM NOW!"

After about an hour of chaos that had frayed their every nerve, the agents heard Leroy speaking in a loud voice.

"We are about ready to start the reaction," he called. "Everyone to the conference room."

A few minutes later, all the members had gathered in the conference room. Most of them stood around the large table. Conversations were minimal and low until Leroy began speaking in a serious voice.

"Lower the lights so we can better see the action," he said somberly.

The lights went out. The agents were left with nothing but grainy snow on the screen in the car. The room was silent. Newport turned up the volume.

"Walter," Leroy continued, "slowly bring up the primary power on the lens."

They agents heard a low humming sound; it increased in intensity until Newport had to lower the volume on the monitor in the car.

Leroy then gave a series of commands in a most serious, almost menacing voice.

"Turn on laser one."

A red spot about the size of a soccer ball was cast down onto the center of the conference table. It was the only thing the agents could see on their screen. It looked ominous.

"Turn on laser two," Leroy commanded flatly.

A blue laser aimed from a different direction cast a spot of the same size on the table, overlapping the red light. The agents stared, transfixed. Newport's heart was beating faster.

"Turn on laser three," said Leroy.

A green laser was activated. There was a long pause. Realizing he was holding his breath, Newport sucked in air just before Leroy spoke again.

"Ready with the ring."

This time, there was an audible reply from a voice they didn't recognize.

"Ready, my director."

"Place the ring," responded Leroy, still in a most serious tone.

The agents watched as a pair of laboratory tongs appeared in the colored light cast by the lasers. The tongs held a metallic ring in their grasp. The ring slowly moved until it was positioned in the center of the laser lights.

"Increase the lens secondary power slowly to its threshold," said Leroy ominously.

The ring lurched slightly and Leroy ordered, "That's it. Hold at that level."

The tongs opened and slowly retracted out of view.

The agents watched, awe-struck, as the ring stayed where the tongs had left it, hovering six inches above the table.

"Increase the lens one portion," Leroy again, his voice as cold and steady as ever.

The agents saw nothing and no one touch it, but the ring rose two more inches from the tabletop and continued to hover there.

"Increase the lens one hundred portions."

Almost instantaneously, the ring shot up and out of view of the camera.

Newport actually heard Bererra gulp.

In the conference room, the members began to speak to each other in hushed, excited voices. The agents could not tell what was being said, but it definitely sounded sinister to them.

"You have done your work well," Leroy continued. "The test went as planned. We are now ready to execute the plan. I will arrange for Dieter to be here Friday."

He paused until the room was completely silent.

"After Friday," he announced, "the world will know of a different egg."

Leroy followed that pronouncement with the most diabolical laugh he could muster. The laugh sent a chill down the spines of the three FBI agents in the car. They still had no idea what was going down on Friday, but it did not look good.

"The world? Dieter? Egg? The world will know a different egg?" Newport sputtered. "Is Dieter a person?"

Chaotic activity once again took over in the building; the participants appeared to be packing up the stuff they had brought. In a reversal of the earlier action, everyone left with what they brought and returned to their homes.

Meanwhile, the agents were dumbfounded. What had they witnessed? What were these folks going to do? What was this no-criminal-record-holding hodgepodge of seemingly ordinary people going to do on Friday?

"This has to be the most deceptive sleeper cell ever concocted," Newport muttered. "No traces of other wrongdoing; all their records are pristine. And the mix of ages and types—that's

436

never been done before. This has to be part of a much larger plot."

Stan and Jose listened to Dolan ramble and wondered if he was losing it. Or was he right, and they had something much bigger on their hands?

92. BACK AT THE BUREAU

Friday was going to be **The Big Day**, and Newport wanted the division boss there to witness the proceedings. He wanted the big boss to be there when Dolan Newport delivered the culprits that had the TSA, the FBI and a dozen other governmental agencies chasing their tails for the last several months.

However, since Newport still didn't know exactly what the little group of misfits was up to, he decided it was best to wait until the last minute to get his boss involved. If he told him too soon, his boss would have a lot of questions for which Newport did not have good answers. Questions like, "What were these law-abiding citizens planning to do?" and "Who authorized the smoke detector surveillance?" Newport also planned to include the Chicago police, but again only at the last minute. He reasoned that it was easier to beg forgiveness after the fact (when he had triumphantly conquered a terrorist cell) than to get permission beforehand.

93. FRIDAY, THE BIG DAY

Like the session two days before, the members hauled in box after box. After Carl and Walter had brought in their heavy box, they both returned to the car for the smaller things. On the way back in, just as Walter took his last step up the stairs to the second floor hallway, he tripped.

The sack he was carrying flew up in the air and its contents fell to the floor. One item, an egg carton, hit with such force that the carton broke apart and the eggs came tumbling out onto the floor. Walter was fine; no damage was done. Once he was back on his feet, he gathered up the eggs and continued on his mission.

"Hey, Stan," called out the video technician. "Is Newport around? I just saw something he might be interested in."

Nowak came in to the technician's little cubby back at the regional office.

"He's not here right now. What did you see?"

The technician replayed the video from the hallway camera.

"Look at that spill job," the technician narrated. "He really took a tumble...now look at the stuff in the sack. That bag must have gone up six feet in the air. Watch... here... Now, see that egg carton? Watch it hit and the eggs fall out."

He re-played the egg-carton scene twice while Nowak scrutinized the monitor.

"Not one broken egg," the technician observed.

"Probably hard boiled for their snacks," said Nowak dismissively.

When Newport returned, the tech shared the incident with him as well. But Newport waved it off; he was busy making arrangements for his giant sting operation.

As before, there was much commotion as boxes were unloaded and equipment set up. Having arrived near Worthington's office, Dolan watched the monitor in his car, which was parked a block away and around the corner. Based on the last session, he estimated he had an hour and a half before the show began.

Newport placed two calls. The first was to his boss, CD Marion, the Midwestern Regional Director of the FBI. The second call was to local police, advising them of the pending action. His boss and the police both questioned why he had waited until now, but Newport put them off by promising that he would explain later.

Marion and the police backup arrived within the hour and gathered around Newport's car. He immediately directed their attention to the video monitor and began explaining the images. Not wanting to give them the opportunity to ask questions, he painstakingly described every detail. Based on what he had seen a few days before, Newport interpreted the blurry images for the newcomers. Assuming that this session would be the same as the last one, he planned to provide the appropriate narration just in advance of each step. He knew this dramatic tactic would make a good impression on his boss.

"Once they are ready, all the moving about will stop and the images will be clearer," Newport explained. "Next, they'll stop talking and the lights will dim."

That sequence of events began a few minutes later. All the agents, the police and his boss were crammed around the car, eyes fixed on the screen. Marion grumbled that the pictures were lousy and he really would like to know more about why they were doing this.

"I don't remember seeing any paperwork on this sting, Newport," said Marion in a skeptical tone.

Newport figured he'd be asked that and was ready, "You were on vacation two weeks ago when it came up, and the Kansas City director approved it. You know how slow the paperwork is."

CD Marion was not put off and insisted, "Who are these people? What are they planning?"

"No time now, but they are somehow going to sabotage the Internet," insisted Newport as he went back to describing the impending events, his eyes never leaving the screen. "First, you'll hear a humming sound that keeps getting louder. I may have to adjust the volume if it gets too loud. They refer to it as a 'lens.' We'll hear someone giving commands. Next, three high powered lasers will be turned on one at a time."

"Lasers?" one of the police officers muttered. This was the weirdest FBI investigation he'd ever heard of.

Then the lasers came on, in the exact sequence Newport had predicted. Next, he described the tongs holding the ring in the lights, and the subsequent hovering of the ring.

When a whitish, egg-shaped object appeared instead of a ring, and was placed in the confluence of the laser light, Nowak flinched.

"Hey, that's different," he exclaimed. "That looks like one of those unbreakable eg—"

Newport cut him off with a chopping hand gesture. The last thing he needed was the rookie calling attention to the fact that Newport's description was inaccurate. His narrative dwindled to silence as he tried to make sense of the new images. He was no longer sure what was coming next. Meanwhile, the authoritative voice continued issuing commands inside the conference room.

"Increase the lens secondary power slowly to its threshold," it said.

The tongs were withdrawn; now the egg hovered unassisted about eight inches above the table.

"Okay," Newport stated, sounding slightly relieved. "We saw that before, except with a ring. Next they increase the lens and it will hover a little higher. Then it will fly up suddenly."

But the egg had different plans.

As the huddled men squinted at the screen in Newport's car, the egg began to transform. Small patches of color appeared to radiate from the egg and move about randomly. The irregular spots turned to vibrant bands of color that darted quickly over the egg's surface, changing direction and orientation quickly. It was like a light show, with the egg as the source of the colored, dancing beams of light.

Newport had fallen silent; he did not know what to make of this change of events. The patterns of light moved more and more rapidly, changing back and forth between spots and bands. The intensity grew until it became difficult to look at. The brilliantly flashing egg began to rise, slowly at first and then rapidly upward. Then there was the sound of an explosion. Suddenly, the screen in the car turned red. The color was so intense that it lit up the car's interior like it was on fire. Nothing else from the conference room was discernible through the blinding red light. Then a strong voice, speaking with a heavy foreign accent, spoke above the din of the explosion.

"The Internet will never be the same again," the voice proclaimed.

The screen in Newport's car went dark. There was silence. The observers' reactions varied from bemused to alarmed. Then they heard the tech's excited voice scratching out from Bererra's radio.

"Hey!" he cried. "We've lost everything. I've tried all eight cameras and NOTHING!"

To Newport, the crescendo of flashing lights, the red screen, the ominous pronouncement followed by profound silence, and the loss of his video and audio, could only mean one thing: a disaster had just taken place. A suspicion that had been growing in the back of his consciousness now leaped fully formed into Newport's (slightly addled) mind. These people were in league with some evil foreign government to compromise the Internet, or worse, completely take it down. Not knowing what exactly had just happened and convinced by Newport's implications that he knew something they didn't, the law enforcement group followed the FBI agent's lead. They felt something big had happened—the floating, exploding egg was unlike anything they'd ever seen in real life. It was enough hype to get them to abandon good sense and listen to Newport.

"We'll sort it out later," yelled Newport. "We're going in!"

In less than a minute, all were entering Nick's factory, with Newport leading the charge.

The society members were chatting among themselves as the agents came into the building, and did not appear to hear them approach. The agents quickly gathered in the hall outside the conference room. They could hear the muffled conversations from within. Newport motioned for Jose to kick down the door. A more pragmatic Jose gave Newport a disbelieving glance and simply turned the knob and opened the door. The agents streamed in.

"FBI! DON'T MOVE!

The view as seen by the agents looked more like a cocktail party. The society members were gathered around in groups having polite conversation and eating snacks provided by Carl's wife. The room lights were on, but no lasers were operating. There were no strange humming sounds. On the conference room table was a damaged carton partially filled with eggs. Nothing seemed to be out of the ordinary.

The group, as ordered, did not move and their pleasant expressions had changed to shock and wonderment. Newport bellowed, "You're all under arrest for conspiracy!"

The fear left many faces, to be replaced by expressions of sheer incredulity. An indignant Nick spoke.

"What conspiracy? To do what?" he demanded.

It was a pretty good question, actually. Newport had not formulated a specific charge yet, because he was still not sure what they had done. He had to wing it.

"Conspiracy to do serious and irreparable damage to the Internet."

Realization seemed to dawn on many of the group members' faces.

"Oh!" cried Carl. "I get it—Leroy, was this you?"

The group was relaxing, taking Carl's lead and assuming they were Leroy's theatre cronies here to play a joke, much to Newport's chagrin.

"It wasn't me," Leroy announced, "but I wish it was! JJ? Did you set this up?"

They thought it was a prank! Newport was incensed.

"This is not a joke! We are the Federal Bureau of Investigation and you are all under arrest."

"That's absurd!" yelled Dieter.

"You guys must be in the wrong place," commented Leroy.

More laughter ensued.

"You just did it, we saw it and it is all recorded" stated Newport.

"What do you mean, 'you saw it and recorded it'?" demanded Leroy.

Dolan knew it would no longer matter how they knew; the evidence was "in the can" back at headquarters. He decided it was safe to reveal his source.

"See that smoke detector?" he asked, pointing to the unit his agents had installed. "That's a camera and microphone. All the detectors we installed are the same. We have been watching you," he said in a menacing voice.

If he had been expecting to shock them, he was disappointed. Some members glanced idly at the smoke detector, but no one expressed much surprise.

"You said we just 'did it,'" Carl demanded, changing the subject rather abruptly. "What exactly did we <u>do</u>?"

"You took down the Internet!" Newport exploded. "We were using the Internet to watch you from our car and whatever you did, it went down. Our technician at headquarters confirmed it."

The Chicago police officers exchanged dubious looks that strongly resembled rolling eyes. Leroy stifled a laugh, but a smirk slipped through.

"What's so funny MISTER?" Newport demanded, catching Leroy's expression. "It won't be very funny after the Feds get through with you. They have been looking for you for a long time!"

"For what?" demanded Leroy, his eyebrows shooting up.

But Newport did not answer. He had just opened his mouth to issue the order to start handcuffing when Carl spoke up.

"You have made a terrible mistake."

"Oh, really?" came the condescending reply from Dolan Newport.

"We are making a movie. That's all," Carl said. "An amateur movie."

"Yeah, sure," Newport replied sarcastically. "What about 'the Internet will never be the same again'? That's exactly what somebody said right before it went off."

"You did not hear my entire line," Dieter replied. "I said, 'The Internet will never be the same again after the kids see our YouTube production of <u>Humpty Dumpty in Outer Space</u>."

He waited a beat, looking around expectantly at the law-enforcement group. Dieter pretended to mistake their astonishment for cinephiles' enthusiasm.

"Da," Dieter exclaimed. "YouTube will be jammed by kids wanting to see this updated version."

There was dead silence. It was certainly quiet enough to allow everyone to hear the stifled laughter of the Chicago Police officers. Even CD Marion raised an eyebrow. The two rookies looked at each other, thoroughly dismayed.

One of the Chicago Police officers had taken out his PDA and touched the shortcut to the department's website. There it was. The web was not down. Unlike Newport, both officers were well versed in modern communication technology. From what they'd seen in Newport's car, the officers felt sure that cellular service had linked the surveillance cameras, not the Internet. The officers started shuffling their feet. They even considered backing out of the room altogether in order to avoid any association with this botched job.

But the officers found that they couldn't look away from the gruesome train wreck that Dalton Newport was turning into right before their eyes.

"So how do you explain the flying egg that exploded?" Newport demanded. "What was that about?"

"Oh!" Carl exclaimed, as if he was glad Newport was showing interest in their project. "That is a technique that has been known for ages."

He nodded to Walter and they lifted a heavy contraption out from under the conference room table.

"It's an electromagnetic induction device used to demonstrate Lenz's Law. It is pronounced like 'lens,'" he added helpfully. "You apply an A/C voltage, and these coils produce an alternating electromagnetic field. Then you take a metal ring and place it over the center of the coil. The fluctuating electromagnetic field makes a current in the ring. The current in the ring makes its own electromagnetic field, which always is in opposition to the one from the apparatus. Thus the ring is always being pushed up. It's the same principle used in electric motors. This is an old unit Walter owns. It's nothing new. Like I said, it has been around a long time. Here, look at the label."

Carl angled the machine so that Newport could read along.

"Midwest Scientific, Chicago, Illinois, RA-67988. Oh my! See, there is no zip code, and the phone prefix of Randolph was dropped years ago. This is not new technology," he said, then added, "I'll bet you never took physics, did you?"

Newport glared at him, positively seething.

"I'll take that as a no, then," Carl said mildly, tipping his head to the side. "Let me demonstrate it for you."

Clearly enjoying the attention of the flabbergasted agents, Carl took the ring they had used in the first demonstration and placed it on the device. He gestured to Walter, who flipped a switch to turn it on. As Walter fiddled with the settings, the ring began to hover like it had done before.

"Yeah, I saw that in your rehearsal the other day," Newport replied. "But today you did it for real with one of those egg-things."

Newport grabbed an egg from the table, turned to Carl and demanded, "Okay, now do it again with this egg."

"Make it fly!" he commanded, placing what he thought was an unbreakable egg on the table where he had seen the other egg.

Walter operated the controls, but nothing happened.

"Just as I thought," Newport announced triumphantly. "You're still hiding something."

Carl calmly inserted himself.

"You failed to be a good observer from your smoke-detector viewpoint," he said, allowing condescension to creep into his tone. "You failed to notice this fine-wire apparatus."

Walter handed Carl a very thin wire structure. It had a heavier ring at the bottom, similar to the ring just used. That ring was attached by three thin wire supports to a wire ring at the top.

Carl took an egg from his pocket and placed it in the top ring. The egg fit perfectly.

"Now," Carl continued, "due to the fine structure of the support, your camera probably was not able to detect these wires."

He had made his point, but he could not help himself.

"Eggs by themselves cannot fly," Carl informed Agent Newport.

Unwilling to let it go, Newport grabbed the wire structure from Carl and placed in it the egg he had picked up from the table.

"Make this one fly," he demanded.

"I would not recommend that," came the stern warning from Walter.

"Okay," Newport said. "If you won't, I will."

Dolan had watched Walter manipulate the device's single control, so he figured he could do the same. He pushed Walter aside and placed the egg and wire assembly on the device.

"I don't recommend that you do that!" Walter said, more firmly this time.

Now, Newport was sure they were trying to hide something.

He grabbed the control and turned it a little. The assembly did not move. He turned it more, but still there was no motion. He tried again and again, with no result. How could they make the egg fly when he couldn't? He was more convinced than ever that they were hiding something. Feeling cocky about his conclusion, Newport gave the control one more quick turn, to its maximum.

Before he could do anything to prevent it, the egg and assembly shot toward the ceiling.

Anyone who has ever played with a Lenz Law unit knows that small variations from one trial to the next can cause the object's upward path to vary. There was no way to predict that the egg would come down a few feet away from the table and land on CD Marion's forehead.

Walter had not been kidding when he advised Newport, twice, against using that egg. Walter knew the history of these eggs. They were real, and they were old. They were very old! It was all a part of Plan B.

But Newport had insisted. And now, the expression on CD's face was simply grotesque. He had turned the deepest shade of red a person can imagine. And the smell from the rotten egg... well, the smell was overpowering.

There was a moment of utter stillness, and then Nowak and Bererra rushed, handkerchiefs extended, and desperately tried to clean the egg from his face, which was set in an expression of incoherent outrage. The police officers held their hands to their faces and breathed through their mouths. The Society members

451

cast about for something to look at that wouldn't cause them to laugh.

And Agent Dalton Newport stood stock still, his face ashen.

"Newport!" CD Marion shouted. "May I have a word with you."

It was not a question. The two men moved into the hallway, but it was hardly far enough from the conference room for anyone to avoid hearing what was said. It was so uncomfortable that Carl began introducing the various members of their group to the remaining law enforcement, in an attempt to drown out the voices from the hall. It was a valiant effort, but ultimately an ineffective one.

"WHO'S IDEA WAS THIS?" Marion was demanding. "WHO AUTHORIZED THE SURVEILLANCE CAMERAS? WHO IS RESPONSIBLE?"

"...and Leroy, who's our resident thespian..." As Carl continued his introductions.

Newport responded that he indeed had done it on his own, but under pressure to get results.

"...With Dieter's accent, he's a natural choice for the villain, I hope you don't mind me saying so, Dieter..." Carl continued.

In the hallway, Newport's boss was not buying his excuses.

"I WANT THIS FIASCO ENDED NOW! GET YOUR MEN AND ANY OF YOUR EQUIPMENT OUT OF HERE! I WILL DEAL WITH YOU LATER!"

Wanting to distance himself from the situation as quickly as possible, Marion stormed out of the building without returning to the conference room.

When Newport returned to the room, he was nervous and shaken; he tried to offer an apology of sorts and instructed the other agents to begin removing the cameras. Carl took advantage of the uncomfortable silence to needle Agent Newport, once and for all.

"Oh," Carl cried, the very picture of the harmless old gentleman, "I forgot to mention the cameraman. You may have missed him."

He pointed to JJ, who stood in the corner of the room holding a small video camera. JJ leaned out from behind the camera and with a big grin said, "Smile."

"Oh my, JJ," Carl said. "Has your camera been rolling the whole time?"

"Yes it has," replied JJ with a grin.

"Is it still rolling, JJ?"

With an even bigger grin, JJ responded.

"Yes, Carl. Yes it is."

"Keep it rolling," Carl said sharply, dropping the act.

"I definitely will," JJ agreed, his grin disappearing.

Newport was dazed and confused. How had he let himself get so deep in this mess?

The lights went out as the rookie agents were scurrying about removing the "smoke detectors," but the outage lasted less than a minute. It was over before any concern could be raised. The camera had a highlights lamp that ran all the time. The video camera kept rolling. The whole affair was being captured, just in case.

Leroy had left the room for a few minutes, unobserved in the commotion. He returned before the chaos had died down. The police officers were engaged in conversation with Laura and Megan, who were explaining their devotion to good science and describing the fun they had with activities like the movie. The cops were tech junkies themselves; they were thoroughly enjoying their conversation. The police officers left, convinced that Newport was a loose cannon.

94. THE AFTERMATH

When the boys in blue and the FBI had cleared out, the Society members collapsed in chairs in the conference room, exhausted and emotionally drained. For quite some time, no one even spoke. Then Laura asked a question.

"Where did the fancy lights projected on the egg come from?"

"You can lay that one on me," Leroy answered. "After the previous meeting, when we were baiting them, I remembered that my theatre group had recently acquired some new robotic spotlights—you see them these days in all kinds of productions. You can do images and light patterns of all sorts. I thought it would add to the presentation."

"Absolutely," said Laura. "It was fantastic. I loved it."

Then L, who had been silent throughout the whole ordeal (and for good reason) spoke.

"What did Newport mean when he said 'You just did it, I saw it'?" he asked. "Was he talking about the red laser pointed at the smoke-detector camera?"

Leroy answered once again: "Oh yes, I didn't have time to tell you about that embellishment, either. I set it up after our last meeting, and there was no way to give you a heads-up. Chalk it up to my theatrical urges, but I came up with a way to knock out their video and audio at a dramatic moment. I kind of hoped they'd mistake it for an Internet failure or worse. The bright red screen was good, but I felt it needed more."

Chuckling gleefully, Leroy went on to describe the transmitter the FBI had attached to the power meter.

"Well, I figured two can play that game," Leroy continued. "I could mess with the signals over the electric wires of the building just as well as they could."

The group appeared to be puzzled by this comment; Leroy set out to clear it up.

"I have these X-10 boxes all over my house. I'll bet many of you do, too," he said. "Well, early this morning, I slipped over here, took off the meter and installed an X-10 appliance module that I had modified. You may have noticed the microwave flashing again this morning, Nick"

"Yes I did," came Nick's amused reply.

"Well I have this little controller here..."

Leroy pointed to an unobtrusive control unit sitting on a small table at the side of the room.

"As you can see, it is plugged into the power outlet," he explained. "I can use it to turn that unit at the meter on or off. It operates by sending signals over the electrical wires. Don't you just love the irony?"

Indeed, the group loved it.

After the adulation, Nick jumped in.

"Then when the power went off just a while ago—"

"I slipped down and removed my unit before they picked up their transmitter and meter-base hardware," Leroy finished Nick's sentence. "Can't let them have our secret." Leroy reached into his pocket and held up the small X-10 unit he had just removed from the power meter. There was more laughter and congratulations.

The break served its purpose to restore some of their energy. It was clear that no further business would be dealt with that day, so the group started to gather the bits and pieces they had brought for the 'movie'. Carl, Leroy and Nick exchanged glances and nods, and Carl called for the group's attention.

"Sorry to interrupt," he said. "But we do have one last thing to do today. Laura, you're probably not aware of this, but we celebrate birthdays here in a special way."

In all the excitement, Laura had completely forgotten it was her birthday. Now she noticed that Carl had somehow managed to sneak in with a box that had not been used for their movie.

"This is a gift specially crafted for you," he said gently, handing her the box.

Laura took it, wondering eagerly what it might contain. She lost no time with speculation and began unwrapping the gift. The outer box was plain cardboard. Inside was another box wrapped beautifully in iridescent green paper. The inner box was about the size of a loaf of bread.

Inside, she found white tissue paper cradling an exquisitely detailed 1930 Model A Ford. As she took it out of the box, ever so carefully, her eyes filled with tears. It was beautiful. The detail was unbelievable. If she were small enough, she could get

457

right in and drive it away. She sat speechless, admiring the little car and then looked up at her friends.

"This is just so beautiful," she breathed. "How did you know?"

When she was a child, Laura and her father had restored an identical car from scratch. The many rides they took in the completed vehicle were among her most treasured memories.

"Carl," she said as realization dawned, "is this one of your creations?"

He nodded.

"There's more," he said quietly, reluctant to break into her reverie.

"More?" she said with wide eyes.

Carl took the model out of Laura's hands, flipped a switch on the bottom and placed it on the table. Then he produced an iPhone from his pocket. Poking at it, he brought up an application with a display that looked like a control panel. He handed the device to Laura.

Seeing the buttons labeled "Horn," and "Lights," she knew just what to do. She touched "Lights" and little headlamps and a taillight illuminated on the car. She touched "Horn" and was delighted to hear, "OOuuuuuugggaaaaa."

The place broke up. Deeply touched, Laura said, "I cannot thank you enough for this! It means so much to me. Ever since I saw the model you made for Nick, I have wanted one, and this is absolutely perfect. Thank you, Thank you, Thank you!"

She turned her gaze to JJ, who had watched her open the gift with nearly as much emotion as Laura herself had shown.

"You told them about the car," she said to her friend. "Didn't you, JJ?"

Of course he had. She thanked him quietly, and before she turned into a blubbering mess, looked back at the control pad on the iPhone.

"You must be using Bluetooth, right?" she asked.

"Right," came Carl's response. He was watching her closely; she thought he even looked impatient, for some reason. She continued to study the display and noticed some arrows. She pushed one and the car moved forward. She laughed in delight. The opposite direction arrow backed the car up and the other two turned it left or right.

"Wow! This has full motion as well?" she asked, like a kid at Christmas.

Everyone in the room was fascinated as they watched Laura pilot the car around the conference room table. Even a realistic, audible rendition of a Model A engine came from inside the car.

"Chknpuper, chknpuper, chknpuper," the toy played.

Laura was having so much fun that she had overlooked a small word at the bottom of the screen.

"More."

When she finally noticed the button, she looked up at the group. Carl, Leroy and Nick were still watching her closely. Now, all three of them looked impatient. Did they want a turn to drive or something? She wouldn't be giving up her car so soon. Ignoring the men, she turned back to her controller and touched the "More" icon.

Another touchpad display appeared. It looked similar to the previous one, except two of the arrows were labeled "up" and "down." She looked at the car again to be sure it was not a convertible. It was not. It occurred to her that sometimes old cars were modified for parades so that the front end of the car would go up in the air and the car would spin around on its two rear wheels.

"Nah, Carl wouldn't do that to a model A," Laura thought, glancing again at the watchful faces of the three men.

She could not resist the button any longer. She pushed "Up." Everyone watching blinked, and stared. Upon her touch of the button, the model car had risen a few inches off the table. And much to her disbelieving eyes, it hovered there. The hovering was a little jerky, but it was hovering.

Laura sat frozen in her seat, staring at the car. Seated nearby, L, JJ and Megan quickly looked under the table to see if Walter's Lenz Law device was still there. It was gone! Carl and Walter had already taken it to the car. They looked up to see if any devices were above their heads. There was nothing that could possibly cause a model car to float in midair. As far as they knew, there was nothing anywhere that could cause a model car to float in midair. And yet, there it floated, albeit somewhat wobbly.

Carl, Leroy and Nick sat in their chairs, each grinning widely as they witnessed the discovery process. Laura touched "Up" again momentarily. She did it once again, and the car lurched up a little higher. Then she touched down, and the car went down.

"What is this Carl?" Her voice was now quite serious.

The others were growing quite anxious for an explanation as well.

"I'll give you the quick answer first," Nick said. "Then Leroy, Carl and I will fill in the details."

He took a deep breath, enjoying his audience's anticipation.

"There is one of Walter's eggs in there, and not one of the smelly ones," he said at last.

The announcement was greeted with subdued, nervous laughter.

"I applied some of the shiny stuff to the outside," Nick continued, "and Leroy noodled up the electronics to attach and interact with the egg. Basically, we're getting that little turntable effect we've been going on about. Leroy is using a battery, which is being used for the electronics (and the lights and sounds). But the motion you're seeing—we believe it's due to the interaction of the fine structure particles of the egg with those 'ripples' in the universe that we surmised are all around us."

The Fine Society members wore frozen expressions. They were almost unable to talk. Walter's legs were so wobbly that he almost fell when he attempted to rise from his chair to get a closer look.

"Are you sure about this explanation?" asked JJ.

"I don't have any other at this time," said Leroy calmly.

Carl and Nick backed him up.

By now, the significance of the accomplishment had taken hold of the Fine Society. They were witnessing a monumental scientific breakthrough. Some were laughing and jumping about like children, others crying with tears of joy; and always one of them had the iPhone in hand putting the Model A through its paces. Leroy, Nick and Carl quietly stood together watching the proceedings with expressions not unlike that of a new father at the window of the hospital nursery. Megan turned to them

"I knew you guys were good, but this…this is absolutely unbelievable!!"

At the end, her tone had shifted from congratulatory to a whisper as her eyes filled with tears.

On the other side of the room, Laura and L took turns putting the model A through its paces. JJ was prancing a bit like the next kid who can't wait to get his hands on the controls.

Walter and Dieter were nearby. Walter smiled nervously as he spoke and Dieter listened. Walter was happy, but his stress level was way up. Occasionally, Dieter could be heard offering him reassuring words of consolation.

The members had loads of questions for Nick, Leroy and Carl. The session could have gone all night, but to keep from arousing suspicion, they reluctantly decided to end their meeting and go home. They were emotionally spent, and each of them returned home a changed individual, having witnessed an event that no other person in the world had witnessed before.

When the members of the Fine Society finally fell asleep that night (for some that took a long time), they did so in the knowledge that they had each contributed to a scientific discovery that might very well change the world.

95. POLICE & NATIONAL SECURITY FOLKS

When government investigators could not put together a case against Devoid Williams, they decided to drop the charges against him and take a new approach. It was suggested that anyone who was smart enough to hijack the Internet was probably capable of misleading those who tried to catch him.

The FBI'S new thinking went like this: Chicago was only made to look like the destination of the final communication, but the final location was really some other place. Chicago, the new thinking established, was a red herring. Across the country, FBI agents scrambled to find leads that might point to the real origin of the security breach. But no one had notified CD Marion at the FBI's Chicago office about the new thinking. As far as Marion knew, he and his agents had to press on. That knowledge, had Newport known, would have spared him untold humiliation and scorn.

One of the Chicago police officers brought in at the last moment by agent Newport for the sting had coincidentally attended high school at Main East in Des Plaines. His physics teacher was Carl Niles. In fact, he knew the whole family. When he saw Carl in the conference room that night, he was immediately suspicious that something was terribly wrong. Carl would never get involved in a plot to do anything wrong. Nonetheless, he kept quiet to see what Newport was up to.

The Chicago police officers who attended the raid had worked with the FBI before. They were familiar with the Bureau's habit of taking credit for collective triumphs and finding scapegoats when things fell apart. From the beginning of this operation, both officers had been uneasy—Newport didn't seem to be playing with a full deck, and Marion had failed to stop the episode before it lapsed into farce.

When it was all over and Newport's boss literally had egg on his face, the officers were relieved that the likeable group members were innocent. The officers were also determined to keep the FBI from shifting the blame for the debacle onto the Chicago Police Department.

When they returned to their precinct office, they regaled their fellow officers with the detailed but unembellished story of the FBI's ill-fated Humpty Dumpty sting. The precinct rang with uncontrollable laughter as the story was told over and over. It passed from precinct to precinct, and even reached the national security team investigating the network incident. Having abandoned the possibility that the incident had anything at all to do with Chicago, they had a good laugh as well.

CD Marion was not in on the joke. The Midwestern Regional Director of the FBI did not want to report Newport's disaster to his superiors. To put it mildly, the botched raid would reflect badly on Marion as the ranking leader in that office. Still, he was required to report all activities on a regular basis.

Worse yet, since this had been an unsanctioned sting operation, he was required to call it in immediately and send the written report later.

He placed the call to his boss, Frank Gerard, at his D.C. area office. He and Gerard started with the FBI at the same time and had been competing with each other for promotions ever since. Gerard usually won. The two men barely tolerated each other.

"Mr. Gerard's office," Gerard's assistant answered promptly.

465

"It's CD. Is he in?

"I'll check," she responded.

Gerard was in a meeting that included most of the FBI people involved in the network case. When he heard it was CD, Gerard had his assistant put the call through. The speakerphone in the center of the table rang. Gerard poked the talk button.

"Is that you, CD?"

"Yes," CD paused. "Do you have me on a speakerphone?"

"That's right. What's up, CD?"

Gerard looked around the room and saw a variety of smirks and grins on the faces of the attendees. Any other time, Gerard would have picked up the handset to speak in private, but he and the rest had already heard about Newport's debacle. He couldn't deny his colleagues the opportunity to hear CD's version of events.

"I think we should speak in private," responded CD.

"It's okay, buddy. Everyone in the room has the proper clearance," Gerard responded, gazing around with a big smile.

Realizing he wasn't going to be able to force the privacy issue, CD reluctantly began his verbal report.

"Well," he began, "it's about our search for the perpetrators of the network problem."

CD stopped again, hoping the sensitive topic would convince Gerard that he should take the call in private. No such luck.

"Go ahead, I'm listening," Gerard responded in a singsong voice.

CD knew he would have trouble sugarcoating this one. Newport had done the damage with the unapproved surveillance and disastrous raid, but as director, Marion was ultimately responsible for the actions of his agents.

"Well, we have not yet had any success tracking down the source of the problem. A few days ago we thought we had a hard lead, but that turned out to be false."

"Tell us more about the HARD lead?" said Gerard.

CD thought he heard a muffled voice say something about being hard-boiled, but a sound that resembled snickering seemed to drown out the comment. He told himself he was being paranoid and continued his report.

"Agent Newport came across a group that…" CD stumbled for words, "The group was acting very suspiciously."

"What sort of ACTING were they doing?" queried Gerard.

"No, they weren't acting— well, yes they were, in a way," CD sputtered hopelessly.

"Were they acting out some sort of play?" Gerard asked.

"No," CD objected, "it wasn't a play—it was a movie."

As soon as the words were out, CD wished he could take them back.

"A movie? Since when is making a movie suspicious?" asked Gerard.

This time, CD could hear the words loud and clear from the other end of the phone line.

"WHEN YOU'RE MAKING A MOVIE ABOUT HUMPTY DUMPTY IN OUTER SPACE!" someone yelled.

The laughter erupted so loudly that CD had to hold the phone away from his ear, but he could still hear the next heckler's punch line.

"HEY CD, HOW DO YOU LIKE YOUR EGGS? HARDBOILED OR ROTTEN?"

He was thoroughly humiliated and miserable by the time the jokes and laughter subsided. He sat silently, holding the receiver to his ear as if it were a form of penance, waiting for his boss to re-take control of the call.

This time, Gerard picked up the handset and spoke—in a voice that was no longer smiling.

"I want a full report in my office by the end of the day, Marion."

And he hung up.

96. THE DAY AFTER THANKSGIVING

The society members had no way of knowing what the authorities were doing, but one thing was certain: agent Newport would be off the case. Most of them agreed that they were probably in the clear with the FBI, but they still didn't want to take any unnecessary chances.

The Fine Society took a sabbatical for a few weeks.

Near Thanksgiving, Dieter and Carl held a series of low-key meetings to arrange a gathering of the society at Dieter's place in Ladd.

It was time for the Society to decide what to do with its potentially earth-shaking new knowledge. They chose the day after Thanksgiving for their meeting so that their travels would not look unusual if they were still under surveillance. The members decided that minimizing their carbon footprint was more important than ducking a tail, so they would carpool rather than driving separately. Nick would bring Megan, Carl and Leroy. Laura would pick-up Walter, JJ and L.

The day after Thanksgiving was brisk and chilly, typical for that time of year. Remaining cautious, the drivers arranged to meet their riders at places other than their homes that morning. After collecting Walter and L at different bus stops, Laura picked up JJ at the Museum. As they headed north on Lake Shore Drive, the sun was low in the sky and was partially obscured by a mantel of cold-looking, wispy clouds. Sunlight reflected off the ground, which was covered by an overnight frost. A beautiful sight, but a reminder that winter would soon follow.

They turned west to catch the Eisenhower and I-88. Even today, the roads were busy. It took the better part of an hour passing cityscapes before traffic thinned near Sugar Grove, IL. Now they were surrounded by corn and soybean fields in various stages of harvest. Here their journey continued on the less busy secondary roads, enjoying the scenery as they trekked to Ladd, IL. It was too early for anyone to feel much like talking, and Walter tended to nod off. L, who had not been out of the city very often, absorbed the sights like a sponge, taking special interest in the farm machinery along the way. In the front seats, JJ and Laura spoke only occasionally, enjoying the scenery and the companionable silence of old friends. Near the small town of Sandwich, L broke the relative silence.

"Before we get to the meeting," he said nervously, "I have something to tell you."

Walter woke from his nap to the tension in L's voice. Everyone could tell right away that it was serious.

"Do you remember when you gave me those problems to solve and I said I needed more processing power?" L asked, directing his question to Laura.

"Yes, I remember," she said, growing more anxious as the old mystery came back to her.

"Well, I used the Internet."

"Lots of people use the Internet," she responded quickly. "I mean, of course you used the Internet, L."

She laughed nervously, glancing at his face in the rearview mirror. But he was not smiling.

"But I used <u>most</u> of the Internet," he insisted.

"What do you mean, you used most of it?" JJ inquired, a note of concern creeping into his voice. L took a deep breath—the rest of his confession came out in a rush.

"I spoofed thousands of computers into helping solve the problem. It's like what the SETI people do all the time," he said. "You know, SETI gets extra processing power from other computers, and they do it with the consent of the people who own those computers? Well, I did what they do, only I did it without permission."

The car was very quiet. Glancing at L's miserable face in the mirror, Laura felt a pang of sympathy. Then she caught a glimpse of Walter's grim face, and she felt anger—L had been utterly reckless.

"I hang out—well, I used to hang out—on the web," the boy continued, "with other gamers. They do this sort of thing all the time, just not on that large of a scale. Most of the time, they do it so they can play some on-line game. They borrow unused computer capacity from machines that aren't being used. The guys I knew never did it for malicious stuff. There are some of those out there, but I kept away from them."

"You said that you <u>used</u> *to* hang out with these gamers?" asked Laura, hoping she had understood what he meant.

"Yes, I used to," L confirmed, "but, Ms. Olson, I realized early on what you had done for me…and then, getting an invitation to be part of the Society, I couldn't jeopardize all of that. I did it several times when I got started, but the last time I used it was for the last big batch of sheets that Carl and Leroy had scanned.

By then, my equations and algorithms had been formulated. I don't need that kind of computing power any more. I can use what I have on much smaller systems."

Laura and JJ began asking L for more details, and he was more than willing to oblige. The kid felt terrible—anyone could see that. They rehashed the FBI visits and the events surrounding those episodes, only now they could see the terror L must have felt throughout that time.

"Devoid Williams!" Laura exclaimed. "What if he hadn't been in the basement watching his movies? L, where would this have gone if he hadn't been there? And the bike accident, and how it destroyed your computer..." she trailed off and peered at him in the rearview mirror.

"Your computer <u>was</u> destroyed wasn't it? L?"

He met her eyes in the reflection in the rear-view mirror and assured her that it had been destroyed. They suddenly realized that Walter had not said a word. JJ turned to look at him. He was staring blankly out the window, his face pale and drawn. Knowing how Walter had reacted to stressful situations in the past, Laura and JJ were concerned.

"Walter," JJ asked, "are you okay?"

Walter barely nodded and continued looking out the window. Laura and JJ exchanged glances, wondering what, if any, action they should take. They drove in silence for several minutes. Laura could see L staring straight ahead, looking for all the world like he wanted to jump out of the car. She didn't know what to say, and neither did JJ. Finally, Walter broke the silence.

"I've been around a long time now," Walter began in a shaken voice. "Over the years I've seen good and bad. No matter how hard we try to be good, the bad always seems to show up."

Then Walter turned toward, and put his hand on L's shoulder.

"I'm not saying that what you did, son, was bad," he said. "In fact, the work you've done with your math skills is remarkable. But it would have been tragic if this effort had been cut short that day at Larabee because of your bad judgment. How long would it have taken before conditions were right again? Days? Weeks? Years? It probably wouldn't happen in my lifetime."

Walter paused for a few minutes before resuming.

"You *are* guilty of bad judgment," he told the boy sounding more like a scolding parent, "but I don't think all the blame can be placed at your feet. You haven't had the best role models in your life. What's really remarkable is the change of heart you described."

By the time Walter had finished, his tone was almost congratulatory. He patted L's shoulder again, like a proud parent.

"It was probably a lesson well learned," he concluded. "For you, and now for all of us."

There was silence in Laura's car all the way to Ladd. Walter seemed calmer now; the color had returned to his face, and he had a more peaceful look. Laura and JJ were relieved, but still preoccupied with L's news. And L, relieved at last of his burdensome secret, slept until they pulled into Dieter's driveway.

Meanwhile, the mood in Nick's car was a reflective one.

Megan, Carl and Nick had been with their families the day before. They were thinking of mashed potatoes, pumpkin pie and children's drawings of turkeys and pilgrims. WFMT was playing excerpts from Copeland's *The Tender Land* and *Old American Songs 1 and 2*. Combined with the fall scenery, the ride to Ladd became an experience for the occupants of Nick's car, rather than just a trip. As they left Chicago, what little talk there was focused on the beautiful countryside and on the music.

Around the town of Somonauk, the radio signal began to fade badly. Nick tried the local public stations, but they were talking rather than playing music.

"It's a shame. I used to get more classical and jazz on the public stations," he said.

He rummaged around for a moment, until he remembered where his music had gone.

"Sorry," he said, "no CDs either. I forgot to put them back in after the car wash."

"That's okay," said Leroy. "We can still enjoy the sights."

"And each other," Megan chided. "You know, some people like to talk when they're in a car together."

They laughed, realizing that perhaps the long silence had not been quite so comfortable for the young woman.

"Sorry about that," Leroy chuckled. "We've known each other for so long that I guess we've run out of things to say."

"But we can think of lots of things to talk to you about, Megan," Carl said, his eyes alight. "Don't worry, we'll start with the easy stuff. How is your genetic research going these days?"

Even as a high school student, Megan had been interested in genetics. Her work was so good back then that she earned an invitation to become a member of the Fine Society when she was only sixteen years old. Since then, the human genome had been mapped and her work in that arena had skyrocketed.

"Why, thank you for asking, Carl," she said, batting her eyelashes comically. "It's actually funny that you ask, because just this week I added two more genes to my special project."

Her expertise was human behavior; she was searching for a genetic correlation for good and bad behaviors. Our environment and culture greatly influence our behavior, but Megan wanted to know if there were underlying genetic reasons that might favor a particular behavior? In the darkest recesses of her mind, Megan secretly wondered if people who became terrorists could have some gene, or lack some gene, that somehow made them more vulnerable to bad influences. She did not mention this aspect to others, nor did she dwell on it even to herself. Rather, she focused instead on the positive aspects of her work. Her quest was to find the genes that favor good, positive, life-affirming behaviors, if they existed.

"I now have consistent data on fifteen genes that are found in the good-behavior category," she told her companions.

They knew that for many years Megan had been getting DNA samples from her acquaintances. She joked that it helped her "get to know people better," which was sort of a twisted understatement. Almost all of her contacts turned out to have only the good genes, but a few turned out to have the "bad" genes. The fate of one of them still haunted her. Her current work revolved around comparing deviations and missing genes in certain subjects to the genetic makeup of the general population.

As they drove through the Illinois farmlands, Megan described the newest developments in her research. To gather additional, potentially bad DNA, she had recently begun receiving samples from anonymous donors who had been convicted of violent crimes. Her sources—correctional institutions—permitted the collection on a voluntary basis. She received the DNA samples along with information about the crimes or behavioral problems, but she knew nothing about the donors' specific identities. Her results showed the deviations she had come to expect, as well as certain missing genes. In a few cases, she had found different genes altogether.

"We don't know enough yet to be able to predict with any certainty which people will or will not be susceptible to specific influences," she concluded. "But I think you'll be happy to hear that so far, all the Society Members have the good gene markers."

Leroy, Carl and Nick acted out great relief by wiping their brows, raising their hands like they were praying to Heaven, and shouting "Halleluiah."

"Okay you guys," Megan laughed. That's enough. Thanks for letting me talk to you."

She was teasing, and the men chuckled. At their age, it was charming to be teased by such a young lady.

"How is it that a bright, attractive person like you is not married?" Leroy asked jovially.

"Whoa, Leroy, be careful there!" Carl joked.

"That's a dangerous question," added Nick.

"Yeah!" Megan cried, feigning hauteur. "Why do you care?"

"Well, I'm serious," Leroy insisted. "You'd be a great catch for an intelligent person who loves science and the fine arts."

"Well, if you must know, I've been seeing someone."

"Who?" came the collective response from the group (for by now, Carl and Nick had let their curiosity get the best of them).

"You wouldn't know him," she said flippantly. "He lives in Columbus, Ohio."

"That's pretty far away for a romance," commented Carl.

"I know, but he gets here on business pretty often, and I attend genetics seminars at OSU from time to time."

"How long have you been together, and is it serious?" asked Leroy, playing up the role of inquisitor and making Megan giggle.

"We've known each other about fifteen years," she said. "We've been…close for the last five. So far, neither of us has made any further moves."

"Well, no sense rushing into anything. What's he do? Is he a scientist?" asked Nick.

"No, he—" Megan paused, but after a moment of thought, she resumed, "He travels a lot, used to be in Public TV, worked with a clown on a TV show, plays in a couple of bands, used to be in the corporate world… but he isn't working now."

This news was greeted with silence. No one wanted to be the first to speak for fear of saying the wrong thing. His credentials did not sound like they added up to "winner" for her.

"But my mom really likes him," she added.

More silence followed.

In a desperate attempt to change the subject, Leroy excitedly said, "Hey! What about those Bears?"

This was enough to trigger a lively discussion among the three men that lasted the rest of the way to Ladd.

97. DIETER'S PLACE

Dieter lived in a bungalow at the end of a short street on the west side of Ladd, adjacent to farmland. Unlike houses in the city, the houses here had ample yards with mature trees, bushes, hedges, flowerbeds and the occasional grape arbor. Leaves covered a lot of the ground. As the members got out of their respective cars, they were greeted by the smell of burning leaves. Out here, some towns still permitted the practice.

Laura's carload was the first to arrive. L pulled Laura aside as JJ and Walter continued toward the house.

"I have one more confession."

She swallowed hard, wondering if she could take another confession today.

"Those CTA passes?" L continued. "I fixed them. They should have worked to begin with, so I only did what needed to be done."

Laura smiled, exposing gritted teeth.

"I hope this is the end," she said, shoving him playfully. "I can't take many more surprises."

"That's all. I swear," said L.

Once inside Dieter's house, guests were immediately treated to a fragrance common to a German Gasthof, that pleasant unmistakable aroma that is unique to the experience. Dieter's place had it.

The rooms were large and comfortable. Decorations were traditional American sprinkled here and there with the occasional Bavarian piece (Like the three Rothenburg scenes on one wall of the living room). The living room was furnished with two couches and two easy chairs, all of which were a dream to sit in, not too soft and not too firm, just right: a large picture window overlooked the spacious porch and beautiful autumn landscape. Dieter had installed a Black Forest green painted woodstove in the fireplace; it warmed the room without the draftiness of an open fire. The flickering of the fire silhouetted the decorative metal and glass detail of the front doors.

The nearby kitchen was warm, cozy and redolent of a bakery. Prior to their arrival, Dieter had been baking rolls. On the stove was a big pot of homemade vegetable-beef soup. Needless to say, the combined aromas in the kitchen were wonderful. In one corner of the spacious kitchen, a small wooden table sat, surrounded by chairs. All but one chair were pushed in; the remaining one was pulled out, as if it were waiting for Dieter to return. From the chair, one had a view of the entire kitchen; on the wall directly opposite the chair hung a picture. It was a portrait of a woman.

The woman's name was Uta; she was Dieter's wife. This had been her favorite room; she had spent many happy hours cooking delicious meals for herself and her beloved husband. Dieter missed her but he tried (successfully) not to be maudlin about it. Instead of weeping over her loss, he celebrated the years they had together. They had loved to entertain, so having the group to visit rekindled some of those happy memories for Dieter.

Upstairs, there were four spacious and equally homey bedrooms. The large basement also offered a finished section that functioned variously as extra guest space, den, and playroom for Dieter and Uta's grandchildren.

When the other carload arrived, Dieter took them on a tour; and Laura returned to the living room, happily absorbing more of the ambiance. Sipping a cup of hot tea, she roamed around, examining the framed pictures on the walls. A small frame near the corner caught her eye. It was not a picture, but rather an old piece of paper with writing on it. She moved closer to see it more clearly

"FEINE GESELLSCHAFT," she read: The Fine Society.

Dieter and Walter must be connected by a previous generation—perhaps their fathers were friends or even relatives. Laura resolved to ask the two men about the image when she had a chance.

With the tours finished and overnight bags stowed in their respective rooms, Dieter invited his guests to partake of soup, cheese and rolls. A few people sat in the dining area attached to the living room; those who were more confident in their ability to balance a bowl of soup in their laps settled in the living room.

"Uta taught me well," Dieter said, responding to his guests' praise for the simple but delicious lunch.

"Take all you want," their host announced. "It will be a while until dinner, but I promise you it will be worth the wait. Tonight we will be dining out at a local restaurant."

Those not familiar with Ladd assumed he was joking; no one had noticed any signs of life as they entered the small town, let alone signs of a local restaurant.

After their lunch, Dieter suggested a walk; he would serve as local guide.

"For those of you who take power naps after your lunch," he added, "Might I suggest the living room? That woodstove will have you dreaming in fifteen seconds."

Carl and Leroy opted for the nap, while everyone else headed out for a reviving walk around the neighborhood. The stove worked its magic, as predicted.

Forty minutes later, the walkers returned, invigorated by the cool fall air. Once they were ensconced in the living room, however, the stove began working its magic on some of them as well. Having anticipated a possible second wave of naps, Dieter used the time to tidy up the kitchen and brew a big pot of coffee.

Thirty minutes later, Dieter, along with a very refreshed Carl and Leroy, served coffee to the remaining sleepy but grateful members of the Fine Society. They woke to the enticing aroma of more baked goods and fresh, strong coffee.

It was time for the meeting to begin.

98. GETTING DOWN TO BUSINESS

There was no formal agenda, not even a kickoff speech. As the group sipped coffee, tea and soda, casual conversations sprang up organically. Laura took the opportunity to ask Dieter about the German sign hanging on the wall.

"I saw that name, 'Feine Gesellschaft,' in an old journal at Walter's place," she explained. "Do you two have a connection in the past?"

"You are absolutely right," Dieter responded. "That's a keen eye you have, Laura. Walter and I are related. My grandmother's mother was a Wallerstein; she was the sister of Walter's grandfather. Ironically, we have known each other for only about forty years. We met by chance when Leroy and I worked at Argonne Labs at the same time." Hearing his name, Leroy looked up and doffed his nonexistent cap, then returned to his conversation with Megan and Carl.

"One day," Dieter continued, "we were talking about our German roots and I mentioned that Wallerstein was one of my family names. Evidently Leroy remembered it, and when he met Walter some time later—one of them will have to tell that story, I'm not sure of those details." He shook his head and waved a hand, as if to ward off the torrent of unnecessary information.

"Anyway, somehow Walter told Leroy the story about changing his name when he was in college, and Leroy picked up on the 'Wallerstein' in there. Well, you can probably guess how the rest of it goes. We got in touch and eventually verified that, indeed, we are relatives."

"That is wonderful," Laura said. She thought about the large number of coincidences that seemed to be occurring lately, and wondered if coincidences weren't so random after all.

Dieter excused himself to join Carl's and Leroy's continued discussion of the Bears, and Laura turned to JJ to further speculate about what the secret ingredient in Dieter's vegetable soup could possibly be. Eventually, Laura looked up to see L and Walter turning away from their chat with Megan.

"Should I bring it up now?" L asked, leaning toward her.

Walter, JJ and Laura looked at each other and silently concluded that this time was as good as any. L meekly stood up and looked at the group. In a moment it was obvious that he had something to say. They stopped their conversations and gave him their attention. Humbly and haltingly, L began to tell his story. As it unfolded, the group members uttered words of amazement and concern. L flinched a few times as he described his encounters with Newport. By the time he got around to apologizing for putting the group and their work in danger, there was not a dry eye in the house.

The members remained silent as they sorted out what consequences L's actions might have for themselves and the group. There were a few gentle questions, which L answered in a most straightforward manner. As Walter had been, the rest of the members were concerned about L's poor judgment. But they understood that there was no malice in L's behavior, merely the recklessness of a young man in need of guidance. Since it appeared that they were no longer under suspicion by the FBI (thanks to a well-executed Plan B), the bullet had been dodged.

Two conclusions emerged from the discussion. First, all members, especially L, must continue to be cautious and take special care to keep their activities legal. Second, they must not let down their guard when it comes to secrecy. Going forward, they must have a Plan B prepared at all times. If what had happened with Newport were to happen again, they might not have time to plan an alternative explanation for their activities.

Dieter told them that he'd periodically been watching the street out of the living room window, looking for any strange cars (which were easy to spot in a small town like this). He assured them that he had seen nothing and felt sure they weren't being watched.

They took a short break to stretch their legs, refill their drinks and watch in amazement as Dieter brought out yet more enticing baked goods. Then it was time to get back to business.

Leroy took the floor.

"When we unveiled the flying Model A Ford," he began, "we said that further explanation would be forthcoming. Well, it's time for us to explain. Nick, would you begin?"

Nick moved to a paper easel.

"Since it has been a while," he said, "I'd like to summarize how we got here in the first place. First, we combined the fine structure theory with L's work to discover the model of what turned out to be an electron. To support that position, we independently sourced data like it's radius and half-life. So we interpret this as a vote in favor of the fine-structure theory.

"Next," Nick continued, "Leroy speculated that the Big Bang would have left a lot of waves coursing through the universe—waves that would even be going through us and everything around us. But as Carl pointed out, if all the little pieces are subjected to the same wave forces that we're subjected to, we would not be able to observe them. Remember our motion on earth relative to our axis? The sun? Our galaxy?

"Then Leroy suggested that if we could put one of the small particles on a turntable and rotate it after it had been pushed by the ripple…"

Nick paused, waiting for someone to finish his recollection.

"The particle would have a motion different from everything around it," answered Megan.

Carl, Leroy and Dieter—the Physics heavy hitters—turned to look at Megan with expressions of mingled surprise and satisfaction. They were pleased that the person with the least Physics had grasped the concept. She smiled at them and shrugged coyly.

Nick continued.

"Of course, the little turntable is just a way for us to picture the effect of moving that little particle after it has been acted on by the Big-Bang waves. Our next step was to presume that if we could do this for one particle, we should be able to get the same result for a bunch of small particles, because the other particles are the same in our fine structure model. Okay so far?"

Everyone nodded.

Nick sketched the theorized event on the easel, labeled it, "Turntable Effect," and resumed his summary.

"It was right around this time that JJ suggested that the buildup from the fine particles to the electron looked like a fractal application. At a subsequent meeting, Carl suggested that there might be a fractal effect, where actions at our level could translate down to the finer structures and essentially down to the smallest particles. That would mean that if we took some action at our level, it would be translated down through the layers of structure to the smallest particles. Carl also reminded us of something called the piezoelectric effect, where certain crystals, when twisted or hit, produce an electric spark and vice versa. I had determined that Walter's eggs were crystalline in nature, so it remained to figure a way to interact with the egg.

"Using electricity applied to the surface," Nick went on, "we could induce the motion we were looking for. But the egg's surface was not a good conductor. However, the silvery stuff from Walter's father saved the day. Pieces of that on the outside gave us the electrical mediation properties we needed.

"For that last step," Nick finished, "Leroy did the work. Since this is the new part, I'll let Leroy do the explaining."

As Nick moved to sit down, the group broke out in spontaneous applause: he had managed to summarize several months' worth of complicated scientific discovery in less than twenty minutes. Laura, having forgotten some of the steps they'd taken along the way, was particularly grateful for the refresher course.

Meanwhile, Leroy had taken his position at the easel. Turning to a fresh page, he began.

"In principle, the next part looks easy; once you get it to work, it actually is easy. But getting it to work? That's not so easy."

He smiled as his audience chuckled: Leroy, ever the beguiling performer.

"I attached six wires at symmetrical points around the egg using the silvery stuff," he said. "Next I planned to apply voltage pulses of different levels, durations, frequencies and phases between the contact points. And that's the hard part. Look at the number of variables! They make for a large number of possible combinations; what I was looking for was the combination that would cause a reaction. We were stimulating the egg electrically to induce it to move. We theorized that the motions could, through the fractal effect, carry all the way down to the egg's fine structure. If the motion was just right, or close, we would be able to observe motion caused by the fine particles interacting with the ripples left over from the Big Bang. I knew that if I hit a combination that came close, the egg would move just a bit. I used a very sensitive optical device called an optical interferometer to detect movement. For those of you who are curious about the interferometer, I'll set up another session."

Leroy stopped, took a sip of his tea and gave everyone a chance to let his words sink in. When he thought they were ready,

"Okay?" came his rhetorical question.

"Now here was the tricky part," he paused for laughter and comments like "Oh sure" and "I knew there was a catch" as if everything up to now had been simple.

"We know that applying a pulsating voltage will cause a crystal to move in our macroscopic world, remember the discussion Carl did on crystal microphones back in the early days?"

The group nodded yes.

"Well, we expect that will happen; but what we want is to see if another movement can be detected due to the theorized interaction at the fine-structure level. You remember the turntable effect. Thus, if I saw a big reaction it was probably the macroscopic effect. But if I got little ones, they may have been what we were looking for."

"Since I knew it would take a lot of combinations and time, I noodled up a program for my PC and used it to drive a group of small power supplies. I used another PC to keep track of the combinations, and of the interferometer's output. The next part was deciding where to start the values. That is, should I start with high frequency or low? High voltage or low? And in what combinations? Then I had a hunch. We all know about conservation of momentum. Right?"

Of course they knew about conservation of momentum.

"Well, I figured that as my application of electrical energy causes a twitch at our level, then the energy of that motion is transferred down the fractal-like layers to the fine structure. The twitch at my level involves the whole egg—that's lots of mass. At the fine-particle level, the particles obviously have very little mass. So, I shouldn't need too much effort at my level to get a big reaction at the fine particles' level. Thus, I decided to start with low voltage and then go lower. Another consideration was that getting just a few fine particles to respond one time would not produce enough motion for even the optical interferometer

489

to detect. I figured I had to hit the right frequency, so that all the little motions added together to produce bigger ones. Essentially, I was hoping to produce a 'standing wave,' of fine particles by shifting those particles as they were acted on by the Big-Bang waves."

Leroy took a deep breath and let that sink in before he went on.

"The computer ran various combinations for several days and nights and I was getting results. The optical interferometer was registering twitches of the egg caused by the power impulses I applied to it. I was interested in the smallest twitches, because these would be typical of the actions we were hoping to achieve down at the fine-structure level. When I went back and repeated the input values that had produced small twitches before, it just didn't work. That was the bad news. These were probably random seismic events. However, <u>some</u> little twitches were the result of the applied impulses. How do I know? Well, I played with the power supply variables, you know, frequency, duration and so on. I got better reactions until…. Well, as you can see from the flying Model A, I was able to find some values for the power applied to the egg that resulted in motion."

"So to make a long story short, we now have the basics for controlling these interactions," concluded Leroy; and he sat down.

Even though everyone had witnessed the car demo, they were still spellbound by the discovery. The ramifications were enormous. Tapping into a yet-undiscovered energy source that extends and self-renews throughout the universe would render all other energy sources trivial by comparison.

Laura broke the silence.

"Now what do we do?" she asked.

But no one knew what to say, until Dieter came up with a most elegant solution.

"Let's eat," he said.

His guests stared blankly at him, their eyes glazed with the stupefying reality of what Leroy had shown them.

"Come on," Dieter insisted. "Shake it off. We'll pick this up tomorrow. We have been so absorbed in our work that I'll bet you don't realize it is almost 6 pm."

Everyone looked at a watch or clock to verify. Where had the time gone?

"The next step," Dieter continued, "'What to do' is a huge discussion and requires clear heads. We've done a lot today and need to carefully ponder those thoughts. And nothing is better for pondering thoughts than fried chicken and ice cream."

"What are you talking about Dieter?" Megan asked playfully. "Chicken and ice cream?"

The others joined her in the good-natured chiding.

Smiling, Dieter said, "Well, like I said earlier, we are going out for dinner. You'll love it. It is just a short walk."

"Walk?" came the collective response. Every last member would have sworn to the fact that no restaurant existed within walking distance of Dieter's house. Hadn't they driven in on the main street?

As he headed for the door, Dieter called out, "Get your coats and follow me, we are going to RIPS for dinner and TORYS for dessert."

The FS members dutifully, if doubtfully, donned their wraps and followed Dieter along the two short blocks to the main street. As they approached the intersection, they could see a line of people extending out of a building a block away. The line snaked along the sidewalk and even around the corner. That must be RIPS, they thought. It certainly was.

Though the line was long, turnover was efficient, so the line moved quickly. The brisk air was stimulating and felt good to the group, whose foggy-headed members had been sitting and thinking for most of the afternoon. As they waited, chatting amiably, a young waiter periodically passed through the line offering "crumbs"–the batter that falls off the chicken in the deep fat fryer and gets cooked to a crisp. The cook at RIPS dredged them up from time to time and sent them out to the hungry souls standing in line. Laura and Megan agreed that this was one of those moments where one must take everything in moderation, including moderation.

When they were finally seated, everyone ordered right away. While they waited for their food, beer was consumed in copious amounts (except by L, who had a cola). Lively, non-scientific conversation and laughter ensued. The delicious chicken, fries and beer would have been more than enough, but Dieter had something else in mind—namely, dessert.

Like the pied piper, he led them two blocks south to TORYS ice cream parlor. This place was right out of the past, with its black-and-white checkered floor tiles, round marble-topped tables and wire-backed chairs. The Swift's ice cream soda-fountain area was the same as it had been in the 1950s. Clerks dispensed ice cream in glass dishes and old-style waffle cones. The old Hamilton Beach mixers whirred, churning out malts and shakes. What a trip it was for the older attendees. L had no idea what they were getting so excited about, but decided it was only polite to play along and order a giant milkshake. Each did what none of them would have thought possible: they ate dessert on top of all the chicken, fries and beer.

They walked back to Dieter's a happy and contented bunch. The concerns of present day were thousands of miles away from their minds. The satisfying feast had succeeded in distracting them, however temporarily, from the reason for their visit to Ladd.

For the night owls, Dieter had a rather vast selection of schnapps, as well as beer, wine, coffee, tea or soda. Hoping to hold on to the easy camaraderie of the evening, all members accepted beverages and sat or stood at various places around the house to engage in more pleasant conversation. Eventually, however, they began to peel off one-by-one, saying their goodnights and shuffling off to bed. It had been a long and exciting day. They needed sleep to refresh their minds for the discussions that lay ahead.

99. SATURDAY MORNING

Dieter had strictly forbidden alarm clocks for the Society's visit, so only the delicious aromas emanating from the kitchen provided motivation to wake up. The genial host set out an array of bagels, rolls, sausages and cheeses as a buffet; it was available all morning. So it was breakfast for some and brunch for others. By 10:45, everyone was gathered in the living room and engaged in casual conversation. They expected today's session to be long and filled with debate.

Dieter was the host, but he was not the leader. No one had been given nor volunteered for that function. The members wanted to have an open discussion with everything on the table; there would be no predetermined agenda. Walter was the first to speak.

"I would propose to the group that the first question we answer is, do we move ahead or do nothing at all?"

They agreed that it was a good place to begin, and JJ offered his assessment.

"My view," he offered, "is that we should go ahead. However, to do nothing would be by far the easiest path to follow—if this has the potential I think it has, then we already have a tiger by the tail. To proceed would change our lives drastically."

Carl spoke next.

"As a scientist I would find it hard to hold back, to always wonder about the 'what ifs,'" he said. "But I agree: going ahead might even be dangerous."

Megan nodded, and began to speak rather philosophically.

"There is something called simultaneous discovery," she began, "where it seems that medical, mathematical or scientific breakthroughs often occur in clusters, to totally unrelated groups or individuals. Walter once mentioned that there were old rumors that many more of those symbol sheets exist. Who's to say that the large cache JJ had at the museum is the only set? Someone else might have discovered, or be close to discovering, the same thing we did. I say it is just a matter of time before simultaneous discovery takes place with our fine-particle breakthrough. And my question is this: will the next discoverers be as altruistic as we would be, or might they have sinister impulses?"

After a protracted discussion, it became clear to Laura that they were talking in circles—they had come to no conclusions about Walter's original question.

"I have a suggestion," she announced. "Let's start from a point where we agree to go ahead, so that we can take up the question of what going ahead looks like."

They liked it. But it took a moment for anyone to know what to do next.

"You've shown us the basic results," JJ said. "But won't it take some pretty major engineering before we'd be able to apply it to real situations? A floating a Model A is fun, but…well, can we hear from the physicists? What do you guys think we should tackle first?"

"When I realized what we might have," Leroy answered, "I thought that using it for power generation would be a worthwhile effort. In time, it could replace fossil fuels and negate the high cost and long lead-times for nuclear power generation—and that's just to mention a few possibilities."

While most of the group members agreed with Leroy, Nick was less sure.

"But look at all of the world economies and how intertwined they are," he said. "If you make a big and sudden change, the equilibrium could be upset; in the short term, you would have chaos."

There was agreement in the group on that point, and they continued their discussion.

"I am extremely worried," Walter said, "about what the malcontents and extremists of the world will do with a breakthrough like this. We are worried about nuclear material getting out of secured areas, into the hands of al-Qaeda and the like; think of what they could do if that kind of limitless energy were available everywhere."

Leroy answered him

"If we think others will make the discovery and we don't know their motivations, then as rational, levelheaded, good-hearted people, we need to do it first," he exhorted. "But we have to do it the right way. That is our real challenge: to do it right; to use our discovery for Good Science, like our buddy Leffler taught us."

Laura's ears perked up.

"Do you mean Professor Wes Leffler?" she asked Leroy

"Absolutely," he answered. "Leffler's a great teacher, a fine person, and he's one of us."

"One of the Fine Society?" she asked.

"Yep, he is a silent member; he does his part by promoting our cause through his work," answered Leroy.

Dieter saw this as a moment to interrupt; he suggested they take a break and get the circulation going again.

"There's plenty of finger food and beverages, so help yourself."

The stretch felt good and gave the attendees a few minutes to ruminate on the day's meeting. The fire in the woodstove could not work its magic today. The topic was far too engaging for anyone to sleep through this conversation. Dieter looked out the window, making another one of his inspections of the neighborhood; all was well. Meanwhile, Megan and Laura huddled in a corner of the dining room. They could not be heard over the others, but they were clearly excited about something. When the group reconvened, Laura spoke up immediately.

"Let me start with a question for the physicists," she said

Jokingly, Carl, Leroy and Dieter looked around and behind themselves.

"I believe I heard you say the effect can be controlled by voltage, frequency and phase," Laura continued, smiling indulgently but intent on making her point. Leroy answered in the affirmative, as the others nodded agreement.

"Well, I think Megan and I came up with an idea that—well, it makes sense to us, but you engineering types need to have the final say."

She had the undivided attention of the group.

"We were wondering," Laura continued, "if a product could be made that could have widespread use, while fitting in with a process that already exists?"

She turned to Megan.

"Did I get it all?" Laura asked.

Megan nodded, then shook her head and spoke.

"But you have to do it in a way that no one knows the technology is there," she said.

"That's it," Laura took over again. "Build something that works better. For example, for years we've heard that if you could just increase the gas mileage of each car by a few miles per gallon, the overall savings—to the environment as well as the economy—would be enormous. Megan, what was the one you thought of?"

"I had a wild thought," Megan replied. "Suppose you could make very efficient electrical motors by incorporating this technology, and you could make the motors available to developing countries to pump water, run communications, purify water, whatever… and because the motors are very efficient, the costs to run them would be very low. We could build the 'critical part' for each motor, and other companies could build the rest; then making motors would actually be someone else's business. I don't know if that's a good example, but do you see what I mean?"

Wheels were turning behind all the eyes in the group. They were thinking of various ways to sneak the technology into all sorts of devices, making them run more efficiently.

Nick spoke up, "It would be a big challenge to make the devices look like we simply made a product that was just more efficient, like super bearings that greatly decrease friction. It's plausible, but could we pull it off? How would we hide what we really had done?"

Megan added, "Small changes like that could fly under the radar, minimizing the chances that the technology would fall into the wrong hands."

The excitement in the room increased palpably, even though no one had spoken aloud since Megan finished sharing her idea.

"This might sound flippant," Leroy offered, "but I wouldn't worry about how to hide it yet. We have to develop it before we need to hide it." The group agreed. It was premature to be too concerned yet. The group once again lapsed into contemplative silence. When Walter finally broke the silence to share his idea, the floodgates seemed to open.

"We could make armatures," Walter said, "the heart of every electric motor. Inside the armature we would have our "egg-tronics,""

The group loved Walter's new word. They laughed and decided that is was an appropriate term. When the buzz died down, Walter resumed.

"We could claim superior bearings and precision machining for the better performance."

With that thought, the discussion escalated to higher and higher levels of excitement as ideas emerged from the group's fertile minds. An hour later, the discussion was still rolling at a fevered pitch.

Leroy clinked a spoon on a water glass.

"If I could have your attention for a moment," he called. "I would like to make an observation. Judging by the excitement in the room, it would appear that that our answer to the first question is 'yes.'"

There was a pause while they sorted out which question he meant.

Then L reminded them: "To go ahead or…" he began.

We will never know whether L actually finished that sentence, because the room erupted with the utterance of one loud, unanimous, unmistakable word.

"YES!" cried the members of the Fine Society.

And so it was. The members decided to develop their findings. The decision was easy to make, but lots of hard work lay ahead as they journeyed toward their ultimate goal: maximum impact with minimum effect.

The end, for now.

www.ingramcontent.com/pod-product-compliance
Lightning Source LLC
Chambersburg PA
CBHW071630260626
47170CB00001B/36